What the critics are saying...

5 Unicorns "... the sex fairly screamed off the page with the most passionate, realistic scenes I have read in months. By and large, All I Want hit all my romance needs while striking every passionate button I have. The action is powerful and the love fiery with intensity. *Ms Painter* has written a wonderful novel." ~ *Francesca Enchanted in Romance*

4.5 Stars Heat level: "...very sensual elements I usually only see in mainstream romances without losing the erotic tone. *All I Want* is a must-have for romance fans..." ~ *Dani Jacquel H Just Erotic Romance Reviews*

5 Unicorns "... not only was I graced with a spectacular novel, but also provided with a story so comprehensive and vibrant that I actually envisioned myself in every scene. This author's ability to make me feel as if I was part of the story, to be a part of the emotional upheaval that Jeanne and Mael went through made this an instant hit and a definite keeper. To anyone who hasn't read this tale, you're definitely missing out on something extremely special." ~ *Rachelle Enchanted in Romance*

4 Stars "*Ms. Painter* brings ancient Scotland into your living room and makes you shiver with longing over all those braw Scotsmen. On top of this, she creates characters that tug at your heartstrings, stir your sense of honor and just literally make you want to hug them...Then she ties it all up in a beautifully satisfying bow and hands us the perfect ending all neat and gift-wrapped. To say the least, *Ms. Painter* just made it into the top ten on my list of must-have authors." ~ *Keely Skillman ecataromance*

"*Sally Painter* does a tremendous job of weaving all the elements of the story together so the reader can follow along and not feel lost...The sex is hot, the characters charming, the history details well researched, and the action fast paced. For a highly recommended summer read, check out *All I Want*." ~ *Angela Camp Romance Reviews Today*

All I Want

Sally Painter

Ellora's Cave
Romantica Publishing

An Ellora's Cave Romantica Publication

www.ellorascave.com

All I Want

ISBN # 1419952676
ALL RIGHTS RESERVED.
All I Want Copyright© 2005 Sally Painter
Edited by Sue-Ellen Gower
Cover art by Christine Clavel

Electronic book Publication April 2005
Trade paperback Publication October 2005

Excerpt from *All I Need* Copyright © Sally Painter 2005
Excerpt from *Fated Mates* Copyright © Delilah Devin, Sally Painter, Charlotte Boyett-Compo, 2005

With the exception of quotes used in reviews, this book may not be reproduced or used in whole or in part by any means existing without written permission from the publisher, Ellora's Cave Publishing, Inc.® 1056 Home Avenue, Akron OH 44310-3502.

This book is a work of fiction and any resemblance to persons, living or dead, or places, events or locales is purely coincidental. The characters are productions of the authors' imagination and used fictitiously.

Warning:

The following material contains graphic sexual content meant for mature readers. *All I Want* has been rated *S-ensuous* by a minimum of three independent reviewers.

Ellora's Cave Publishing offers three levels of Romantica™ reading entertainment: S (S-ensuous), E (E-rotic), and X (X-treme).

S-*ensuous* love scenes are explicit and leave nothing to the imagination.

E-*rotic* love scenes are explicit, leave nothing to the imagination, and are high in volume per the overall word count. In addition, some E-rated titles might contain fantasy material that some readers find objectionable, such as bondage, submission, same sex encounters, forced seductions, etc. E-rated titles are the most graphic titles we carry; it is common, for instance, for an author to use words such as "fucking", "cock", "pussy", etc., within their work of literature.

X-*treme* titles differ from E-rated titles only in plot premise and storyline execution. Unlike E-rated titles, stories designated with the letter X tend to contain controversial subject matter not for the faint of heart.

Also by Sally Painter

༄

All I Need
Fated Mates

About the Author

༄

A native North Carolinian, Sally lives with her husband and cat, Bow, in the Blue Ridge Mountains.

Growing up just outside Charlotte, NC, Sally spent summers playing on the beaches of the Carolinas and learning to "shag" — a form of beach dancing.

Born in the South and into an Irish/Scottish family meant storytelling was as natural as breathing. Everyone had their own repertoire of jokes and stories and growing up in North Carolina, famous for its ghost stories, meant scary ones, too. Sally knows a lot about ghosts since she's lived with them all her life, very much like the film, *Sixth Sense*. Invited to participate in a three-year paranormal research project, she at long last embraced her Celtic seer heritage and even runs an online paranormal workshop featuring paranormal research professionals.

Trained in commercial art, Sally discovered writing fulfills her creative energies, especially Romantica™. When not writing, she can be found tending to her flowers and jungle of houseplants, studying all kinds of subject matters, and setting out on new adventures with her soul mate husband.

Sally welcomes comments from readers. You can find her website and email address on her author bio page at www.ellorascave.com.

About Kilts

ಲ

Historians believe the Scottish kilt did not exist until the late 1500s (see Concise Scots Dictionary) and the clan tartans some time earlier. This is concluded because of a lack of documented evidence depicting the Scottish kilt prior the 16th century. When faced with this kind of information, invariably a writer is going to ask, "What if the lack of evidence only means no evidence was preserved?" Ancient Romans and Old Dynasty Egyptians all wore kilts. Is it too farfetched to believe the Scots and even Picts may have worn them also? In my fictional world-building of 1250 AD, Jeanne McBen discovers kilts did exist during this time in history. This poetic license was invoked because a kilt is just too romantic to be omitted in a fantasy time travel.

Clan Hierarchy

ಲ

Clans = members of extended family, included other families (called 'branches' or 'septs') related by marriage or wished protection against other clans. Most had different surnames. There were many clans. Each clan had a chief and each chief had many chieftains.

Clansmen =Overall population of the clan.

Chief = Bloodline descendant (usually), son, brother, nephew, cousin, etc. Some clans had female Chiefs. Clan Chief governed clan, resolved disputes and collected land rents.

Tanist = Successor of Chief, nominated by chief. Gaelic = Tanaiste

Chieftain = Head of branch and sept of clan.

Dedication

☙

*To my husband, Wayne,
two great friends and critique partners,
Lori Soard and Linda Colwell,
and my wonderful editor, Sue-Ellen Gower!*

All I Want

Chapter One

Mael MacRaigl tried to relax in the corner booth, but his knees kept hitting the table. He stretched his legs out in front of him, but his feet came up against the other seat. Laughter and tinkling glass clashed against drifting conversations as more people filled the diner. Each voice jerked his attention in its direction, only to have his anticipation crushed. *It wasn't her.* He closed his eyes, willing his composure to hold fast. The nervous expectancy was like fingernails raking down a chalkboard. There was no relief from its irritating presence. He sighed. The nervous tide receded and Mael opened his eyes. A loud crashing of glass from the kitchen shattered his momentary peace. He stared out the diner window in an attempt to insulate himself from the din.

Low-swag metal lamps pierced the window with harsh reflections against the blackness outside. He tugged on the shirt collar and hastily loosened his tie. It had been a long time since he'd been in such a crowd. She shifted in the booth, he flattened his sweaty palms against his pant legs and willed the anxious trembling in the pit of his stomach to calm. He had waited for such a long time. It was difficult to believe he was actually here.

The familiar prickle started at the base of his neck and rippled down his spine, a sensation not felt for what seemed like an eternity, yet was expected. It felt just like the first time he had experienced it. She was here! Their bond remained. Relief washed over him. Not even the passing years had been able to break their connection. He quickly reined in his excitement and trained his stare on the open doorway. Waiting. His gaze jumped from one patron to the next, following the ever-present flow of people moving in and out of the crowded diner. There she was! His breath lodged in his throat. She paused long enough to glance about the room.

Mael forced himself to remain seated, balling his hands into white-knuckled fists. His gaze traveled her oval face framed by dark, wavy hair, shorter than he recalled. Each curve, laugh line and dimple was imprinted on his very soul. His heart pounded out his need, pulsing to his groin. Unsated hunger smoldered until his need burst to silent heat and seemed to stretch across the room, groping for her.

She tilted her head as though sensing his presence. He could almost feel her against him. His cock hardened. Her lips beckoned him. How he remembered their sweet taste. He would part their moistness and claim her mouth in one long kiss. She'd be his once more. Her lips pursed together in an expression he quickly recognized. She was angry, but struggling to keep it under control.

The faint night breeze rushed past her and breathed across the room carrying her sweet scent to him. He closed his eyes and groaned. He could almost taste her. The urge to rush over to her and gather her in his arms strained against his self-control. She belonged with him. He pushed his heels into the tiled floor, willing himself to remain seated. She was his! He could take her right there in the diner. He didn't care. He would spread her long silky legs apart and taste her, feel her writhe under his tongue teasing her clit. She belonged to him!

She glanced his way. Heat erupted inside him. Would she recognize him? He wanted her to come closer, but knew it would not matter. She'd not remember him. The words he'd practiced came rushing to his lips, but he clamped his mouth shut against the need to call out to her. He had fantasized a different reunion, one where she'd fall into his arms and he'd tell her everything. He could almost feel her excited tearful kisses showering his face. In his daydream, once he'd calmed her and answered her questions he'd make love to her again. It would be sweet release to bring her to the edge of climax just as he had so many times. He would slip his swollen cock into her pussy and ride her. She would cry out in shuddering pleasure, and he would join her as they came together. It would be just as it was before. It had to be!

Her gaze flashed across him. His heart pounded out a staccato beat. If only she would remember, then at long last she'd be his—again. Mael straightened in the booth with his stare steady, ready to face his biggest fear. When her stare dashed past him to the booth across the room. He knew his fantasy would remain a mere fantasy.

Jeanne McBen moved closer. She was so beautiful. His heartbeat drummed louder in his ears. He sought her gaze, but she didn't even notice him. Instead, she brushed past him.

Hope collapsed with him back against the seat. He watched her walk over to the far end of the diner. Her jeans hugged the perfect curve of her hips—how well he remembered the feel of her curves. Her hair used to brush past her shoulders and down her back, but now it

All I Want

stopped slightly above her shoulders. His stare moved down the short-waisted jacket she'd no doubt grabbed at the last minute in her mad rush to get to the diner by midnight. She wove her way through the Fifties-style diner and stopped in front of a man crouched over his coffee mug.

Mael trained his attention on her mouth, focusing on hearing her words rise above the noisy diner.

"I can't believe you did this," she said to the man who snapped alert. Dressed in a fine wool suit, he unfolded his tall frame and stood from the booth while she slipped into the seat across from him. He was taller than Mael remembered, but just as lanky. He marveled at how predictable some things were. Even though she'd agreed to meet this traitor who'd become her fiercest enemy, she had chosen wisely. The diner was very public and always crowded.

The world faded from him, leaving only his beloved. How could she not recall their life together, or the love they had shared? He grasped the coffee mug, tightening his fingers around its smooth shape. All that was about to change. This night she would remember him. This night he would send his wife back in time to him. To when they met.

The man lifted his head.

"I didn't do anything, Doctor McBen."

"Why are you so formal, Gregory? Is that what happens when you become a thief?" She sat down in the booth.

"Thief?" His laughter grated against Mael's ears. He leaned forward, training his power on hearing their drama unfold even though he knew what would be said, what the man wanted, and what she would end up doing. His expensive leather shoes gave easily under the staccato poundings of his toes. How he longed to have her lift her gaze to his. He could force her to notice him. The temptation eased from him. Instead, he sought her lips as she spoke. He sought her voice among the roaring din of the diner and focused on the soft lilting.

"Let me in my lab, give back my research, Gregory, or I'm going to the police."

Mael's fingers itched to stroke her silky dark hair, knowing the sweet scent her soft curls would release should he bury his face in their length. His stare traced the slender curve of her neck to the base of her throat where he used to shower kisses evoking shivers and delighted giggles from her. She'd always loved it when he let his tongue trace an imaginary line down to her navel and over her flat stomach. Heat stoked in his belly and he shifted in the booth hoping to ease his discomfort.

"Jeanne." Her name escaped him, the final "e" lingering on his tongue like a whispering sigh. Mael glanced around the noisy diner, knowing no one paid him the slightest attention. He frowned and shook his head at the waitress who tried to refill his coffee mug. The young woman flashed a wider smile than necessary and ignored his refusal.

"Don't you want a little more?" She licked her lower lip and leaned over just enough to allow a generous view of her ample breasts. Mael shook his head, recalling bar wenches from centuries past who had made the same kind of cloaked offers. He glanced away from the disappointed waitress and found Jeanne's lips once more.

"You're a thief!"

"I didn't steal a damned thing. It's my lab you're using. You're little more than an employee, in case you forgot."

Rage flashed over Mael, and he reminded himself to focus on the reason he was there. Still, the memories were bitter, and the pain too deep to ignore.

"Trench," he ground his teeth against the name as though he could crush the man between them.

* * * * *

"I'll call Channel Eight, Gregory." Jeanne tightened her trembling hands around the coffee mug to keep from throwing its contents into his smirking face. How dare he think he could just steal her work. "They'll be very interested in what you've done. In fact, everyone in the research community will be interested." She glared across the booth at him. How could she have been so wrong about him? Her stomach pitched. His angular features spread into a sneer, transforming him into someone she no longer recognized.

"Call the media? Do you think that'll change anything?"

She looked from him, letting her gaze sweep the crowded diner. She couldn't bear the coldness reflecting in his blue eyes. For five years he'd been her mentor and colleague. How could he suddenly be her enemy? How could he have done this to her?

The day's events were a blur. It was nearly midnight, but it felt early. The world was out of sync. She'd been trapped in its unnatural

All I Want

rhythm ever since she'd found herself locked out of her lab that morning. Resurging panic had traveled with her throughout the day as she waited for this meeting. Waiting until she could finally confront him. Gregory Trench had betrayed her. She found his stare again, and rushed to finish what she'd rehearsed on her drive to the diner.

"*Doctor* Trench," she said, somehow his title making it easier to challenge him, "I've worked damn hard, almost three years, on the *Next Gen* virus. If you think I'll just sit by while you steal my antiserum…" Her bravado slipped from her when his lips widened into the cruelest smile she'd ever seen.

"*Your* antiserum?" He covered his laugh with the napkin. "Granted, I've been living in Scotland this past year, but it is still *my* lab. I control the funds. I own the work. You signed away all rights when you came on board. Remember?" The tone in his voice sliced through any remaining hope she had that it had been some horrid mistake and this midnight meeting would resolve it. She fumbled with the spoon in her coffee cup, but her hand shook so badly she released it.

She glanced at the couple sitting in the booth across from theirs. They were only teenagers, around the same age as her brother, Ryan. Her pulse quickened. "Until last week they were doomed." She nodded to the high schoolers. "They—"

"Can now be cured." His voice sliced her next sentence. "Have long lives and some might even have children, depending on how advanced the virus is. Thanks to my lab."

"My work, Gregory. It's my work that produced the cure. I just don't understand why you've locked me out of my lab. I don't understand what's going on."

"The why's easy, Jeanne. Because I can. It's my lab. If you're as brilliant as I believe, you'll turn over the disc, as I requested. That *is* why you agreed to come here, isn't it? To return my property?"

She ignored his demanding tone. He had her records, all her work. She was not going to give him the only pawn she had to stop whatever he was planning. This was irrational. There was no reason to lock her out of the lab and confiscate her work.

"Give me the disc, Jeanne, if you want your brother to remain safe."

"My brother." Her heart seemed to stop beating. "What does Ryan have to do with this?"

His smug grin set her pulse racing.

"You made Ryan a part of this when you took his blood sample. It was his blood you used to unlock the mysteries of this virus, wasn't it?" His eyes widened with an anxious glint as though he were enjoying her discomfort.

"You touch one hair on Ryan's head—"

"How cliché of you." His laughter chilled her. "I don't want to harm Ryan. He's too valuable."

"You leave Ryan out of this, you son of a bitch!"

Trench raised his hand to halt her words. "You don't want to cause a scene here in Penington's most nostalgic haven." He glanced about the busy restaurant.

She followed his stare. Three couples paused long enough to squeeze into the booth across from them. The twenty-four-hour diner grew louder as the steady stream of partygoers sought a place to top off their night of revelry, crowding the diner beyond its capacity.

"I'm sure your small-town paper would love another sensational story about North Carolina's most gifted scientist. They could run a background feature on your parents' tragic death and how you managed to raise your younger brother while putting yourself through med school."

She closed her eyes, struggling against the sorrow over her parents' brutal deaths. Tears threatened past her attempt and when she opened them, it was to Trench's triumphant grin. She glared at his sharp features, thinking he resembled a hawk. No, a vulture.

"Why have you stolen my work? What are you going to do with it?"

"*Next Gen* is a death sentence to the world. I got the first stats this week. That's why I flew back. It's spreading faster than we anticipated. In more ways than you can possibly imagine your discovery is timely. Your antiserum is going to make me the wealthiest man in the world.

"People will pay whatever I charge for the antiserum so their prepubescent offspring can avoid the plague and its sterile side effect. Look about this diner. It's too late for most of these teenagers, but the next generation will be the final hope for all of mankind. With your antiserum, the *Next Gen* virus will be little more than a vague nightmare."

All I Want

She stared at the young faces so full of life and hope as they reveled on the threshold of adulthood, ignorant of the vile organism growing inside them.

"This is about money? How could you, Gregory? My antiserum isn't for ransoming to those who can afford to pay."

"You're so naïve, Jeanne. But I knew you wouldn't relinquish without a fight. That's why Ryan is staying with me." He sat back.

"What?" She jumped from her seat but he grabbed her wrist and pulled her back to the booth.

"Sit down." He glanced about the diner.

Wincing under the harsh grip, she followed his stare, realizing several conversations had halted with her sudden outburst. She jerked from his hold and sat back down, but her mind screamed as tragic scenarios flashed in front of her.

"Ryan's only sixteen years old! He's of no value to you."

"Are you serious? I know Ryan's the sole bearer of the one element that'll stop this horrendous plague ravaging our world."

She must not have covered her shocked reaction because the slow cruel lifting of his lips widened. His smile radiated his triumph.

"So, you see, it's up to you. If you don't turn over the disc, the next generation born will be the last—ever. And your brother will die."

Gripping her purse to her chest, she leaned forward, trying to still the quake, but his threat thundered through her.

"And Ryan? What are you going to do with my brother? I'll go to the police. You can't do this!" Her own words echoed in her ears with childlike tremors, hardly intimidating to the devil sitting across from her. His silent stare chilled her. She had to find some way to stop him.

"Your brother will remain as my guest, and you'll say nothing to the police. His future depends on you, Jeanne." Trench tossed his napkin on the table in front of her.

"What do you want?" She tried to stop the plea in her tone, but it slipped past her attempt. His blue eyes widened with bright excitement.

"What I asked for when you first sat down in this booth—the disc."

"There's no disc."

He rested his clasped hands on the table until his knuckles whitened, then released a harsh sigh. Slowly, he leaned forward.

"You're amazing. You grew up surrounded by research scientists. Your own parents worked in my lab. How could they have created such a gullible child?"

"You disgust me," she countered, feeling very much like a helpless child.

"Where's the disc?" His gaze hardened on her.

"What assurances do I have you won't harm my brother?" If she could use the disc to leverage some bargaining power, then she might have a chance to defeat him.

"Use your pretty head." He flattened his hands against the table and stood, his heartless gaze trapping her eyes. "Ryan is too valuable to harm, unless you force me. I've run tests. I know he has additional proteins. If we had a couple of years, I could hire enough scientists to work it out, but the world can't wait. I need the formula now." He reached inside his suit coat and flung a ten-dollar bill onto the table. "For the coffee." His thin-lipped grin reflected the same cruel enjoyment mirroring in his eyes.

"What about Ryan?" She reached for his arm, but he jerked from her grasp.

He tugged on the gray suit sleeve and smoothed the fine material.

"Gregory. Where's Ryan? You'll release him, won't you?"

She reached out again, but he sidestepped her.

"In spite of my instructions, you didn't bring the disc. Don't test me further. The disc for your brother's safe return. It's up to you," he said.

"I don't have the disc. You took all my research when you locked me out of my lab this morning."

He stepped closer, bracing himself with one hand on the back of her seat, and leaned forward so his face was only inches from hers.

"What kind of idiot do you think I am? You've read my books. You know my philosophy on research. *Back it up*. You didn't keep the complete formula on the hard drive at the lab. You're too smart to take such security risks. Give me the damn disc," he said between clenched teeth. "I have all the time in the world. You don't. Ryan won't come home until I have what I want."

Before she could react, he turned and pushed his way through the crowd. Her thoughts were jumbled. Where was her brother? Would

All I Want

Trench harm him? What was she going to do? She was helpless. No, she was not helpless. Never again!

She unzipped her purse and frowned at the way her hands trembled as she fumbled for the cell phone. She tottered on the edge of hysteria until her fingers closed over the familiar shape and the panic eased.

She'd call Ryan. He'd answer by the third ring like always. It was after midnight. He'd be watching the Friday night horror show. Trench was lying, he was!

Her purse slipped from her lap. Jeanne watched the phone slide across the checkered floor. The realization that everything was just beyond her reach paralyzed her. It was all her fault. She should never have involved Ryan in this research. What had she been thinking? In her passion to find a cure, she'd ignored the rule to never cross that line separating family and research. So focused on her brother, she didn't see the man standing there, until he stooped to retrieve her things.

Had he been standing there long? His auburn hair covered his face when he stretched forward to pick up her phone. Her gaze rose with him as he straightened. Holding her purse cradled in the crisp folds of his shirtsleeves, he looked down at her. A hint of a smile tugged the corners of his lips.

Her stare locked with his. Instantly, she thought of her father's favorite pair of tiger-eye cufflinks. Unlike the cold amber stones, the two orbs staring back at her were like molten bronze. Her heart skipped a beat. She strained to break from his stare. Then, just as suddenly as he had seized her stare, he released it, turning his attention to her purse.

"'Tis yours?"

Without a word, she grabbed it, mumbled a thank you, and brushed past him. Pulling her jacket closed about her T-shirt and faded jeans, she zigzagged through the crowd.

The exit was a welcome sight. She shoved the heavy door open and escaped into the cool night. Her pulse throbbed as imaginary scenes of her brother being held in a dark room at the mercy of Trench flashed through her mind. She glanced about the dark parking lot looking for Trench. He was gone. Her car, hidden in the shadows at the far end, seemed miles away. Even with brisk strides, Jeanne felt she'd never reach it.

"Excuse me, lass," came the thick accent behind her.

Her pulse spiked and she spun around, nearly colliding into the man from the diner. He reached out to steady her.

"There, there, lass. I dinna mean to startle ye." He gripped her upper arms, but she struggled from his hold. "I just wanted to return these to ye." He held something in front of her.

The lights from the diner outlined his silhouette in radiance. His hair lifted under the soft breeze then fell once more in waves to his shoulders.

"These?"

Her attention jumped to the jangling keys suspended from his finger.

"Thanks…again." She snatched them from him and sprinted toward her car.

"Ye are in no condition to be driving, lass."

She clamped her hand against the startled scream, for he was leaning against her car with his arms folded over his chest. Glancing over her shoulder toward the diner then back at him, Jeanne tried to rationalize what had just happened. How had he done that?

God, he was tall, certainly taller than any man she wanted to meet after midnight in a parking lot. His dress shirt, opened at the throat, was tucked into dark trousers. He looked as though he'd just removed his coat and tie after a long day at the office. From shimmering depths of gold, his intense stare beckoned her. Goose bumps prickled down her arms, while her breath escaped between her lips in a rush.

"Are ye okay? Perhaps I could be of some assistance to ye?" He moved toward her.

She shook her head, keenly aware of her vulnerability. A car turned into the parking lot with its headlights glaring. He shielded his eyes as it slipped into a nearby space. Seizing the opportunity, she hit the unlock button on the key fob and jumped inside behind the steering wheel. He grabbed the door and blocked her frantic attempt to shut it.

"Ye have nothing to fear from me, lass. Were it my intention to harm ye, I'd have done so before now."

"Look. I don't need your help. Move out of my way, or I'll hit the car horn." Her attention riveted to his eyes. Sudden heat washed over her. The sound was soft, like the lazy breeze rustling overhead in the huge oak trees only it was his low, rumbling laughter.

All I Want

"I'd never wish to cause ye alarm. I merely thought I could be of assistance seeing how Trench upset ye."

"What did you say?" She froze in the new attempt to slam the door in his face.

In the dome's light, his handsome face seemed to transform into one of an ancient warrior. Every feature sharpened under the light, the most prominent being his eyes, then his angular nose.

Suddenly, she saw him brandishing a heavy sword, with a tartan plaid draped over one shoulder while a knee-length kilt lifted slightly from a sweeping gust of wind. Behind him, lush, green hills arched and cascaded into other hills.

"Aye lass, I know Trench has taken your brother hostage in hopes of keeping ye quiet while forcing ye to relinquish your antiserum." His words jolted her out of the momentary reverie.

"How… How could you *possibly* know that? Just who the hell are you?"

"Mael. Mael MacRaigl. Trust me, Jeanne lass, ye canna go to the police. Trench will kill Ryan."

"How do you know my name? How do you know about Ryan?" she asked.

"I know more than ye ken, Jeanne. Trench has stolen your work. All those years of sacrificing shall be for what? So he can line his pockets by preying upon the fears of others?"

"How could you know this?" she asked. His words seemed to hit her in the pit of the stomach for her breath pushed between parted lips.

"Jeanne." His low voice soothed the rising panic. "Ye are in no shape to be driving anywhere tonight. I want ye to get out of the car."

She blinked at him, hearing his words, knowing she should slam the door and lock it. Instead, she climbed out of the car. It was as though she were separate from her actions, as if she watched herself from somewhere else. Why didn't she run? Why didn't she get back into the car? She was like a puppet doing his bidding while her mind screamed for her to resist.

Her pulse sharpened when she lifted her gaze to his. The world around her blurred, moving in slow motion. He pulled her into his arms and pressed his hard body against hers. His breath was warm against her cheeks. His touch…familiar.

She struggled to tear from his gaze and break the spell. Startled, she realized she was not in his arms at all, but stood like a statue in front of the open car door. What had just happened? She must escape and strained to raise her arms, but they were dead weights. Drugged. He'd drugged her! Her mind raced back to the past few minutes, when she'd taken her things from him in the restaurant. She'd been in such a state he could have pricked her with a needle, anything and she'd not have noticed.

"Ye can trust me, my Jeanne." The dome light was harsh against his handsome face. He raised his hand and tapped the door handle. It slammed closed. Darkness now shrouded him, but she found his gaze, only this time it was calmness, not fear that swept over her.

"What have you done to me?" She struggled to push the words past her lips. It took every ounce of energy she had to raise her voice above a faint whisper. A haze masked her thoughts with a warmth encasing her. Sleep beckoned.

"Close your eyes, Jeanne." His words held mysterious promises in their baritone depths.

"I have to find Ryan—" She reached for the door, but missed and fell forward. She cried out. His strong arms caught her and lifted her against him.

"I'll take ye to him, lass, but we must wait until the time is right. 'Til then, sleep."

Chapter Two

Jeanne reached out to steady herself against his hard chest. She pulled away, but his arms tightened around her.

"Ye are all right, lass. Sit down over here. Gather your wits." He guided her to the huge rock beneath a pine tree.

She blinked, desperately trying to focus, but the night engulfed her, so she couldn't get her bearings. Bowing her head, she rubbed her eyes then looked up.

"Where are we? How did I get here?" Her heart pounded. Why couldn't she remember? The night breeze lifted her hair, capturing a thin wisp. The wild strand danced in front of her face. Absently, she swatted at it, but the wind snatched it from her grasp and dropped the dark curl back to her shoulder before moving on to her companion.

Though groggy, she was acutely aware he seemed separate from everything around them. She noticed how even nature dared not disturb him when the breeze abruptly changed direction to rush into the thicket beside him. Everything spun in front of her.

"I'm really dizzy." She bowed her head and fought to quell the rising nausea.

"It shall pass." His voice pierced the night.

"You *drugged* me." She strained to see his face hidden in the night's shadows. Questions and fragmented conversation of her meeting with Trench and her flight from the restaurant tumbled over each other.

Clouds swept across the black sky, revealing a full moon. Its light cascaded through the trees and bathed everything in a gray shimmer. His handsome face shone pale, but his eyes were sudden shards of brilliance.

Her breath caught in her throat. Hypnotic eyes. Was that possible? Had he hypnotized her? She didn't remember any woods near the diner. Willing the trembling in her body to calm, she flattened her hands against her legs. Just what had happened after she left the diner? She'd been on her way to the police. Had she made it to the station?

"Ryan. Oh my God, I have to find my brother." She moved to stand, but everything tilted sideways. His strong arms supported her.

"Easy, lass. Ye need to take a moment to recover."

"Recover?" she scoffed out loud. How could she do that with his hard body pressed against her? Her senses sparked alive with his closeness. What kind of drug had he given her? Night smells rose on the wave of a new breeze. Everything smelled differently. It all felt so—

"Ancient?" he finished her thought. Had she spoken out loud?

"What?" She glanced up at him, and then looked away, trying to recognize the surroundings. "Where are we?"

"Where Trench has brought your brother. They arrived this morning." He lifted his hand to smooth her hair from her face. His fingers brushed against her skin. The contact shot through her, and her knees turned to water.

"This morning?" She felt as though she had been plopped down in the middle of a dream. "Are you saying it's *Saturday* night?" Panic trembled to her arms and legs, and pounded out a staccato heartbeat in her ears. "That's impossible. An entire day passed? Oh God! Why can't I remember anything?" She rubbed her temple.

"A cruel fate was bestowed upon us. For now that I have found ye, I canna have ye. But soon, soon, ye shall understand. We're running out of time."

"Time?" She shook her head, unable to believe she'd lost an entire day. And what did he mean *have* her? Did he think she was going to have sex with him?

"Come." He released her and started across the meadow toward the hill. "We need to hurry, Jeanne." The sound of his voice burned through her. It was so familiar. Where had she heard it before? Had she met MacRaigl at the lab? No, she swallowed hard, she'd have remembered him. A man like him was not easily forgotten. She might be a dedicated scientist, but she certainly would have found time to get to know any man walking into the lab looking like that. Did he work for Trench? Was that it? Had Trench sent him to keep her under control?

Once more clouds blotted out the moon, casting shadows to race over the strange terrain. Large boulders dotted the grassy meadow and bulged into hills that rose high above the woods. She was not on the Carolina coast. That much was certain. Had he driven her to the Blue Ridge Mountains? Was that where she was? She watched him walk up the steep rocky terrain. He was leaving her behind!

All I Want

She jumped up and ran after him. He knew too much about her to have been sent by Trench. Trench wouldn't have divulged anything, so how did MacRaigl know about her formula? More importantly, how did he know where Ryan was?

"Who are you?" She caught up with him and grabbed his coat sleeve jerking against his arm. "Where are we going?"

He spun around so quickly she nearly lost her balance.

"This is Scotland. My homeland." He looked down at her with his dark gaze devouring her. She swallowed hard against her hammering heartbeat. "And this is where your brother is being held prisoner."

"*Scotland*?" Her voice echoed around them. "Are you crazy?" Her legs threatened to collapse beneath her again. Okay, not a good thing to ask an insane person. His laughter was deep as he slipped his arm around her waist and tugged her to him. For a moment she thought he was going to kiss her. For a brief split in reality, she could see him doing just that, but in another setting, a more barbaric surrounding. He looked different, too, sporting a short beard and longer hair braided along the sides of his handsome face. But his laughter was just as deep and rich. It burned through her as though it were hot coals. When had she met him? She shook her head vigorously.

"I don't understand any of this." She struggled from him. "I don't remember boarding a jet. That would be, what? A five-hour flight with about that much of a time difference? Why can't I remember anything?"

"Ye have no memory of it, or me. Do ye?" he asked with disappointment edging his voice. He moved from her.

"You're the man from the diner. But I don't remember flying. If this is Saturday, then I've lost an entire day." The sinking feeling entrapped her. "Oh, God, what have you done to me?"

"I've brought ye to the place Trench is holding your brother prisoner."

"I was out for an entire day? Look here, I want some answers." She planted her hands on her hips.

"I've kept ye safe, Jeanne, until it was time. Now, we must go." He moved.

"Whoa! You have to answer some questions before I go any further with you, highlander."

A smile tugged the corners of his mouth in response to the title.

"I don't remember leaving the diner parking lot."

"Ye lost one day. 'Tis forever gone. Ye canna regain it, but Ryan shall lose forever if ye insist on answers now. There's more at stake than just your brother. The future of the world rests squarely on your shoulders. Your science canna explain what has happened, my Jeanne. Science requires proof, and my magic requires faith. Do ye have any faith left within ye?"

"What?" Somehow, she knew he could see there was no faith in her. Sadness dulled his brown eyes.

"Then it'll be a difficult journey for ye." He stroked her cheek with the back of his hand. His touch blazed a trail of heat through her. Her clit tingled in response, and she swallowed against the unexpected twinge of arousal. Suddenly, he turned and resumed the climb up the rocky hill.

"Wh-what does that mean?" She mentally shook herself. The clouds fled from the moon, brightening the landscape. "You're full of riddles that have no answers," she yelled after him. He paused mid-stride. The cool moonlight bathed him in an eerie radiance.

"I believe 'tis yours." He held a blue disc in front of her. The moon's brightness glinted off it like a reflecting mirror.

She plunged her hands inside the jacket pockets. Her fingers groped for the disc, but it was gone. Her attention shot back to the stranger.

"Give it back, damn you." She dug her heels into the ground and ran up the hill after him.

"Ye must come with me to have it returned."

"Do you have any idea what's on it?" she yelled while running toward him.

"Aye." He nodded.

She stopped in front of him then bolted to block his path. "Then you know how important it is to *everyone*," she panted and stood with her feet planted apart, hands on hips. The disc was just beyond her reach. She wanted to lunge for it, but dared not risk damaging the only remaining copy.

"'Tis your formula for your antiserum." He held it in front of her. "When Trench learned he dinna have the complete formula, he asked ye to meet him at the diner last evening and bring it to him, only ye pretended ye dinna have it. Without the last equation," he paused and glanced at the disc, "'tis all worthless. Trench has nothing."

"Just what do you want?" Her fingers itched to snatch the disc from him. She wanted to find Ryan. She wanted everything to return to the way it had been.

"Had ye gone to the police, your brother would now be dead. We gave Trench time enough to arrive here and be lulled into a false feeling of victory. The man is certain no one can stop him. But he's wrong. I'm here to help ye stop him and get your brother back."

"How do you know so much? Just who the hell are you?" She bit her lower lip, trying to gauge the truth in his piercing stare.

"Someone ye can trust," he said and glanced at the horizon. "We need to hurry."

"Trust," she choked. She didn't trust anyone or anything. She was not about to trust this mysterious stranger who had kidnapped and obviously drugged her.

"Aye. That thing ye dinna believe in. When did ye lose that part of your soul? Was it when your parents died that fated New Year's Eve, and ye realized some things in life canna be explained away with scientific logic?"

"Just who the hell do you think you are?" She clenched her teeth. "What gives you the right to bring me here, wherever here is and then tell me about my parents? And just for the record, they died New Year's *Day* 2000, not New Year's Eve."

"Always focused on the details, Jeanne. Always the scientist." He looked into her eyes. A chill rushed over her. "'Tis going to require something other than chemistry or physics or even state-of-the-art technology. It requires a leap of faith. Can ye manage such a thing?"

"I'm not leaping anywhere with you." She folded her arms over her chest.

"Then ye condemn your brother to death. It'll be dawn soon." His stare swept the late nightscape, and then once more settled on her.

"What happens at dawn? Do you turn to dust or something?" Her sarcastic tone filled the night. She startled when he grabbed her and jerked her against him. His hard cock pressed against her belly. She throbbed as his fingers threaded through her hair and tilted her head back to receive his kiss. She blinked up at him but her breath caught in her throat for he was standing almost a foot away. It was the second time she'd experienced the sensation. What was it? His eyes seemed too bright for the darkness. A frenzied current sparked and throbbed to her pussy, wetting her panties. Her cheeks flushed hot and she looked away.

"Come." He turned.

She jolted from her trance and gasped for air, realizing she'd been holding her breath. He was leaving her!

"Hey! My disc." She sprinted after him.

Early morning dew greeted her with the heavy scent of sod. A sudden silence fell over the night, even the wind stopped. Just above the treetops, the moon gleamed in luminous splendor, only it appeared to be growing larger. She glanced at the valley, then back at the moon. It was hurtling toward the earth! She widened her gaze and watched the moon descend into the trees.

A primordial stirring fluttered in the pit of her stomach rousing a memory. She struggled to summon it to the front of her mind, but it retreated into fleeting shadows with voices echoing in their wake. A cool breeze held on to the magic with Celtic melodies drifting to caress her face like a lover's touch. The lonely whine of a bagpipe resonated deep inside her. Jeanne looked in his direction. He was now at the bottom of the hill, but where was the piper? She spun around. No one was there.

"Hurry, Jeanne, we're running out of time." He stood on the ledge overlooking the valley floor.

Her breath escaped between parted lips. Familiarity and recognition of the moment went beyond all she knew. Her soul filled with the melody of memory, so clear yet so distant. Glancing back, she swept the line of trees for the moon, but it was gone. How was that possible? She'd witnessed the moon falling. Just as she knew she'd heard pipes. Trapped within a flickering span of time, she sensed all mysteries beyond her understanding lay in wait. All she had to do was reach out with faith and the invisible veil would fall. What faith? The enchanted moment fled just like the moon. Confusion flooded the void.

"What's going on?" Frantically, she searched the tree line for the moon.

"We're almost there." His baritone voice beckoned her. It had been so real. "Jeanne."

Hesitating for a heartbeat, she glanced at the horizon one last time then ran the rest of the way and made the descent to where MacRaigl waited. His lips stretched into an understanding smile.

"So ye take your first leap of faith, Jeanne lass. Now your journey begins." The light in his eyes softened.

"Journey?" she asked.

"Do ye like castles?" He nodded toward the valley floor.

She followed his stare to the valley below them. It stretched toward a wide meandering river crested by another rising hillside and a— She squinted her eyes shut then opened them again, but the wide towers jutting from the building below were still there.

"A castle?" her voice rang through the silence with incredulous timbre.

* * * * *

"How did you know about this passage?" she whispered.

MacRaigl led the way through the wooded area surrounding the estate.

"My business to know," he said, never breaking his stride. She marveled at his soundless movements. He stopped and raised his hand in a gesture for silence. She held her breath, straining to hear.

"There are dogs," he informed her.

"Dogs?" She strangled on the word. "Did you say dogs?" The world pitched. She grabbed a nearby tree branch to brace herself. Her body stiffened with familiar panic. Perspiration chilled against her skin.

A distant owl's hoot startled her. Had she been superstitious, she would have stopped right there and fled. Instead, she quickened her stride to catch up with him. Snarling hounds with sharp teeth bared in a fit of attack was not a sight she wanted to see ever again.

"I know ye are afraid, lass, but I shall not let them near ye." He waited for her. If she could have seen his eyes in the faint light, Jeanne knew they'd mirror the sympathetic tone of his voice.

She stared up at him, silenced by flashing memories. Post-Traumatic Shock Disorder. She knew all the clinical stats on her condition, yet knowing did not prevent recurrence. Her breathing was rapid. She tried to calm the hyperventilation by forcing her breath to slow.

"I promise ye, my Jeanne. I'll not let the beasties near ye." He grabbed her hand.

His touch sent electric shocks coursing through her. She could not place the feel of him to anything she knew, yet the contact of his flesh against hers broke the familiar cycle of relapse. She blinked up into his bright eyes. How was that possible? What kind of power did he possess? Nothing had ever stopped the PTSD episodes.

"I forget ye dinna know me." He squeezed her hand then released it before starting across the damp meadow. She stared after him, trying to comprehend his power over her.

"What kind of dogs?" She hurried to catch up with him. Even therapy had not diminished the power of her fear. Her heartbeat pounded so loudly she couldn't hear anything, much less a stalking, killer canine.

The trauma had molded her, against her will, dictating her choices and haunting her dreams. And here she was defenseless, out in the open, vulnerable to her greatest fear. Dogs! Her legs trembled, threatening to fail her. The vision of falling to the ground and becoming an easy prey of the animals quickened her pulse.

"Ye are safe with me, Jeanne. I'll always protect ye."

She tried to focus on his words. She couldn't keep up with his long strides toward the castle. Sprinting across the wide meadow, her feet pounded against the ground almost as hard as her heartbeat. Slowing her pace, she matched his stride and timidly slipped her hand into his confident one. Empowerment was immediate. How did he do that? She glanced over her shoulder, searching the darkness for any movement, anything that might be one of those bloodthirsty creatures lurking, watching and waiting. Goose bumps prickled down her spine.

Long shadows darkened the ground, mirroring the tall towers. MacRaigl stepped into the blackness. She was quick to follow him. They stopped in front of the stone wall and he glanced down at their clasped hands. She followed his stare. Her breath tugged from her. A delicious warmth rushed through her, drawing her nipples tighter. Consciously, she met his look. Were those tears she saw or an illusion of the night?

MacRaigl's eyelids closed against her probing, and he lifted her hand to his lips. Jeanne held her breath in anticipation. His lips touched her skin and delightful shivers rippled up her arm and fluttered against her heart sending it into an erratic pounding. His lips lingered, welding his breath to her flesh.

Suddenly, his strong hands closed over her shoulders and he tugged her to him, pressing his powerful body against hers. His lips covered her gasp. Demanding lips of fire scorched a path of longing to her very soul. She whimpered with desire so arresting, she let his tongue part her lips and take full possession, darting and teasing her tongue.

Images flashed through her mind as though a fast-forwarded movie. Scene after scene of an ancient time, swords, highlanders, a sea of faces and echoing voices filled her mind.

Mael's arms molded around her and the familiarity of his touch, his very taste, overpowered all protests, dissolving into blissful internal welcoming as though a long awaited reunion. Vignettes of conversations and scenery cascaded around her. The light from a fireplace so real she could smell the woodsmoke. The visions were so powerful, she shuddered and his kiss melted through her.

The image sharpened. She saw herself lying naked in his arms with the shadows of their passion dancing on the stone wall. *Ye belong to me now, Jeanne love. No other man shall lie with ye, ever.* She could feel his tongue flicking against her clit. The raging need to feel him inside her, shocked her, yet the vision felt so natural and oh-so very right. The penetration of his cock... His tongue teasing hers... She struggled from the scene, pushing it from her mind, but it was as unrelenting as his dark fiery kiss. *I want you, Mael, now!* Her shadowy form gasped and clung to him as the warrior pounded his cock into her.

Jeanne groped for something real to find her way out of the delusion. She pressed her palms against his broad chest and shoved back, breaking the consuming kiss.

"My Jeanne," Mael MacRaigl rasped, panting as he moved to recapture her lips.

"No!" She managed to push the breath from her chest and his arms fell from her. Jeanne stumbled back, touching her fingertips to her searing lips. This was a new twist to her trauma. She was now hallucinating passionate sexual encounters. Embarrassed, she cleared her throat.

"Are ye all right?" He reached out to touch her shoulder, but she sidestepped him. She needed distance between them. Somehow, she knew he was the reason for the images. She didn't understand how, but she could not afford physical contact again.

"This place." She tried to rationalize her behavior. "It reminds me, I mean. I feel like—" Her breath jerked in short pants against her strained control. She tried to disentangle herself from the vision. "It's like a fortress."

"Aye, built to withstand the fiercest of attacks."

"It was?"

"Completed in the year 1240 A.D.," he said with the crease in his forehead deepening. "'Tis been added to over the centuries, but the core of its center is as ye shall remember it."

"I've never been here. I'd have remembered it." She stared up at the massive building. As soon as the words tumbled over her lips, she knew they weren't true. "It's the strangest feeling." She shook her head.

"As though ye *have* been here before?" He finished her sentence once more and smiled down at her. "Perhaps in another life?" He tried to lighten the moment, but his words only made her more anxious. She needed to focus on something else. Anything.

"This is where Trench has been living?" she asked.

"He leases the estate. Come." He held out his hand.

She shoved her hands deep into her jacket pockets and followed him around the massive wall to a thick underbrush of ivy.

"I don't understand why he's in Scotland, of all places," she said, shocked that she accepted she was indeed in Scotland.

MacRaigl pushed through the ivy and was swallowed up by the dense vines.

"There's the door. Come." His hand emerged from the camouflage of leaves, but Jeanne ignored the offer and pushed the vines aside.

"How did you know about this?" She stepped inside the stone passageway.

"I know everything about this castle. 'Tis mine." He shrugged apologetically then started down the dark corridor. Short beams of light flashed on as he passed. The diffused light fell onto the stone floor and guided their winding trek.

"Yours?" she asked and hurried to keep up with him. Her earlier misgivings returned. How did she know he was telling the truth? She could not be certain about anything at that moment. Even if he could help free Ryan and stop Trench, how could she trust what he said? She had thrown all logic to the wind and was following him deeper into what could be a trap.

All I Want

She swallowed hard. It had been a very long leap of faith, all the way to her ancestral homeland, Scotland. In a saner moment, she'd have fled in the opposite direction. The memory of Trench's sneer as he'd tossed the money on the table jarred her. Was anything about Trench and his diabolical plan sane? Somehow it felt logical to be illogical. And this man she was following through a castle, no less, what about him? Who was he? What did he really want?

"Ye can trust me. Trench's mind has begun to deteriorate in his quest for power." MacRaigl turned to her, speaking as though he had read her very thoughts.

His presence filled the narrow tunnel. Her nostrils pricked with the scent of his cologne and woodsmoke but there was more. A strange mingling of scents like incense and other ancient aromas tugged her very soul, teasing a singular thought, but retreated before she could grasp it.

She stood even with his broad, strong shoulders, which she instinctively knew could bear the weight of the world if needed. Now, how could she possibly know that? But she did, deep in her heart. She also knew his anger could spark quickly just as she knew his humor could erupt into a deep, infectious laugh.

She drew a long breath. It was not logical that she knew anything about this man. She'd never been prone to over-imagination, but then she'd never been in such extraordinary circumstances, accustomed to dealing with facts. There were no facts to support these imaginings or feelings.

Excited pulses fluttered from her stomach to her groin and desire rushed warm and moist, dampening her panties. That had never happened before! How could the mere thought of him evoke such a physical reaction? She knew his touch. As surely as she knew her own name, she knew what it felt like to be possessed by this man. Her breathing sharpened. She wanted to be possessed by him so badly. She ached raw with a need stronger than any sexual desire she'd ever experienced.

"I'm here for one reason only, my Jeanne, and that's to ensure ye stop Trench."

The mere sound of his voice made her knees weaken. Was it possible he knew what she was thinking? She struggled to focus on anything other than his handsome face, or the images flashing through her mind or recalling how hard his cock was against her when he'd embraced her.

"If you know who Trench is, and what he's doing, then why lease him your castle?"

"I always keep my enemies close."

"Trench is your enemy?"

"He's yours, is he not?" His gaze touched her eyes then slowly moved to her lips.

She tucked her lower lip underneath her teeth.

"Some things always remain. We must hurry, Jeanne."

On wobbly legs, she followed him. No man had ever had this effect on her. Before she could further contemplate her mysterious ally, he paused in front of an arched door.

The same feeling of cognizance washed over her. Jeanne took a deep breath to still the riotous hammering of her heartbeat.

"Do you know where Ryan is? What part of the castle?" she asked.

"I'll find Ryan and free him, but ye must follow Trench."

"Follow?" Her stare snapped up to his eyes—such incredible eyes.

"Ye shall understand when we get there. Just know I'll protect Ryan, Jeanne. Ye must follow Trench," he said before turning to open the door.

"What?" She wanted to spin him around to face her. She needed answers not mysterious remarks that only raised more questions. Instead, her attention was drawn to his long braid of auburn hair intertwined with thin strips of leather. Fleeting phantom images stirred in the furthest recesses of her mind and mingled with erotic longings she'd never felt before.

"Ye must go first, Jeanne. I'll search for Ryan. But ye go the rest of the way alone." The light from outside the tunnel fell over his face, but his eyes seemed to glow with an inner fire. "I wish I could accompany ye. But 'tis your own journey ye make from this point forward."

Her pulse spiked, and her mouth dried with unspoken questions.

"I have lived in *Tír na-Óc* too long, my Jeanne. To be trapped within *Annwn* was my choice. Ye must remember this. I dinna regret my choices. To be here this day has been my single purpose in all I have done." He lowered his face to hers.

Her heart slammed against the wall of her chest when his lips brushed hers. Cool lips that heated her flesh like an open flame. She wanted more and moved her arms, prepared to encircle his neck. It was a familiar fire racing through her—a fire only he could stoke to flame and only he could quench.

He broke from their kiss and whispered, "Godspeed."

She blinked up at him, not understanding a word he'd said. Her nerve endings tingled alive with his closeness. Before she could react, he opened the door and placed a firm hand on the small of her back, guiding her through the doorway.

She started to turn and voice concern about waltzing in on Trench when MacRaigl closed the door behind her. She panicked. Certain he had been locked out, she shoved against the door, pushing with all her strength, but it didn't budge.

"Doctor McBen." The high-pitched voice of her enemy resounded overhead. "I guess I underestimated you, again."

Chapter Three

Jeanne watched Trench descend the staircase, seeming nonplused by her intrusion.

"Where's my brother?" She glanced about the massive foyer, noting the uneven stone floor. It really was a castle! Where was MacRaigl? Was he waiting on the other side of the door for the right moment?

Trench gestured and two guards rounded the front hall corner.

"Not her. I can handle a woman, you idiots. Check, through that door, the tunnels and the grounds, just in case she's not alone. You are alone, aren't you, Doctor?"

The guards pushed past her and to Jeanne's surprise, the door opened easily. Where was MacRaigl?

"My castle's protected by *dogs*. Did you know that?" His lecherous smile made her stomach churn. "You must have encountered my Dobermans. No?" His eyebrows arched high over his beady eyes.

The air stirred warmer, and the room pitched, threatening to fade from her. She steadied herself against the wall.

"Please, come into my parlor." His face broke into a twisted grin. "Perhaps a scotch or brandy?"

He gestured to the Queen Anne chair while he strolled over to the sideboard. "How was your flight? I just arrived this morning. Of course, I have my own jet now. Did I mention that before?"

She closed her eyes, trying to remember how she'd come to be here. She should be able to recall the flight. Her mind filled with images of MacRaigl. Where was he?

"Doctor McBen?" He held up a glass of brandy.

"I want to see my brother." Jeanne ignored the proffered drink and folded her arms across her chest. Her gaze flickered over her shoulder to the foyer. Anxiously, she held her breath, listening for any sounds from the underground passage. There were none.

All I Want

"You did come by yourself, didn't you?" He paused as he filled the snifter.

"I want to see—" Her words latched in her throat, for hanging over the large fireplace at the end of the room, was an oil painting image of Mael MacRaigl.

"Striking, isn't it?" he asked, following her stare. "You should see his descendant, the owner of this estate. He's the perfect image."

She couldn't resist and moved closer to the mantel, staring up at the full regalia of the kilted highlander. She studied the bronze eyes set in the strong tanned face framed by long brown hair which hung in side braids intertwined with leather and plaid strips. Mael MacRaigl.

"How did you find me?" Trench's voice jerked her out of her trancelike fascination of the portrait.

"I want to talk with my brother." She spun around to face him, delivering what she hoped was a defiant look.

"How did you find that old entrance into the estate? Only the groundskeeper and I know about the underground tunnel to the wine cellar. How could you have possibly known about it?"

"I want to see Ryan. Now!" she said.

"Okay." Trench nodded, but to her consternation, lowered his lanky frame into the tapestry-covered chair.

His surrender caught her off-guard. Her shoulders relaxed, and she flattened her sweaty palms against her jeans. Ryan was still alive. Once she saw him, she would be okay.

"I'll allow you to see your brother, if," he paused and smiled at her, "you give me what I want."

"You have my work and my brother. What else could you want?"

"The same thing I wanted Friday night. The disc. The downloads from your lab were incomplete. It appears you left out a step. A very important step, Doctor McBen. The last piece of data that reveals the plasmid vector and, of course, the right protein DNA. Without those—"

"You don't have a cure," she finished, feeling victorious over him.

"It's all worthless." His irritation etched across his sallow face. "But you know that. That's why you created the file without the final data. Very clever. The disc?" He turned his palm up and raised his head so he looked down his nose at her.

"I don't have it." She told the truth, recalling MacRaigl still had it. "I don't know where it is."

"Surely you can be more creative."

"I've been upset about my brother and my antiserum. *My* antiserum, which you stole from me." She clenched her fists by her sides. "The antiserum I had to create because you and your associates wouldn't listen to warnings issued by my father. You didn't care about the potential immune response. And that's *your* gift to the world — death. You've stolen the future from the world."

"Stolen is such a harsh word." He lifted the brandy snifter to his nose and inhaled. "Ah, I love Russian cognac. And as for your poor washed-up father, he chose his direction in the science community — totally against the mainstream of popular opinion. He committed professional suicide."

"My father was right! He's revered."

"Wouldn't surprise me if they tried to make him a saint." The sarcasm in his tone shot through her.

"You stole my antiserum and kidnapped my brother. Those are serious crimes, *Doctor* Trench." She took a step backwards, trying to edge her way into the hall.

Had he planned this from the beginning? Had he taken her under his wing and brought her on board, right out of med school because he'd known she was on the path to finding a cure? How quickly life had pivoted. Saving the world from one of the worst diseases to plague history now meant her brother's life would be forfeited. Fear pounded so hard she couldn't move.

"Do you think I'm concerned about such a trivial thing as kidnapping? I'm going to soon rule the world, Jeanne. With the antiserum, I can—"

"My antiserum is for the world, not for you to exploit." She clasped her hands in front of her, lest she slap that smug grin off his face.

"You always were an idealist, Jeanne." He tilted the glass and finished the brandy.

"Better than a thief," she spat, looking toward the staircase and the upper level. Where was her accomplice? Had the guards captured him? Was he hurt? Captured? Her heart skipped a beat. Dead?

All I Want

MacRaigl was not going to help her. Her confidence crumbled. She'd followed him right into a trap. She'd made it so easy for Trench. Her breath rose and fell in faster waves.

"You need to learn the ways of the world, particularly those of research. We're a close-knit community and those in very high positions have been watching you for some time. Do you think I do all this on my own volition?" He gestured for her to sit down in front of him.

"So, the government is behind your theft of my antiserum? And I thought it was DEC Corporation."

"Sit," he insisted.

Again, she ignored the request and folded her arms over her chest. She fought the urge to run up the ancient staircase just outside the room and scream Ryan's name. Instead, she glared at Trench.

"I'm glad you realize your research was not financed by mediocre government agencies."

"I understand you're a thief. But you forgot one thing—you can't mass-produce." She bowed her head. "That's been my one obstacle."

"The lack of AB negative blood is no longer an impediment."

She snapped alert.

"That's the *only* impediment to my antiserum being readily available."

"I've solved that minor detail. As I was about to say, I've several projects related to your research. You'll be relieved to know your brother and those like him won't have to be sacrificed, if all goes well."

"Sacrificed?" she repeated and broke into a cold sweat. He was willing to drain Ryan of his precious blood. Every beat of her heart was painful.

"I also found it odd I could not isolate the DNA protein needed for your antiserum. It was easy enough to check the DNA protein of all AB negatives. I assumed it was a singular common protein of that blood type. But even with my endless resources and exhausting all avenues to duplicate the proteins, I'm embarrassed to admit, I'm stumped."

"You did all that?" Realization threw her panic to a heightened level.

"Several months ago. But what I couldn't discover was which protein or combination makes your formula successful. I need that disc."

She felt as though the air had been knocked out of her. All this time he'd been watching her, attempting to duplicate her research. She was grateful she'd been so careful and never left the last equation of her formula at the lab. She'd been worried this very thing would happen, only the espionage would come from competitors, not her own boss.

"The disc. I'm getting tired of repeating myself."

"We can't recreate the protein synthetically. Ryan doesn't have enough to mass-produce. We can never give the world a cure for *Next Gen*. There's not enough blood supply to produce the antiserum."

"The only conclusion I reached was he and perhaps other AB negatives are genetic throwbacks. Possibly throwbacks to here. Scotland," he informed her with a smug smile cracking the hard lines of his face.

"That's impossible," she said, shaking her head. "Only one percent of the population is blood-typed AB negative. To create the kind of blood supply needed for adequate production requires at least one out of three. My research showed the thirteenth century might have supported that large of a population with AB negative blood, but that's speculation."

"There's proof, right here. You discovered it last year." His smile widened.

She drew her arms tighter into her chest, straining to contain the anger coursing through her.

"The DNA from my ancestor's grave?" Her mind whirled with what she knew he had concluded. "The bloodstain on the burial garment was not conclusive. The integrity of the remains was in question." Her voice cracked, and the words lodged in her throat when she met his smug look. "That's why you're here?"

"Your conclusion from that one DNA sample was proof the blood type existed."

"You've misinterpreted my findings. You can't be that sloppy. You wrote the textbooks on research protocol. You know it doesn't prove AB negative was common. It only points that the remains were in all probability my ancestor's, who had AB negative blood with the necessary protein. That's all it proved."

"You're such a brilliant scientist, but it's a shame you didn't stay in America, instead of following me here. We could have been a great team."

All I Want

"You stand for everything I loathe."

"I've exhumed other tombs, other gravesites and all are AB negative. The key to gaining enough AB blood is here in the heart of the Highlands, tucked away in this remote location. This castle provides the necessary alchemy for my experiment."

"Alchemy?" Her laugh was strained. "I see you've advanced your science into the realm of what...witchcraft? A little eye of newt, Trench?"

"You think I'm mad?" His eyes slid closed then opened. "Once I have all the blood I need to sell to DEC, then maybe you'll grasp the scope of my genius."

"So all you care about is the money?"

"What else did you think? Science?" He crossed his legs and brushed his hand over his slacks.

"How could I've been so wrong about you?" she spat, trying to judge the distance to the staircase. "You have no conscience."

"I guess I really don't." He stroked his pointed chin, letting his gaze move over her.

Jeanne stiffened her spine, refusing to be intimidated.

He glanced past her to the grandfather clock with widened eyes.

"It's almost time." He stood abruptly.

"I won't let you exploit my work. You're the reason a cure's needed. Had you listened to the warnings years ago about DNA antiserums and the experimental drugs you and your backers were using on the unsuspecting public..." She paused when the color rose in his face.

"I found my father's journal recently. I now know about your secret experiments, and how easily you'd stepped into the research program straight from Harvard. Those experiments spawned a greedy scientist who didn't give a damn about the damage he created.

"You didn't care about your moral obligation to the world. You and your partners used science to make yourselves rich and to hell with the next-generation mutations your drugs created. *You* gave the world *Next Gen*. What happened to 'do no harm'?"

"Ideals of the young. When you get to be my age you'll realize it's all empty idealism. The only thing that gets you what you want in life is money and the power it wields. Had it not been me, there would have been someone else to carry out the work. Destiny has its own agenda.

Besides, each generation spawns a brilliant scientist, like you, who can counter the ill side effects of the previous one."

"Ill side effects? Are you serious? Next Generation Syndrome is more than a side effect. You've created a sterile society. The death of the human race is a lot more than an ill side effect."

"It won't come to that, since I have your antiserum. Just give me the disc and we can stop all this."

"I told you, I don't have it and there's no other copy. How do you intend to retrieve it from my mind?" She jutted her chin out and met his unwavering glare.

The veins in his forehead bulged underneath his skin. He grabbed her arm. She cried out.

"Then you sentence your brother to death." The digital beeping interrupted him. Trench raised his wrist and tapped the watch stem. The beeping stopped. "We're out of time."

"I won't let you do this!" she yelled and broke from him. "Ryan!" She ran up the staircase.

Chapter Four

"Who the hell are you?" The youth backed from the door with fear flashing in his blue eyes.

"I'm here to rescue ye," Mael announced to the five-foot-ten-inch wiry lad with short, cropped blond hair. Ryan looked like he belonged on a surfboard, not in an ancient castle being held hostage.

"Are you with the military?" he asked, backing away from him.

"I came with your sister."

"Jeanne? She's here? Where?" he yelled, relief washing over his face.

"Downstairs talking with Trench."

"Damn man, *he's* the one who brought me here. We have to save her."

"We have to wait here." Mael closed the door.

"Are you crazy?" Ryan tried to dash past him. Mael picked the youth up by his shirt and lifted him from the floor.

"I said we wait." Mael lowered him to the floor and the teenager backed away.

"How did you do that? Are you one of their test subjects? One of those GI power fighters?" he asked, pacing in front of Mael, running a shaky hand through his short hair.

"I'm a vampire," Mael spoke calmly, keeping his stare leveled on the boy.

"Okay, man, whatever," Ryan laughed. "But, this guy, Trench, he's dangerous. I-I think he killed my father."

"Why do ye think that?"

"Because my father worked for him and opposed the research that created Next Gen."

"Ye know about that?" Mael was surprised Jeanne had shared such confidential information with her brother.

"Of course. My sister found the cure. Trench wants it and will make everyone pay a fortune for it."

"And ye are just a pawn?"

"Yeah, man. That's me, a fricking pawn. When I tell Jen what I overheard—"

"What's that?"

"Something about a legend and an eclipse. I tell you, man, Trench has lost it. He's crazy. He thinks he can go back in time. Now, let me out of here so we can help my sister." He started toward Mael again.

"I know this is difficult to understand, but ye are helping her by staying here with me."

"You're full of shit, man." Ryan lunged at him, but Mael was quicker and soon had the lad's arms pinned behind his back. He slammed him against the wall with his face scraping against the rough stones.

"Ow!" he yelped. "Just let me go, man. I promise I won't tell no one. I just need to get my sister out of here."

"It's too late." Mael glanced out the window. "The sun will rise soon. Come. We're going into the tunnels." He dragged Ryan behind him and led him out the door.

"What tunnels?"

"The ones where I can keep an eye on ye until it's dark."

"That will be too late to save my sister."

"I made a promise to Jeanne and I intend to keep it."

* * * * *

Jeanne scaled the top step and bolted down the long corridor, but Trench's hand closed over her hair. He jerked her backwards, and she fell against him. Her cry of defeat echoed down the ancient stairwell.

"I've been waiting for this moment since I first heard the legend," Trench huffed, dragging her toward the landing, "and you won't interfere. I'd been turning over the problem of the DNA protein needed for your antiserum, when I remembered the forensic on your ancestor. I did a little investigating and stumbled across the Legend of MacRaigl."

"MacRaigl?" Her breath caught in her chest.

All I Want

Trench towed her behind him, down the steps and toward the cellar tunnels. "What you don't know is I did my thesis on displaced energy and a hypothesis on creating a vacuum in time. I've never abandoned my theories." He pulled the door open and pushed her through it.

She glanced around for MacRaigl. Had the guards found him? Was he waiting for the right moment to come to her rescue?

"Let me go!" She jerked against his grip. Her voice echoed through the twisting passages. "You've completely lost control, Gregory."

"You challenged me. I want you to see where your research has brought us." He halted in front of an arched doorway. "If you want your brother to live, you'll cooperate."

The cold look in his blue eyes paralyzed her. When he lifted the heavy door pull, it groaned open on its hinges, revealing a dark exit. He dragged her through the ivy arch, which only moments earlier she'd entered with MacRaigl.

Gray mist rose along the hillsides. Late night had stretched into early morning with the hint of sunrise along the horizon. He stomped through the damp high grass, pulling her behind him toward the distant knoll.

She jerked against his hold.

"Keep up this resistance and I'll just whistle for the dogs. Do you want to fight off a pack of incensed hounds?" His words gripped her like a cold vise.

She relaxed against his hold.

"Legend is a powerful thing, Jeanne. It lives long after those who create it."

"Your greed has driven you insane," she screamed.

His complexion darkened into a fine red hue. His fingers tightened around her arm.

"Insane? I'm a genius." His intense stare assured Jeanne he fully believed it. He shoved her ahead of him into the bramble. Prickly thorns seized her jacket and held her captive within their mass of gnarled vines cascading over the stacked-stone wall.

"It's only right you witness what your antidote has spawned." He jerked her from the briars. Her jacket ripped under the force, leaving shreds of material dangling from the wicked thorns. He towed her along and scaled up the hill, then descended into a glen.

"How far is it? Don't you have a jeep or something?"

"It's faster on foot. Can't drive a jeep where we're going."

They moved along the hillside, but the mist hampered their efforts. He tried to see his watch in the darkness. Obviously, he had a timetable, Jeanne pondered.

"The key to your creation lies here in this mountain a few yards ahead." Surprised how high they'd climbed, Jeanne marveled at the elongated drifts of rising mist.

"I didn't create your twisted agenda," she spat but came up short in her tirade when they crested the hill and stopped a few feet from a stone archway that divided two long, irregular three-foot walls. The walls cascaded down the hillside in opposite directions.

"What's that?" she asked, eyeing the opening with a sudden feeling of dread. He jerked her toward the arch, but she dug her heels into the ground. They stood about a foot from the opening. The air was static. Her skin tingled and a chill coursed down the length of her spine, making her stomach flutter. She knew whatever lay ahead was unnatural.

"You feel it too, don't you?" He moved closer to the archway.

"My God! What is it?" She held her hand out in front of the entrance. An electrical current greeted her fingertips. Jeanne marveled at the magnetic pull pulsating from the opening.

"This entrance was built in 1253 A.D. Three years after the event. It marks the mouth of the cave. A very special cave. It was all walled up. I had it excavated."

"What event?"

"A total solar eclipse that darkened all of Europe. It was the kind of event ripe for birthing a legend. And it did, a legend about a man and a woman who loved each other so much each gave their life for the other."

"I never thought of you as sentimental, much less romantic," she jeered, hating him with her entire being.

"Don't be absurd. Romantic garbage. The woman thought she was sacrificing her life so her lover could live, and he gave up his soul so she could live or some kind of nonsense. It's the legend that holds the key."

"Then I never realized how superstitious you are."

All I Want

"It's not superstition. During that eclipse a portal connecting the future with the past was opened. According to legend, this eclipse occurs every seven hundred and fifty-five years."

"A portal?"

"Straight through there. Legend says he shoved her through the portal so she could live."

"He shoved her into the past?"

"No!" he growled, exasperated with her questions. "He shoved her from the past, to here, the future."

"Why? What was he saving her from? And what happened to him?"

"All that matters is the eclipse and the legend."

"But you said he gave his soul so she could live."

"Some ridiculous romanticism obviously added to embellish the legend. He sent the portal keeper into another time then walled up the entrance so no one could ever use it again. Something about a bargain with the devil. All those legends have something about a bargain with the devil. Like I said, it's an obscure story. The only important part is the portal and the eclipse. That's what I'm interested in."

"What was the woman spared?"

"Something your brother won't be if you continue to refuse to cooperate." He pushed her into the dark opening.

"Is that how you intend to get the last equation from me? Kill my brother? I think that'll be real incentive for me, Trench." She hoped the sarcasm dripped from her words.

"Ryan will remain my guest for life, if I don't get what I want."

Her blood chilled with the calm threat, so easily said without emotion.

"Think of it as your final contribution to mankind, Jeanne. Since your antidote can't cure you and you'll never have children. But your antiserum will give birth to a new world."

A burning knot rose and thickened in her throat as tears welled in her eyes. She looked away, refusing to give him the satisfaction of seeing how much his malicious comments hurt. He shoved her and she stumbled into the pit of darkness.

"You're a twisted son of a bitch!"

The sound halted her. A horse? Cautiously, she squinted past the jagged opening. The horse's nervous neigh resounded from inside the cave, only this time, louder.

"We're almost there." He produced a palm-size flashlight from his pocket and held it over his wristwatch. "The portal should open in fifteen minutes."

"The eclipse is now?" She turned to face him. The sun had not crested the horizon. No radiance pierced the haze. "There's no sunrise. Shouldn't it be morning? How long does an eclipse last? Ten minutes or less? That doesn't give you much time, Trench. To obtain the quantity of blood you would need requires much longer. This is doomed to fail, even if the legend's true."

"Totality only lasts about three minutes. The moment just before the eclipse becomes total, there are brilliant shards of light—"

"Yeah, Baily's beads," she interrupted.

"It's more complicated than we have time for. We'll be inside the cave when totality happens and the portal should open then."

"*Should* being the operative word," she sneered.

"If the legend's true, the portal will open again one year from today, as time bends back into itself, like a rubber band snapping back. It's said to remain open the entire witching hour. Which was considered to be midnight. After that, it won't reopen until the next total eclipse seven hundred and fifty-five years from now."

"But there are eclipses all the time. It's not logical to risk so much on an obscure legend."

"There's only one eclipse like this one. It happens when all the planets are aligned perfectly, remember the one in 2000 when all the planets were aligned to a certain configuration in the sky? The last time that particular eclipse with planetary alignment had happened was at the time around the birth of Christ. It's the same kind of unique alignment. I've spent the last two years analyzing data. This is it! This is the time the legend spoke about. Look at the horizon, there in the east. See how dark it is?"

She followed his stare. "Sure because it's night."

"No," he said, "it's six-thirty in the morning." He held his watch up to her, shining the flashlight's beam on it.

For the first time, she noticed the very color around them seemed to be draining from the earth itself.

"But there was a full moon! I saw it. I know enough about eclipses to know there can only be a solar eclipse when there's a new moon not a full one."

"There wasn't a full moon." Trench looked at her as though she were crazy.

"Yes, there was."

He shook his head and jerked her toward the cave.

"Your attempt to confuse me is worse than lame. The last signs of the approaching eclipse began a few days ago. These signs distinguish this eclipse above all others. I've done the calculations. It's all very precise with specific placements of planets in line with the Eastern hemisphere. These alignments began moving into place over a year ago.

"I have it all worked out, down to the most minute detail. The equipment's inside the cave. I can extract then convert the plasma protein and store it until the portal reopens next year. I'll be able to monitor the planets once on the other side and calculate the exact moment the portal will reopen. And then, I'll bring my precious cargo back to this time period before the portal seals again." He held his hand up to direct the flashlight's beam into the cave.

"I have a portable lab right in here." He moved the beam to reveal a crude cart covered with an oily canvas and a very nervous horse tethered to it. "I had to bring the cart up the other side of the mountain. Too steep the way we came. See? I have cases of collection bags, syringes, a solar generator to power a refrigeration unit, and even a hydro generator, just in case, as backup. I've thought of everything."

"You're crazy!" she shouted, fearing he was not insane and what he was saying was more than legend — It was history.

"I hadn't expected you."

Before she could react, he grabbed her. His fingers closed over her wrists and pinned her arms behind her back.

"Let go of me!"

He wrapped something around her hands and wound it tight about her chest. She struggled against the elastic binding, but he pushed her to the floor. She kicked at him. He had the advantage and bound her legs together.

"I left instructions for the cave to be guarded until I return, so one of the guards will find you tomorrow and keep you safe until I return. That should give you plenty of time to realize you've no choice but to give me the formula. I'd advise you not to leave the cave. You could hurt yourself. There are all types of wild animals roaming around."

"I can't imagine you risked staying in North Carolina until the last moment. You must have been sweating bullets trying to get back here in time." She tried to distract him and somehow keep him from going through with the diabolical plan.

"I had no choice. I needed the complete formula. Kidnapping Ryan and bringing him back here with me was a stroke of genius. I had plenty of time. When you showed up, my fantasy was complete. You can be a witness."

He stood from the task, staring down at her with his arms akimbo. "I know how close you and Ryan have become since your parents' deaths."

She looked away, hoping he'd not seen the pain in her eyes. She'd never give him that satisfaction, damn him.

"You protest now, but in the end, you'll do just as I want. You have a brilliant mind but believe your life's governed by logic." He leaned down so his face was only inches from hers. "But as a scientist you're flawed because you have a sentimental heart. You try desperately to hide it. You even think you control it, but you don't. You never will," he jeered.

"I'll never give the disc to you." She glared up at him, hoping he could feel the hatred searing through her.

He retrieved a cigarette lighter from his trouser pocket and lit a nearby lantern suspended from the crude cart that looked as though it belonged in a museum. The horse snorted and stomped about nervously.

"You believe people are basically good and life is colored in gray. Idealistic drivel. Your brother is the last living relative you have. You would lay down your life for Ryan without hesitation." He stooped over to set the lantern on the ground near her.

"Until this past week, I thought—believed—that perhaps my father was wrong." Bile churned in her stomach. "How could I have ever thought you cared about this project for what it could give the world?"

"Because you're a romantic, Jeanne. You actually believe in that oath you took." He stared down at her with a disgusted sneer twisting his narrow features.

"Untie me, damn you!" She jerked against the restraints. The straps gave slightly under her writhing, then snapped back tighter.

"During my absence, you'd be wise to concentrate on developing a submicron self-replicating computational system."

"It isn't possible with this protein."

"I believe you. In the meantime, this journey back in time is my last hope."

"Last hope? You sound desperate."

"As I said before, you don't know the real world of research and what's at stake."

A loud unearthly groan vibrated from the far end of the cave. The horse whinnied and stomped about, but Trench was quick to grab the reins and control the mare. A brilliant blue light sparked along the back cave wall. His voice drummed in her head.

The cave wall pulsated, resembling heat waves on a car hood. The hair on her arms prickled as the blue light gathered momentum and spun into a vortex. It grew brighter and stronger as it gyrated. Undulating and pulsing, it spun counterclockwise. And the faster it spun, the larger it grew.

"The legend awakens." He pivoted toward the light.

Her pulse throbbed in her throat. She watched in horror as though it were a big-screen special effects movie recreating in front of her.

"It's true! It's all true." His eyes were dancing orbs of blue.

She jerked against the straps. The whirling noise echoed louder in the cave.

"Enjoy the show. I'll see you in a year. Remember, you give me the equation, and I'll give you Ryan." With that said, he grabbed the horse's reins and pulled the reluctant mare behind him, walking toward the light which had grown the full height of the cave. The animal neighed and tried to rear, but Trench was strong and managed to pull the helpless steed, cart and all, into the light.

Powerless, Jeanne watched as he entered the brilliance. Her heart pounded against her chest. This could not be happening. Brilliant sparks of bluish-white light emitted from the tunnel.

The noise intensified into a crackling similar to lightning, followed by a burst of electric blue light. Gregory Trench along with the horse and cart were swallowed up within the chaotic waves of light and vibration.

She watched, unable to stop him. Time seemed to drag into eternity. She sat staring at the whirling, crackling vortex gyrating in front of her. He was gone. How was that possible? Trench along with the horse and cart had vanished! Suddenly, a silhouette began to sharpen in the depths of the whirlwind and Trench emerged from the light.

"I did it, Jeanne!" He stood just outside the vortex. She'd never seen him so animated. "I was there! I saw the village down in the glen. It's just as the legend portrayed. All of it!"

He rushed over and grabbed her, pressing long fingers around her upper arms. She winced under the painful hold. He was going to do this. He was going to destroy the world. He would use her work to hold the world hostage. It was all her fault.

"I'm going to be rich beyond anyone's imagination!" His blue eyes were wild, as crazed as any drug-overdose victim she'd seen during her ER internship.

"No," she cried out, "don't do this, Trench. Please!"

"There's not much time, I must go back. I just had to test the portal to be certain I could come back. Now you have something to think about while I'm gone." He released her.

"You can't do this!" she screamed, jerking against the straps, not believing he had actually gone back in time. It was an elaborate trick.

He paused in front of the portal.

"It will close in a few minutes, Jeanne. You see how easy this is for me? Do you see how I control even the past? It's pointless to resist. You can still save your brother. You'll have time to think it over." He stood in front of the kaleidoscope of colors.

"You're going to stand out. You'll be killed as a demon," she jeered. "An appropriate ending for you!"

"You're wrong. I've spent the last few months tracing my ancestors. And I know where to find them. I should have an ancestor about forty miles north of this very castle. I'll claim kinsman. A clansman always protects his fellow clansman." He stroked his pointed chin then bent down to retrieve the lantern. "I'll be needing this more than you." His laughter spiked goose bumps down her arms.

"Lots of things different in this old world I'm going to. I've spent the last year learning Gaelic," he said and paused at the opening of portal. "Difficult language, but here's a word for you. *Annwn.*"

She froze. It was the same word MacRaigl had used. *To be trapped within Annwn was my choice. Ye must remember this.*

"What does that mean?" Her head throbbed. Her arms were numb. If she sidetracked him, he might not get back through the portal in time.

"Has a lovely sound, doesn't it? Befitting since it means the supernatural realm." He bowed to her with great flourish.

She fought against the bindings. MacRaigl's words echoed in her mind and suddenly she knew what he meant. *Ye must follow Trench.* How had he known? How could he have possibly known about this?

Trench walked into the pulsating energy but turned to her with the lantern swinging slightly under his gait.

"My ancestor is going to be very helpful. Just imagine coming face-to-face with the seed responsible for my being here. I wonder what my ancestor would do if he knew?"

"He'd slit his damn wrists if he knew what he was going to create," she yelled as he was swallowed up in the portal one last time. "Don't do this, Trench! Stop!" She dug her heels into the hard dirt and pushed with all her strength, rolling over. She realized she'd need to roll several times to close the distance between her and the portal.

She must follow him. It was the only way to stop him. MacRaigl had known! She must travel back in time, if that was in fact what was happening here. Time travel? Was it possible or just part of Trench's insanity? The wavy blue light shifted and danced about. Wherever it led, she was going to follow him, somehow. If the portal closed, she would never be able to stop him. Everything would be lost. Her brother, her life—the entire world. Gone. Destroyed by the greed of one man.

"I'll be damned if I let him do this!" Her face scraped against the dirt floor as she rolled toward the portal. It pulsated smaller then surged wider. It was closing. Her heart pounded faster, pumping the drug through her. Where was MacRaigl? If he'd known all this why hadn't he stayed to help her? He could have stopped Trench. She rolled over one more time and came to rest just a few feet from the portal's threshold. It seemed like minutes had passed, but logic told her it had only been seconds since it was still open. It grew smaller only to pulse wide once more. The totality of the eclipse must be ending.

She twisted her bound torso so her feet fell only inches from the surging current. A loud pop resounded from inside the light, and the air seemed static around her body while motion swirled about her. The sensation reminded her of the time she'd been in an electrical storm while flying home from Washington, DC. It had been an electromagnetic discharge and had surrounded her like an aura.

The current tugged against her foot as though it were alive. She raised her head, straining to see around the cave. Her breath caught in her chest. There at the cave opening stood Mael MacRaigl. She would recognize his silhouette anywhere. "MacRaigl. Help me!" Her voice was lost in the crackling noise. A magnetic force tugged against her feet. Before she could call out again, she was jerked into the whirlwind. Jeanne cried out and saw him rush from the cave entrance toward her, and then halt across from her. He stood watching her.

"Dinna fight it, my love." His words were garbled and stretched as though they were taffy.

She tried to call out to him, but the force of the vortex bore down on her, making movement impossible. His image distorted into watery veins of color. Again, she tried calling out, but her words were garbled in a world that seemed thick, like syrup.

The pressure intensified so strongly she could not lift her head. A roar followed by a swooshing sound preceded an acceleration that seemed to suck her right into the core. A kaleidoscope of brilliant colors spiraled around her. Her ears rang.

The elastic bands holding her expanded and tightened against her arms and chest. She screamed when part of the band sparked and ignited, and her clothes smoldered from the small fire. Her flesh stung and burned.

Acrid fumes choked her, stealing the air from her lungs. She gasped for fresh air. Fearful she would burn to death, she struggled to free herself from the burning straps. Suddenly, they fell away, and she hit the ground hard. The whirling noise ended. She lay panting, not daring to move. Her entire body ached.

The vortex expanded followed by a loud crackling then silence. She blinked, struggling to adjust to the blackness around her. The only sound was her ragged breathing. Her nostrils filled with the same dank smell of the cave. Where was she?

She lay on the floor of the cave listening to the silence around her. Cool air rushed from the opening, tunneling to her. She sucked the fresh air into her lungs, clearing the smoke and easing the heat in her throat. Tears burned trails down her cheeks. She lifted onto her hands and knees, but her limbs trembled under the effort. She cried out and fell to the ground again.

Her arms ached from the scorched paths left by the fiery bands. Rolling over onto her back, she gasped for fresh air, reminding herself of a landed fish desperately gulping for air. Turning over onto her stomach, she dragged herself out of the cave. Excruciating pain greeted each movement and once outside, she collapsed onto her back, staring up into brilliant sunlight.

"Oh my God." Her voice cracked with silencing pain searing her throat. Her ears roared, and her vision darkened. Had the smoke singed her vocal cords? The edges of unconsciousness threatened. She needed a hospital. Where was MacRaigl? Pulling herself up onto hands and knees again, this time she found herself in a high stand of grass. She was outside the cave! Jeanne crawled over to the shade of a nearby tree and collapsed.

Waves of darkness threatened unconsciousness with each unbearable assault of pain. She leaned against the trunk, shivering uncontrollably. Was she slipping into shock? She looked about the lonely hillside. That highlander had disappeared again. She must find help. Had she truly journeyed back in time? Was she in thirteenth-century Scotland? Was that possible? Pushing onto her feet, Jeanne steadied herself against the tree. Her stare bounced along the rise of the hills where the roofline of the castle taunted her.

It looked the same, as best she could tell. Perhaps she'd merely passed through a vortex of pure energy and nothing more. Maybe it had been a huge show of natural phenomenon that Trench had staged for her, not anticipating she would pass through the energy field, too. He could be on his way to the airport and back to North Carolina only to return a year later portraying he'd actually traveled through time. How would she have been able to disprove his claim?

A slow grin parted her lips. Well, she could now. Just as soon as she made her way back to the castle and a phone. Where *had* MacRaigl gone? He'd been standing in the cave only moments earlier. Why would he desert her like this? He could have helped her stop Trench.

The air rushed between her parted lips, but her voice was silent in the sighing. Rough bark bit sharply into her arms and she examined the ugly thin strips of charred skin lashed against the tender part of her arms.

She glanced over her shoulder at the cave entrance and was startled. The stone archway was no longer there. In its place was a rough opening slightly hidden by scrubby vines. Before she could contemplate how it was possible her stomach pitched and everything faded to dark.

* * * * *

When Jeanne came to, it was to a canopy of brilliant stars. Disoriented, she raised up on one elbow, quickly realizing she was not in any shape to walk back to the castle. How long had she been unconscious? She searched the horizon and immediately saw a tiny beacon of yellow light bouncing toward her. It drew closer. She struggled to stand, but the pain brought her back to the ground.

The light grew brighter revealing a shadow behind it. Silhouetted in the light's brilliance, the hooded figure was dark and foreboding. She fell back into the grass. The shadow halted a few feet from her. She could feel the stare penetrate from beneath the hood. Everything slipped away with a feeble voice echoing around her.

"It appears ye weren't as fortunate as your companion. Never heard of travelers being hurt when passing through the sacred portal. I had to return to me cottage to fetch me cart. It took longer than I wished, but ye needed many things. Come, Verica will take care of ye until the portal returns."

Chapter Five

The voice fell over Jeanne, jolting her awake. She squinted against the dim light. What language was that? She reached through the fog clouding her mind, trying to understand the cadence that carried the dialect.

She opened her eyes wider and met the tired stare of the old woman.

"There ye be," she spoke in English.

Jeanne looked around for whoever the woman had been talking to, but they were alone in the dimly lit cottage. A fire crackled in the fireplace across from the pallet where she lay. Her breath caught in her throat as her gaze settled on the strips of cloth bound around her burns. Gingerly, she touched the tan cloth and winced under the pain, but the soothing coolness of a salve shifted slightly under the pressure of her fingers.

She strained to speak, but the sound was little more than a gasp. Wicked pain scorched her throat and she grabbed her neck trying to quell the burning. Tears streamed from her eyes. What had happened to her? The stoop-shouldered woman leaned against a crooked walking stick. It hadn't been a dream. This woman had found her last night.

"Glad ye woke. Such a slip of a lass ye are. How are your arms?"

She spoke English? Relief washed over Jeanne. She tried to talk, but the same fierce pain pierced her throat. She clutched it and swallowed against the burning.

"Canna ye speak?"

Jeanne shook her head.

"But ye do speak?"

She nodded. Had the fumes of the burning strips singed her vocal cords? Her pulse pounded harder at the other possibility. Laryngeal nerve damage. She prayed it was not so drastic, that she'd somehow damaged muscle tissue instead of the nerve.

"Ye suffered an injury to your throat?"

Jeanne nodded. Slowly, she raised her arms but winced under the movement.

"Aye, your burns shall heal nicely. A special salve I applied and no scarring shall trace your injury. As for your voice, 'tis a potion I can make.

"The confusion shines wide in your eyes. 'Tis all very simple really. Ye came through the cave portal, where time stands still, time rushes forward and time moves backwards all in once space." She paused and must have seen the disbelief in Jeanne's expression because she laughed. "Don't try to understand. Impossible it may seem, I lay witness to it many times. Ye are me fifteenth. And for ye, time must stand still so ye can heal. I know ye wonder how I come to speak English."

She was flabbergasted. Just who was this woman? Was she part of Trench's plan to make her believe she'd traveled back to medieval Scotland?

"All who come through the portal want to know how I speak their tongue. 'Tis a simple thing for me since those who travel here speak the English tongue. Verica, 'tis me name, keeper of the portal. Just like me *máthair* before me and hers before her." She leaned closer, her voice dropping into a whisper. "There are those who say I am bewitched," she said with a cackle. "But ye can judge for yourself, I reckon."

Jeanne tried to speak once more, but the pain only drew a gasp from her.

"There now, dinna be fretting yourself. I saw the sun in its odd light yesterday morning and said to meself, Verica, today ye have a visitor from the other side. Imagine me surprise—two travelers. I never had two at the same time, so I ask meself what could possibly bring me two?"

Jeanne's heartbeat quickened.

"The man's business must be serious to come prepared with his own cart. He rode off before I could climb the mountain to greet him. I watched him race across the glen as though the devil's hounds gave chase," she said.

Jeanne tried to talk, but the acrid burning brought new tears to her eyes.

"There now, ye can tell me once ye heal." She pushed Jeanne's chin up and examined her throat. "No burns on the outside at least. Some warm milk and honey will heal ye promptly. 'Tis surely maddening to be filled with questions and canna speak them. Ye be a curiosity to me as well. The manner in which ye arrived says to me that perhaps ye were an afterthought." She shrugged. "Never ye be of mind. Several years have passed since me last visitor. A man of the year 5045 A.D., if ye ken. I canna imagine time so advanced." Verica moved to the fireplace to stir the suspended iron kettle.

"No need for fear. Verica shall take good care of ye. And ye can go home. Just not now. We shall mark the days so ye know when your portal returns."

Jeanne closed her eyes, then opened them again, but the woman was still there, dressed in a doeskin dress and a tartan shawl draped about her shoulders. It was all so fantastic. Had she actually traveled through some kind of time portal as Trench had claimed? Her mind clouded with pain.

"If ye miss the portal's return, then ye canna go home. Simple in how it serves. So we must assure ye return to your time." She moved to stand by the bed once more.

Jeanne tried to talk again, but the pain slashed up her throat. She clutched the old woman's arm and shook her head.

"Dinna worry, lass, ole Verica will help ye. I know how to mark the days and return ye safely to the cave when 'tis your time. One year exactly, not a day less or more. Now, ye must trust me, lass." She patted Jeanne's hand. "Been doing this since I was a wee lass helping me *máthair*. As for your companion, I suspect he is more enemy than friend?"

She nodded quickly.

"I understand."

Jeanne didn't understand any of it. How was this possible? How could she be talking with this woman from thirteenth-century Scotland?

"None who have come through have understood in the beginning. And try as I might to explain, how does one explain that which is a mysterious thing?" she chuckled. "I guard the secret of the portal. Only I and those who journey through know of its existence."

That was it! She must prevent Trench from going back through the portal. Her mind began to whirl. If there were some way she could return while trapping him here in the past then she could save Ryan *and* her formula.

"I see your mind turning it over, lass. Aye, 'tis always another portal. There are many portals to many places and times. But where it would take ye, now that ye canna know. But I do know ye would not be back to your starting point. So, we mark the days from the time ye arrived. That assures ye return to your proper time. Do ye understand?"

She nodded. If she prevented Trench from returning to their time, what would stop him from going through another portal, possibly into the future or the past? There was only one way to ensure he did no further harm. She swallowed the aching in her throat. She did not think she could kill. It went against everything she held sacred. She'd have to find another way.

"People come to me from many times, not just from the future, but many from the past."

Her pulse quickened. Trench in the past would be just as tragic if not more so than in his own time. He could change history.

"The portal has its own rhythm," Verica continued to explain. "'Tis a living thing. It opens every few years. I canna explain why. From your time, it may open every hundred years or perchance ye come from a place where it opens only once. But for me, it opens every three sometimes four years."

What the woman described was more than she could logically accept. How was it possible? If this were true, then the portal had its origin *here*.

"Now." Verica moved closer. "I change your bandages and when ye regain your voice, ye must tell me about your time. I hold all the stories passed on to me from those who journey through the portal. 'Tis me legacy. I preserve their tales for those who come after me. Alas, I have no bairns and must find someone, before I die, to entrust me sacred watch. And they must learn me tales and those of me ancestors before me.

"I made ye a special healing potion. Ye shall use it every day until ye can speak again and tell ole Verica your story. Everyone has a story, and I know them all."

Had she not been in so much pain and confusion, Jeanne would have been intrigued with the woman's chatter. Her main thought was Trench and where he was and, more importantly, how he planned to get blood from these people. She must heal quickly so she could go after him. He must be stopped!

All I Want

* * * * *

"I am here to see my uncle," Trench spoke in the well-practiced Gaelic. The tutor had been worth the cost. The young man's face twisted as though trying to recognize him. He turned and ran up the stairs to the Great Hall.

Trench sat in the wagon, prepared to flee should his ancestor's hospitality be less than welcoming. He'd researched his family tree and chosen to masquerade as an ancestor in France. The only drawback was he had no physical description and that was the one element of risk in this plan. Hopefully, the family genetic pool had endured through the generations, and he'd be able to pass as one of them.

The door jerked open and he jumped in the seat, causing the horse to shift nervously. A large stocky man, wearing a blue and black plaid emerged from the house. He stopped at the top of the staircase and glared down at Trench with his hands fisted on his hips. Trench frowned at the man's large physique and quickly realized his plan might not have been sound.

"Ye claim kin?"

"Aye." He sat, waiting to be invited from his wagon.

"What proof do ye offer to such a kinship?"

"Ye are Cullen de Mangus?"

"Aye. And who might ye be?"

"Gregory de Trench." He swallowed hard. According to his family records, his contemporary namesake would be in France for the next six years. If he could pose as Cullen's nephew from France, then he would be able to wield the power needed to accomplish his mission.

He'd purposefully chosen the ancestor for whom he'd been named.

"Son of Hillary de Trench of the Gallaway Valley. I offer this." Trench held out the brooch he'd inherited from his mother. His lips twisted at the irony, for standing in front of him was his fourteenth great-grandfather. To be talking with the man who was solely responsible for his existence was more than he could contain.

Cullen nodded to the lad who rushed down the steps to retrieve the token.

Reluctantly, Trench handed the gold brooch to the lad and waited while Cullen held it up to the late evening light, squinting at the jewels adorning the rather large piece of jewelry. It had been a long ride here and he was tired. He wanted something to eat and a bed. If this masquerade failed, he'd flee to the valley and find a safe haven. Getting the blood would be more difficult. So far, his painstaking research had paid off. He'd found his ancestor just as his research had revealed. It was a perfect plan.

"This belonged to me grand-mere and bequeathed to my sister, Hillary de Trench," Cullen stared down at him. "I have not seen ye, Nephew, since ye were but a wee bairn. Step down so I might have a better look at ye."

His heart pounded heavier. He swung down from the cart, keenly aware that his tall, slender form was no match for his ancestor's bulky one.

"Aye. Ye look just like me sister," his voice boomed overhead. "Welcome, Nephew!"

He'd done it. Relief washed over him. Somewhere in the generations of the family gene pool, he had followed someone other than the grandfather standing before him. Trench found himself embraced in the bear's arms and ushered into the Great Hall. His expectations had all been met and now, the real work would begin.

Chapter Six

Jeanne lay in his arms. Rays of sunlight touched her naked breasts and warmed a trail down her leg. His hard body moved beside her, and her arousal was immediate.

"I waited so long, my Jeanne," he whispered then planted small kisses down her neck to her breasts where he flicked his tongue over her erect nipples. She groaned and eagerly spread her legs to receive his probing hand. Long thick fingers traced her labia, slipping between them, and spreading her so his fingertip could tease her clit. She squirmed under his caresses, needing more.

He lifted from the bed and planted tender kisses over her flat stomach and down to where his fingers teased her pussy. His tongue danced over her clit, and she moaned, wiggling against the stimulation.

"I want you," she moaned, writhing under his artful lovemaking. "Now," she breathed, and her demand was met when he spread her legs wider and shifted between them. He eased his cock deep inside her, slowly at first, until the walls of her pussy relaxed around him.

"Aye, ye want me, lass, but not as deeply as I need ye." His words were warm sunshine on a cold winter's day against her flesh. He moved in and out. She reached up and grasped the braids on either side of his face and pulled him into her possessive kiss.

"No woman will ever love you the way I do, Mael."

"Aye, Jeanne love," he breathed and pressed into her kiss, devouring her with his passion. A raging heat flashed over her, snaking up her spine, rising with each thrust.

"Ah, ye awaken."

The voice jolted her. Panting, Jeannie blinked against the bright light cascading through the uneven slats of wood and sod that served as a roof. Her nostrils filled with the dank scent of earth and the bubbling stew Verica stirred. She took a deep breath and tried to compose herself. The raw aching need pulsated between her legs.

"How do ye fare this morning?" Verica left the fire to bend over her and examine the poultice bandages. The woman's wrinkled face crinkled like parchment and the creases deepened. She smiled down at Jeanne.

"Ye begin to heal. I shall change the bandages after ye eat the stew."

She nodded, trying to ignore the throbbing between her legs. Heat rushed over her face. Dream or no dream, she was aroused and very frustrated. Why would she dream of Mael, especially like that? He was practically a stranger, and yet something about him had seemed familiar. Her dream had felt so right as though they belonged together. And it had felt as though it were a memory. She pulled back the plaid and, with the woman's assistance, stood. Pain shot up her arms, displacing any remnants of the dream. She walked over to the table and slowly sat down on the crude bench while her hostess spooned the thick, creamy stew into a wooden bowl.

"We have venison. Killed it meself. Eat and this shall be a day of rest for ye. I must gather herbs and make a tincture for your wounds, then I visit the village. When I return, I shall tell ye about me very first visitor when I was but a wee one. Would ye like that?"

She nodded and took the stew and crusty bread Verica handed her.

"I can also begin to teach ye me native tongue. A wise thing for ye to know the language should ye have a need. But first, I shall share a bit of history about meself. All visitors seem interested in me ancestors since they were Druids."

She snapped alert. Her curiosity must have shone, because Verica's face cracked into a wide grin.

"Aye," she spoke in a hushed voice and leaned forward, "some of them were Picts. Would ye be interested in them as well?"

Jeanne gave several short nods.

"I dinna speak of it amongst those in the village. Superstitious lot find solace in their new religion and condemn that which they canna understand. So 'tis best to keep to meself. Like I do about me visitors."

Jeanne nodded again, while trying to comprehend that this was actually happening, and she was truly in the past. If Verica was aware of her ancient ancestry, then perhaps she knew some of the ancient secrets. Jeanne's pulse spiked. Although she'd ridiculed Trench, she knew alchemy was the original science. Such an opportunity to learn was mind-boggling.

All I Want

"Once ye grow stronger and healed ye can accompany me to the village. Your lack of voice might serve ye well. They shall think ye tetched and not ask questions of ye. The village folk believe me visitors are kinsmen from other regions." She laughed and Jeanne imagined Verica rather enjoyed the drama of her life.

She agreed wholeheartedly with the old woman that the less anyone knew about her and how she came to be there, the better. She took a bite of stew. The hot liquid scorched her throat, burning a path to her ears. Her eyes watered.

"This shall help." Verica shoved a pottery mug into her hands. She sniffed the steaming white liquid.

"Milk and honey." She winked. "Shall quiet your throat."

Cautiously, she sipped the warm, sweet milk. It was like a soothing balm as it rolled down her throat. She smiled widely at Verica and pushed the thoughts of non-pasteurized milk from her mind. The old woman had probably milked the cow only minutes earlier. If her vocal cords were singed then the only way to heal without proper medicine would be time—if she could avoid complications such as an infection. She cringed at the thought of not having any antibiotics to combat the simplest of infections.

"Soothing, aye?" Verica turned back to the bowl and pestle. "Now I make a poultice to replace that one about your arms. Trust Verica. I shall heal ye, lass."

Over the next few days, she rested while Verica told her about her ancestors and taught her Gaelic phrases. Still unable to speak, she silently mouthed the words along with Verica. She'd always had a natural talent for language, having learned Latin names for everything from bones to plants from her parents long before she'd ever attended school.

They soon fell into a daily routine, rising at the sound of the lone cock, and after chores and breakfast, Verica would set out for the village. The days faded into each other and were it not for the stones Verica added to the large crock near the fireplace, Jeanne would have lost count.

Her dreams grew more intense, to the point she dreaded sleep, fearful she might respond to her dream lover and embarrass herself. While she suspected Verica was slightly deaf, she certainly was not blind.

This morning was not much different than the others as she stood inside the crude barn watching Verica milk the cow. The heat from her dreams still throbbed between her legs.

"Ye try." Verica stood from the chore.

Reluctantly, she settled onto the stool and allowed Verica's calloused hands to cover hers as she massaged and squeezed the cow's udders. Soon a strong stream of milk shot into the large wooden bucket. Steam rose as the warm liquid clashed with the cool morning air.

"Ye have the hands of a lady, not accustomed to hard labor," Verica remarked without any emotion. Soon, the bucket was full, and Jeanne carried it to the cottage, placing it on the table.

She was continuously amazed how time-consuming the morning chores were and the effort required just to survive. If they did not attend the livestock and harvest the milk and eggs daily, then they would not eat.

By the time they sat down to the morning meal, she was famished. Breakfast usually consisted of game stew or roots. She'd shown Verica how to make an omelet, and it was now the woman's favorite with a side dish of meat, usually rabbit.

They finished up and set about gathering the daily herbs. Sometimes, Verica would show her how to find a new precious herb either beneath other plants, moss or sometimes hidden underneath rocks. Occasionally there would be a variety that grew out in the open beneath lofty pines, but mostly they had to hunt for the delicate plants. Today, Verica was in a hurry and wasted no time in gathering the herbs. As they made their way back to the cottage, she turned to Jeanne.

"I believe your companion has revealed himself."

Her heart pounded harder. Pausing along the path, she stared at Verica.

"There have been rumors the last few times we visited the village. I dinna want to upset ye, but the gossip grows each time." Verica reached over and patted her shoulder.

She tried to speak, but her voice was little more than a rasping breath.

"Ye canna get excited. Straining your voice shall not help it heal."

Jeanne took a deep breath and tried to still the impatience.

All I Want

"There are rumors of several mysterious deaths. Eight over the last few weeks. The villagers are frightened. They say a vampire walks amongst us—again."

Jeanne's heartbeat thundered in her ears. Trench! That was how he was getting the blood. His insanity was feeding off the superstitions of these poor people. What could she do to stop him? Her breath came in short quick puffs. What did Verica mean by "again"?

"Aye, 'tis more." Verica grabbed her hand between her rough ones. "A new rumor that Cullen de Mangus and his nephew, who arrived around the time the portal opened, plan to challenge the new Chief. I suspect 'tis your companion in masquerade. If Mangus challenges the new Chief, it shall mean war within the clan. Granted, 'tis their right. Yet, Mangus would not challenge unless incited. I suspect your companion creates a diversion for whatever mischief he plans."

Filled with questions she wanted to ask, Jeanne struggled to force the words out, but quickly regretted the attempt when ragged streaks of pain raced up her throat.

"Nae, dinna strain so. We shall keep our ears open when we visit the village this morning. First we make our tinctures then we tend to the sick." She patted Jeanne's hand.

Daily remedies were made and carried to the village so Verica could treat wounds and illnesses. In exchange for her healing charms and potions, she was given food or clothing and sometimes a pig or chicken.

Jeanne tried to still the rising panic as they neared the village. Several weeks ago when the mother of a sick child had spoken to Jeanne in French, not Gaelic, Jeanne had tried to respond, but found her voice had still not returned. That was all it had taken to start the gossip that she was indeed tetched and possibly a witch.

Verica had scoffed at the accusations. Jeanne had begun to understand much of the dialect and strained to hear the villagers' murmurings as she followed Verica through the crowded streets.

She caught snatches of words and phrases, enough that by the time they were on their way home Jeanne knew there had been suspicious behavior the last few nights, and the villagers were on edge. She'd heard the mention of a clan, and the nephew who had arrived around the same time she had. Verica was right. It was Trench!

"The old Chief died nearly one full moon hence," Verica explained as they were making their way back to her cottage. The sun had warmed with brilliant gold shimmering along the late afternoon horizon as the day slipped from them. She raised her eyebrows in what had become their silent language of her needing further explanation.

"He was the Chief of our clan and left no bairns, but has a nephew who is the rightful heir. The Mangus family shall challenge his claim. This discord over his assuming the title should never have happened. MacRaigl has been trained since a wee bairn. He is the Tanaiste. Your time would call him, Tanist, the one chosen by the Chief before he died to be his successor."

She grabbed Verica's arm and shook it.

"Lass?"

She mouthed the name.

"Aye, MacRaigl," Verica said.

"Mael?" She mouthed the name in silence.

"Ye know the name?"

Jeanne nodded in short jerks.

"The nephew from France who incites the clan must know him as well. If he has his way, there shall be a war. When challenged, MacRaigl shall defend his birthright as Chief. This newcomer insists the title be bestowed upon his branch of the clan, foremost to his uncle, Cullen de Mangus."

"Who?" Jeanne formed the word. "Name." She pressed her lips together to form the silent word.

"The name of the nephew? 'Tis that what ye ask?"

She nodded vigorously.

"Gregory de Trench, 'tis the instigator's name."

Her knees were water. She stumbled in the path, quickly leaning against the pine tree that canopied the forest. Her breath came in short, hard puffs. Her ears rang, and the world shrunk from her into darkness. She was going to pass out. She bent over, struggling to remain conscious.

"Here lass." Verica supported her, drawing her to a nearby rock. She sat down, and grabbed Verica's hands, staring into her wise eyes.

"'Tis the man who came through the portal before ye?"

Jeanne nodded, tears welling heavily in her eyes.

"What he's about 'tis a dangerous thing. A war that dinna happen before. I know 'tis true from those who have passed through me portal. Mael MacRaigl was unchallenged." She shook her head. "This could change things not just in me world but in yours."

Chapter Seven

Mael MacRaigl squinted against the morning sun and looked out the window of his sister's new home.

"Would ye be wanting anything else, me laird?"

He turned to look at the woman. She was dressed in a plain brown dress and blushed when his gaze lingered on her face.

"Nae, lass. Be off with ye and tell my man, Ian, to make haste. I would be leaving for MacRaigl Castle this morn and not this eve."

"Aye, me laird." She curtsied but was unable to mask the disappointment in her voice. With a longing glance in his direction, she closed the door behind her.

Mael turned back to the open window and sucked in the crisp air through flared nostrils. Instantly, he regretted the thoughtless dismissal. It had been some time since he had enjoyed such a willing lass. His cock hardened at the temptation to call her back into his room.

Irritated, he closed the window against the lush, rolling mountains across the valley. He had important business to finish. He must be off. What had delayed Ian? Impatient with his servant's tardiness, he sat down in the chair beside the fireplace and pulled on one of the boots. He was lacing it when the door swung open, and the flushed, bearded face of his servant peered inside.

"Me laird!" Ian wheezed and ran to take over the task of booting his master. "Apologies, Laird MacRaigl. I dinna know ye had risen."

Mael sat back in the chair and sighed heavily. "'Tis important business we must attend this morn, Ian." He cast a brief glance about the chamber. "I think I should like to take our morning meal with us. Tell the cook to bundle it, will ye, Ian? I can finish my boots."

"Ye be in such a rush to leave before saying goodbye to your own sister?"

Mael settled his stare on the older man and snorted at the perplexed look centering the tired blue eyes.

All I Want

"It should be evident to ye I wish to return home." He finished lacing the other boot and stood from the servant. Ian bowed and nearly sprinted from the chamber. Mael paced back over to the window and clasped his hands behind his back. The brilliant sun had risen high above the trees. It might be too late.

The rap on the door was timid and would have gone unnoticed had he not been expecting it.

"Enter." His voice sounded loud and harsh to his own ears.

The timid childlike girl shuffled into the room, eyes downcast and visibly shy at being in the presence of the great laird. She stood with hands clasped behind her back.

"Ye have a message for me from my sister?" he demanded.

"Aye, me laird." Surprise mirrored in her face with the unspoken question how he knew she'd come to deliver the message. Instead, she held out the linen envelope. He immediately recognized Tryon's seal and waved the girl away. His glare narrowed on the other seal, melted so closely to Tryon's that the two red seals merged into one while clinging jealously to the stationery folds.

The silent message of using not only her own seal but that of Tryon's was not lost on him. He tried her seal with his forefinger, letting it glide over the impression. His hand trembled against the fine paper as he folded the letter into the seal and it cracked under the pressure. Slowly, he unfolded the message. His sister's elegant handwriting swept over the page.

My dearest brother,

As you read this letter, you now realize your darkest fears have manifested. I shall not return to MacRaigl Castle with you as you demanded. Instead, I choose to stay with my new husband, Alexander. 'Tis now my place.

My attempts at explanation went unheard. I say once more, I love my husband. Contrary to your accusation, I chose to be his wife. Alexander dinna coerce me into the decision. My heart demands I remain with him, dearest brother. I canna rescind my decision even if my mind wished it. I prayeth thee stay until this evening when we shall discuss further. There remain many things unsaid.

'Tis of grave concern for me that the clan shall gather in less than a month's passing and yet rumors stir there may be a division of loyalties. Cullen de Mangus threatens all we hold sacred. United, we can overcome all obstacles

placed before your rise to Chief. Dinna turn your back on me, brother. The future of our clan depends on us rallying together.

I plead with ye, remain at Fernmoora and allow me audience this evening. By our blood we share, I implore you.

Your loving sister,
Ishabelle

"I-sha-belle," he gritted his teeth against white-hot anger, "what have ye done?" Her letter had one purpose, to rile him into confrontation. Balling his hand into a fist, he clamped his teeth into his own flesh. His agonized groan filled the room, startling the hounds in the Great Hall downstairs into a round of barks and frightened yelps.

He relaxed the bite, pulling his fist away and glared at the impression he'd made in his own flesh.

"Damn it all to hell. The bloodsucker!" he choked off and spun on his heel. "Ian!" His voice boomed through the quiet castle as he stomped down the spiral stairs. "Ian!" The impatience in his soul surfaced and would not be held at bay any longer.

"Me laird?" Ian appeared from the shadows of the Great Hall just as Mael bounded onto the landing. "We make ready."

"Good. Be it none too soon. Let us leave this foul place." He stomped across the massive hall, threw open the door leading to the courtyard and descended the stone steps without another word.

The groomsman took a frightened step back when Mael neared him. Ignoring the youth's wide-eyed gape, Mael jerked the reins from him. The horse snorted, and he relaxed the hold.

"Me laird, Me laird." A servant girl ran after him, carrying a cloth bundle bound with a leather strip. "Ye forget your morning meal."

He paused in mounting his horse and turned to her. The look on her face was one of sheer terror, and he realized the full brunt of his frustration must have shown in his expression. The unsuspecting girl trembled as she held out the bundle. He tightened his grip on the horse's reins and struggled to contain the outrage.

"Thank ye, lass." He took the parcel. The leather gloves he wore stretched in his grip around the linen package. "Tell Missus McLarty I am pleased." Mael stiffened his shoulders and gritted his teeth tighter together lest he yell his aggravation, awakening his sister and her new husband. He swallowed back the threatening words and glanced at Ian who had mounted the mare beside him.

"Here." He tossed the bundle to the older man then swung himself onto the steed. The stallion pranced nervously and whinnied, sensing his charged emotions.

"Ye not be seeing Ishabelle before we leave?" Ian questioned. "Ye owe her that much."

"I owe her nothing after last evening. Ye were in attendance." He shifted in the saddle.

"But she still remains your sister. She needs ye now more than ever. What if she should need your protection?"

Mael froze in his actions and glared at Ian.

"Are ye daft? Ye think the likes of Alexander Tryon needs *my* protection?" He watched the color drain from the old Scotsman's face.

"'Tis your sister. I've watched the two of ye grow from wee bairns. Ye canna disown your own flesh. Your only kin."

"As long as she's with Alexander Tryon, she canna be my kin. To be with him means she turns her back on all I am." Mael felt the intensity of his own stare on Ian, but the servant wouldn't back down.

"But 'tis *Ishabelle*."

"No longer the Ishabelle we knew. And damn well, ye know 'tis God's truth." Mael challenged.

"But me laird, if a clan war comes, and should Cullen de Mangus have his way, then the allegiance of Alexander Tryon shall assure our victory."

"I shall not align myself with the devil." Mael reeled the horse around and dug his heels into the steed's ribs.

* * * * *

Morning brought an occasional rooster crowing against scattered sounds of chopping staccatos and wagons rumbling through the village streets. Jeanne hurried along the dusty street, wearing the borrowed clothes Verica had given her.

"Ye will save this boy, then the villagers will accept ye." Verica gave her a gaping grin.

She took a deep breath. She'd learned enough Gaelic dialect to understand what was expected of her. She wanted to tell her benefactor that she could not perform miracles, but knew it was pointless.

Suddenly, Verica changed to English, casting an amused glance at her. Jeanne looked about to make sure none of the villagers appeared to understand English. She was relieved at the curious looks of those they passed. To them it was a foreign tongue. It was Verica's little joke, and the old woman used it to instill greater fear in them.

"These imbeciles canna understand us. 'Tis true, because ye dinna speak they fear ye a witch." Verica hobbled slightly ahead of her, leading the way to the cottage where they'd been summoned. The sheep corralled in an irregular fence made with young saplings, trotted over to the edge of their pen to blink at them.

"Me *máthair* before me and her *máthair* before her were accused of being witches. These poor ones depend on us, but were they to ken ye came through the portal—" Verica paused to glance back at her. "For now we heal this laddie."

Jeanne slowed her gait when she saw the big highlander pacing in front of the low thatch-roofed home.

"Nae, 'tis but an overgrown pup." Verica's withered hand closed over hers. "Give him the bundle as I instructed." Her guardian hailed the burly bearded creature.

"Angus, we come to heal your bairn," Verica stated matter-of-factly and slipped past him when he blocked the doorway.

Jeanne swallowed hard and handed him the brown bundle, then ducked inside as his huge hands quickly untied the folds and retrieved the shortbread Verica had baked that morning. She didn't stay to see if he was pleased with the offering.

Stepping inside the dark cottage, she quickly found Verica stooped over a pallet on the floor near the open fire grate. She met the mother's frightened stare with what she hoped was a reassuring smile. After all, she was a doctor. She had been trained in the twenty-first century and anything these villagers contracted, surely she could identify and treat.

Couldn't she? She was grateful for the historical medicine coursework she'd had during her premed schooling. She had learned about natural remedies made with herbs and along with what Verica had taught her that knowledge had come in handy.

All I Want

"He burns with fever." The woman pulled her down beside her in front of the pallet. Verica leaned over and whispered, "He is like the other one, yes?"

Jeanne examined the child, letting her fingers glide over the swollen neck glands. Verica instructed the child to open his mouth and held a candle closer so Jeanne could see into the child's mouth. Scarlet streaks ran the length of his throat.

She looked at Verica and nodded. Without proper diagnostic equipment, she could only guess. It had been five years since she had worked in an emergency room, although that experience was proving invaluable. The boy had an infection similar to modern strep throat. She marveled at the various illnesses she'd treated, so similar to those found seven hundred and fifty-five years into the future. All except *Next Gen*.

She forced her attention to the task at hand and reached into the dress pocket, retrieving the medicine pouch Verica had made her. She removed the tiny clay pot, only four inches in diameter with a leather strap securing the lid.

She soon had the bread mold worked into a paste while Verica tended to boiling water over the hearth. Together, they made a crude tea and with the mother's help, managed to get the child to sip it.

"She shall return this evening to give the lad another tea," Verica informed the mother.

Jeanne saw the mother's skeptical expression. Wanting to allay her worries, she reached out to touch the young mother's arm.

The woman cried out and jerked from her touch.

"Leave her," Verica hissed, pulling her from the crude hut. "She's ignorant and knows nothing of the arts."

Jeanne glanced back at the small family as Verica ushered her down the dusty street.

"Stupid woman!" Verica spat and tapped her cane against the hard earth. "She accepts your help, but her superstitions rule her miserable life."

Disdain edged Verica's words and she suddenly understood Verica was an enigma in her own time.

"There, ole witch." A lad dodged in front of them taunting with childish gestures.

"Get out of our way," Verica barked.

The youth jumped from Verica's flailing attempts to hit him with her cane.

"Old woman," he spat. "Ye and your mute healer. Ye think ye now be the village queen? A few witch's tricks and ye gain the respect of the whole village?"

"I not be needing any respect from the likes of ye." Verica shoved a path through the crowded street.

"No tongue and nowhere to run." Several children joined the chant, following them through the village.

Jeanne's pulse quickened. She silently prayed for Verica to stop baiting the boy and concentrate on getting them back to the haven of her cottage in the forest. Over the past four months, she had seen the power of superstitions in thirteenth-century Scotland and taunting the village into a frightened mob was not wise.

"If ye think us witches, then best be getting out of our way. Cross me path again, lad, and I shall put a curse on ye."

She saw the brittle look in Verica's eyes and had she not known better, she would have believed the old woman truly was a witch.

The lad made a face at Verica, and she swung her cane at him again.

"Witch witch, curses and spells, witch witch."

"A curse on ye, then, forewarned ye were." Verica halted mid-stride in the middle of the street. Jeanne nearly tripped over her and before she could regain her composure, the entire village had frozen like a DVD on pause. They all stared astonished as Verica continued her theatrics.

The old woman let out an eerie wail and held her arms high above her head. She swung the cane in a circle above her head and muttered unintelligible gibberish.

"Unto ye will befall, just as a tree does suddenly uproot, so shall ye. And when we wake upon the morrow, our hearts no longer filled with taunting sorrow for this bitter thorn that tears me flesh shall be seen nevermore."

She turned on the lad, staring into his frightened face. "And children shall chant, beware the witch Verica, not cross her path should ye too suffer the fate of Roth," she hissed the final words at the youth. His complexion turned to a sickening pallor.

All I Want

"The witch doth curse me, all ye lay witness." His blue eyes were huge with fear.

"We bear witness to your taunting. Ye brought it upon your own head." An old man spoke from a nearby doorway. The crowd was a wave of murmurs and hands making the sign of the cross over their chests.

Much to Jeanne's relief, Verica lowered her cane and continued toward her home. The woman's laughter grew louder as they neared the forest and started through the thicket that masked the narrow path leading to her humble cottage.

"Let their superstitions keep them awake this eve," she cackled. "Aye, I see the fear in your eyes, lass, but their worries of evil can only make us richer. They dinna ever burn a witch in this village. They fear our wrath too much. They think this fever 'tis the result of a *vampire*."

She bit her lip, longing to voice her concerns about Verica's theatrics. Frustrated, Jeanne shoved her hands deep into the pockets of her skirt and fell in behind Verica. Did Verica believe in vampires, too?

"They found another one, dead. The body was floating in the river. Heard them speaking of it earlier. 'Tis twelve it makes since ye arrived." Verica glanced over her shoulder. "I dinna be thinking ye responsible, but perhaps the friend ye seek?

"I know the stories. Heard them all me life as a child. As keeper of the portal, many strange things have been made witness to me. 'Tis part of *Annwn*. Such have their own rules of creation.

"But what perplexes me most 'tis what your friend be doing with the blood. None who come through the portal ever committed evil. Most merely desired to go back home." Verica paused at the turn in the forest path and let her gaze settle on Jeanne. "They all had puncture wounds about the neck and were drained of all blood. What other explanation do simpletons have but vampires." Verica leaned heavily on her cane, then turned up the path again.

Jeanne frowned. There was only one explanation—Trench.

"There be a man, several days ride from here. Rumors of him years ago, when I was but a lassie. His name, Alexander, best I recollect. 'Twas rumored to be an ancient one. Were the stories true, then he be well over a hundred and fifty seasons, ah, years." She gave Jeanne a cockeyed grin wrinkling her face. "Were he still alive. Or should it be dead?" Her laughter echoed in the lofty pines overhead. "I imagine vampires be a bit of both. Aye?"

She rubbed her throbbing temple and longed for the crest of the hill that would suddenly rise in front of them, almost startling her each time she journeyed through the forest and climbed the path.

Even in her limited understanding of the native tongue, she knew their actions were scrutinized. If the lad, Roth, fell ill or died during the night, then she and her benefactor would be killed.

The glen greeted her like a soothing balm against her jangled nerves. She followed Verica into the thatch-roofed cottage and collapsed onto the straw pallet.

"I know what ye be thinking, quiet one, but the lad shall not be stricken with more than a sleepless night." Verica spooned the wonderful-smelling stew into their bowls.

She shook her head when her hostess lifted the bowl of steaming rabbit stew.

"Come eat and quit your fretting. Ye must go back this evening and tend the Gardners' bairn with another tea of that foul-smelling bread." Verica sat down at the crude table and slurped from the bowl of stew.

Reluctantly, Jeanne sat down beside her but continued to worry about what the old woman had set in motion. It could make things more difficult for her when she went back tonight, alone.

"Eat your meal. We have more spells to cast and the ancients' blessing after our meal. Soon, ye understand me ways and me tongue as I understand yours." She paused to stare at Jeanne. Her angular features were sharper than she recalled. "Ye have an ear for language."

She understood most of what the old woman said and marveled how quickly she'd gained understanding. She nodded and surmised she had a latent natural talent for the language aided by an ancient cell memory that somehow had been activated when she traveled back through time.

She would not rule out the possibility that Verica's repetitive chants and constant chatter helped stimulate that awakening memory. She could no more explain the phenomenon than she could explain being in the past. She grew weary trying to analyze what had happened, and how it was possible. It just was.

"Eat, lass. Autumn has arrived. We have wood to chop, herbs to pick and tinctures to bottle this day. Much work ahead of us. Let us eat our morning meal before another interrupts with someone needing our services."

All I Want

Jeanne ate the stew contemplating the victims. The first had been found in a nearby village. There were numerous reports of bite victims. Trench must be instantly blood-typing potential donors.

It depended on who told the stories. Some said hundreds were killed, while others said a handful. She suspected he would wait until closer to the time the portal reopened to collect the bulk of the blood. Clearly, he was orchestrating it all by inciting his ancestors. He would time the clan uprising to mask his final collection and ultimate disappearance.

With each death, her sense of urgency heightened. She had to find where he was hiding and storing the blood. She had to expose him to the village. Chills gripped her. They would kill him.

"Ye think he dinna deserve death?" Verica's annoying habit of reading her thoughts amazed her.

She shared the guilt. Had she never discovered the cure— Her thoughts were interrupted when Verica stood from the table and scraped the remains of her stew back into the pot suspended over the fire.

After her visit with the Gardner boy tonight, Jeanne would resume her nightly vigil along village outskirts and wait. She'd find Trench, eventually, and confront him, exposing his charade. He didn't know she had followed him through the portal. Surprise would be her biggest ally.

Jeanne had no idea how she would force him to return with her to their time, much less release Ryan. How could she protect the world from Trench's greed? She was only one person, lost in the thirteenth century.

She stood and carried the bowl over to the fireplace. It was too overwhelming to think about. She scraped the leftovers into the pot and lifted her stare to Verica's tired gaze.

"I hear your thoughts, lass. Ye might be able to follow him, but ye canna be strong enough to stop his evil. Not even a man can stop a demon."

Chapter Eight

It was over a day's ride back to MacRaigl Castle and they spoke very little. Mael rode the horse hard, expending his frustration and anger in the ride. By evening, the beast was near exhaustion so he dismounted to walk.

"Ye must reunite the chieftains and declare your birthright as Chief. Since your uncle had no son, ye are the only male heir," Ian spoke for the first time since leaving Fernmoora. "There are disgruntled chieftains who seek to further their own holdings. A few will use this opportunity to challenge ye."

"I expected challenges, but I never suspected they would come from Cullen de Mangus. My uncle and I overlooked that man's ambitions."

"'Tis the way of our people." Ian shrugged. "Any man can challenge ye even though ye are the Tanaiste."

Mael had spent much of the past few years working with his uncle planning strategies to maneuver himself and his family to retain the Chief status.

"All the planning and staging of tactics canna anticipate the nature of man," Ian said. "There still remains one goal necessary to bring it all together so no man can challenge further."

Mael shot him an angry look.

"Ye resist all ye want, Mael. It remains undone." Ian shrugged when he snorted. "She need be a suitable woman to share your governing of the clan. Plenty of eager lasses await your choice. All ye need do is choose."

He groaned. What Ian and even his uncle never understood was he sought a certain woman for his wife. The one who held the spark and wit he craved. After all, she would be the *máthair* of his children, his hearth and his very home. He did not wish to marry for convenience as expected, if he could find his true mate.

"If ye allow your heart to prevent ye from accepting anything less than your ideal, then all is doomed. Ye must choose soon. Cast all

All I Want

personal desires aside for the sake of the clan, man. Ye mustn't delay marriage any longer than ye delay laying claim to your birthright. Ye should have claimed it immediately—"

"I'm well aware of my duties, Ian," he practically snarled. Ishabelle's sudden marriage had delayed the ceremony. Now there was unrest. As for his wife, Mael waited for the mate of his soul to arrive as foretold by the seer on the day he was born. He knew she was in the world—somewhere. He would know her when his gaze fell upon her. That was also the way of his people on his father's side.

"Ishabelle recognizes your delay shall harm the uniting of the clan. 'Tis why she married Tryon, to assure the MacRaigl line continues. Just on the perchance her brother dinna fulfill his moral obligation to the family name," Ian said.

"So she uses as an excuse. I dinna believe it shines as her true motivation." Mael kicked at a stone blocking his path and sent it sailing underneath Ian's horse. The mare snorted and pranced faster. "Such mixing of MacRaigl blood with the devil himself. I can never forgive her," he said.

"Ishabelle always was headstrong." Ian reined his horse to a slower pace.

Mael picked up a twig and turned it over in his hands. "I shall find my bride and claim my place as Chief soon." He did not add if his beloved never showed, then he would sacrifice his heart's desire and marry just for his clan. But he still had time and intended to make full use of it.

"Ye now have greater worries than your sister's rashness. The greatest challenge awaits—to unite the clan before Mangus can tear us all asunder."

"Aye. He used my absence to incite the clan. I shall approach the chieftains upon my return."

"A rightful first step. Your uncle, Sirus, struck the pact with our neighboring clans when he ascended to the position of Chief nearly forty years ago. 'Twas by his side even then," Ian said and gave a wistful frown.

"I shall renegotiate the pact."

"Good. 'Tis expected. With support of the clans and your chieftains, even one rogue chieftain such as Cullen de Mangus shall not oppose such solidarity." Ian seemed to relax in his grip on the reins.

Perhaps Mael had finally reassured his confidant that he'd do his part. He knew how to bargain for the clan's loyalty. His uncle had trained him well. If he could retain the support of the other clans as well, then Mangus would relent.

"Be about your return home without me, Ian," He spoke abruptly.

"Me laird?"

"I wish a bit of solitude."

"But ye shall soon to be Chief. Protocol demands I escort ye. 'Tis my duty. The Chief should never be left unprotected—I mean, unescorted—me laird."

"I am yet to be Chief, Ian. Ye see before ye the same man as when my uncle lived. I have defended myself well enough my entire life. Now leave me to my privacy."

"I could be put to death for neglecting ye. I served your uncle for—"

"As long as I can recall, Ian. Ye served my uncle well. I am yet to don the mantle of Chief. I require privacy this eve. Homeward." Mael reached up and clasped his clansman's arm.

Ian hesitated, as though weighing his duty against Mael's determination.

"Know that I dinna agree with this decision." He nudged the horse with his heels and guided it around Mael's horse. Mumbling under his breath, Ian started the descent to the village.

Satisfied he would have his privacy, Mael stopped along the river, hoping a night in the open wilds of the hills would soothe his soul. Nestled in the rocky hillside above the village and his castle just beyond, he had a clearer view of his lands as he sat in front of the smoldering campfire, wishing to hold on to the night's enchantment.

If only he had a willing wench to share the canopy of stars and a heated night of lust. He stoked the fire with a broken branch. The need for a wife plagued him. There were many to choose from, but a fitful match might mean joining with a rival clan to forestall the looming challenges to his claim.

The moment clouded with plaguing thoughts of Ishabelle, and the newfound peace shattered. Ishabelle had sealed her fate. Now he would seal his. The last thing he wanted was a clan war. The transition of power must be smooth. If only Ishabelle would remain at Fernmoora

All I Want

and not incite the clan further. Alexander Tryon was not an ally to any clan just as he was not a man to challenge.

When news of their sudden marriage leaked out, the clan would be furious. They would not await the ascension of the heir within the allotted time. They would feel betrayed because Ishabelle embodied the spirit of the clan. And she possessed the second sight, which brought all clansmen seeking her guidance. He shoved the stick into the dying fire, stirring the embers. His sister had become his greatest enemy.

Anger rekindled in him and Mael growled between his teeth. Why had she married Tryon? He poked the fire harder. She had sounded like some chambermaid with her head filled with Tryon's grand promises. She'd spoken of her heart having been captured. His hand closed around the twig. How had Tryon enchanted her? Why had Mael not been ken to his sister's seduction? Surely, Tryon had stolen her soul, and she was merely following it. The twig snapped under his grip.

If Ishabelle remained out of the bid for Chief, then he could be assured an easier rise to power. She had even threatened that if he did not marry and sire a child within the allotted time, she would seek the title and, with her new husband, sire a kingdom of MacRaigls. 'Twas her right as his sibling, but this had never been part of their plan. She had helped their uncle plan the strategy for Mael to be the successor. She had agreed he should be Chief. Her role as the seer of the clan was the role she preferred. It had been agreed upon by the three of them.

He stood from the fire. Damn Ishabelle! He'd pursued her to Fernmoora, only to arrive too late. The deed had been done, the marriage sealed. He kicked dirt over the fire, smothering it. He could not reconcile the marriage. He had lost his sister forever.

Shaking his head, Mael wondered at what moment she had started hating him— hating him enough to marry Alexander Tryon. He mounted the horse for a slow descent to the village below. Resigned to spending the remainder of the night traveling to his home, he dug his heels into the horse's ribs, driving it into a hard gallop across the valley floor. The village nestled at the bottom of the mountain was swallowed up by a mist rolling off the river.

* * * * *

The street was nearly deserted with the thatch-roofed houses gaping darkly at Jeanne as she ventured into the village. The night had grayed with a fog settling over the countryside. She was late, having been caught up in fascination as Verica made tinctures from the fresh herbs they had harvested.

A figure darted into the lane ahead of her, and Jeanne ducked behind a nearby cart. He wore a cape that fell to the ground and when he turned to look behind him, her heart leapt.

"Trench." The word rushed from her in a soft outward push of air. It was the first sound she'd made in months. Fear quickly replaced the relief in having voice again. She swallowed against the slight burning in her throat. Just how was she going to stop his insanity? She bit her lower lip. "Trench," she repeated, testing her newfound voice. Elated over the ability to speak again, Jeanne paused to test it once more. "I'll stop you, Trench." Her voice sounded alien to her ears.

She'd almost given up hope of regaining it, just as she had in finding him but there he stood like some B-rated movie version of Dracula. Where was he going? He glanced over his shoulder and disappeared around the corner.

She must be careful. The least thing she did would certainly be interpreted as that of a witch. Verica's morning performance had sealed their fates. The muffled sound ahead alarmed her. Just as she rounded the corner Trench plunged a syringe-like instrument into the youth's neck. He covered the boy's scream with a cloth, probably chloroform, she reasoned. It would be like Trench to be that cliché.

The boy slumped forward as the whining sound of a pump hummed from beneath Trench's cape. He shifted the boy's weight, revealing the syringe was attached to a tube that emptied into a long silver cylinder strapped about his waist. So that was how he was doing it—a vacuum system to a holding tank. She gauged the cylinder could hold at least eight pints. He'd kill the boy!

"Trench!" Her voice was hoarse and lower pitched than normal. She tore through the quiet street, alarming a nearby dog into a harsh barking fit. Even in the moonless night, she could see his startled expression.

"What are *you* doing here?" He let the youth fall to the dirt street and started toward her. "How did you get here?"

Lights began to flicker as torches were lit.

"Come." He hid the syringe inside the lining of the cape and grabbed her arm, yanking her down the street. The surge of villagers pouring into the streets to see what the commotion was about halted them. Their murmurs followed by gasps at the sight of another victim. Several crossed themselves and mumbled words of prayer.

"Keep your mouth shut, and we'll live to return to our own world. Remember Ryan," he hissed between clenched teeth with bony fingers closing tighter around her arm.

The agonized wail of the lad's mother pierced the night, echoing like a tolling bell as the woman rocked her dead son in her arms.

Jeanne watched in horror.

"He caught the witch," a man shouted from the crowd, pointing to them. Trench took a step back.

"This is going to get ugly. We need to leave, now." He pulled her backwards with him.

"Catch them. *They* did this!" came another shout.

Trench released her and fled into the shadows just as the crowd engulfed her. Before she could react, someone grabbed her arms and tied them behind her back. Struggling against the steely grip that shoved her into the village square, she glanced around for Trench, but he was gone. The mob's shouts roared in her ears.

Her heart pounded harder. She bit her lip to keep from crying out. She must stop them. If she spoke, their ancient fears would be confirmed. Only a witch could heal her own muteness. How could she escape this?

The sea of angry faces, illuminated by sputtering torches, undulated as they forced her toward the center of the village. She looked about for Trench. Where was he? Her heart leapt with hope that Verica might have heard the uproar, but quickly crushed when she realized Verica was so near deafness she was probably sleeping through the entire event.

A man behind her jerked a coarse rope around her neck. Her heart slammed against her chest.

"No! No! Trench!" she screamed.

The crowd froze in a massive wave as her words echoed into the night. Shock and then fear washed over their faces followed by murmurs that soon rose to shouts of renewed determination.

"Hang the witch!"

"No, burn her!" someone shouted.

Jeanne stood in the circle of sputtering torches. Acrid air seared her nostrils. She coughed and gasped for fresh air but the smoke burned a path to her lungs and stung her eyes. She blinked against the tearing. Panicked, she struggled to see beyond the mob, searching the woods.

Verica had not heard. There would be no rescue. The mob moved closer. The flames from their torches blasted her in a wave of dry heat. Rivulets of perspiration trickled down her back and she licked her lips, longing for a cool sip of water from the well only a few feet away.

The men lifted her onto a rickety wooden barrel. Helpless, her senses charged alert when one of the men threw the other end of the rope over a tree limb. She struggled from the threatening jerks against the noose as her hangman took up the slack.

He pulled the rope taut, and the noose constricted around her neck. She stood on tiptoes trying to ease the choking, but the hangman jerked the rope tighter and she gagged. Panic overrode all thought, with only one mandate—escape. A man rushed up and tossed straw about the barrel.

"We burn her, too. Let the fire purify her soul." His action started a new frenzy. Others rushed to find more kindling and tossed it on top of the straw. Soon, they had constructed a menacing wall of sticks and straw around the barrel. Her chest heaved high as one man lowered his torch. Her throat closed around the scream that bubbled from her chest and trapped it into silence.

Suddenly, a shadow moved from the line of trees bordering the village. Hope welled in her. Verica! The night stirred cooler, and the mob hushed. Sensing the presence, they turned en masse to peer behind them.

He emerged from the depth of blackness. Silent. His broad frame cut through the mist and smoke with the hilt of his sword glinting from the torches' light. The villagers parted in a wave, whispering to each other. A few dropped their torches to the ground and ran from the circle, while some of the women fell to their knees wailing.

Her knees were water and her pulse, a riotous throbbing in her throat. His auburn hair lifted around the thin long braids that ran both lines of his jaw.

The blue and black plaid of his clan flapped around him as an angry gust of wind seized the village. The kilt hugged his trim waist. The hem stopped just above his knees with a slight venting midway his thigh whenever he took a step.

All I Want

"MacRaigl." Jeanne's breath escaped her but her own voice was lost beneath the wicked roar of torches and a sea of murmurings.

"What is the meaning of this?" His hard gaze moved from one gaping stare to another, finally settling on hers. His eyes narrowed on the thick rope cinched about her neck, and the stack of kindling beneath her. Jeanne searched his stare for a sign of recognition. There was none.

"The burning of a witch. She killed Roth! She must die. She's turned her sacred powers to the work of black magic. She must die!" The man pointed to the lad. His mother still cradled him in her arms. MacRaigl took long strides over to them. Jeanne saw his stare narrow on the puncture wounds in the lad's neck. The color drained from his face, and he tightened his fists by his side.

"Nonsense! Silly superstitions." His voice boomed over their heads and he turned back to her. "Untie her! Now!"

The men beside her jumped at the command. The tremor of his voice vibrated in the hollow of her chest and stayed. His face was set in angry, cruel lines. He was her rescuer, wasn't he? She should feel gratitude, not fear. She braved another look into his eyes.

Raw, barbaric rage flashed in their brown depths until he met her look, then suddenly, the glint in his eyes spiked hot. Naked hunger greeted her probing stare before he masked the thought. She looked away, but could not escape what she'd seen in his eyes. Lust. Her pulse throbbed.

How had he come to be here? Had he jumped through the portal at the last minute? That was the only explanation. But where had he been all this time?

No one challenged him. The tension on the rope eased, and she gasped for air. The man beside her lifted the rough noose over her head, slightly scraping her nose in the clumsy attempt to do as commanded. He stepped back from the makeshift execution block, edging away from MacRaigl.

"Now, go home. All of ye. If I ever see any of ye so much as gaze upon this woman, I shall have your heart and eat it for my morning meal."

The tone in his voice mirrored by a dark scowl assured Jeanne that he would do just that. The villagers cowered from him and scurried from the square, retreating to their homes. Several men stooped to assist the mother with her son's corpse. Jeanne scrambled from the barrel and took a timid step toward him, then stopped.

He stood with arms akimbo, watching the villagers flee, and then turned to her with a slight grin parting his lips. She took a step back.

"There, lass, I saved ye. Had I wanted harm to ye, I would not interfere." He raised his hand to his lips, and she noticed for the first time he'd grown a short beard. His shrill whistle sliced the night. A sleek stallion, as black as the night that hid him, answered the call. The animal stopped beside his master and pawed the ground. She recalled the painting hanging in the Great Hall at Trench's castle. This man looked as though he'd stepped from the portrait.

Was this MacRaigl's ancestor? Of course, that would explain the beard and why he had not recognized her. He swung his mighty self onto the back of the animal and reached down to her. Jeanne stared up at him.

"Ye best be taking my help, lass, if only for the night. Come morning light ye can be about your affairs. But for this ill-fated night, I bid ye." He reached for her.

She hesitated. He certainly didn't seem to know her. Her own hand shook as she reached for his. His touch was warm, strong, and commanding. Effortlessly, he hoisted her onto the back of his horse.

"Not accustomed to horses?" he chuckled, flashing a devastating smile. She must have looked confused because he tilted his head back to release a deep laugh. "Take a hold." He jabbed his heels into the stallion's ribs and the horse lunged forward.

Grasping for anything to hold onto, Jeanne struggled to stay astride the horse. His rock-hard arm came around her, and before she knew what had happened, was plopped into his lap.

"Dinna lose your hold, lass."

She clutched for the stallion's mane but he swung the beast around and dug his heels harder into the animal's ribs. The jolt threw her against his steel chest. Icy shivers raced down her spine. The brisk wind whipped about them, clearing the torch vapor.

"The night belongs to us!" he yelled and dug his heels harder into the horse's sides.

They tore through the night with man and beast moving as one while she jerked and bounced about desperately struggling to keep from slipping from his lap. A low chuckle vibrated from his chest. The horse bounded up the hillside and Jeanne slid sideways but his firm arm came across her chest. He held her tightly against him, crushing her breasts against his muscled arm.

All I Want

"Relax, lass, move with the beast. Feel his rhythm." The warm golden tone in his voice had the same mysterious effect on her frayed nerves as his descendant's. It was a familiar balm to her innermost panic.

He was like a sturdy tree as she settled against him, with his firm thighs hard like the rocks jutting from the mountainside. She relaxed the vice-like clamp of her knees against the horse's sides and attempted to meld with man and beast. She could fit better on the horse if she allowed herself to press her buttocks into Mael's— She stiffened. His cock was as hard as his thighs. There was no mistaking it. That was his erection poking into her.

She closed her eyes against the relentless, tearing wind. His slow easy breathing clashed with the labored breath of the horse and somewhere between the two was hers, short and shallow. She focused on slowing hers to the steady rise and fall of his chest but the bulge against her seemed to be growing. Could he truly be that big? Fire torched her blood. Excitement coursed through her in giddy anticipation. The horse moved beneath them with its hooves cutting into the soft sod.

The naked power of this man, a true Scottish Highlander, set her heart pounding harder. Here she sat in his lap, streaking across the rising hillsides in the dead of a September night. Her senses tingled alive. She was aware of sounds and smells she had never experienced in her world.

Had modern mankind barricaded itself from nature so much that such sensations were lost? Or was it more than the absence of distractions that made life in the past more vibrant?

"See," he said, with his low voice drifting through her hair pinned within the slight space between his chest and her back, "he rides better when ye dinna struggle against him. Ye have poise and the strength, all ye need 'tis a wee bit of practice in how to mount and ride him for the sheer pleasure of the ride."

The image he conjured sent flickers of fire scorching over her. She was grateful he could not see her burning cheeks, yet sensed every cell in his body knew the imagery his words had traced through her mind.

"He feels what ye feel, lass," he continued, showing no mercy for her growing embarrassment. "He possesses a sense about such things. Can tell when his mount is nervous. Makes him skittish. Difficult to handle. When ye relax, he relaxes and is able to perform like he should." He shifted slightly in the saddle, leaving no doubt it was indeed his stiff cock pressed against her.

She gasped.

"Just give him a bit of rein, and he shall show ye just how wonderful 'tis to ride him all through the night, aye."

A hot ache pulsed between her legs. He was just the way she remembered him from her dreams. It took all her willpower not to squirm in his lap. The warmth of his thighs against her chilled ones was more than she could stand. His arm scorched against her breasts.

She gulped in the night air and the fog clouding her thoughts cleared momentarily. A canopy of brilliant stars distracted her for a split second, but it was impossible to focus on anything other than muscled arms, sexy bare thighs, and the throbbing cock barely separated from her own flesh by an askew skirt. One slight bounce from his lap, and she'd be mounting *him*. Her pulse throbbed.

The starlight cast a pale radiance over the rolling hills and distant forest. But along the horizon, just above the silhouettes of trees, she saw a castle looming with dark round towers. Uncannily, as though reading her very thoughts, he spoke.

"Aye, 'tis my home. MacRaigl Castle." He pulled the reins back and brought the horse to a halt. Relaxing his arm, he rested both hands between her legs, dangerously close to the aching need he had aroused in her. "'Tis the home of my great-great-grand-mere, who came from Norway to marry my grandfather." He bent over so his lips were against her ear. "The original castle was burnt, but we rebuilt a finer one. Ye shall like it here," he declared with heated breath curling down the outer rim of her ear and winding a fiery trail deep inside. Without warning, he jabbed his heels into the stallion, urging him up the steep embankment leading to the winding road home.

She struggled to keep from pressing deeper into his lap and against his cock. The higher the horse climbed, the more her body pushed against his. As the horse neared the crest, Jen slipped even higher in Mael's lap.

Unable to reposition herself, her hips shifted and his cock beneath his kilt pressed harder as she squirmed to move from him. His hot breath fell in heated waves along her neck down the slope to her breasts. Urgent spikes of heat pulsed to her clit.

"Ye best sit still, lass, unless ye wish to fall from my lap and down the side of the mountain," he chuckled.

She stole a peep over his arm. Her breath caught in her throat. Her vision filled with the darkness of the steep mountain slope shaded by stunted Rowan trees twisting from the rocky edge.

"Aye, then, to my castle we make haste." He jabbed his heels into the horse's ribs, and it seemed to charge forward with greater power.

The stallion made the last climb onto the ridge and regained its steady gait. Jeanne sighed with relief.

"Ye shall discover my castle has all things necessary for a comfortable life. Mind ye, there are no witches." His chuckle was warm against her ear and bore genuine amusement in its deep tones. "Least none ye can tell. The rumors of the ignorant and superstitious can follow us even here."

She had to silently agree with him. Trench had preyed upon those superstitions to wage his campaign of terror.

The horse's gait tossed her up in MacRaigl's lap. He groaned slightly. She bounced again then resettled against him. His moan eased from him. A small smile slipped over her lips. Served him right.

They drew closer to the castle. The outer wall perimeter ran the length of the entire castle and grounds inside. She noticed large holes in the stonework and recalled the cross-like shapes were used for crossbows. Two round towers balanced either side of the gatehouse. They started over the drawbridge.

She looked over his arm into the depthless dark waters of the moat. The stallion's gait echoed through the night as he carried them over the bridge into the castle. She thought of MacRaigl's twenty-first-century descendant and the castle she had visited. She'd approached it from the cellar. Was this possibly the same one? Her mind whirled with the fantastic possibility.

There were multiple round towers and a network of exterior walkways along the upper walls that connected the towers. The MacRaigl of her time had said he'd added onto the original castle. As they approached, the grille-worked gate within the castle wall groaned and slowly rose over the arched entrance. The sound of the portcullis sliding up the grooves was like nothing she'd ever heard. Ancient. Primitive. The clatter rang loudly in her ears. This was real, all of it. Even if it had been real some seven hundred years before she'd been born. It was too astonishing to comprehend. He shifted his weight underneath her and the feel of his body assured her it was real, especially *him*... She squirmed in spite of her attempt to ignore his closeness. It had been a long time since she'd been with a man. She mentally paused... Come to think of it, she'd never been with a man over seven hundred years old. She bit back the giggle.

The gatehouse torch sputtered bright in the darkness. The sentry bowed his head when they rode past him through the arched entrance. Once inside, the metal scraped against itself and the iron gate lowered. Two dark figures rushed to secure the heavy wood doors with a thick wood beam. The drawbridge cranked up against any other visitors. It was a new sound, but one that filled her with a feeling of safety she'd not felt since being delivered here by the portal.

They rode through the quiet square. The horse's hooves clopped over the cobblestones. Jeanne looked about them, amazed that within the thick walls was indeed a village. Marveling over the wide towers and various dwellings within the castle, she recalled pictures of castles and moats. Sure, she'd read about such places, but never had she thought she'd actually see one as it truly was, in its own time period.

She'd watched numerous movies depicting medieval times, but they had not captured the true essence. It was nothing like she'd expected. It was all so vivid. Even the vegetation was more vibrant than in modern times. Barking dogs startled her from the reverie. She jumped and shifted in his lap, quickly finding the animals.

The canines rushed to greet them, followed by an angry shout. Some were hounds while others looked like modern border collies. They yapped and jumped about the horse. She trembled and pressed closer to MacRaigl. The horse stomped nervously then jerked against the reins.

She pulled her legs up, struggling against the awkward position she now found herself in and buried her head into MacRaigl's hard chest. The scent of horse, leather and man filled her nostrils. Her heartbeat pounded so loudly in her ears, she could barely hear the dogs.

MacRaigl brought the horse to halt.

"Ye fear doggies?" he whispered with his lips pressed close to her ear. Jeanne didn't know which sensation was more intense, her fear of the dogs, or his warm breath caressing her skin.

"Tie the beasties," his voice boomed overhead.

She peeped around his arm and saw shadows running ahead of the animals as the men led them away. Her gaze moved up the wide stone steps.

"The dogs are gone, lass. 'Tis safe."

The huge double doors at the top of the steps scraped open. Golden light spilled down them seeming to chase the older man running toward them.

"Me laird! Did I misunderstand ye? I thought ye were to return on the morrow." His words broke off when he saw Jeanne sitting in MacRaigl's lap.

"Aye," was all MacRaigl offered and he shifted under her. Without warning, his hand came around her waist and he lifted her off the horse with him, then setting her on the ground. Her knees wobbled but she steadied herself by leaning into his hard body. She spun around to make sure the dogs had not returned.

"Tell Missus MacRay we have a visitor, Ian." He bowed slightly to Jeanne. "If ye will lead the way, me lady. Just follow Ian." He gestured to the older man, who also wore the same type of tartan slung over his shoulder.

She fell in behind Ian eager to get away from MacRaigl, instantly missing the warmth of his body pressed against hers. A gusty breeze blew against her, raising goose bumps over her. It was a strange feeling to be separated from him after so intimate a ride. Her stomach growled as she hurried up the steps. The open doors welcomed her with light and warmth. Unlike its modern version, this castle didn't have a foyer, instead it opened directly into a massive hall. She stepped over the threshold, glancing back to make sure the hounds were not following, and met MacRaigl's curious stare. It was amazing how much he resembled his twenty-first-century descendant. Upon entering behind her, he paused and closed his hand around her wrist. Her heartbeat quickened.

"'Tis safe, now." His intense brown eyes brightened, and a slow grin stretched over his face while his stare touched her lips. Her cheeks stung with patches of warmth and she looked away not feeling at all safe from his passion.

His low chesty rumbling sounded behind her. He knew how much he affected her. She was mortified. Was it so easy to read her emotions? She'd not blushed so much since she'd been a teenager. Forcing her concentration on Ian, she slipped from MacRaigl's grasp and started up the winding stone steps.

Ian lifted a sputtering torch from the wall bracket and led the way up the tower. She followed him with her hand outstretched against the cold wall to maintain her balance. Daring a last glance over her shoulder, she met MacRaigl's gaze. He stood at the bottom of the staircase with one foot resting on the first riser and his kilt revealing a bare knee.

Her attention riveted to his long legs, afforded a wonderful view with the gapping vent his stance created in the kilt. The thick, cross-strapped leather boots stopped just below his knees. Her heart palpitated. Desire fanned over her. Cute knees, her lips formed silently before she could stop them, grateful he did not speak English and better yet, he thought she was a mute. Had he noticed?

She lifted her stare to his. Oh, yeah, that was definitely a look of confusion and curiosity. She must be more careful, but her attention was pulled back to his sexy legs. Wet heat rushed from her pussy, dampening her inner thighs. Her mind replayed how it had felt to sit between those sexy man legs. She straightened her shoulders and resisted the temptation to look again, knowing he still watched her.

"What is this?" A woman's voice broke across the silence of the hall with fierce consternation riding its high pitch.

Jeanne jerked around, pressing her hand into the curving stairwell. The scene below seemed like a movie playing in front of her. The woman, dressed in a deep green velvet gown with gold braid hem along the cuffs, bodice and waist, seemed to glide from the side room. Her long auburn hair cascaded wildly about her shoulders.

She tried to mentally overlay the modern floor plan to the one below. It was the same room she had sat in nearly seven centuries into the future, listening in complete disbelief as Gregory Trench had revealed his vile scheme.

"I've been waiting for ye, Mael. What took ye so long? And—" The pale oval face lifted. Inhuman dark eyes widened into a catlike stare over her. A surge of chills tightened her nipples into hardened rounds. The woman had called him Mael. Was it possible? Was she his wife?

"Who is *she*?" the woman demanded as only a lover or a wife could.

Jeanne was awestruck by the woman's beauty and could see how a man like Mael would be captive to her forever. A small pang of jealousy coursed through her. Her palms grew sweaty against the cold stone wall. Nonsense. Once she returned to her own time, these people would be mere shadows of the past. Dead. Ghosts of ancient times. The thought ripped through her with unexpected sadness.

"She is my guest. No one ye should concern yourself about." Mael MacRaigl's gaze swept over Jeanne. She saw the same depthless glow in his eyes as she'd seen in the twenty-first-century MacRaigl and hugged herself. Perhaps it was just this castle, and the unpleasant memories it held.

"Come. I would have a word with ye." Mael grabbed the woman's forearm and urged her back toward the room.

"Is she the reason it took ye so long to return?" the woman laughed as he pushed her through the doorway, closing the heavy door loudly behind them.

She tried to understand the muffled voices raised in bitter anger. Ian cleared his throat.

"Now that our entertainment 'tis over if ye will follow me." He started up the stairs once more. "The laird shall handle her, dinna worry yourself about her," he added as they wound their way up the tower. He lit the wall torches lighting their way up the curving steps.

She followed him, unable to shake the deep fear that had seized her when she'd met that creature's gaze. Who was she? The question pressed against her lips, begging to be voiced, instead she bit the insides of her mouth.

Ian paused on the first landing, but only long enough to light another torch.

"'Tis me laird's private solar," he informed her, nodding at the closed door then continued up the tower. She hoped the servant would explain who the woman was, and why she was so angry, but it was soon apparent he was not going to offer any further explanations.

When he paused on the second level, he lit another torch, and nodded to the door to her right. "Me laird's bedchamber," he said, and then motioned toward the door across from it. "Me laird's garderobe and for your use as well." She noted the location of the bathroom, if one could call it that, was halfway between the two levels and was grateful she'd not have too far to go. Of course, she assumed there would be chamber pots.

On the third level, he stopped and swung open a door and then entered the musty, cold room. He quickly set about starting a fire in the huge grate. She marveled at the size of the fireplace, surmising three people could easily fit inside its grate. The room was as large as the tower was round. She stared at the unlit logs and shivered. Wrapping her arms around her torso, she realized the mammoth logs had apparently been placed there some time ago in anticipation of a guest during the course of the winter. The kindling caught fire and flames licked against the monster logs.

"Shall take the yules a bit to catch fire and warm the room." He turned to her with a frown creasing his bearded face. "Had me laird a wife, then this chamber would be her wardrobe. We need a bed set in here for ye."

Her pulse sharpened. So Mael was not married. She mentally shook herself. She could not think of Mael, or any man that way. She could not afford to have feelings for him, but, she licked her lower lip, there was no denying the intense longings his touch had ignited. Absently she wondered if she could just have sex with him and not lose her heart. What was wrong with her? She mentally chided and reached out, fanning her hands in front of the weak fire.

"Since there's only me laird, I use this room for storage. I'll have these removed and placed in the solar's basement."

She started to protest all the inconvenience her unexpected visit was causing, but dared not break her illusion of being a mute.

"Do ye no speak, lass?"

She shook her head.

"That could cause ye some difficulties. Perhaps we best say ye are from a foreign country and dinna speak our tongue." Ian seemed to consider something then added, "I think ye should return with me to the kitchen for a bit. Missus MacRay will fix ye a nice supper, and ye can warm yourself by the kitchen fire. By the time ye finish your supper, your chambers shall be cozy warm."

She glanced about the room, doubting the stone-floored, stone-walled room ever got warm. Eagerly, she followed him back down the winding staircase to the landing and the Great Hall below. As they walked across the expanse, the voices from the adjacent room raised in angry shouts. Well, Mael's was raised in a definite shout, drowning out the softer feminine one.

"Ye left without a word. How can ye treat me so callously? Ye possess a cruel soul, Mael MacRaigl."

"At least I *possess* my soul!" he shouted so loudly the door vibrated.

"Dare ye speak so to me, Mael. After all we have been to each other. What of our ties? Ye may sever the love we share, but ye can never break the ties of blood."

"Ye betrayed our blood! I am not the one who lay with the devil himself and then flaunted the sin in my face."

Her scream was raw. Jeanne imagined the woman had flung herself against him with her talons bared.

"If ye will follow me, lass?" Ian gave her a disapproving frown.

Reluctantly, she turned to follow him across the Great Hall, but the sounds from the room halted her again.

"Get out of my home." The door jarred open, slamming into the stone wall. The menacing shadow of the highlander filled the archway.

Chapter Nine

Jeanne watched in horror as he stomped across the expanse with the writhing woman in tow. He held her by her upper arms but she fought him with flailing arms and legs striking the air in vain attempts to wound him. Her unearthly screech echoed in the vaulted hall.

"Release me," she spat, striking at him, trying to dig her long nails into his face. "How dare ye treat me this way!"

Mael paused long enough to jerk open the heavy door that led to the courtyard. "Out of my castle and off my lands. Ye are not welcome in my home."

He shoved her through the doorway, but she reeled with her own rage heaving high in her chest.

"Ye see the world so clearly, do ye? Ye know better than the rest of us poor miserable souls who are not allowed to make our own decisions in life? Ye dinna own me, Mael MacRaigl."

"Nae," he said so softly Jeanne had to strain to hear his words. "The devil owns ye now."

The raw hatred etched over the woman's face, transforming her beauty into ugliness. She moved as though to lunge at him, but he slammed the door in her face. Her muffled outrage against the heavy door soon silenced.

Ian cleared his throat, but Jeanne continued to stare as the emotions played across MacRaigl's face. Just who was this woman? What had she done to warrant such treatment?

"She shall not be allowed entrance into MacRaigl Castle ever again." His look shot past Jeanne and hit its mark squarely on Ian.

"Aye, me laird," he mumbled behind her.

"Why did ye allow her entry this eve knowing how I felt?"

She took a step backwards, fearing MacRaigl's anger might find a new target.

"I dinna! I swear, me laird. She arrived some time before meself."

All I Want

"A broom she must have ridden, then." He turned on his heel.

Jeanne watched as he reentered the side room, slamming the door behind him.

Ian's sigh of relief was in unison with hers.

"Now that the final act 'tis over." He nodded toward the door at the end of the wide room. "Shall we see about a hot bowl of stew for ye and maybe a bit of bread and mutton?"

She fell in behind him, glancing over her shoulder one last time, before following the servant out the side door. A covered walkway led across the courtyard to the separate structure he identified as the kitchen. She walked briskly behind him, eager to get out of the chilling night air.

* * * * *

"Awake, lass," came the chambermaid's soft voice.

Jeanne blinked against the morning light and snuggled deeper into the voluminous folds of the down comforter.

"Nae, me Laird bids ye join him in breaking the fast. Ye must hurry and dress." The woman pushed the linen curtains from the bed and draped them over the bedpost hook then tugged at the covers. Jeanne shivered from the unwelcome drafts of cool air. "Please, lass, dinna make me master angry. He grows rather loud when crossed."

She squinted into the servant's fearful eyes, remembering all too well the laird's anger and rose from the bed.

She was a solid goose bump when she splashed the cold water on her face, shivering uncontrollably. How she missed central heating and hot water. She toweled her face dry, moving closer to the fire. What she'd give for a cup of black coffee and a lemon-filled donut. Her stomach rumbled and she mentally shook the longings from her mind. She'd taken her world of conveniences for granted. How many times over the past months had she reached for her cell phone or thought about turning on the TV to watch the news. She'd never realized what a creature of habit she was. Living without electricity was impossible to put into thought. It took two, sometimes three times longer to do everything. For the first time in her life she understood how servants had come into being and how vital they were to daily life.

The chambermaid brought her several kirtles. Two were clearly for daywear while the other three were more ornate and formal. Jeanne wondered if the garments belonged to the woman from last night and chose the light green linen one with a leather girdle, which the maid helped her lace.

Next the maid brushed her hair and worked it into a thick braid that fell to her back. When the girl tried to place the barbette and linen cloth over her head, Jeanne refused. The maid frowned, but gave in when Jeanne stood from the table, indicating she would not be coerced into wearing the contraption. She didn't care for the chinstrap headgear and didn't intend to wear it.

Once ready, she followed the maid down the tower steps to the second floor. The girl motioned for her to continue alone and turned back up the steps, no doubt to tidy up the bedchamber.

Exploring the castle and becoming familiar with the layout was the first thing she must do. Of course, she might not be here long enough. She couldn't return to the village. Verica would learn about the mob and how MacRaigl had saved her. Perhaps she could get word to the woman that she was safe.

Upon entering the Great Hall, she was surprised by the number of people sitting in the enormous room. Rows of trestle tables lay perpendicular to the large table where Mael and Ian sat with two other men on what appeared to be a slightly raised platform, like a stage. Three risers ran the width of the dais. She quickly noticed that his table had the comfort of chairs while the other tables had benches. Most of the diners were men, with only a few women in attendance.

MacRaigl lifted his gaze from his conversation with Ian to meet hers. She smiled slightly. He was quick to his feet. The other men, dressed in tartans, all the same color as his, stood from their meals. Some exchanged quizzical expressions.

"My guest has arrived." He held up a silver chalice in a toast. "Join me, lass, sit by my side."

She quickly caught the wide-eyed glances the men and women gave each other and realized this was not an everyday occurrence. On shaky legs, she made the long distance to her host, trying to appear nonchalant. He held out his hand and placed a quick peck on her cheek. The gesture shocked her. She'd not expected such genteel manners from a warrior, but the touch of his lips against her flesh caught her off-guard. Swallowing the pounding pulse, she tried to mask the effect his nearness had on her.

"Be seated." He pulled out the chair beside him and held it for her.

She sat down. Her gaze met his and her body blushed hot. She looked away. It was impossible to search those brown eyes without feeling his molten passion bubbling beneath the surface.

"I trust ye slept well," he inquired as he poured her a goblet of dark wine from the clay pitcher.

She nodded and stared at the young man who came over to her with a large bowl of water. She noticed the small towel draped over the youth's arm and realized she was supposed to wash her hands, but Mael shooed him away before she could react.

"Ye are with tongue?" he asked and tilted his head as though expecting her to open her mouth for inspection.

Jeanne pursed her lips together and again nodded. This seemed to satisfy his question. The same young man reappeared, carrying a wooden bowl with a large slice of white bread and slab of cheese. She smiled at the youth.

"Have ye always been without voice?"

She shook her head and avoided his deep piercing stare.

"So what mishap stole it from ye?" He lifted the goblet to his lips as though expecting her to speak.

"Would that such a fate befall me wife," came a chuckling voice across the room, followed by loud bursts of laughter.

"Aye. Dinna complain, me laird, count your blessed stars."

The woman sitting beside the man slapped his arm and whispered something. His fit of laughter choked off. A low murmuring swept over the room. Jeanne caught the words "tetched" and "witch". Two Gaelic words she understood clearly.

"Hear me," MacRaigl spoke between mouthfuls. "There shall be no nonsense and superstitions between these walls."

"Aye," came a weak unison response.

"'Tis merely a lass who met with misfortune. I am told she is a healer. Aye, lass?"

She greeted the kind look in his eyes with a grateful nod. A few more mumbled words brought him to his feet. He pounded the table with his fist, jarring all the goblets and bowls.

"Hear me! Ye shall treat my guest with the same respect ye give to me. She can care for our sick."

"Aye, me laird." The men nodded and MacRaigl sat back down, giving her a satisfied nod.

"Aye, Timmons, once Alyce gets ahold of ye after this meal, ye shall be in need of a healer," one of the men guffawed. The room echoed with laughter, and the tension receded.

MacRaigl's laughter rang above them all. It was deep and came easily. She could not stop the grin that broke across her face. He glanced at her and winked. The rest of the meal was a constant bantering between the men and their laird. She marveled how even the span of centuries had not altered the social nature of small talk. Grateful the attention had shifted from her to that of everyday life in the MacRaigl Castle, she ate her meal in peace.

* * * * *

Jeanne was leaving the Great Hall with MacRaigl to start a tour of the castle when Ian rushed up to them. His usual robust complexion was a sickly pallor.

"A word with ye, me laird," he whispered so the stragglers could not hear.

"Speak it, Ian. The girl can tell no one."

Ian looked at her with brief consideration, then turned back to his master.

"I found the chambermaid, Rachel, dead."

Her pulse quickened.

"Dead?" The harsh tone in MacRaigl's voice shuddered through her.

"Aye. Ye must see." Ian gestured toward the outer door leading to the garden that separated the two wings.

"Come, lass, since ye know the healing arts."

"'Tis dead she be, me laird, no healer can help the lassie now."

He frowned at Ian's sarcasm and gestured for him to lead the way.

She followed them out the door and through the herbal garden past the dormant vegetable gardens into the wing she assumed was the servants' quarters, judging by the numerous bedchambers that opened along its hall.

They entered one of the rooms and she immediately noticed the bloodstains splattered across the sheets, and a faint trail leading to the partially opened window.

MacRaigl rushed over to the prone body. The woman appeared to have collapsed on the floor. All color had drained from the body, leaving it a grayish-blue hue. She bent down beside him and stretched out her hand to brush the long reddish tresses from the girl's neck.

Recoiling as though she'd been stung by a hornet, Jeanne stared at the two puncture marks that bruised the ashen skin. Dried blood discolored the wound, making it a hideous injury.

"She has no relatives," Ian spoke behind them. "We could easily bury her without anyone knowing."

Jeanne jerked around and met the servant's pleading stare.

"She would not do this." MacRaigl lifted the lifeless body into his powerful arms and carefully laid the girl on the bed.

"And what other explanation do ye offer? Ye know—"

"Enough. Ye shall not speak it." His voice was hoarse.

Pain dulled his dark brown eyes so deeply that her breath caught in her chest. It was an agony that ripped through the soul. She recognized that pain. She'd felt it when she'd helplessly watched her parents savagely killed. She'd felt it again when Trench had taken her brother prisoner. Yes, she blinked up at him, she knew his pain.

"Me laird, ye canna ignore this. Ye must send word to her."

"I canna believe she would seek revenge this way." Mael moved to the window with his back on them.

"Ye disowned her. Ye banned her from her own home," Ian reminded him.

Jeanne snapped alert. This was the woman's home, too? Then she *must* be his wife.

"Ishabelle may be many things I canna accept, but I canna believe my sister to be a murderess."

She looked from him to Ian. Last night suddenly had meaning. MacRaigl had fought with his *sister* and disowned her. What had happened to make a man like MacRaigl do such a thing? She could never disown Ryan.

Instinctively, she reached out to clasp his hand, but was not prepared for the sensation of his fingers entwining with hers. The contact was just as powerful as his descendant's had been. Warm and comforting. Too comforting.

His large hand closed over hers and squeezed tightly. She held his stare. Unspoken understanding coursed through their touch. It was a connection she'd never experienced with another person. She swallowed the rising excitement.

"The lass doesn't believe it either," he argued. His eyes filled with a gentleness belying his power. "We saw another like this, aye, lass?"

She considered the question, dropping her clasp of his hand to link her hands together behind her back. Her gaze wandered back to the puncture wounds. Shifting her stare to him once more, she nodded.

MacRaigl's breath escaped him in a loud release.

"'Tis like the body we found at Tryon's." Ian's voice was low and monotonic.

"That dinna mean Ishabelle, my sister dinna—" MacRaigl turned from them. Gripping the bedpost, his shoulders slumped forward.

Tears pooled in her eyes. Was it the reminder of her own loss of Ryan that caused her to cry? Her blurry vision filled with the highlander's dejected stance as he struggled to compose himself.

"Tend to the burial yourself." He straightened. "Ye sew the shroud so none shall see, and we shall hold the service immediately."

"Aye, me laird."

When MacRaigl turned around, she noticed the redness in the rims of his brown eyes. "The lad in the village had these markings."

She met his questioning look. Should she reveal she had a voice and dare risk having to explain more than she could? She could attempt to speak the language she'd learned over the last few months. Moving toward the window, she looked into the sky. "In the village. The lad had similar wounds."

She nodded.

"Do ye know who was responsible for that death?"

She looked from one man to the other, trying to gauge their reactions. If she implicated Trench, what would they do? Was their justice like that of the villagers? She could not afford to have Trench killed. She had to know for certain that Ryan was at the twenty-first-century MacRaigl Castle. And there was the question of being able to return to her own time. Since she and Trench had come through the portal together did it mean they must go back together? If Trench were killed could Verica still return Jeanne to her own time? What if she could not get word to Verica? What if something had happened to the old woman? Jeanne was not certain she could even find the cave again, much less calculate the exact time of return.

But, Trench knew where the cave was and he knew when the portal would reopen.

"Do ye know, lass? Who killed the lad?" His tone was reined but impatience gripped each word.

If Mael killed Trench, wouldn't that be taken as an act of war since he was Cullen Mangus' nephew, at least in disguise? She gnawed on her lower lip. And if he succeeded in killing Trench, then she might not be able to go home. There were too many risks in telling the truth. It was best to hide behind silence. She could not afford to start a chain reaction that could escalate her current situation.

"Dinna ye understand my question? Do ye know who killed the lad in the village?"

Slowly, she shook her head and looked down at the floor. Lying had never been easy for her.

"Are ye sure, lass?" came his plea. She knew the truth would release him from the agony he felt believing somehow his sister was responsible for this death. But why would his sister have done this? Revenge against him? How had he come to such a conclusion? She nodded, hating herself for the lie. She couldn't tell MacRaigl the truth.

If she wanted to return back to her own time, then she must see that Trench stayed alive. If Trench had killed the girl, then it meant he had followed Jeanne here.

"Ishabelle could have gone to the village first. She arrived before us, me laird."

"Enough!" MacRaigl turned on his heel taking a menacing step toward the servant. "See to the arrangements. I have other matters to attend." With that he stomped out of the room.

She stared after him, feeling responsible for his torture, wanting to assuage his guilt, and her own.

"Ye dinna understand, do ye, lass?" Ian began to wrap the linens around the body. "Much here canna be understood. I must fetch needle and thread and a burial shroud. Will ye stay and not allow entry while I fetch the articles?"

She nodded. Once alone, she quickly closed the door and hurried over to the window. Her gaze searched the mortar sill speckled with blood. Opening the window further, she noticed the blood trail along the outer ledge where it ended. She looked down the two-story drop where the tall brush had been crushed and broken.

"Trench," she whispered. The sooner she found him, the sooner she could stop the carnage and wait until the portal reopened.

"What are ye doing?"

She pivoted sharply on her heel and shrugged, hoping he would accept her response.

"The task of telling Missus MacRay about the lass was not pleasant. Laird MacRaigl instructed me to say the lass died in her sleep. We dinna know why." He dropped the heavy dark wool cloth onto the floor.

"I dinna hope ye faint of heart, are ye?"

Jeanne shook her head.

"Good. I need ye to spread the cloth underneath the corpse. I'll lift her. Can ye do it?"

She nodded then quickly picked up the shroud.

Once the body was wrapped, Ian pulled the ends of the burial cloth together and began to sew. Seeing that his skill with the needle was not nimble, she gently took it from him. She had sewn up hundreds of cuts and stab wounds in the ER. Sewing a shroud should be child's play.

"Pftt." Ian watched her. "I never seen anyone sew like that. Ye have a fine skill there, lass." He leaned over to examine the finished end. "Why, appears as though Rachel sewed herself up from inside." His gaze was a mixture of awe and suspicion. "Be careful, lass. There are some within these very walls who would lay witch upon your door stoop without further cause."

Her pulse quickened. He was right. She recalled how she'd been greeted at breakfast.

"The laird has taken an interest in ye and that alone sets some of the lasses into a mêlée. Many a female desires the attentions of Mael MacRaigl, knowing he must marry within the year lest he lose his lands and claim to the title of Chief. It shall all go to his sister should he be forced to forfeit. To claim Chief he must procure himself a wife soon."

All I Want

She didn't understand. It must have shown on her face, because Ian was quick to explain.

"There's the matter of the MacRaigl line continuing. If he dinna find a wife soon, then according to our clan's tradition, the land shall revert to the next married sibling. That would be Ishabelle. Ye met her last evening."

She was beginning to understand last night's event. Ishabelle had married so she could inherit the lands. Mael MacRaigl had been betrayed by his own sister.

"Ye understand a bit now?" Ian nodded. "Let us be about."

He lifted the shrouded body effortlessly, while cradling the girl's lifeless form in his arms as though he didn't wish to disturb her. She followed him outside and down the narrow steps. Why did she continue to feel there was more to the rift between MacRaigl and his sister than an inheritance? Why would MacRaigl and Ian suspect Ishabelle of this girl's death, especially the way in which she died?

What had driven him to disown his sister? Certainly, an ill-fated marriage or the challenge to his claim as Chief of the clan was serious enough to hammer a wedge between the siblings. History was full of such stories. And Trench was altering it. She had to stop his madness.

"Dinna take the lass's body through there," came MacRaigl's voice from the courtyard. She stepped out into the light and met his stern look. "Take her to my chapel," he ordered and glared at her. "Why do ye have this one with ye?"

"She sewed the shroud," he informed his master.

She noticed MacRaigl's fists clench white-knuckled by his sides.

"That was your task, Ian." His glare filled with such raw emotions, Jeanne took a step backwards.

"She-she," Ian stuttered and shifted the weight of the corpse in his arms.

She stepped between the two men and planted her hands firmly against MacRaigl's hard chest. The contact was electric, sending currents through her hands, trembling all the way down her body. Her stare locked with his, and she knew by his expression he too had felt it. Slowly, she shook her head. His muscles relaxed.

"Take the body to the chapel. Missus MacRay and her lasses await ye. Ye shall have to say the words."

"Aye, me laird. Damn sin no priest has come to take Father Jacob's place," Ian sighed, casting her a grateful nod.

She smiled slightly.

"No fault of the priest that he died. He was an old man. We shall have a new one by spring."

"Will ye be attending, me laird?"

"Nae. I have other pressing matters." He stomped off in the opposite direction. She thought it odd that he would not be officiating at the service and ran to catch up with him.

Slowing her pace to his, she jerked on his sleeve, marveling at the feel of the homespun linen. He broke stride and looked down at her. She wanted so much to tell him that it was Trench and not his sister who had murdered the chambermaid, but she couldn't. Not yet.

Instead, she reached up and stroked his tanned cheek, letting her fingers trail down the length of his short beard. The heat rose in her. She longed to feel his hands warm against her breasts. How would it feel for his lips to claim hers?

"Aye, lass, I know ye possess a tender heart. I scared ye." He took her hand, turned it up and bowed over it so his lips touched her palm in a tender kiss.

Her breath rose full in her chest. His kiss sent pulses throbbing between her legs. Visions of him making love to her set her on fire. She mentally shook herself. This was not what she needed. She could not afford to get involved with a barbarian highlander. She had a mission. She must find Trench. She could not lose her heart to this man. She jerked free and spun on her heel, running across the courtyard toward her chamber tower. He certainly didn't act like any barbarian she'd ever imagined.

Mael watched her disappear into the castle. What was the mystery surrounding her? Perhaps the village rumors were true. Could she be a witch? He certainly felt bewitched. Ever since he'd first seen her in the village, he'd wanted her. Riding with her in his lap had required all his self-control to keep from taking her. She was soft and round and full of mysteries. He longed to explore her body, suckle her nipples and explore her passions.

His cock hardened with his thoughts. He considered her a moment longer. A woman like her would be a hot wild ride, and he knew once he'd tasted her, he'd want more. He shook his head and turned in the opposite direction. His quick strides through the arched wall brought him to the front courtyard just beyond the keep and into the north bailey of the castle. Renewed anger quickly abated his lust. He headed for the stables, where he found the lad holding the reins to his horse, saddled and bridled as he'd ordered. The youth glanced up at him.

"Your horse, me laird."

"Good lad." He took the reins. "Tell Ian I shall return in a few days' time." He swung onto the horse's back. The stallion shifted slightly under his weight.

"Aye, me laird," the boy grinned a gap-toothed grin.

"Me laird!" Ian rushed through the archway. "What are ye about?" The fear in Ian's eyes assured him that his old friend knew exactly where he was going.

"Mind your own business, Ian, and I shall be minding mine. Ye have a service to attend."

"I canna let ye do this. 'Tis no evidence."

"All the evidence I need 'twas in front of my eyes." Mael jerked the reins and guided the stallion toward the gate. He dug his heels into the horse's sides and galloped from the castle.

"Ye canna do this! Ye canna!" Ian blustered. "'Tis a mortal sin to slay your own flesh."

Chapter Ten

Jeanne sat down on the window seat as the world outside blurred under the tears welling in her eyes. Cradling her head in her hands, wave after wave of despair seized her. She worried about Ryan. Trench's madness was stressing her out beyond her ability to cope. It was bad enough being trapped in the past. And then, there was Mael. The look in his eyes would forever haunt her. She was responsible for it being there. She should have told him about Trench.

There was only one way to help him end these rumors and set his clan back on its natural course through history. She lifted her head and stared out the window and beyond the confines of the castle to the glen. As soon as it was dark, she would find Trench and put a stop to it all.

The sound of an approaching horse drew her attention out the window. The rider drove the horse into a hard gallop through the open gate. Immediately she recognized Mael. Now, just where was he going? Realization thundered through her. She was on her feet, taking the stone stairs two at a time. She bounded from the tower and out the door into the courtyard, slamming right into Ian.

"Aye, lass." He righted her. "He took off. Gone to his sister's. I know ye dinna understand. He blames her for the maid's death. I tried to stop him, but stubbornness runs deep in the MacRaigl family. I dinna know what else to do."

She knew! She grabbed the plaid draped over his shoulder and jerked him toward the stable.

"What lass?"

She pounded her forefinger into her chest, pointed to him and then in the direction MacRaigl had gone.

"We canna follow. 'Tis foolishness to try and stop him."

She stopped and folded her arms across her chest, staring at him.

"Ye truly think ye can help?" His rigid conviction of a moment earlier waned. She seized the opportunity and nodded frantically.

"I know how he looks at ye."

The warmth spread over her cheeks.

"The pass may be dry enough to let us cross over the mountain and make the glen before he does. 'Tis worth a try." Ian rubbed his beard.

The smile broke over her face as involuntarily as her swift embrace of the stout Scotsman. Blustering, Ian disentangled himself from her hold.

"There. There. Save all that for the laird. Come." He took her hand in his calloused one, and they raced to the stables.

Within minutes their horses' hooves were digging into the rambling green hillside as they raced to stop Mael. She wondered what she would do once they found him. Should she just blurt out the truth? She couldn't do that.

They rode hard. Ian led the way down the treacherous mountain slope, strewn with huge rocks jutting from the lush green hills. She clung to the horse's mane, jostling over the steep mountainside. She tried to stay in the saddle and clutched the reins. Not an accomplished rider like Ian, she'd been on a horse one time in her life. She grappled to guide the horse and finally gave up, concentrating on staying in the saddle.

"Are ye fairing well, lass?" He cast a worried look over his shoulder. The treacherous path narrowed with the terrain pitching steeper.

She managed to break her concentration just long enough to nod.

"Never ridden a beastie before, have ye?" Concern rose large in his eyes. "Clutch her sides betwixt your knees. Hug the mare as though your knees be your arms." He ducked as his mount took him through an unexpected thicket. "Beware, branches—"

She wasn't quick enough in her reaction, and the thorny bush caught her in the face. Her scream ripped across the mountains as the wicked thorns tore her flesh. Her horse bolted, sending her backwards.

Jeanne clutched for the horse's mane, but toppled from its back, landing painfully on her side. The force sent her sliding down the slope toward the jagged cliff edge. She grabbed for something to hold on to as the hard boulders and scrubs scraped against her legs. Thorns slashed her hands. She clutched at every twig and vine she slipped past but the wide mouth of the valley below lay poised to receive her. Fear ripped from her throat once more as the open space below her dangling feet sucked her legs into its vacuum. She clawed at the dirt, but the ground continued to disappear from her grasp. Suddenly, bands of steel clamped around her wrists and she stopped falling. Suspended in midair, Jeanne glanced up and met Mael's dark frown. Effortlessly, he lifted her from the edge of the cliff and pulled her into his powerful embrace, swinging her up into his arms. He carried her up the mountainside.

"Thank God." Ian crossed himself. "I dinna know where ye came from, me laird, but praise the Lord for sending ye here."

MacRaigl snorted as he stomped passed Ian and gently lowered her to a nearby rock, safe from the mountain's perilous edge.

"Are ye unharmed, lass?" He put his hand under her chin and lifted her face for inspection. "Aye, the tumble left several gashes. Ye need tending." He gathered her into his arms again and mounted his horse, leaving Ian to follow with her horse in tow.

Although she was in pain, Jeanne took comfort in the refuge of his strong arms as they rode back to the castle. She certainly had not intended to go to such lengths to stop him. Had he not appeared, she'd be dead. It was the second time he had saved her.

"I saw ye leave the castle and knew ye were on a journey of disaster. Ian dinna know as I did that ye are no horsewoman. I feared 'twould be too late."

She trembled in his arms.

"There now, 'tis from coldness or fear?" He wrapped his tartan about her. The warmth from his own body still heated the wool and she snuggled against his chest. His body felt as hard as the rocks she'd fallen over. The tartan fluttered about them and she quickly heated against him. There was only him, and she longed to stay in his arms forever.

"Missus MacRay shall brew one of her teas and soothing balms. Ye shall feel better soon." His words comforted her but the sensation of his touch made her forget the cuts and bruises.

The luxury of being a mute made life uncomplicated by lengthy explanations or inappropriate responses. Since no one expected her to speak, no one expected anything from her, at least that was what she thought.

* * * * *

All I Want

Mrs. MacRay came in, followed by a young girl carrying a tray. She set the pewter tray on the table by the bed and handed the housekeeper the brown crock. Jeanne stared as the two women lifted the lid and dipped strips of linen into the ointment. They were gentle as they tended to her scratches.

"Ye be a lucky one now, lass." Mrs. MacRay spread the cooling balm on her temple and pushed her head to the side. The young girl leaned closer and stared over Mrs. MacRay's shoulder as she examined Jeanne's neck.

She pulled from their probing and glared up at them.

"There now, we had to be certain. All of us are examined regularly since the scare began," Mrs. MacRay admitted and dipped the end of the cloth into the white cooling balm. She touched it to Jeanne's face.

She wanted to tell her the truth about the maid who was killed and who Trench was. The women moved to treat the scratches and scrapes along her arms. While they dressed the scratches on her legs, Jeanne sipped the tea. The warm herbal blend began to work its potent magic and by the time they were finished, she could barely hold her eyes open. She was promptly tucked away in bed and forgotten, until the heavy door creaked open and Mael peered inside.

"Do ye sleep?" he whispered.

She shook her head and he entered, stopping beside the bed.

"Ye feel like a bit of company, lass?" He reached down and gently brushed a stray strand of hair from her face. Jeanne stiffened under his touch and sat up further in the bed, pulling the covers underneath her chin. She nodded and he dragged the nearby chair closer, sitting across from her.

"Did Missus MacRay take good care of ye?"

Again she nodded.

"Do ye need anything? Can I get ye something else to eat? More blankets?"

Shaking her head, she caught the look of doubt in the depths of his brown eyes.

"Do ye have everything ye need to make ye comfortable? I know your fall was frightening."

She moved her head with jerky nods.

"I feared ye would go over the edge before I could reach ye."

113

She fidgeted with the heavy covers running her hand over the top of the thick blanket, feeling vulnerable in his presence. He covered her hand with his. She looked up into fiery eyes. His clasp tightened, halting her nervous fidgeting. His hand was rough and calloused but as warm as a huge mitten. Her breath caught in her throat tightening against the heartbeat pulsing thicker into a choking lump.

"Ye tremble, lass. 'Tis from the cold or be it from the heat?" He leaned closer.

She bit her lower lip and averted his stare, tugging her hand from underneath his to clasp hers together around her knees. Aware of his intense stare, Jeanne rested her chin on her knees and stared into the blazing fire grate.

"I feel the fire, too." His voice washed hotly over her.

His presence was like a blazing sun beside her. She wanted him with a need that grew stronger each time he looked at her or touched her.

"Such a mysterious lassie. Ye surely be bright, 'tis shown in the way ye notice everything. But one thing puzzles me."

She stared up at him. His handsome face was set in a perplexed frown. Her fingers itched to stroke the line where his beard met tanned skin, remembering her spontaneous gesture in the courtyard that morning. Instead, she laced her fingers tighter together.

"I am befuddled, lass. I know ye to be a mute yet ye talked before injured."

Jeanne nodded slowly.

"Could ye speak again?"

She fell into his deep gaze.

"I think 'tis possible, lass." He grew animated and rested his arms on his forelegs, clasping his hands together.

She shook her head.

"I believe 'tis. How else could a mute scream at the top of her lungs for every ounce she be worth, not once, but twice? Do ye remember doing so?"

Panic gripped her. She had betrayed herself by an involuntary reaction. How could she explain it?

"Perhaps 'tis a first sign. I hope ye might try to speak to me. That ye could rather practice — with me, so as not to frighten others. After all, we have enough superstitions flying about our heads without creating new ones."

She gave a weak attempt at a smile. Her world of silence had become too comfortable, providing a safe distance between her and the hostile elements. As much as she wanted to talk with Mael, she could not risk giving up its protective shield. Not yet.

She longed to tell him how his touch made her heart flutter and her deepest desires stir hot. She needed to tell him how much she wanted him to kiss her right now. She longed to feel his tongue against her clit like he'd done so many times in her dreams. If she told him these things, then she'd eventually have to explain who she really was and why she was here. It was impossible. He would surely claim her witch or mad. It was best to keep the distance between them that the silence provided.

"Perhaps ye be too exhausted from the accident. We can try on the 'morrow. No rush for ye. We own all the time in the world." The chair scraped against the wood floor and he stood.

Jeanne watched his tall frame unfold to full height. His tan linen shirt was laced with a silk cord venting just below a sharp collar. The full sleeves of his shirt folded within the tartan that was draped over one shoulder. Her gaze slid over his broad chest to his narrow waist and the wide leather belt that held the plaid in place. Her gaze involuntarily traveled to his knees where the kilt and leggings of his laced cloth boots met. Her heart palpitated and heated desire licked her throat, traveling down her chest to join the aching between her legs.

"Would ye speak just one word to me, lass?" He suddenly sat down on the mattress with her.

He lifted his hand and cradled her face. Her breath hung in her throat.

"So comely a lass. I find myself thinking of ye all day, unable to attend the business of my estate. When midday strikes, I find myself unable to attend the hunt, because my mind 'tis clouded with your beauty." His soft laughter was easy. "My men shall soon fear me besotted. If only I had a name by which to call ye. 'Twould ease the ache in my heart a wee bit."

She tumbled into the bottomless bronze eyes staring so intently at her. He smelled of the highlands—clean, crisp, fresh, and that ever-present, distinct, earthy smell of the hills. He moved closer and lowered his face to hers. Her pulse raced. She'd never wanted to be kissed so badly in her entire life. She ran her tongue along the inside of her lips in anticipation.

The air between them sizzled. Her senses shocked alive with her heart pounding heavier. His warm breath fell over her cheeks. She closed her eyes just as firm lips captured hers and she greeted his taste. His entire presence enveloped her, smothering her with his essence. Encircling his powerful neck with her arms, Jeanne longed for him.

His beard pricked tender skin, but she didn't flinch. The taste of his lips intoxicated her. Aroused by his tender passion, she explored his mouth, pressing her breasts into his chest, needing to be closer. To melt into his desire would be so easy, all she had to do was let go and lose herself in his arms. Mael pulled her onto his lap. His cock hardened beneath the heavy material of his kilt. She longed to wrap her trembling fingers about his stiffened shaft and stroke him into mindless pleasure.

The thought was like a dousing of cold water. She stiffened, realizing she couldn't do this. To risk surrendering to her desires was suicide. If she didn't break free of him now, she'd never be able to let him go. Oh, she had no wish to escape his touch. All she wanted, he could give.

His arms tightened around her. His kiss deepened with his tongue darting inside her mouth, demanding a response. Her fingertips tingled as she traced the line between his beard and smooth skin. The contact of his flesh underneath her touch was electric.

Mael lifted his face from hers to place hungry kisses along her cheek and down her neck. Her breath rushed from her in a muffled whimper. She didn't want him to stop. She needed him to finish what he'd started. She needed to feel him inside her. She wanted him more than anything she'd ever wanted in her entire life.

Cradling her face between his hands, Mael tilted her head to meet his stare. She closed her eyes against the probing look not wanting him to see how desperate she was for him.

"Ye canna hide from me." His voice was full and rasped with passion.

Once more firm lips seized hers. The hunger burst between them. Groaning under his touch, her need was fierce, coiling and snaking upwards from her throbbing clit. If he continued to kiss her like that she'd come just from the intense anticipation.

She glided her hand up his neck, stretching her fingers into his thick hair. Her hand brushed over the single braid woven at the base of

All I Want

his neck with fabric and leather. Her pulse sharpened. Everything about him excited her. The leather and tartan plait, coarse against her fingers, reminded her this was an ancient warrior, like those she'd read about in history classes.

The realization she was not kissing the man she'd met in the parking lot but his ancient ancestor, a man who'd existed seven centuries before her birth, jarred her. The spell broke. She tore from his kiss and scooted off his lap into the cold folds of the bed linens.

"What?" Confusion creased his forehead as though trying to see the answer in her eyes. Slowly, he stood from the bed, straightening his clothing, and positioning the tartan over his erection.

"I dinna mean to take advantage of ye, lass." Was that remorse she saw in depths of his eyes? He squared his shoulders. "'Tis late and I keep ye from your rest."

She was amazed how easily he recovered from the rejection. Without another word, he turned and closed the door behind him. She released a ragged breath then collapsed against the mound of pillows, rolling over with the covers snug about her. His passion still burned her lips. With her tongue, she traced the hot trail his kiss had left imprinted on her lips, forever. She hated herself for denying him, for denying herself. But the last thing she needed was to fall in love with a seven hundred fifty-five-year-old man. Her laughter bubbled in her throat.

"Talk about an age difference." She buried her giddy laughter into a pillow, but it quickly transformed into sobs.

* * * * *

Mael stomped down the curving staircase to his chamber, still burning with the flame she'd stoked. His cock was as hard as the stone his feet stomped against. He wanted her. He needed to feel her come with him inside her, but she'd stopped him. Why? Although she was a stranger, somehow he knew her. He threw open the door to his room, slamming it loudly behind him. He'd never had an erection ache so badly.

"Me laird?" the woman's voice greeted him.

"Not this evening," he barked at the woman who sat in the middle of his bed, dressed in a soft, revealing gown. It would be all too easy to take her. He was aroused and in need of a good fuck.

"Me laird is upset." She rose on her knees and reached for him.

"I said, *not this evening.*" Instead of taking her, he turned his frustration on her.

"Oh." She hung her head and slid from the bed. "I misunderstood, me laird."

"Nae, lass, the misunderstanding rests with me. Forgive me," he said and reached out to stroke her arm. "Be a good lass. Leave me now."

"I can make ye forget your troubles. I know what a man likes," she assured him, moving around the bed.

"Surely a comely lass as ye knows what a man desires. I'll send Ian around in the morning to see that ye get your regular purse."

"Aye," she sounded disappointed. "But for ye, me laird, there'd be no purse. A night with a man such as yourself would be purse enough." He watched her eyes widen as her gaze took in his body.

Suppressing an irritated yet amused grunt, he nodded toward the door. "Your compliments would be best served to someone purchasing them, lass. There shall be an extra amount for ye inconvenience. Ye shall find Ian in the Hall waiting to escort ye back to the village. Leave me now." He turned his back to her and warmed his hands in front of the fire.

"And ye dismiss me as though I were but a servant?" her voice rang with the indignation of rejection. "And what of your sister and her devil husband?"

Mael spun on his heel just as the dagger sliced the air an inch from his ear. Her screech was that of a banshee. He grabbed her wrist and quickly disarmed her. Drawing his other arm around her, he pinned her flailing attempts to gouge his eyes.

"Who sent ye?" Anger pumped through him.

"Those of us who would rid the highlands of your kind and your she-devil sister."

"Ye stand as judge and God, do ye?"

"To the devil, aye, on that we do."

"Let us find out just how many of ye there be." Mael jerked her into a tight hold against him, with his arm around her neck, daring her to struggle. He led her through the door and down the stairs toward the Great Hall.

"Me laird? What is the meaning of this?" Ian rushed over to them as Mael towed the girl into the room.

All I Want

"I have the same question on me tongue, Ian. Seems this lass was to be my assassin, only not too adept at her chosen profession."

"Aye?" Ian eyed the girl. "What say ye, lass?"

"'Tis known throughout the valley that Ishabelle, banshee of the devil, bridesmaid of the dweller of darkness, came here and left a chambermaid dead in her evil wake. 'Tis our pledged duty to rid the world of her kind."

"Perchance ye dinna see well enough to distinguish 'tis Mael MacRaigl ye attacked, not his sister?" Ian laughed. Mael was momentarily amused at the girl's dedication regardless how misled.

"Enough," he said. "Place her in the lower chamber for the evening. We shall escort her home in the morning. Then perhaps her people shall be appeased."

"We shall not be appeased until all MacRaigls and Tryons are dead, beheaded and their hearts served for our morning meals," she spat.

Ian took the writhing woman from the room and dragged her toward the door leading to the lower chamber.

"The curse has befallen ye, MacRaigl. Think ye sealed in your position as Chief of the clan? The clan will not unite behind ye! Ishabelle brings death upon the lands of MacRaigl. Others shall follow me. I am but one of many. Many who shall never cease until ye lie dead."

"Take her from my sight, Ian." He slammed his fist hard against the table.

"God as me witness, MacRaigl. Your clan shall be purged from the Highlands. From the very face of our world. We shall not rest until ye lay destroyed. We rally your own chieftains to our cause. Ye shall never be Chief over your clan. Never!"

"Get thee hence," Ian barked and jerked her from the room.

Mael poured a full mug of mead and downed it with vigor as the woman's voice echoed along the corridors while Ian hauled her toward the stairs. He poured another one and carried it back to his chamber. He wished he'd never gone to visit his sister and her new husband, and regretted he'd sent Ian for a wench earlier that evening. It was worthless to have regrets. He bolted his chamber door and downed the remainder of the mead then fell onto the bed. He flung his arm over his eyes, willing his thoughts to unbind, but the vision of his lovely guest flashed through his mind. So silent, yet so loud.

Damn it, 'twas a haunting to his soul. He shifted on the mattress. 'Twas the way her eyes filled with what? Sadness? Fear? Desire? He wasn't sure which it was. Such mystery surrounded her. 'Twas that very mystery which intrigued him almost as much as her silence frustrated him.

Was she somehow involved with the conspiracy to rid the world of MacRaigls? He laughed out loud at his own musing. How could a mute slight of a lass be any more than what she appeared? If she held dark secrets, he had not unlocked them.

Turning over her lovely vision in his mind, the desire resurged through Mael. Her sable hair curled so softly around her delicate face. Such beauty was a rare find. But there was something else about her that bespoke what? She was an enigma, not a typical lass. She dinna seem to quite belong with the locals. It wasn't anything tangible. Nothing to which Mael could put a name, perhaps it was because she was a mute. He could see so much in her eyes. Gorgeous eyes which masked thoughts and emotions he occasionally glimpsed whenever she was unaware he watched her. She guarded a secret, that was clear, but was it the secret he feared, or one he could never guess? 'Twas the puzzle that kept him awake that night.

He sucked air into his lungs and held it there, feeling his heart pump harder. He released it in a heated rush. That afternoon, on the cliff, he'd heard her scream. She had voice. Somehow, he must find a way to get her to use it.

He must have drifted off to sleep, because he awoke from the dredges of a deep slumber, knowing a distant sound had interrupted his rest. He was awake and on his feet with dirk in hand.

"Me laird," Ian said and pushed his way into the room, "the lass, your intended assassin, has escaped."

Chapter Eleven

Jeanne jerked awake. What had startled her? She lay in the darkness, holding her breath, and waited for it to resound. Low shallow breathing assured her someone was in the room. Chills gripped her.

Flickering light danced from the fire grate when the shadow stepped forward. She held her breath, keeping the heavy covers about her neck as the intruder moved closer.

"You felt me, didn't you?" came his hoarse voice. "You knew I'd find you."

"Trench!" She jerked straight up in bed.

"You can hide within the confines of MacRaigl's castle, but you should have known I'd find you. What to do with you is my dilemma."

She was on her feet, scrambling in the dark for a weapon, anything, but he jumped on her. She crashed to the floor with him on top of her as he pinned her arms above her head.

"Get off me, you son of a bitch." She thrashed under him.

"Had I wanted you, Jeanne, I could have taken you any time. But I've been busy planning a way to get to you when that big brute wasn't around. I think you've bewitched that highlander."

"Mael will kill you." She brought her knee up but her nightgown caught her leg and she missed her aim, clipping only his thigh.

"I have MacRaigl preoccupied tonight. He's in no shape to come to your rescue."

"I don't need him." Her pulse quickened. What had he done to Mael? Suddenly, her fear for the Scotsman overshadowed concern for her own safety.

"I think you need him more than you realize," he said and shoved his knee between her legs, separating them.

"I'll kill you myself." She jerked her arms free and clawed at his face, but he recaptured her wrists and pinned her arms above her head.

"I like your fire, Jeanne. I never realized how passionate you are. I think I'll take you back with me and keep you as my personal hellcat." His laughter raised goose bumps along her arms.

"I want Ryan freed," she heaved.

"God, you have a fucking one-track mind." He straddled her legs.

"Give up now, Trench. Before it's too late."

"What do you intend to do? How can you possibly stop me? I've set things in motion. I think I'll just leave you here, trapped in this time period. Would you like that, Doctor McBen?"

"I'll like it when you're brought to justice in our time." She wiggled under his hold, longing to dig her nails into him.

"I think I'll just leave you here where you aren't a threat to my work. You've trapped yourself with your own stupidity in adopting the persona of a mute so you can't tell anyone about me and if you did, who'd believe you?"

She froze in her struggle. He was right. No one would believe her. She'd be condemned a witch again or worse, demented. Either way, they would kill her.

"I just need one thing from you, Jeanne. Tell me and when I return, I'll free Ryan."

"You will?" she asked.

"I give you my word."

"Your *word*!"

"A trade. Your life for his. I'll leave you here in this time and free Ryan when I return."

"What do you want?"

"Don't try my patience by playing ignorance. The disc. I still want the damn disc!" He pushed his arm against her throat. Pain choked her and she gasped for air.

It was her turn to laugh. It bubbled unbeckoned from her chest and strangled in her throat.

"The disc is in the twenty-first century, asshole. I can't begin to tell you how to retrieve it. I have to go back. If anyone else tries to retrieve it, it'll be destroyed."

"If you don't cooperate, I'll kill Ryan, slowly." His words stilled her. "Where's the disc?"

"You'll never find it without me. We both go back. We both get what we want."

He lifted from her and jerked her to her feet. A chill wind greeted her and for the first time, she noticed the window stood ajar. Confused she looked at the chamber door, then back.

"You just need to realize there's no negotiating." He looked at the open window again. "Come. You're going with me now." He dragged her toward the window.

"I'll go back with you willingly, but you'll free Ryan when we return before I give you the disc. If you do that, I'll help you with the final process."

He stood in front of the window, his silhouette elongated with the reflection from the fire.

"What assurance do I have that you will honor *your* word once Ryan's free, Jeanne?"

"I've never gone back on my word to anyone."

"I'll let you see him, but you'll turn over the disc before he's freed. Come on. The way back to our world is just a few short months away. I've a relative about a day's ride from here, Cullen de Mangus. He believes I'm his nephew from France. Has made me quite welcome. So welcome that I've been able to convince him that *he* should be the next chief instead of Mael MacRaigl. I couldn't have orchestrated it any better." His laughter chilled her. "We'll stay with Cullen until it's time for the portal to return." He held out his hand to her.

She didn't trust him to keep his word, but if she could at least return to their own time, then she might have a chance to free Ryan and stop him. She lifted her hand and took a step forward.

"I'll see you keep your word, Trench." Reluctantly, she placed her hand in his.

He opened his mouth to respond, but the bone-chilling echoes of snarling hounds bounding up the stairwell interrupted them.

"What the hell is that?" He jerked from her. The beasts crashed against the door, growling and clawing to get in. Trench bolted for the window.

"Wait." She ran after him, but he grabbed the rope he'd used to climb into her chamber and rappelled down the tower wall to the ground.

Her heart pounded to her throat. She'd never attempted the sport he'd so enthusiastically pursued. She had no idea how to follow him down the high wall. Just as she reached for the rope, the metal hinges on the chamber door groaned and splintered the wood. The door tore from the metal lock and crashed open.

The hounds lunged into the room. Her scream echoed against the granite walls. The fierce animals snapped and bit at the air. She backed into the drapery.

"Leash the beasts!" Mael bounded in behind the dogs, and grabbed her, enfolding her into his embrace, shielding her from the dogs with his body. "There, lass, the dogs are gone," he soothed.

Fear dragged her into the dark recesses of memories, but the sound of his voice pulled her from the flashback and for the second time, she didn't fall into the pattern of recall. Panting, she stared up at him. It was a battle to see beyond the memory that played in front of her. She searched his face. Was it possible his genes had traveled through generations so intact that his twenty-first-century descendant could pass for his twin brother? Even to the inflection of his voice? Even the ability to halt her PTSD episodes?

"Are ye harmed, lass?" He brushed her hair from her face. "Ian discovered one of our guards murdered and our prisoner escaped." He stroked her cheek with the back of his hand as though he needed reassurance she was alive and unharmed. "I unleashed the dogs. But it was my intention to startle him, never ye."

Shaking, Jeanne collapsed against him. He hushed her sobs. Trench was gone. She'd been so close. The realization was like the lifting of floodgates and tears spilled down her cheeks.

"Where is he?" Mael spoke over her head.

Ian stomped past them and peered out the window then turned back to them.

"Escaped, me laird."

"Find the girl. I want the guard doubled and those responsible for the assassins gaining entry into our castle brought to me. We have a traitor amongst us and that traitor shall be put to death."

"Aye, me laird." Ian rushed to do his bidding.

She clung to Mael. The tone in his voice frightened her. He would not tolerate what had happened tonight. Someone would pay. His arms tightened about her, and she welcomed his strength.

"Are ye certain ye remain unharmed?" He pulled her closer to the fire so the light bathed over her, and tilted her head. He examined her face then brushed her hair from her neck. His gaze narrowed on the curve of her neck dropping to her partially exposed shoulder. She felt his chest expand as he held his breath. She knew what he was searching for — the telltale puncture marks. He released his breath.

"Ye have no marks." He tried to still the rushing heat pumping through his veins. His hand trailed the tuft of lace that edged her gown to the ribbon drawstring in front, brushing the softness of her breasts in its path. Immediately, her nipples tightened with the shock of his touch.

"Ye are so lovely, lass. I was fearful for ye." He searched her upturned face. "I wish I had a name to put to ye. 'Twould ease my mind." He stared into her large blue eyes.

He let the back of his hand brush her breasts again, moving it slowly and deliberately. When she didn't pull from his touch, his heart pounded harder. She wanted him. The look in her eyes assured him she could be his. All he had to do was claim her. She stared up at him and he felt her barriers drop.

"I ask myself how one lass so quiet can wreak such turmoil in a man's life in such a wee bit of time?" He raised his hand to cradle her face, moving his thumb to trace the fullness of her bottom lip. She closed her eyes to his probing stare. Disappointment dropped over him yet he could feel her desire as surely as he could feel his own.

She opened her eyes to his tender smile, noting how his short beard moved when his lips parted for his sigh. She searched the endless depths of his bronze eyes and found the soul she sought. Her pulse spiked.

Was it possible to own the heart that governed that soul? She needed him as a woman needs a man, only it was more than a physical need. Mael MacRaigl calmed her fears just as his descendant had that fated night. She lifted her hand to trace the corner of his mouth, and he stiffened from the current that shot between them. Knowing his desire was as strong as hers sent hot pulses to her clit.

"I dinna find any signs of him about the outer walls," Ian interrupted, shattering the moment. "And the lass still unfound."

"Search the castle." Mael threw over his shoulder, never breaking his stare. Ian's running footfalls sounded from the stairs. "Can ye talk? Can ye tell me who this intruder was? What did he want from ye?"

She dropped her stare and bowed her head lest he see her agony. How could she make him understand things that would not be reality for over seven hundred years?

"Ye think I canna know what 'tis to be different from others. The differences in ye lie in many ways. The expression in your eyes. The way ye startle so easily. 'Tis though ye dinna understand our ways, lass. Are we so different from your clan?"

His finger trailed the curve of her face, pausing under her chin. He tilted her face and recaptured her stare with his. She tried to turn from him, but his hand was a vise about her arm. He pulled her closer with a strength she had underestimated.

"Please dinna fight me, lass. I only seek the truth. I think ye seek the same."

She stopped struggling and settled her stare on him.

"I can help ye, lass, but ye must tell me where to find this shadow creeping into my home and nearly stealing ye from underneath my nose. He created a diversion. 'Twas well planned only he underestimates me."

Her mind whirled with the possibilities. If she broke the barrier between this charismatic man and her, then she might discover he was able to understand, even help her. She glanced down. There was such power in silence. It held her voice captive. Even if she wanted to speak, she was not sure she could. Her gaze wandered to his broad chest where his shirt laces had come undone, revealing a thick mat of auburn hair. She swallowed back the sparking flames. If she didn't tell him the truth, she was defenseless against Trench. She nibbled on her lower lip.

"'Tis fine, lass." He drew her into the folds of his arms again, placing her head on his chest, while he stroked her head. His heart pounded hard against her ear. Desire radiated hot and etched a streaking path to her groin. She so needed him to fuck her. But she couldn't risk feeling more for him than she already did. She would leave soon and return to her own time.

"I know ye need time to know me. Then my trust shall win your dark secrets. I dinna think our shadow shall return this evening, but should the cur decide to test my patience further, ye shall sleep in my chamber," he said.

Jeanne stiffened and pulled from him. Such closeness would surely be the end of her resistance. Perhaps that's what he wanted.

"Nae, lass. I shall have Ian make me a pallet on the floor."

All I Want

She released her breath.

"Ye think I would take advantage of ye during this time of vulnerability, lass?"

She shook her head, feeling foolish. She had met so few honorable men in her time. Mael MacRaigl would be honorable in any century.

"I would not come to ye that way, when ye be distraught. Not for our first time, lass."

Jeanne bowed her head. Her cheeks warmed at the thought of making love to him.

"When I take ye," he said with his voice deep and full, "shall not be when ye be scared and seeking comfort. Nae, I shall take ye when ye burn with passion and seek the fulfillment only I can give ye."

His promises scorched her cheeks as surely as the blistering of the fire burning in the grate. His low chuckle stoked her heat to a furnace-like roar. Without another word, he turned and led the way to his chamber.

They met Ian on his way up the curving stone staircase.

"A bed of pallets for me, Ian, in my chamber. The lass shall have my bed."

"Aye, me laird. I shall be about it." Ian paused as though weighing his next words. "We found Clemmons by the West tower. His throat cut in the same fashion as Mason's. The assassins must have turned on him, once he aided their entry over the wall."

"I want every man questioned. If he had another helping him, I want him found." Mael's voice held a steady strength in its depth that assured her if there were other traitors within the castle walls they would be dealt with swiftly.

"Aye." Ian turned to do his bidding.

Weak-kneed, she followed Mael down the stairs to his chamber just beneath hers.

"Ye dinna think I would see ye placed too far from my protection did ye?" He opened the door and allowed her to enter first.

The room was a golden glow of candlelight. A huge fire roared in the monster fireplace. Her stare found the long tapestries hung from the walls in an array of scenes, the like of which she'd only seen in books and museums. Immediately, her attention was drawn to the pair of swords hanging over the mantel. She turned from the fireplace and came face-to-face with the massive bed.

In spite of her attempt to ignore the ornate bed, she was lured to it. Its curtains were drawn, with one panel pushed aside. She imagined he'd been about to retire when Ian had roused him about the woman's escape. Just who was this woman, and what had she done? How long had he kept her imprisoned in his castle? She longed to ask, but clung to silence.

Her attention riveted to the exquisite bed. The heavy, hand-carved headboard depicted a scene of couples entwined within each other's arms and was repeated in the footboard. She wondered how much such an artifact would be worth in her time.

She reached out and stroked the carved post at the footboard, overwhelmed by the majestic power of the sculpted scene. She glided her hand over the smooth curved wood, her fingers tracing the sensual dip of the carvings as though she caressed a lover.

Her fingertips tingled against the wood where each detail had been meticulously shaped, sanded and oiled. The mysteries of this ancient culture had been captured within the scenes. A groan escaped her before she could stop it.

"I knew ye had voice." Mael spoke behind her so close that his breath fell against her shoulder. He closed his hand over hers, trapping it against the erotic scene that tapered down the post to the footboard and forged into two nude lovers intertwined in a passionate embrace.

She didn't move. She dared not stir, lest she lose the frayed control that kept her from pulling Mael down onto the mattress with her.

"Me laird." Ian's voice broke the spell. She jerked from him. Surely Ian had a sixth sense with such untimely interruptions. Mael turned and she caught the dark scowl he gave the servant.

"'Tis the last of the mattresses." Ian dropped the thick mats onto the floor beside the bed. He set about stacking the mats on top of each other and then spread the linens over them. The final touch was a pillow he tossed onto the makeshift bed and then turned to Mael.

"Post a guard outside my door." Mael paced over to the door to give Ian further instructions. He spoke so low, Jeanne had to strain to hear his commands. "I shall leave for my sister's at first light. Send a rider to Fernmoora now to warn her ."

Ian mumbled something then left.

She stared down at the jumbled covers askew at the foot of the bed which tumbled over the footboard cascading to the floor. It looked as though he'd leapt from the bed. She glanced over her shoulder at him. Her heart skipped a beat. He still wore his day attire, so he must not have been in bed. How had it come to be so disheveled? She swallowed the lump in her throat and took a cautious step toward the bed. Her body ached for rest. It had been a strenuous day, and she yearned for sleep.

"Go ahead, lass, 'tis a fine bed." He smiled widely at her, turning her embarrassment into mortification. How did one climb into a man's bed gracefully while he watched?

"Allow me." He took long strides over to her, threw back the other panel, and lifted the covers so she could slip underneath them.

Her heart fluttered as she climbed into the majestic bed. Surely it would make a king-size bed look like a bunk bed. Her imagination was rampant with thoughts of Mael lying in it. There was only one reason for a man to have such a large elaborate bed. She swallowed the rising fire.

How many women had he taken in this bed? Was he as good a lover as she suspected? She chastised herself as he pulled the covers over her. She needed to think about something else other than the way Mael MacRaigl's broad chest tapered to his trim waistline. Or the way his hard cock had felt against her.

Her stare flickered over him. His open shirt revealed thick matted hair that trailed in a thin line over his abdomen and beneath the waist of his kilt. Her pulse was a hot drumming. She took a deep breath but the burning continued down her chest, fanning hot between her legs, and once more the aching need to feel him inside her drove throbbing waves to her clit.

Snuggling down into the softness, Jeanne breathed in his scent. It surrounded her like a warm protective cocoon. He had slept in this bed. He'd rested his head on the very pillow she scrunched beneath her. Delight and a mixture of sensations twinged through her. His hard, muscled back had pressed against the linens where she now lay. Her fingers stroked the soft material. The image of Mael's belly flinching underneath her hand ignited a fiery current, streaking through her blood. She took a deep breath, trying to still the longing but it wiggled past her attempts and traveled after the flame. Heat coursed over her breasts, tugging her nipples into hardened tender nubs as the rising ache rushed to her pussy. She looked up at him. He moved.

Her skin tingled in anticipation, feeling his heat when he leaned over her. Her eyes scorched when she met his look. Did her own desire show in her own face? Her heart pounded against her chest. Reaching down, he stroked her cheek with the back of his hand. Her pulse raced. Without a word, he turned back to the mat in front of the fire and crouched down.

She watched him unlace his boots and unpin his tartan from his shoulder. Licking the dryness from her lips, she forced herself to turn her back to him, but she heard every movement he made. Had he removed all but his long-tailed loose shirt? Her breath came in short pants. Had he removed all of his clothing? Moist heat flared between her legs. She tried to push away the vision of his naked body sprawled out on the narrow mat only a few feet from her. She knew he had disrobed. She'd remembered reading somewhere that people during this era had slept naked. Mael certainly seemed the kind of man to sleep naked.

She forced her thoughts to move to something else. Anything. His kilt and his cute knees flashed with memory of their first meeting. She squirmed under the cover. Of course, there was that famous controversy surrounding kilts and exactly what men wore or didn't wear underneath them. She was positive during this time period, there was nothing worn beneath them.

When she snuggled deeper under the covers, Mael's scent wafted up and filled her senses. What was it like to sleep next to him? She mentally shook herself. She must get a grip on her thoughts. She had to think of something less—exciting. His deep, even breathing resounded, making anything other than thoughts of him impossible.

She imagined him pulling her down into the mattress. She could almost feel her body curl into his hard one. Slowly, she flattened her hand against the linens and stroked the bed, imagining his back beneath her touch. Releasing her breath, she closed her eyes and felt the coziest she'd ever felt.

The day's tensions flooded from her and with it scenes of the past events. Where was Trench? Where did his cousin live? She must try to find the manor before it was too late. Her thoughts slowed. The drifting haze just before sleep seeped into her mind, but something distant roused her from the beckoning pool of mindlessness. What was that? She pulled away from the ethereal world of sleep.

Something moved at the foot of the bed underneath the covers. She sat straight up. Her scream lodged in her throat when a hand closed around her ankle and dragged her toward the footboard. The sharp glint of steel flashed against the dim light.

All I Want

"Mael!" she cried out as her assailant rose from the covers, poised to plunge the blade into her chest.

Chapter Twelve

Jeanne kicked and scratched her way across the bed. Suddenly, the death grip around her ankle released. She turned and saw Mael's silhouette against the fire's glow as he lifted the flailing banshee from the covers. The flash of steel blinded Jeanne.

"Mael!" she screamed and moved to help him, but the covers bound her to the bed. She jerked against the linens and freed herself. Her feet slapped the cold floor as she hurried to his aid, but the female silhouette vaulted toward the windows, jerked the handles and threw open the heavy windows.

"Halt!" Mael raced after her, but the woman dove through the open window.

"Oh my God!" Jeanne ran to him.

He froze in front of the open windows, looking down.

"She jumped! She jumped to her death." He shook his head.

"Me laird!" Two burly guards ran into the chamber.

He stood totally oblivious of his nudity, and the guards. Finally, he turned to talk with them, but Jeanne's attention was riveted to his sleek, hard body. He stood in front of her with his fists resting on his hips revealing hard, muscled arms, totally unaware of the image he cast in the fire's light.

One of the guards brushed past her to look out the window and then turned back to Mael and shook his head.

"Tend to her body. Rouse Ian, we need three horses readied."

She stared at him unable to move as though cemented to the floor. The men seemed oblivious to Mael's undress, while she blistered from the ripping need ravaging her. Was it heightened by the sudden fright of the assassin's attack? The overwhelming relief they were both unharmed? Her stare traveled down to his trim waist and tight muscled abdomen, then stopped at the thick mass of hair and his cock.

"Are ye harmed?"

She forced her stare to his amused look and shook her head. Her jagged breath rushed between her lips and raw sensations pulsating through her. Never had she wanted a man as much as she did Mael MacRaigl. She trembled. Her need for him was a survival reaction. She glanced at him again. Of course, it could just be his incredible body. She turned her back to him and closed her eyes, gritting her teeth against the urgent need to throw herself on him.

"We canna stay here." He grabbed her by the arm and led her toward the bed.

She stumbled by his side, acutely aware of his nakedness brushing against her. She craved his strength, needing reassurance they were safe. Were there more assassins lurking beneath the covers? She glanced down at the disheveled bed.

"Are ye harmed?" He lifted her arms to examine them. His chest was a thick curly mass of chestnut hair that trailed in a thin line all the way to his groin. His cock was thick and long. If that was his normal size in repose... Her breath rushed between her parted lips.

"Nae, she dinna cut ye. Stay here while I get your clothes. Once we dress, we leave," he informed her and pushed the dirk into her hand. The leather handle slipped in her sweaty palm, but she tightened her fingers around the shaft. He turned his back to her, and she continued to watch him, transfixed on his tight buttocks, watching the strength in his legs with each step he took. Her mind reeled when he walked over to the pallet and retrieved his clothes. She clasped her trembling hands together, trying to focus on the dirk instead of Mael's backside. Donning his shirt he walked toward the door while drawing his kilt around his hips and belting it. He jerked the door open and said something to the two guards.

"Well, they sure don't wear anything underneath their kilts," she whispered to herself and collapsed onto the bed, gripping the bedpost with one hand and holding the knife poised to defend herself in the other.

"No one enters." His voice fell to her ears. "One of ye inside with the lass while I gather her clothes." The largest of the two men entered the chamber and stood just inside the room, staring at her. Feeling uncomfortable, she pulled the drapery panel about her and listened to the sound of Mael's bare feet as he padded up the stone steps to her chamber.

It seemed to take him forever and several times she was tempted to go in search of him. She gnawed nervously on her lower lip. At length he returned with her clothing. She noticed he had taken time to pleat his kilt and pin the tartan over his shoulder. He'd even laced his boots. He was a man for detail, she mused.

He dumped her clothes beside her and slipped the dagger from her clutch, placing it inside his shirt to slide it into the sheath underneath his arm.

The guard stepped back outside to resume his watch, closing the door behind him.

"Dress, lass. Ian shall accompany us."

She stared up at him.

"Speak it." He seemed amused by her silence. "Ye had voice enough to call me out thrice."

Jeanne bowed her head, refusing to speak. She could no longer make it appear to have been a fluke.

"I shall give ye privacy." He turned his back to her and stood in front of the fireplace.

She hurriedly donned her medieval garb and laced her shoes, then tapped him on the shoulder. He glanced at her and nodded.

"We go now."

She gave him a questioning look. Wanting to ask where they were going.

"We go to Fernmoora. My sister's home."

Her eyes widened.

"Aye, the sister I tossed out the door and banished forever. But, blood, 'tis blood and those ties canna be severed. Our inept assassin let it be known earlier this evening that a conspiracy is afoot. The man who entered your chamber this night must be one of them. They sent the lass to kill me, and she'd have killed ye as well. Someone incited them and now they shall not stop until we all lay dead. They have sworn to kill my sister and her husband. I sent a rider to warn them.

"'Tis clear they shall not rest until their swords run blood. Our blood. Two assassins in my castle this very eve bespeaks a planned conspiracy and a traitor within my own court. It serves us to draw them out and have them follow us away from my castle. Then, we shall know who be loyal, and who be a traitor."

Jeanne nodded.

The castle was alive with sounds common for the day, not the middle of the night. Stomach-rumbling smells came from the kitchen across the courtyard. Maids scurried from the Great Hall and buttery to the kitchen, doing Mrs. MacRay's bidding. Jeanne followed Mael into the Great Hall.

"The horses await us," Ian greeted them. "Missus MacRay set us with bread and cheese—even a flask of mead. The men await with the horses."

"Nae, we go without escort." Mael frowned at his servant.

"But me laird, 'tis not safe. Already twice this night your life has been threatened and the lass's— Once we leave, any would-be assassins follow."

"Do ye think me incapable of protecting myself and the lass? I shall not have my castle left unguarded, or my men forfeited by ambush. 'Tis my sister who wrought this night's revenge upon us. No more shall die. It ends this night."

"At least allow me to accompany ye."

"Upon that I agree, Ian."

This seemed to appease the servant because he grinned widely then turned to see about their horses. Jeanne's mind turned over the events of the last few hours. Trench was gone. Would he track her down to Fernmoora?

She knew he would never give up until he had her formula. The only comfort was Ryan would remain alive as long as Trench needed her. She took solace in that thought as Mael led her down the steps.

Several men with torches stood waiting for them at the foot of the steps. Some appeared to have been roused from their sleep while others appeared to have been taken away from their nightly drinking and revelry. A gust of wind whipped through the courtyard sputtering through the torches. She shivered beneath the heavy fur Mael draped over her and pulled the tartan shawl into a hood over her head.

"We accompany ye, Laird MacRaigl," a rough-looking highlander spoke.

"Aye, we do." The man beside him nodded.

"Aye," the others chorused.

"We vowed to protect the next chief and so we shall." A man, larger than Mael, stepped forward as though he represented the group.

She recognized him from the meals in the Hall. He always wore his dark hair in several small braids that ran down the sides of his face.

"Julian," Mael said, "your loyalty 'tis accepted, but your death's not wanted."

"Death?" came a shout.

"Ye speak to warriors. Why should ye believe 'tis death we seek this eve?" another challenged.

"Aye! At least not our own!" the chorus of voices was vigorous.

"Ye all have families, here," Mael said, "'tis a personal matter betwixt Ishabelle and myself. Honor my request. Stay within the castle and protect those we leave behind."

"If ye insist on riding about the night and being easy target for the assassins, Laird MacRaigl, then we shall protect ye. 'Tis what we swore to do," Julian insisted.

"Aye," Mael agreed. "But the assassins believe their attempts this eve have set me to cowering within the walls of my castle. They shall not suspect a nightly journey. We have the element of surprise."

"Spies roam the countryside, me laird." Julian was unrelenting.

"I pray ye stay and do my bidding. Protect our people and our land during my absence," Mael's voice boomed, and he turned from them. The discussion was over. He was, after all, the laird. There were several mumblings and even a few disgruntled shouts but eventually the men conceded and disbanded. Julian remained behind.

"A word, me laird." He touched Mael's arm and motioned for him to walk so they might have a private conversation.

"My pardon." Mael turned from her.

"Me laird," Julian's voice was low, but the wind shifted and carried his words across the courtyard to her. "As your Captain, 'tis me duty to advise ye that ye make too little of what ye undertake. 'Tis dangerous and where ye ride promises to be laden with assassins. Their snipers abound."

"But ye forget the territory we venture into."

"Nae. Laird Tryon surely has his minions but his enemies outnumber them. I beg ye, reconsider, Mael," his voice dropped an octave. "Allow your guards to accompany ye. Think of the future of our clan. Ye are the destined one."

"Then know as such I make the right decisions." Mael placed his hand on Julian's shoulders.

"I've known ye since we were bairns, Mael. Ye and Ishabelle—the things ye do and she does, lie not just betwixt the two of ye, but affects the clan."

Mael bowed his head and released Julian's shoulder.

"And so I go to mend the breach." Mael pivoted and walked over to her. Julian stood watching, his expression was one of pained frustration.

Mael wasted no time and hoisted her onto the horse. She grabbed for the reins and attempted to sit straight on the animal's back, marveling at the enormity of the beast. Fear fluttered in her stomach when the animal shifted its weight slightly.

"Guard MacRaigl Castle, Julian," Mael instructed before swinging up onto the stallion's back and jerking the reins. The horse spun around toward the drawbridge. Mael stared at her.

"Are ye sure ye can handle the mare? Ye can ride with me."

She met the mischievous glint in his brown eyes. Oh, that grin was wicked. She nodded slightly at him and swallowed her rising excitement. How could a mere look turn her into such a quivering mass of desire? Was he a devil?

Mael dug his heels into the horse's ribs and the animal bolted from the courtyard. Jeanne nudged her mare to follow with Ian bringing up the end.

"Safe journey," Julian called after them.

They rode out of the courtyard and over the bridge in silence. Mael turned his steed toward the mountain range. Jeanne, still following at a slower pace some distance behind, didn't dare try to keep up with him. She was amazed she had managed to stay on the back of the horse for so long.

Chapter Thirteen

The terrain was steep and soon became rocky. It was the roughest ride she'd ever endured. Her body ached from what seemed to be hours of abuse and she finally slumped forward in the saddle, wrapping her arms around the mare's neck as best she could.

"The lass has fainted," Ian called behind him. Mael jerked his horse to a halt and guided it over to hers. When she lifted her head, he was instantly relieved.

"Not fainted, Ian, exhausted." He reached over and lifted her slight weight from the horse and settled her onto his lap.

She didn't offer any resistance. Instead, she seemed to welcome the change and nestled against his chest, wrapping her arms about his waist.

He startled from the unconscious gesture. She was so fragile. He felt a giant in comparison to her small frame. Excitement dragged him to the edge of self-control. What was her mystery? Why did she hide behind silence? Guiding his horse up the final climb, he knew the terrain would level onto a ridge and beyond lay Fernmoora.

What would he find once they reached his sister's home? Would she and her husband of one week be dead? Murdered as he and his household might have been that very evening had the assassin not been so inept? Who had sent her? To which rival clan did they claim allegiance? Or had they been of the Mangus family?

Mael mulled over the possibility that Cullen de Mangus had become bold enough to attempt the assassination and possibly aligned with another clan. He tightened his arm around her while clutching the reins in his free hand. Somehow, she was connected to all the bizarre events.

Clearly, she used her muteness to hide her knowledge. There was intelligence in her eyes, quickly masked of thought each time he probed too deeply. His arm brushed her breasts slightly and he shifted in the saddle. She had passion. He'd felt it in her kiss. Her softness rekindled his desire and once more his body responded to her. His cock rose and hardened against her.

Innocence was one thing he'd not seen in her eyes. Fear, panic, worry, mistrust, yes, but never innocence. She did not look at him like a maiden. Her eyes held experience in their blue depths as though she knew what kind of pleasures he could give her.

"Do ye think Ishabelle's in danger?" Ian asked beside him.

"She has Tryon to protect her. Rachel's death gave old superstitions new life."

"The tales surrounding Tryon were never dead," Ian reminded him bitterly. "Do ye forget what we witnessed?"

"To forget, Ian, would be the blessing I seek." Mael took a deep breath, letting the early morning air fill his lungs and clear his head. His gaze was drawn to the woman in his lap. She'd fallen asleep. He knew only sheer exhaustion would allow such escape from discomfort.

His gaze caressed the tender curve of her chin where her hair cascaded to her chest. She'd clutched his tartan tight about her, unintentionally creating a barrier to his hungry stare. He looked away, training his stare on the distant knoll. His senses were vibrant every place her body molded into his. Desire surged and filled his heart to overflowing.

"Ye shall be Chief, Mael. Your word 'tis law. Were ye to declare Tryon—" Ian's voice broke off when Mael glared at him. "Ye could decree Tryon and your sister be left in peace." He finished in a lower voice.

"A decree such as ye speak of would serve as validation of the deepest fears. Were there no threat, then no need for any decree. Nae, Ian. I shall parley with Tryon myself."

That said, Ian fell silent and guided his mare ahead of Mael's stallion. He took Ian's gesture as bitterness. His friend had been angry ever since they'd left Fernmoora. Ian could neither accept the life Ishabelle had chosen nor fully admit to the danger she'd brought upon them.

Once he was officially proclaimed Chief by the clan, he envisioned life would return to normal. Being Chief had certain dangers that were a part of everyday life, but the last few days had been far from normal dangers.

The advent of Ishabelle's marriage had brought with it other events Mael had never expected. The woman in his arms stirred. If only he knew her name. He steeled himself against the surging need to taste the sweetness her lips promised with full softness. His arms shook against the urgency and he fought to control the base desire coursing through his blood. Sweat slid down his back as he overpowered the need to fuck her as he'd never fucked any woman. The pleasures he could bring her would surely be matched by those she'd bring to him. He shifted in the saddle and cleared his throat. Beads of sweat popped across his forehead and he brushed his hand over his face.

"Who goes?" Ian's voice cracked through his thoughts. He jerked alert as did the woman in his arms.

Jeanne tried to push the sleep from her mind. She opened her eyes and was greeted by mist and shadows. Mael released his hold on her, and she grabbed for the horse's neck. The sound of scraping metal told her he'd drawn his sword from its sheath. She laced her fingers though the horse's mane.

"Hold fast, lass." He dug his heels into the horse's sides. The animal grunted, then jolted into a gallop. Its hooves dug into the sod as they thundered through the night and up the steep hillside. Where was Ian? They crested the ridge, just in time to see shadows rise from the ground and surround rider and horse. The silhouette was dragged from his mount, his sword slipping from his grasp.

"Ian," Jeanne gasped.

The yell was barbaric and so savage, she shuddered. She glanced over her shoulder and realized it had come from Mael.

In one swift movement, she found herself dethroned and unceremoniously plopped onto the damp moss. She stumbled to steady herself. He charged over the knoll toward the pack of dark shapes lunging at Ian's flailing attempts to fight them off.

She squinted into the fast-moving mist. Were they animals or men? The snarling assured her they were dogs, but they stood on two legs. She shuddered and cowered behind the nearby rock. They could not be dogs, they *had* to be men. She panicked with the all too familiar edges of relapse as the memories flashed in front of her.

She'd never experienced medieval fighting, she was just confused. After all, they were not called barbarians for nothing. Something moved toward her. Terror paralyzed her then suddenly she realized it was her horse. She collapsed against the mare with a hot sigh.

All I Want

"You scared me," she mumbled, and the mare nuzzled her with a low nervous neigh. She stiffened, vaguely remembering Mael lifting her from the horse and Ian leading the mare behind him.

Cautiously, she patted the horse and tried to climb back on, but the nervous animal shifted away from her attempt. At length, she was astride and gathered the leather reins, trembling as the horse pranced about.

The loud clash of swords echoed around her. The horse stomped about, obviously sensing her inexperience and fear as she jerked the reins. It was as though the world shifted in the space of a breath. Sudden morning light crested the hillside, shining like a beacon through the thick fog, bathing the world in blinding brilliance. Her breath rasped from her throat. A fierce wind gusted up the ridge and parted the fog in its wake.

Mael stood swinging his mighty sword over his head, bringing it down in swift, bold strokes against the dark creatures clawing to pull him from his saddle. The mist pushed from the ridge, allowing magnificent shafts of light to flow into the cloaked hillside.

The ambushers cried out then—vanished. Jeanne blinked. It was as though they had evaporated. The mist disappeared, revealing the green hillside. Frantically, she kicked her heels into the mare's sides and forced the steed up the hill. Mael dismounted and stooped over Ian. She slid from her horse to join him.

"Is he dead?" she asked, rushing over to him.

Mael cradled the Scottish warrior in his arms.

"Nae, lass, but we must get him to my sister's."

Jeanne stooped beside Ian and tilted the unconscious man's head back so she could examine him, stunned by the amount of blood that covered him. Her first instinct was to retract her hand before she came into contact with it, but mentally stopped herself. She was conditioned to a disease from her century. She sighed, noticing how the older man's gray eyebrows and face were streaked with blood.

Frustrated, she met Mael's look.

"Where's his wound?" Her Gaelic was stilted and broken.

"Here." Mael, turned Ian's head slightly revealing the large ugly bruised area where the blood pumped from several puncture wounds. They were like the wounds Trench had left in his victims. Did Trench send these attackers? Was that possible? She tore at the hem of her gown. The material ripped under her grip.

"Apply pressure to the wound. I'll get his horse. We must hurry." When she returned, Mael had placed a stone on the bandage and bound a piece of Ian's tartan about the wounded man's neck, turning it into a pressure bandage.

He hoisted the huge man over his shoulder as though he were a sack of flour and slung him over the horse's back. He took a leather strap and lashed Ian to the animal. Turning sharply on his heel, he picked Jeanne up and plopped her onto the back of the mare.

"Your voice has a habit of vanishing almost as often as these assassins."

Surprised, her mouth fell open.

"Aye, lass, your secret 'tis in the open now." His expression was a mixture of anger and triumph. She looked away. "At this moment, I have Ian's life to preoccupy me, but once his care is assured, I shall come to ye for answers, lass, and best ye be prepared to give them to me this time."

She gulped at the threat mirrored in his eyes, now two hard chips of brown. Gone was the fire and mirth, the laughter and warmth of soul. It was as though Mael MacRaigl had transformed. At that moment, he was the epitome of a Scottish warrior—determined, ruthless, barbaric and unbending. He was used to his demands being met. He was soon to be a Chief, she reminded herself. She could not afford to confuse this Mael with his modern heir.

He walked over to his horse, his plaid kilt swinging with his strides. His long legs arched over the saddle as he mounted the horse. Glancing briefly at her, he reached over and gathered the reins to Ian's horse.

The early morning was a brilliant backdrop offering a stark comparison to the previous night. He led them down the hillside to the next slope where the valley converged into a lush, protected Eden complete with a wide stream coursing through the valley floor.

Jeanne immediately recognized the fortress. It was like so many she'd seen in storybooks as a child. Gold-crested red flags fluttered above the tower walls. As they drew closer, she realized unlike MacRaigl's castle, this one was strange and foreboding.

The silence was the eeriest of all. It was as though they had arrived in a ghost valley. The large gates stood open. Unprotected.

All I Want

Anxiously, she looked at Mael, who appeared calm although he held his sword poised to strike the first blow.

He led them over the drawbridge and through the gate, and once they were inside, he dismounted to lower the gate and close the heavy doors. Hoisting the wide wood beam, he barred the doors. Without a word, he quickly mounted his horse and led them through the inner village until they reached the castle courtyard.

It was deserted. Her heart pounded with the realization they were too late. The assassins had already been there. That was the reason the gate was unprotected and stood open. Mael dismounted his horse with his sword still drawn.

"Watch over Ian," he ordered and started up the steps of the castle.

Her gaze fell on Ian's bloodied face. She gulped. He looked dead to her. The large door creaked open, and a young man peered around it.

"Laird MacRaigl!" He bounded down the steps. The wide grin on his freckled face, fell as soon as he saw Ian. The lad's shoe ground against the stone step as he pivoted and ran back up the steps, calling out.

Before Jeanne could dismount, several men rushed outside the castle and down the steps. She looked on as they carefully eased Ian from the horse. Mael stood on the steps waiting.

"Get guards on the gate and raise the drawbridge, now." His voice boomed across the courtyard. A man broke from the task of carrying Ian and ran toward the gatehouse.

She trembled. Once in the Great Hall, Mael drew his arm around her waist and held her safely to his side. She didn't struggle, drawing strength from his nearness. She looked about the ornate hall as he quickly surveyed their surroundings.

The elaborate carvings on the staircase depicted scenes of various animal hunts. Once more, she marveled at the craftsmanship of the era. She was growing accustomed to castles and villages, but she would never get used to horses. She groaned under the angry ache in her legs.

"Your mistress?" his voice boomed. "Where does your mistress rest this night?"

Her heartstrings tugged as the youth's face washed red. He appeared to be Ryan's age. She tried to calm the panic trembling in her. Ryan was all right, she assured herself.

"Me lady retreated to her chambers, Laird MacRaigl. 'Twas a tragic night." He led them up the winding staircase. Mael grabbed him by the arm and spun him around.

"Is my sister well?"

"Aye, me laird. Me lady lives."

"And your master?"

The youth hung his head. "Struck down."

Jeanne gasped. Her hand went to Mael's arm as she sought to console him, but quickly realized there was no remorse in him.

"My sister, though, she remained unharmed?"

"Aye, me laird. We were able to fight them off," he said, then blushed. "The soldiers fought them off and gave chase, hence the gates were open when ye arrived."

Her heart ached for the youth's clumsiness, knowing he must feel the overwhelming power of Mael MacRaigl to his very bones.

"Let us tend to my man," he instructed, and the procession once more clamored toward the tower and the third floor.

"I shall summon a healer," the youth assured them as they caught up with the men carrying Ian.

"We have our own healer." Mael nodded toward Jeanne.

Chapter Fourteen

Jeanne glanced at the lad and then pushed past him into the sunny chamber. She waited for the men to lower Ian onto the bed and took the unconscious man's wrist. Her forefinger immediately found the slow, faint pulse.

"He needs a transfusion," she spoke before realizing what she'd said.

"What?" Mael echoed with the same look of confusion vexing the other faces around her.

"Away with you." She shooed the servants from the room then turned to Mael. "I need your help. I know you wish to tend to your sister, but Ian needs us," she insisted as she set about checking the compression cloth. "I need water and cloth stripped for bandages. And I need herbs—tarragon, comfrey, hyssop, some mugwort for his pain and yerba santa. A pot over the fire so I can make a poultice. Do you think your sister has these herbs? I need you to drain a cow of its blood and bring the blood to me quickly."

Mael stood staring at her.

"Yes, I'm speaking. We don't have time to discuss it. I need a needle and thread, too. We have to work fast if we are going to save him." She surprised herself at her own command of his language.

"So be it. Ask for it, lass, and ye shall have it. But the cow's blood?"

"I have to replenish his blood. I'll make a soup of the cow's blood." Jeanne tried to remember her medical history classes, and what would help the body replenish its own blood supply short of a transfusion. She knew ancient healers had made soups from cows' blood. She must somehow get fluids into him, but he was unconscious. Saline and dextrose infusions would provide a temporary benefit. How could she rig an IV? Immediately, she thought about Trench and knew he had the necessary equipment. But how could she find him? There was no time.

The supplies were brought to her in a volley of servants moving in and out of the room. She set about sewing the wound. Mael returned with two women each carrying a bundle of herbs.

"We need a bucket of clean water and some salt," she instructed, ignoring his confused look as he left the room again. She motioned for the maid to sit beside Ian and instructed her to fill the skin flask with the saline solution she'd mixed. Next, she filled a second flask with plain water and instructed the girl to alternate the two liquids and squeeze them into Ian's mouth.

She then set about creating a poultice. It was a tedious night filled with vigil, waiting and praying. Mael left to find his sister, and Jeanne spent the time wondering why this had been done to Ian. Why would Trench resort to this kind of drama? Was it part of his plot to terrorize the locals into believing vampires ravaged the night?

Ian began to spit up the saline and she discontinued it. When the young maid fell asleep, Jeanne took over, focusing on getting the water into him. She nursed him through the night managing to mix some of the blood soup until it was thin enough to trickle down his throat. Not too much or he'd lose it, too. It was early morning when fatigue overcame her. She collapsed in the nearby chair and slept. Her dreams were filled with demons and snarling dogs. She startled awake.

Mael stood in the open doorway surveying the room.

"How is Ian?" He moved past her and over to the sleeping man.

"Better, I think. And your sister?"

"Grieving," was all he said before turning and leaving the room again.

By midafternoon, Ian regained consciousness and attempted to sit up. Jeanne was quick to wrestle him back onto the mattress. As though sensing his servant's awakening, Mael entered the chamber.

"You have to stay in bed for the next day or two. You must allow yourself to heal," she insisted.

"A miracle has occurred. Ye found your voice, lass." Ian gave her a faint smile.

"Aye, but we yet to witness if 'tis a miracle or a curse." Mael winked at him.

Ian rumbled with laughter, and she shot Mael what she hoped was a withering look. He didn't seem to notice her disdain.

All I Want

"I shall have some food and drink sent up for both of ye. Tryon's men just returned from their pursuit of the assassins. I wish to speak with them." He stopped by the door to glance back at them. "I am relieved ye seem to be on the mend, old friend."

The servants arrived shortly after he left with mutton pie, mugs of mead and wooden cups of milk. They also brought another bed and set it up in the corner of the large room.

"Laird MacRaigl says 'tis for the lass," the burly man spoke to Ian before stomping from the room.

When Mael returned it was early evening, and she'd just finished spooning a broth into a very disgruntled Ian.

"How's your sister?" she asked, sitting on the edge of the bed beside Ian.

"She grieves for her husband." He collapsed in the chair beside Ian. "How do ye feel, old friend?"

"Much better."

"He's a strong man." She smiled faintly, feeling self-conscious. She'd not had any conversations in over five months. It felt strange to speak, especially to him. "Was her husband the reason you banished her from your castle?" Jeanne lifted the pottery mug of water to Ian's lips and allowed him to sip. Her back ached. She wanted to sleep.

"Some things remain best kept within the circle of family." His rudeness incited her. His brown eyes quickly masked the emotion she saw in their depths.

"It doesn't take a rocket scientist to see you didn't like your brother-in-law."

"*Rocket scientist*? What do those words mean, lass?" His gaze swept over her as though attempting to understand who she was and where she came from by that one phrase.

Jeanne realized she should guard her choice of words. No matter how limited her Gaelic was, her use of English words like rocket and scientist had served to whet his curiosity.

"What I meant was a simple fool could see you were not fond of her husband."

"The truth ye speak. But we shall speak no more of Alexander Tryon."

She met his angry scowl with what she hoped was an indifferent shrug. Let him be that way. If he wanted to growl and huff he could.

She had a patient to tend. She turned her back on him and continued to encourage Ian to drink more water.

"Ye try to drown me, lass," Ian protested in a weak whisper.

"Probably the most water you've ever had," she bantered back with the old warrior. Mead or wine appeared to be the drinks of the day. She wondered if water was ever considered for anything other than stews and distilling liquor. Perhaps if they knew to boil it, they'd drink it.

It was nearly midnight when she fell fully clothed onto her bed, faintly aware Mael covered her with a blanket.

"Ian. Watch Ian," she murmured.

"Worry not, lass. I shall watch over both of ye." Mael smiled down at her, feeling such tenderness his hands shook as he tucked the edge of the quilt about her narrow shoulders. He was exhausted and longed to lie beside her. He ached for the solace he knew he would find in her. To feel her in his embrace would soothe his very soul. Instead, he released a weary sigh and fell into the chair beside Ian's bed.

"Ye are exhausted, me laird."

Mael lifted his gaze to the familiar pair of tired eyes.

"I thought ye slept." He leaned forward. Resting his forearms on his legs, he clasped his hands together.

"Ishabelle? Tryon?"

"Tryon lies dead and Ishabelle," he said, meeting knowing look of his friend, "'tis so grief-stricken I canna console her. She blames me." He concentrated on the thread hanging from his tartan.

"Ishabelle dinna think clearly. How could she hold ye responsible?"

"She claims when I disowned her 'twas a public proclamation that she and Alexander were no longer under my protection. That I condemned them to death because I showed no fear for Tryon's revenge."

"But did ye tell her that your life was nearly taken last eve?"

"Nae. She shall not hear the truth. Her anger gives her comfort. I shall allow her to have it for her companion."

"The lass always was headstrong, me laird, even as an infant she insisted having things her way."

All I Want

Mael felt a stab of sorrow for his beloved sister, lost to him when she married Alexander Tryon, now lost forever in Tryon's death. The realization that Ishabelle hated him as much as he had hated Tryon was the final blow.

"My sister no longer claims to be my sister," he said and closed his eyes. "She swore revenge upon me for the murder of her husband. 'Tis not for myself I fear." He shot a worried glance at the sleeping woman, who although now talked to him, had yet to tell him her name.

"Ishabelle embraced the dark," Ian spoke softly and crossed himself.

"Aye. That we witnessed." He gritted his teeth against the overwhelming anger. His body ached for rest, his mind yelled for escape while his soul agonized for his sister's redemption.

"When shall we return to MacRaigl Castle?" Ian whispered.

"When ye are well enough."

"I am." Ian moved to rise from the bed, but Mael was quick to react. With one hand, he overpowered the blustering man back onto the mattress.

"Ye have the strength of a wee babe," Mael jeered. "We shall leave soon enough. Rest now." He sighed wearily and turned from his friend, staring at her. His body hungered for the place beside her. Instead, he leaned back in the large chair. His groan matched the ache in his legs as he rested them on the edge of Ian's bed, crossing them at the ankles.

* * * * *

Jeanne didn't stir, keeping her eyes shut against the room and the two men, although she longed to see Mael's expression. Had it matched the sadness in his voice? She heard him collapse into the chair across from Ian and knew it was a poor substitute for a comfortable bed. Straining to hear any further conversation, the only sounds were those of Ian's snoring and Mael's deep breathing.

She had understood parts of their conversation, enough to realize Mael was just as superstitious as his servant. His brother-in-law was dead and his estranged sister had declared revenge on Mael. Suddenly, she felt as though she had been dropped into the script of a movie. Everyone knew how to play their roles except her. As an intruder into the past, she had no rightful role. Was her presence here altering the future she longed to rejoin? Perhaps Ian was meant to die.

She knew the worst aspect of being here in thirteenth-century Scotland was growing attached to these people. Her desire for Mael was wild and made her abandon all logic. She feared it would transform into something even stronger if she stayed with him much longer.

Her mind twisted over the paradoxes time travel presented until she could no longer lie still. Taking the quilt with her, she made her way over to the roaring fireplace. Mesmerized by the hot blue and red flames licking the thick logs, she stared transfixed, watching the gigantic logs hiss and pop. She glanced over at him. His breathing was rhythmic and deep. Her gaze traveled the length of his tall, strong body stretched languidly from the chair to the bed. His bare knees were the only light area in his silhouette.

Her heart pounded faster, and she strained to make out his form, imagining the way his hair fell in waves over his shoulders. Broad shoulders that had shielded her from the elements, angry villagers and savage dogs. Perhaps Mael MacRaigl was a bigger enigma than she. Drawing the coverlet tighter about her, she luxuriated in the fierce heat that warmed one side of her body. Never had she imagined how damp and drafty castles could be. This one seemed worse than MacRaigl Castle.

The sound from the door startled her. She jerked about, expecting to see a shadow along the stream of light at the bottom of the door, but there was none.

"Stay with Ian," Mael spoke beside her, startling her so much she gasped, but his hand clamped over her mouth, trapping her scream. "Shhh," he hissed and pushed her behind him. Before she could protest, he had drawn his dagger from inside his shirt and moved toward the door.

She watched with held breath for what seemed an eternity until the heavy door creaked open, and the shadow entered. He lunged forward and effortlessly held the intruder prisoner with his dirk wedged menacingly against a pale throat.

"Are ye the true assassin, brother?" The feminine voice was like the snarl of a trapped animal. Lighting a taper, Jeanne turned and gazed into the familiar brown eyes set in the palest face she'd ever seen.

"Ishabelle," she whispered and saw the anger wash over Mael's face.

"Seeking your revenge so soon?" He spun his sister around to face him and let the knife blade slide down the side of her neck coming to rest sharply at the hollow of her throat.

"I should have known ye would bring your whore to my home." She looked from him to Jeanne.

"She dinna resemble ye in the slightest," he rasped.

"Damn ye!" Her long-nailed hand came up and struck at his face, but he was faster and pinned her arm to her side. "'Tis your fault. Just as surely as your hand drove the blade into his heart. My beloved slain from your anger and now ye lie in his house with your whore, comforted with her in your bed while I lay alone in the coldness of mine," she screamed while writhing under his hold. Her sobs were jerks of screams and tears. Jeanne wanted to reach out to comfort her, but knew the woman's grief would lash out like a wounded animal at anyone who moved to help her.

"'Twas not my hand that struck Alexander Tryon down." The pain contorted his handsome face, and Jeanne stood frozen, unable to hold either's suffering. "His destiny was imprinted upon his soul by his own choice. Just as ye have marked yours."

"Release me." Ishabelle jerked against him.

Jeanne looked from one face to the other, trying to connect their features into some pattern of similarity. Unlike Ryan and she, these siblings shared no common physical attributes other than their bronze eyes, and the undeniable fact both were charismatic. It was obvious they shared the same passion.

Mael released her. Ishabelle tripped and fell into the fireplace, or at least it appeared she had. It was so swift, Jeanne had to tell herself she'd truly seen the woman fly from the contact. Ishabelle whirled around to face them.

Mael stepped beside Jeanne, using his body as a partial shield between his sister and her.

"I know what ye have done to my brother, *witch*." Ishabelle leaned forward and let her blazing glare narrow on her. The chill started at the top of Jeanne's head and ran down to her feet. "I know the arts myself and recognize another of my kind. My Alex and I were so happy." The sadness in her eyes was quickly masked. "I heard the rumors of ye way before my brother took ye into his bed. Bewitched him, ye did."

Ishabelle's fine features were framed by the voluminous waves of dark reddish hair.

"Ye know such things are superstitions." Mael took a step forward.

"Aye. Just as the superstitions of *vampyres*." Her laughter was sharp and cold. "I came to tell ye to leave my husband's home with first light." She turned her attention to Ian, who lay glaring up at her from his bed. "Even ye have turned against me, Ian?"

"Nae, lass, never against ye. Ye always were a bit headstrong, but carried within ye a kind heart. Your brother dinna hate ye. Canna ye see the worry in his eyes when he looks upon ye?"

Ishabelle glanced at Mael. "All I see in his cold eyes is hatred."

"'Tis the one thing I agree with ye about." Mael took another step toward his sister. "I brought us here to protect ye, Ishabelle. Ye still be blood."

It was almost a sob that gurgled from her throat followed by a tirade of cursing that Jeanne could only partially understand.

"I am *Alex*'s blood, Mael MacRaigl. I am part of him for all eternity. My ties to ye are severed forever!" She pivoted. Her black velvet dress swirled with her movement and she hurried from the room.

Mael started after her, but Jeanne grabbed his arm. "Have the two of you not wounded each other enough?"

"Stay away from things ye dinna understand." He jerked from her and stomped out of the room. She started after him, but Ian's voice halted her.

"Leave them, lass. He shall not harm her. I know the two of them since they were birthed. They always scream and fight with each other."

"They act as though they hate each other."

"Aye. That part 'tis new. Headstrong they be and more alike than any twins I ever know."

"Twins?"

"Aye. He canna harm her any more than she can harm him. He would console her in her grief, but she shall not allow him. The only thing keeping her heart from breaking is that anger so he shall let her keep it."

She sat down on the edge of the bed, dumbfounded. Mael and Ishabelle were twins? She had done a thesis on twins. She understood the physiology of their connection as well as the emotional and almost psychic bond they shared. Mael in all probability felt many of the things his sister was experiencing.

"What did you mean when you said Ishabelle was part of the dark?"

"Eavesdropping on me, lass?" Ian frowned at her.

She pursed her lips tightly together. She had stepped out of the protective silence so she must now answer questions not just ask them.

"How is Ishabelle part of the dark?" She ignored Ian's comments, determined to understand the rift between Mael and his sister.

"'Tis now a being of the dark." Ian sighed heavily.

"Being?"

"She lives differently from the rest of us. She sleeps when we are awake."

"So she's a night person?" She studied the expression on his face, finding it unyielding.

"Aye." His laughter was abrupt and loud.

Jeanne wanted to pursue the conversation, but the door opened, and Mael stomped inside.

"Ye find Ishabelle?"

"Aye," was all he said and fell onto the bed. "My apologies, lass, bone weary I be and in need of your bed. I must sleep." He dragged the blanket from the floor and turned his back to her. "We all need sleep. We leave first light."

She wanted answers and was too curious to go to sleep. Instead, she waited until the room vibrated with both men's snores and then slipped out of the room. Just as she was closing the door, she sensed someone behind her.

Chapter Fifteen

"Ye either be a daft witch or a very brave one," Ishabelle said.

Jeanne jumped.

"Brave?" she echoed, clutching her chest as she gasped for breath.

"Ye leave the protection of my brother to seek me out. Ye came to find me, dinna ye?"

"I did." She noticed the way Ishabelle's skin had an almost translucent texture.

"And why dinna ye fear me? Ye think my brother can keep ye safe?"

"He has so far." She stiffened her back and held her head up so that she looked right into those angry eyes.

Ishabelle turned down the long, winding stairwell. Jeanne hurried to keep up with her. They entered the large Hall and at the end was a room draped in black linens. Ishabelle seemed to almost glide across the massive hall. Unlike MacRaigl castle, this hall was ornate with several large tapestries hanging from the walls. The rushes and herbs crunched under her feet as she quickened her stride to follow Ishabelle.

"My husband's body lies here. Do ye wish to pay your respects?" Ishabelle motioned for her to enter.

Curious, Jeanne followed. A wave of heat blasted her with the overwhelming scent of sage and cedar incense burning in a metal globe suspended from the wall. The room was a mass of burning tapers supported by what appeared to be solid gold candlesticks. The body was laid out on a huge table, draped with the clan's plaid.

"Are ye like my brother and think my beloved damned for all eternity?"

"Why would Mael think such a thing?"

"Why indeed?" Ishabelle turned her stare on Jeanne. An eerie sensation crept around her neck and slithered down her spine.

"I don't understand." Jeanne shook her head and looked away.

"Ye understand more than ye dare to voice. Ye understand the roots and herbs, dinna ye?"

"I'm a healer if that's what you mean."

"A student of the arts."

Jeanne shrugged and took a step closer to the corpse.

"He sleeps the eternal sleep. Lost unto me for now." The tears in her voice pierced Jeanne's heart.

"I am sorry about his death."

"'Tis death ye think has befallen my husband?" she snickered and moved to stand in front of the prone body of the man she claimed beloved husband. She let her hand brush over his head. "He merely sleeps. He shall awaken when 'tis his time. Until then," she said and caressed his hair, "I wait and don the robes of widow. I spend my nights in lonely longing for his embrace."

Jeanne ventured closer and examined the body as best she could without being obvious. She could not risk touching the corpse not knowing how Ishabelle would react. This was the first time she'd seen the woman in a fairly calm state. She hoped to find out more about Ishabelle and Mael and just what had driven them apart. The thought of such an estrangement happening between Ryan and her made her pulse quicken.

She strained to see beyond the dim candlelight. The body appeared untouched by rigor mortis, but was a bluish hue, certainly in keeping with a corpse.

"So how long will he sleep?" She focused on Ishabelle once more, deciding it best to fall in with the woman's denial.

"'Tis difficult to say." Her hand moved to stroke the handsome man's jaw. His black hair was straight and combed neatly so every hair was in place. He was dressed in his Scottish regalia, and his sword lay by his side.

"Why?" she asked.

"Because I am new to this. I am told he shall rise again—" Her voice broke off and she turned from Jeanne, signifying their brief conversation was over.

She stood staring at Ishabelle and the corpse wondering how she could argue with centuries of superstitions and mysticism. How could she disprove what Ishabelle and Mael considered their reality? Exasperated, she turned from the room and retraced her steps to the chamber. When she entered, Mael gave her a disapproving frown and rose from the bed.

"Where were ye, lass? Dinna I warn ye to stay with me? The assassins are everywhere. Even here we are in danger."

"I wanted to talk with your sister."

"Did ye now? And do ye like conversing with the devil's whore as a midnight pastime?"

"How can you speak about your sister that way? It's shameful. She's a woman grieving for her dead husband."

"Aye, she tell ye this, did she?"

"She didn't have to tell me. I have eyes." She glared up at him.

"Aye and a voice, too. Since ye are awake, perhaps ye can explain to me how ye found your voice?"

"I never lost it." She shoved past him toward the bed.

"So, ye pretended to be a mute? And for what purpose did it serve ye?"

"It saved me from answering nosy questions like yours," she huffed and lay down in the bed.

His laughter was low and full. "Your spirit is that of a Scottish lass, but your accent betrays ye. Where do ye come from, lass?"

"America," she groaned and snuggled under the covers. His warmth still clung to the linens and his scent greeted her as she settled against the pillow. It was a wonderful scent of woodsmoke and forest.

"And where lies this land of yours? America?"

"Far across the ocean. A land you could not possibly know about."

"Why did ye hide behind silence?" He was not going to let her escape his questions. She frowned up at him. He stood peering down at her with muscular arms folded over his chest.

"I'm tired and wish to sleep. I'll explain tomorrow on our ride back to your castle. Is that acceptable to me laird?"

Mael seemed to consider her a moment. "Aye, 'tis acceptable." He stepped around the bed and climbed in beside her. She sat straight up with an indignant gasp.

"You are *not* sleeping with me."

"As ye said, lass, I, too, am exhausted. 'Tis no other bed. I shall sleep here. If ye like ye can sleep by the fire. Take the coverlet and make

All I Want

yourself a pallet beside Ian." Even in the dimly lit room she could see his grin. It was maddening. The fire in the grate popped in response to his mirth.

"Keep to your side," she forewarned.

"See here, lass, were I a mind to take ye, would not be with Ian sleeping beside us. Ye think me less than a rutting stag?" He released a weary moan. "Were I taking ye to be serious, would find my soul wounded to its very quick by so low an opinion of me."

"My apologies," she said with the warmth rushing over her cheeks, "I meant no insult."

"Aye." He turned on his side and faced her. The heat from his body radiated around her. She managed to pull the covers about her so they created a barrier between them. He raised his hand and stroked a strand of hair from her cheek.

"I find no insult in your concern, only insult that ye think me less than a man of honor. 'Twould never enter my mind to expect ye to willingly accept my attentions without my gentle warming of your affections."

Electric currents shot through her where his fingertips glided over her skin. The contact pitched her into a quivering wave of feverish desire. Her raw need for him threatened to overtake all good judgment.

She longed to taste his lips and feel his hard, muscled body pressed against her. Was it mere abstinence, or his untamed sexuality that catapulted her to the frayed edge of control? Would he be a tender lover, or a fierce, passionate one? Just what did medieval men expect from their women? She was a jumbled mass of sensations. Finally, she turned from him, giving him only her back to focus his intense stare upon. She cursed the circumstances that had brought her here.

Immediately, her thoughts flashed to his twenty-first-century counterpart. If she ever returned to her own time, would she be able to find that MacRaigl? And was he as exciting as his ancient ancestor? She tried to remind herself that the two men were individuals but it was so easy to mesh them into the same man. Her thoughts became a collection of disjointed conversations, floating in the mist between sleep and consciousness. Voices echoed in her dreams as she fell into a deep sleep.

* * * * *

"Ye can return without me." Ian's voice pierced her slumber. Jeanne opened her eyes to brilliant morning light. Her gaze quickly found Ian lying on the pallet, frowning up at Mael.

"I shall not be going anywhere without ye, Ian." Mael threw his tartan over his shoulder and pinned it in place with the gold brooch.

"I canna ride yet, 'tis no choice in the matter but to leave me. Once healed, I shall ride back on me own."

"Ye dinna hear a word I said to ye, Ian. Ishabelle is tossing *our* arses out. 'Tis not by choice we leave."

"Ishabelle needs someone to watch over her," Ian defended.

"And that would be ye? Lying here unable to defend even yourself? I tell ye now, Ian, the assassins sprung from the belly of the evil deaths. 'Tis fear in its worst manifestation. Ye think they cease their attempts because ye fell to a knife wound?"

"Knife wound?" Ian tried to sit up further in the bed. "'Tis what ye claim brought me nearly to death's door? A mere knife wound?" His outrage blasted across the room, and she paused while pulling on her shoes.

"'Tis what I saw."

"'Twas no knife did this to me. Ye know 'tis true."

"And ye think they give ye time to heal before they try to kill ye again? The only reason they dinna return to Fernmoora was because their biggest fear, Tryon, lies dead. They know Ishabelle's importance to the clan. Her arts protect her and none shall defile her revered position as seer to the clan. They did what they set about to do. They killed her husband to set her free—free to serve the clan once more."

"So Tryon's death was all they wanted within these walls? And ye saw his body?"

"Aye. Had they thought the bastard survived, do ye think they would have left my sister alive, Ian? Why would they flee after felling the devil himself and leave his demimonde of a wife to walk about the night? Only one answer. Tryon was the only one they wished dead." Mael sat down to lace his boots.

Jeanne was on her feet. She'd had enough of these ridiculous superstitions.

"Tryon is dead. And the assassins left. That's all you know. Anything else is speculation. Ian suffered severe bites. Not a knife wound, but some kind of animal bite. Not assassins, Mael, but animals."

Both men raised their stares at her intrusion into their argument.

"So it might appear." He smiled slightly, letting his gaze touch her lips. She willed the warm rush that crept over her body to stop, but it continued down her neck all the way to her feet. She averted his stare, meeting Ian's confused one.

"Ye dinna understand the tales surrounding Tryon, lass." Ian tried to sit up on his pallet and settled for resting on his elbows.

"I think I can fill in the blanks," she quipped and both brows furrowed deeper, trying to understand her slang expression. She mentally reminded herself to talk like them. "What I mean to say is I have imagination enough to know about the superstitions surrounding Tryon. I believe the word is *vampire*?" The caustic tone of her voice echoed in the chamber.

Ian visibly paled and mumbled something under his breath. Mael seemed perturbed that she'd spoken the word out loud, because his longing gaze hardened into anger.

"Ye think 'tis superstition?" He finished lacing his boots and straightened to full height. She swallowed the fire lashing her throat. Somehow this barbaric setting was having an inexplicable effect on her.

Absently, she wondered if there were some kind of genetic regression occurring in her body responsible for the intense sexual desire his presence stirred in her. Before she could wrap her mind around the possible theory, he moved closer, making all thought processes impossible. Her skin tingled as he closed the distance between them. She knew if she put her hand out, she'd feel the same physical force of two repelling magnets.

Her gaze locked with his fiery one. Her breath rushed from her. Only they were not polar opposites. Indeed, she knew her body would fit his, perfectly if she would only allow it.

"The lass dinna think 'tis superstition." Ian's loud voice cracked through the air.

She looked from Mael to Ian, who struggled to rise from the pallet. Both were quick to aid the older man and managed to deposit him into the nearby chair.

"But I do think it's superstition, Ian." She trembled, knowing she tread on thin ice. What she was about to say would create a battle, one she would lose. But her medical knowledge prevented her from pretending to embrace their backwards beliefs. "Vampires are a creation of misunderstood medical facts."

"'Tis the truth now? Medical? What kind of word do ye use?" Mael seemed to be amused by her claim to knowledge and sat down in the other chair. He folded his arms over his broad chest, waiting for her explanation with a smile teasing his lips. Delicious humor reflected in his eyes and Jeanne looked away.

"Yes." She decided it best not to elaborate. "Every symptom exhibited by a person accused of vampirism can be medically explained."

"What does medically mean?"

"Medical. By the rules of medicine used in the art of healing. Science. There lie reasons behind the appearances of the person. A cause and its effect."

"Aye, Ian suffered the effect, and the cause, he believes, was vampire," Mael said then burst into a fit of laughter. Ian was quick to join in. He considered her a moment, then stood. "I shall borrow a wagon from Ishabelle to make your journey easier, Ian, but we leave before Tryon awakens."

"He is *not* going to awaken. He's dead. The smell, although cloaked with all that incense, is definitely the stench of death, not to mention, he is a death blue."

"Ye know this for fact?"

She nodded. She would not back down. If one thing she knew even in the thirteenth century, it was there is no such thing as a vampire. Science still held the same truths seven hundred plus years in the past as it did in the future.

Mael moved so he stood only inches from her with his handsome face looming down at her.

"Ye canna trust what ye saw, lass. What appears to be death is for Tryon mere sleep."

"This is insane! You people cannot realize there's more to life than your silly superstitions of magic potions, faeries and yes, vampires?"

"Ye people? And if we be so absurd in our beliefs and thinking, then why are ye with us? Why are ye not with your own people, since they must be so wise as to not need magic and faeries?"

"It's a long story."

"We both like stories. Dinna we, Ian?" Mael winked at Ian.

"Aye. Storytelling 'tis one of my favorite pastimes." He winked back at Mael.

"For an ignorant group of people, lass, we understand the pleasure of storytelling. So tell us the story of how ye came to be so far away from your home. That would be the home that lies beyond the ocean?" The two men's laughter seemed to prickle against her very spine.

She clamped her mouth shut and stood with her fists resting on her hips. How could she explain so it didn't sound wilder than their own superstitions? Exasperated, Jeanne closed her eyes and bowed her head.

"I think the lass has lost her voice again, Ian," Mael snickered and punched his friend.

"'Twould appear."

"'Tis a convenient thing, lass, to lose your voice when it serves your purpose."

"I can't explain it to you. You wouldn't understand." She regretted the words as soon as they slipped past her lips.

"Not only are we superstitious oafs, Ian, but now we seem too simple-minded to understand her stories. I think she insulted us once more." Mael turned to address his next words to Ian. "As a superstitious simpleton, I shall be tending to the wagon, Ian, so ye can ride with little pain." Mael glanced at her. "It may appear I am not a man of strong mind to one who claims to live on the other side of the ocean, lass. But when ye speak of things like medical, rockets, science, and America, dinna ye think ye sound a bit daft and filled with superstitions yourself?"

She wanted to slap the smug expression from his face, but he left the room before she could react. His laughter echoed from the stairwell.

"There, lass, ye know he has a great sense of humor and enjoys a good spar of words with ye."

"He's an arrogant superstitious jerk," Jeanne growled between clenched teeth.

"Jerk?" Ian's face scrunched up.

"Never mind." She shook her head and started collecting her things in preparation for their journey back to MacRaigl Castle. She pulled on her leather leggings and began lacing them.

"I dinna believe I've ever seen him so taken with any woman as he is with ye."

She froze in her movements and glanced over at him.

"Aye. 'Tis as evident as that nose on your beautiful face. The way ye toss his words back at him," Ian chuckled. "No one has ever dared to talk to the Laird that way, except Ishabelle." His fit of laughter had left him wiping tears from his cheeks.

"You need several days of rest before traveling."

"Ye dinna know Mael MacRaigl the way I do, lass, or Ishabelle. She made her feelings clear. We shall not be welcome beyond this morning."

"Tell me, Ian." She seized the opportunity. "Tell me about them? You said they are twins." She moved from the bed into the nearby chair.

"Aye. Born within ten breaths of each other they were. Not a sound he made, blinking, looking about the room as though he already be the laird. But Ishabelle entered the world screaming at the top of her lungs and crying to be fed and held. Always demanding attention and having things her way. And they have been the same ever since."

She could imagine it true based on what she had witnessed.

"Their poor da could not control Ishabelle, and young Mael became so smart he surpassed his teachers. Their *máthair* never recovered from their birth and died two years later. The old laird did his best by his bairns, but Ishabelle, with no real guidance, roamed about the hills like a wild thing. 'Tis no wonder the stories followed her, and she ended up losing her heart and soul to Alexander Tryon."

"How old were they when their father died?"

"Ten seasons when the old laird died. Mael agreed to be schooled in France, but Ishabelle refused the gracious education offered her. Her heart beats with that of the land. The lass would not leave the highlands. They share the same passion. Mael understands how to use it. Ishabelle lives on the edge of her emotions without a thought to guide them. 'Tis not to say Mael be a coldhearted man. Rather trained to discipline. Ishabelle's education was conducted by the highlands. She embodies the mysteries of our land. She became the faerie and the faerie dust, all in one."

Jeanne wanted to probe more into Mael's youth, but didn't know how to without being obvious. Ian paused in his storytelling.

All I Want

"What of your family, lass?"

She felt the all too familiar jab of pain. "My parents died five years ago. I have a younger brother, Ryan." She tried to make her words sound nonchalant, but the truth must have mirrored in her eyes for Ian reached out and took her hand in his big rough one.

"Ye miss them, dinna ye, lass?"

She could only nod, to speak would release the tears that burned her throat.

"I see the pain in your eyes. Ye miss your home. Why canna ye go home, lass?"

She blinked away the tears. They both jumped when the door flew open.

"Just as I suspected, Ian, ye have other things on your mind than your wound." Mael's voice rang with edged humor, but his glare blazed on their intimate handholding.

Jeanne flushed warm and silently cursed herself for such schoolgirl things like blushing and handholding. Again, her mind turned over the possibilities of a genetic disturbance. She was on her feet and moving back to the bed, gathering her animal skin wrap before Mael could make another comment.

"My sister wishes to serve us for break-the-fast. The servants set a table in the hall." He raised his hand. "Nae, stay, Ian. The cook shall send yours up with a comely lass. Perhaps ye can hold *her* hand whilst ye eat." He turned to Jeanne.

"If ye shall join me, lass." He paused as though remembering something. "Your name, lass. Now that ye have your tongue, give me your name."

"Jeanne," she informed him. "McBen."

Both men exchanged looks with raised eyebrows.

"'Tis McBen?" Mael's laughter was so intense, she straightened her shoulders. "I know the clan McBen. They live five days ride to the south." He shook his head. "Come, lass," he called over his shoulder as he left the room, "ye can tell me all about your clan, and why ye believe them lost on the other side of the ocean."

She groaned. Her story sounded absurd even to her. She hurried down the staircase in the wake of his deep laughter. When she entered the Great Hall, she found him waiting for her by the table. Just as she descended the last step, Ishabelle's voice echoed behind her.

"Your horses lay readied and await ye in the courtyard." She looked at Jeanne briefly, but her attention anchored on her brother.

"Aye, Ishabelle." He waited for Jeanne to sit down. She did so quickly, trying to feign interest in the fine white linen cloth and silver table setting.

Ishabelle watched them from the landing. Jeanne grew uncomfortable under her hostess' stare, but Mael seemed undaunted by his sister's watch.

"Are ye joining us?" he called to her never once looking up.

"I prefer to dine in private," she mumbled just barely loud enough for them to hear. Jeanne dared a glance in her direction. "Ye shall leave after your meal?"

"We shall be in just as much haste to be away from Fernmoora as ye seem for us to leave."

"Good." She nodded. Her long skirt whirled as she turned from the stairs. "Leave Ian here. I am in need of his protection."

"The hell I shall." Mael jumped to his feet, slamming his fist onto the table.

Chapter Sixteen

Jeanne caught the pitcher of wine and righted it, but the silver goblets toppled over from the force of his outburst. She watched one roll from the table and clatter to the stone floor.

"Ian needs rest. He canna ride." Ishabelle looked down at the spilled goblets and continued as though nothing had happened. "Age has taken its toll upon him, Mael. His healing powers no longer equal those of a man your age. Canna ye see how weak he grows?"

"She's right." Jeanne spoke beside him, intrigued by the softness in Ishabelle's voice when she spoke of the servant.

Mael's glare shifted to her. She met the chilling look with an apologetic shrug. Instantly, the hardness in his brown eyes softened and blazed with unmasked desire. Her breath caught in her chest. How did he manage to do that to her? She willed her pounding heartbeat to slow.

"I ask this one thing of ye, brother. 'Tis so hard to find compassion for me in your heart? Is your hatred for me so great to cause Ian to suffer?"

Mael's body went rigid beside her, and he balled his hands into white-knuckled fists.

Without thought, Jeanne reached over and covered his hand with hers. The sensation flashed through her. He lifted his stare. It was a brief exchange, but so powerful she trembled. He broke from her stare and looked up at Ishabelle.

"The decision rests with Ian. I shall abide his wishes." He sat down beside Jeanne without another word.

She watched as the hard lines in Ishabelle's face relaxed, and the brittle look in her eyes warmed. She marveled how alike these twins were. They could both be ice one moment and the next melt into intense heat. Ishabelle turned from the ornately carved banister.

Jeanne decided it best to eat in silence. An hour later she followed him into the courtyard where their horses waited. Ian's mount pranced nervously at the end of the reins as the groom struggled to control it.

A dense fog hung in the early morning air, and she pulled the hood of her fur cloak over her head. When she tried to put her foot in the crude stirrup, she slipped and nearly fell to the ground. Chuckling under his breath, Mael took long-legged strides over to her and unceremoniously hoisted her from the ground, plopping her onto the hard saddle.

"Do ye think ye can keep from falling off, lass?" His broad shoulders shook with laughter as he walked back to his horse.

She watched the way his kilt swayed with his gait and his sexy muscular legs. Her heart leapt in response to the sight he cut. He swung his handsome self over the saddle with the full tartan across his chest, pinned to his shoulder with the gold family crest. His linen shirt, laced and tied at the neck, had billowy sleeves cuffed at his wrists. Her stare lowered to the boot lacings, which screamed sexy. She tried to remind herself one more time that she must leave him soon and couldn't give in to her longings. But when he sat on his horse, laughing with such ease, she wondered how she could ever leave him.

Mael reined the horse, waiting on her. She glanced from Ian's horse to the double doors at the top of the wide steps.

"Ian chose to stay. He always had a soft heart for my sister," he said to her unspoken question.

"And you have no such place in your heart for her?" she asked, unable to keep the smile from creeping over her lips.

"Once." He jerked the horse's reins, guiding the steed toward the bridge.

"Oh?" She nudged her mare to catch up to his. "But you granted her request for Ian to stay behind. Did you not grant it because of that same soft place in your heart?"

He reined his horse to a halt and leaned over so close that his breath brushed hot against her ear.

"Nae, 'twas my soft heart for ye, lass," he whispered, then brusquely righted himself and dug his heels into the horse's ribs. She sat staring after him. Excitement rushed over her.

His stallion bounded over the drawbridge, and the thick morning mist quickly engulfed him. She jabbed her heels into the horse's ribs and hurried after him.

They rode in silence for what seemed hours. Surprised, Jeanne was able to ride the horse in a more assured manner. The heavy mist clung to her cloak, weighing it down heavily on her shoulders. As they drew closer, the gray shapes distorted by the haze became snarled trees and craggy rocks. The world seemed to close in around them and for the first time she *felt* the mystical powers of ancient Scotland.

Insight shifted in her like the fog. It was the *land* that created the superstitions, not the people. The only sounds around them were the labored breathing of the horses and the digging of their hooves into the soft sod. The air smelled of earth. Its fragrance encased them. It was as though the very essence of the land filtered into her body and absorbed her.

Was that how these people felt about their land? She had never been connected to the earth. Nature had always intrigued her from a scientific interest, but she had never considered nature existed for its own purpose. It lived and breathed all on its own with or without people.

She shifted in her saddle and the horse moved beneath her. Even the mare seemed to be an extension of her. The sensation overwhelmed her. *This* was what she had remembered standing in the mist staring at the moon so long ago with the other MacRaigl. She had remembered it. She had felt this moment over seven hundred years into the future. But...how was that possible?

The paradox twisted around her like the ancient roots of the gnarled trees just ahead of them. It was not until they stopped underneath one of the lofty trees for their noon meal that she braved to meet his stare, but quickly averted the contact. The soul-deep longing still centered in his bronze eyes. They were alone. No servants and no Ian to interrupt them. Again, the feeling of déjà vu instantly transported her back this time to the night Mael had rescued her from the angry mob. Rubbing her clammy hands together, she shivered.

He removed a plaid from his saddle and flicked the heavy cloth in front of her. The air between them hung as heavy as the fog along the hills. He spread the tartan beneath the tree and she sat down, awkwardly focusing her attention on the brown leather pouch he handed her. She untied the leather straps and unwrapped a loaf of bread and large chunk of cheese. He turned back to his horse and retrieved the skin flask of grog. Flashing a satisfied grin, he settled on the blanket beside her and shifted closer. His arm brushed her as he lifted the flask to his mouth.

Frenzied waves of desire washed over her. He appeared unaware of how heightened her senses were with his nearness. Jeanne forced her stare away from the seductive profile he made with his kilt askew above his long legs, revealing muscular thighs toned by the highlands' rough mountainous terrain. He was, she reminded herself, a barbarian compared to his twenty-first-century descendant.

Absently she wondered what the modern Mael was doing at that moment. What was her brother doing? Was he safe? She pushed the painful thoughts from her mind and tore some bread from the loaf before handing it to Mael. The haze shifted slightly, allowing a few shafts of light to penetrate through the trees. He reached inside his shirt. The glint of the dirk caught her square in the eye as he retrieved it from its sheath and began to slice the cheese into manageable pieces. Intrigued, she watched him wipe the blade on the plaid before returning it inside its sheath.

Handing her a slice of cheese, he took one for himself, then settled against the tree trunk with a groan. The late morning fog lifted further with the afternoon sun, and the day quickly warmed their respite into a perfect autumn day.

He sat, enjoying the food, watching her. The heat of his stare sent a giddy fluttering to her stomach. Jeanne managed to push the meal past the excited lump in her throat, but her appetite quelled under his relentless stare.

"So tell me your story." He passed her the skin flask.

She took it, welcoming the task to stall her answer. How could she possibly explain the truth so he would understand? The harsh brew scorched a path down her throat, fanning into thick flames to her stomach. She cleared her throat then wiped her mouth, catching the droplets of grog that trickled from her lips. She glanced up at him, noting the excited gleam in his gaze. Blushing, she handed it back to him.

"I have no story."

"Everyone has a story, lass." He tilted back his head and squeezed the grog into his opened mouth. Her stare fastened on him. Everything about this man excited her. The simplest of tasks were acts of teasing.

"Not a story that would be of great interest." She straightened her back and braced for his questions. He was not a man easily put off. He had been as patient as she could hope. She feigned interest in rewrapping the leftovers.

"You're very adept in the art of avoiding the parley of question and answer."

All I Want

"I don't attempt to avoid anything." Her voice tightened around the words.

"Did ye think I would allow the questions to remain unasked?"

"What questions?" she asked. Unable to feign interest in her task any longer, she lifted her head and met his harsh glare.

"All the many questions surrounding ye as though they were a shroud." His eyebrows arched high above his brown eyes.

"I'm no mystery. I lost my voice due to an injury. The villagers misunderstood my muteness." She stood and turned from him, folding her arms over her chest. She stared out over the mountainous range. "By the time my voice was healed, their superstitions had already condemned me to be a witch. So I decided to remain mute. After all, why speak and give them further cause?"

"But ye use words I dinna know."

"My people use those words."

"Aye, in your village that lies beyond the ocean?" There was no laughter in his voice this time.

"It's true. As strange as it may sound." She dropped her gaze.

"Aye, 'tis strange."

She braved a glance and quickly regretted it. His stare seared through her very clothes, scorching her flesh.

"I shall solve your mystery. If I know no other thing about ye, this I know." He came to his feet. His words struck her core with a white-hot piercing. Her pulse throbbed, sending heated surges to her groin.

He took a step over to her, stopping in front of her. His fingers closed firmly over her shoulder. Jeanne froze. She couldn't think. Her body rushed with fiery tingles. Every cell in her body cried out for him. Cupping his other hand to mold against her face, Mael let his forefinger trace the curve of her jaw. Jeanne's heart slammed against her chest, pounding every urgent need through her. She quivered in anticipation.

"I shall discover your mystery." His breath flamed against her cheeks.

"Hmm," Jeanne moaned and tried to turn from his lips so tempting and too close to hers. She knew if she kissed him, her defenses would shatter and she'd tell him anything he wanted to know. He tilted her face, positioning to receive his kiss. With one final attempt to resist him, she stiffened her back and planted her hands firmly against his chest. God, his chest was hard.

"Would ye push me away, Jeanne lass?" He enveloped her in a powerful embrace.

Her legs wobbled under her when his lips brushed against hers ever so lightly. Poised to resist his advances, her defenses crumbled under the contact. He pressed harder and she tried to refuse him, but his ardor was fierce. His lips claimed hers as though she had always belonged to him. His embrace molded her to his hardness. It was as if she had once been a part of him and somehow separated and now, at long last, rejoined.

She relaxed and slipped her arms around his torso, longing to mold herself to him. Liquid fire poured from him. Her lips melted against his kiss. His passion turned her into a quivering embodiment of heated need. She ached to feel his fingers press against her pussy, his hard cock stroking in and out of her. His passion unleashed, Mael swept her into his arms and laid her upon the plaid beneath the tree. His powerful body covered hers as the world spun around them.

His tongue parted her lips and plunged deep inside her mouth. A throaty groan vibrated from her and seemed to incite him, for his tongue captured hers in an urgent passion.

Tugging at the ties of his shirt, she struggled to free his chest to her anxious touch. His hands moved over her, trapped within the folds of material that separated her aching clit from his touch. It was torturous, and she moaned against his kiss, freeing her own hand to help him find what he sought. His fingers found her thigh and glided over the inside of her legs to firmly separate them to receive his probing. Her breath escaped in short, hot pants.

The first warm stroke of his finger against her pussy sharpened her pulse. She moved her hips in response to his seeking and cried out when his hand lifted from her. He released her lips to trail tiny kisses along her neck, pausing briefly where the pulse throbbed at the base of her neck. His tongue traced small circles along the tender spot while he stroked her clit, just barely touching it with the pad of his fingertip. She burned with a fierce need to feel his finger pressed harder into her hot flesh, but he continued to tease her with light, tender strokes. She lifted her hips in search of the pressure of his hand, but he moved from her writhing. The need burst with an edgy longing for his touch. She could not endure the teasing and clasped his hand between hers, driving it deep into her flesh, thrusting her hips against him.

All I Want

Suddenly, he rose from her, supporting himself on one arm. A frustrated wail jerked from her when he pulled away, again. Dismayed, she opened her eyes and met his distressed look.

"What is it?" she asked and drew her arm around his neck, trying to pull him back to her.

"Me damned kilt," he grunted. "'Tis wedged beneath ye, lass." His frustration darkened his handsome face, but his eyes were molten with desire.

Her heartbeat leapt. She quickly shifted, freeing him. He moved over her.

"Is it true you wear nothing underneath that kilt?" she whispered as her mouth sought the excited warmth of his again.

"I wear a very hard pain for ye underneath me kilt, lass." His hot breath brushed against her cheek.

"I can relieve that pain for you, Laird MacRaigl." Her laughter caught in her throat when his hardness touched hot against her thigh. "Oh my." Her breath rushed from her and she closed her hand around his thick cock. He groaned and she moved down the shaft of his cock with quick, tight strokes. Her touch aroused him further for he moved her hand from his cock, seeking the moistness of her pussy. She guided him to her, tilting her hips to receive him, hoping she was able to accommodate such a large man.

"Ye are so lovely, lass." His voice was low and deep with desire. He placed one hand on the ground beside her head and supported his weight as he maneuvered between her spread legs. The tip of his hot cock brushed against the raw throbbing between her legs. He eased deeper, as though testing her readiness. She wanted him to fuck her, but he taunted her, barely pressing the swollen head of his cock past the lips of her pussy then retreating to the outer edge of her opening.

She grabbed his butt with her hands and pushed him into her, crying out as he plunged inside. His full thickness spread the walls of her pussy wider, raking past tender flesh, moist and ready to receive him. She knew she was tight, and perhaps it was a surprise to him since he pulled from her and teased the outer lips of her pussy, with the tip of his cock, driving her to the edge of frenzied need. He worked his cock in and out, pressing past her wet lips, going deeper each time. The slight friction bristled up her spine, exciting her further, and she rolled her hips, longing to seduce him back inside.

His steel-hard cock poised on the outer rim of her opening, teasing and retreating until liquid fire rushed from her pussy, drenching his cock and aiding him to slip inside through her fleshy walls. She relaxed around his thickness, allowing him full entry.

Mael thrust deeper and pulled his length from her only to ram it harder into her again. She clung to him, letting her hands glide over his corded muscles, longing to strip him of his shirt.

Suddenly, he lifted his head so his stare locked with hers. Jeanne's heart throbbed in her chest as she met his bronzed eyes, blazing with open passion. His stare forged a bond so deep her very breath jerked from her in a tearful gasp.

He plunged his cock into her, all the while his eyes beckoning her into his stare, holding her captive as he fucked her. Neither spoke. No words were needed. The air was charged with their scorching passion. Sweat rolled down his chest, clinging to her bodice. She searched the depths of his brown eyes. He knew. Just as she did—they were made for each other. Their joining was perfect. Every sensation he stimulated fueled her desire, driving it stronger, leaving her unsated, building her need for him. Lost in the smoldering desire sparking within those brown depths, her thoughts cascaded into the passion raging between them, lost forever with only one thought, one need—Mael. And at that moment, they both knew, it was destiny. They were meant to be together. Their lives had been spiraling in opposite realities toward this very moment on this grassy hilltop, where they were fated to make love and consummate their destinies.

Her heart throbbed harder and the heated need quickened, driving her against him, seeking fulfillment. His pace slowed as he drew his cock from her, then slowly plunged deeper, drawing her closer to the edge of orgasm. Jeanne undulated against his deliberate massaging strokes. The sensations intensified. She needed faster, not slower to ease the urgent melting between her legs. She gripped his shoulders and moved up and down his shaft, quickening her rhythm while he maintained the slower movement. Heat prickled over his skin as her frantic need burst and she shuddered against the waves of liquid fire. He groaned and moved over her, stroking her hair. He planted a tender kiss on her lips, then lifted his face to stare down at her.

His expression reflected the overwhelming pleasure she felt mingling with the powerful realization. The corners of his lips lifted slightly and he nodded as though to assure her that he, too, was thunderstruck by the moment.

Her desire quickened as she fell into his deep brown eyes once more. She rolled her hips and he responded by ramming his cock harder into the depths of her silky heat, sending new waves of intense pleasure to her clit. He closed his eyes and groaned, filling the ache within her, driving it, stoking it into a roaring flame that consumed her completely.

She undulated under him, rotating her hips in short circles, clamping the walls of her pussy around his heated shaft. He pumped faster, slipping his cock in and out of her, the smacking sound exciting her further until she was left craving more. More kisses, more touches, more rubbing of his chest against her aching breasts still trapped beneath her dress bodice.

Her nipples throbbed to be suckled. She tightened her legs around his hips, pushing into each new thrust. The sucking sound grew louder, and he pressed hot kisses along her neck, while he grunted and clung to her with a burst of wild unleashed passion. The sounds from their lovemaking filled the air—sounds only they could make together. It was as seductive as any touch or words spoken in husky whispers. Her heart soared. She longed for his touch against her breasts and as though reading her mind, Mael bent his head, flickering his tongue along the soft place where her breasts rose above the dress bodice. Slowly, he positioned his weight on one arm and moved his other hand to let his fingers trail over the warm soft cleavage, following the path with his tongue darting between the leather laces that still bound her. His breath was hot against her flesh while his fingers worked the laces loose. He tugged on the lacings and her breasts spilled from the strict confines.

Mael grunted with obvious delight. His desire surged from him into her and his strokes quickened. Firm lips captured one of her hardened nubs between their moistness. He tugged, sucked and licked her nipple, sending pleasure in rapid lightning streaks to her clit.

"Aye, my Jeanne." His words fell between his kisses. "Ye be such a treasure." His tongue flicked over her hardened nipple to the other one, then back.

Warm arousal surged once more to her pussy. She was a frenzy of unfulfilled desires, taken to the edge of sensations, tottering on the edge of orgasm.

"Take me now, Mael," she insisted and grabbed his buttocks, pulling him deeper into her undulating hips. "Fuck me," she demanded and dug her fingers into his ass.

"Aye, lass, ye seem ready," he whispered in her ear, moving in and out of her moist softness in a powerful plunge. The pressure of his fucking eased the surging need, then drove it higher, pushing her beyond thoughts, driving her into a frenetic urge and yet, climax eluded her, driving her to rock harder into each of his movements. Did he want her to beg? She squinted her eyes. For the first time in her life, she felt possessed. If he didn't bring her to orgasm she was going to scream in frustration!

He released his breath in a chesty groan. His lips were like warm sunshine against her breasts. She worked the material of his linen shirt until her fingertips tingled with the feel of his hard, muscled back. The rough scraping against her arm was a vague sensation lost somewhere among the urgency of his passion. Lust was the drug, and she surrendered to its potency. Her thoughts transformed into echoes lost among the waves of delightful sensations. Their need roared to flame and gained momentum. He ground into her, each thrust pounding against her clit. It wasn't enough, she needed more, she wiggled against him, gaining the needed friction against her swollen clit. The dagger's sheath strapped to his chest scraped her flesh again. He thrust harder, and she called out, wrapping her legs tighter around his hips so she could press against him, dragging her clit against his hair tuft.

The frenzy of their passion stretched with heat radiating and throbbing, demanding its own fulfillment. She could not get close enough to him. She pressed her lips against his shoulder, and scattered kisses over his hard muscles. His flesh tasted sweet and strong. She let her tongue trace circles over his chest, delighting in his essence.

Mael supported his weight with his hands planted on the ground and drove harder and deeper into her. The smacking of his balls against her as his cock slid in and out of her pussy, echoed around them.

Longing for his closeness, she mimicked his posture, supporting herself with her hands so that her breasts brushed against his thickly matted chest. The sensation excited him beyond expectation. His arm came up and pulled her against him, rocking back onto his knees, taking her with him, so that she straddled his lap. His other hand gripped her buttocks as he continued to pump himself into her, groaning with each downward thrust she made as she rode him.

Rivulets of perspiration rolled down the curve of her spine. Her hair cascaded over her face and lashed against his with each thrust. His skin was a furnace of heat. Sweat broke free of his pores, and he groaned between clenched teeth, pumping harder, tightening his grip

All I Want

on her buttocks. Mael pulled her forward, lifting her slightly and Jeanne found herself flat on her back against the plaid while he pumped vigorously, driving her to the climax she so desperately craved.

She clung to his strong body, lost in the raging senses of frenetic pleasure. She longed to reach the heated pinnacle that ebbed and rose, teasing her when it receded, then rising higher. She clung to the pleasure edged with hot searing sensations that only this side of release could maintain. Her head burst in an array of lights and release teased her into frantic thrusts as she chased the sensations. Fiery streaks gripped her entire body and pulsated into climax. She moaned, gasping for air. Her release was complete. She cried out and gulped in the brisk air. Warmth spread through her in sweet spasms. Mael shuddered with her and groaned his pleasure as the powerful muscles in his back flexed and relaxed and flexed again. His cock throbbed inside her, wave after shuddering wave, pulsating bursts of his heated come spilling inside her, rushing past their heated joining.

She held him to her with all her strength, never wanting him to leave her. Never wanting the moment to end. He buried his head into her breasts and his hot breath caressed her tender flesh. Slowly, he rose onto his forearms and shifted his weight. He smiled down at her and stroked her face with his hand, turning her chin so he could nibble on her lobe while whispering unintelligible endearments to her. She was a mass of sensations and quivering pleasure.

"My Jeanne," he breathed and planted the softest kiss she had ever tasted upon her lips. It was tender and unhurried. The kind of hot lazy kiss only lovers can cherish in passion's ebbing.

She lowered her legs so he lay between their v-shape. Slowly, ever so gently, he slipped his cock from her and rolled onto his back beside her. Neither spoke. He reached over and gathered her into his arms, kissing her forehead. Never had she felt so completely sated. Sleep beckoned her. She nuzzled against his neck and allowed passion's final dredges to overtake her.

"Mael. I want to tell you—"

The cry was unearthly and came from behind them. Mael rolled from her and came up wielding his sword just as the attacker's sword whooshed downward threatening to rip through his chest. The striking metal resounded along the hillside.

Groggily, she watched, paralyzed, unable to scramble from the plaid. Mael recovered with less than his normal agility, but managed to come to his feet. His kilted form, disheveled with his shirttail blowing in the breeze, was poised for the assailant's sword as it sliced through the air. He blocked the move.

Brandishing his sword in a large circle above his head, he released a warrior's cry. The sound chilled her blood. She blinked, trying to clear her mind, struggling to grasp what was happening when only moments earlier, they had lain entwined in each other's arms. Was this warrior standing only a few feet from her the same man?

The would-be assassin backed from him, stumbling to the ground. He screamed out as Mael's mighty swing found its mark. She covered her scream with her hand and turned from the ghastly scene. Panicked, she stumbled to her feet, clawing her way up the hill toward the tethered horses.

Incited by the slaying, the man's comrades lunged from the brush and boulders. Their cries screeched in her ears as they rushed toward Mael, but he was beside her, pulling Jeanne to her feet and dragging her toward the horses. In one fluid motion, he tossed her onto the back of the horse, while swinging the enormous sword against the attacking men.

She held onto the horse's mane, struggling to free the reins from the tree branch. The horse pranced about nervously jerking against the tethering. Mael slammed against the mare, pinning Jeanne's leg against the animal. Her scream tore through the battlefield.

An attacker raised his sword over his head with both hands, and Mael released another savage shout. She watched in silent terror, knowing he could not dodge the strike without leaving her open to the blow. The man's face contorted into a pained expression followed by a red stain spreading into his shirt. Mael pulled his dagger from the man's chest and the assailant fell facedown at his feet.

Without a break in stride, he lifted his sword in a fluid downward motion and sliced the reins from the tree. The mare bolted with newfound freedom, and Jeanne locked her arms around its neck, using all her strength to hold onto the frantic beast.

"Mael!" she screamed as the animal took her in the opposite direction, leaving him to fight the remaining assassins.

Chapter Seventeen

It was several miles later before Jeanne was able to coax the horse to stop. With no reins, she managed to turn the steed back in Mael's direction.

Her heart was a riotous drumming. Scenes of blood and torn flesh flashed in front of her. What if the assassins had overpowered her brave warrior? What if Mael had been wounded and lay dying? Her stomach pitched. She bit her lip so hard, she cried out in pain.

Eternity spanned between her and the mountain ridge. When the horse crested the hill, Jeanne spotted the slumped man draped in a green tartan. Struggling to stop the horse, she slid from its back. Her feet touched the ground but her legs threatened to collapse beneath her. A mist had recaptured the knoll and cloaked the nearby trees and rocks. She measured each step as she climbed toward the giant tree where earlier she had spent her passion, thrilling under Mael's touch. Now, he could be lying beneath it, dead. The sob caught in her chest.

She glanced about for his horse, but there was only another fallen assassin, lying beside a boulder. Her knees were water by the time she crested the hill. Pausing beside the tree, she peered around the trunk, searching the ground. The tartan was gone. Her heart skipped a beat.

"Aye, all dead, lass," he spoke behind her.

She spun around with tears spilling down her cheeks. Her arms came around his neck as she jerked against the sobs. Mael crushed her to him. Her heart filled to bursting.

"Oh, Mael. I was so scared." Her arms tightened about his neck. Her entire being trembled in relief. She would never let him go. Never!

"I know ye were, lass, but ye be safe, now." He squeezed her gently before holding her at arm's length. "We must hurry. There shall be more. We shall not be safe until we reach my castle." He pulled her alongside him and hoisted her onto the horse's back, then swung up onto his horse.

"Stay close to me, lass." He leaned over and caught the horse's bridle with a leather strap and soon had her in tow behind him, urging the horses into a hard gallop across the endless ridges.

Jeanne struggled to stay on the horse's back, constantly glancing over her shoulder for assassins. They rode all afternoon and as the sun began to slip behind the distant mountain, the air stirred cooler with dusk settling over the world.

Every inch of her ached from the jarring ride. They scaled the last mountain ridge and the flickering lights of MacRaigl Castle greeted them from the noble hillside across the valley.

Her heart flip-flopped at the welcomed sight. Relief escaped her, parting her lips with a low sigh. She could not remember ever being so weary. Her muscles seemed to stretch then relax like a worn strip of elastic.

Mael reined the horse, startling Jeanne into an unexpected stop.

"The danger lays in wait, lass," he informed her in a hushed voice.

Adrenaline rushed to her head, clearing the fog that had seeped into her weary mind.

"What?" She blinked against the dark monochromatic landscape.

"They shall try to stop us from reaching the castle. We must ride swiftly through the valley floor. 'Tis where they shall await us. The second wave shall strike just there." He pointed at the base of the hill that rose beneath the castle. He reached inside his shirt, retrieving the dirk.

Her mind flashed to the last time she'd seen the weapon embedded in an assassin's chest.

"Take it, lass. At least ye have a means of defense should I—" He didn't finish and thrust the short hilt of the blade into her hand.

She tightened trembling fingers around it. Her breath was a shallow rasp.

"I don't know how to use this." She stared with horror welling in her chest.

"Ye surely know how to slice a boil, dinna ye?" He gave her a lopsided grin.

"I'm a doctor, not a warrior," she frowned.

"Doctor?" His voice held more than confusion in its harsh tone. "Lass, I dinna have the time to figure out your language. Should I fall,

All I Want

use the dagger if ye must to save yourself and get to the castle. If ye are unable to fight them off, then turn the blade upon yourself. 'Tis a better fate than becoming prisoner."

Before she could argue further, he leaned over and locked his lips to hers in a hard kiss, then released her.

"Ye own me heart, lass. Now and forever!" He tossed the reins into her lap, and she fumbled to catch the leather straps while he unsheathed his heavy sword. Her heartbeat leapt to her throat. Was Mael saying he loved her?

"Steadfast, now, lass. Dinna fall behind. I canna fight and keep ye in my sight."

She nodded. It would be a treacherous ride to the castle. She struggled to still the trembling in her body. He had taken care of them so far, why should she doubt his ability now? Maél MacRaigl was not a man to fall victim to any man's sword.

"Ye must stay close to me, lass. Whatever happens—should I fall to a blade, ye must ride toward the castle. Dinna stop for me or anyone," he instructed, then flashed a wicked grin. "The devil best clear our path."

She gulped, searching his face for traces of fear but only determination shone in his eyes. He dug his heels into the animal's ribs. She mimicked his actions and drove her mare into a gallop, staying close on his horse's heels.

The early night half-moon barely peeped above the mountain range. The horses' breaths were labored with the pounding of their powerful strides resounding beneath them. She felt exposed as they streaked across the glen and toward the flickering lights beyond the valley floor.

Mael leaned into the wind with his sword poised by his side. She marveled at the image he cut and wished she had a camcorder to capture him for all eternity. His braided hair streaked behind him while his tartan flapped about his muscular frame. He moved with the stallion as though he were a part of the animal. Her breath quickened with the sight, but her attention soon turned to her own struggle to stay on the horse.

The horses' hooves drummed out an urgent beat in night as they descended to the valley. All her senses were looming shadows highlighted by sputtering torches alon She willed the horse to quicken its gallop. Her skin ting of sweat quickly chilled by the night air. They reached the valley floor and the castle lay only yards ahead. So close, yet it might as well have been miles away.

Her breath came in ragged gasps. She tried to move with the horse. Her very heartbeat seemed to lurch to a halt when she glimpsed the first shadow along the tree line. It was quickly followed by another movement then another.

"Be alert, lass, they await." His warning was brisk. His voice sounded strained. Her palm sweated against the hilt of the dirk. She tightened her grip on the leather reins. The sensation was too familiar—terror. It was her bitter enemy, and quaked through her as though it owned her.

"Me laird!" the voice sliced the still night. A figure moved from the groove of trees.

Mael didn't rein his horse, instead he dug his heels into the horse's sides. She mimicked him, driving her heels harder into the mare's ribs.

"Halt, me laird, 'tis me, William, your loyal servant."

"Ride hard, lass," he yelled and raised his sword higher above his head.

"Stand down, me laird, 'tis your clansmen, here to escort ye to the castle," came another voice, joined with a unison of male voices.

"Aye. 'Tis Robert and Andrew, your ever-loyal servants, Mael MacRaigl."

"Stand down and let us pass," Mael's deep voice boomed across the valley as he drove the horse toward the shadows.

The men did not move, but seemed more determined to stop him.

"Me laird. Halt. Dinna ye recognize your true servants, here to protect ye from would-be assassins. We bid ye halt. We're here to lend escort to the castle."

"Assassins lay in wait along the moat and bordering lands," another voice sounded from the blackness.

"Be ye true, then stand aside." Mael swung his sword over his head releasing a bloodcurdling yell that startled the men's horses. The shadowy figures jerked about as their horses pranced underneath them.

Mael, unheeding their calls, raced toward the castle bridge. She held the dagger in front of her, bouncing about the horse's back, yet poised as best she could to defend herself.

All I Want

The men finally relented and reined their horses aside. Mael and Jeanne raced past them toward the bridge.

"Open!" he demanded and reined his horse so he was now behind Jeanne, allowing her to cross the bridge first. As the heavy doors creaked open, the light from inside the courtyard was a joyous sight. Her breath escaped her in a rush as she entered the sanctuary inside the castle walls. The men she recognized as his army surrounded her. She reined the mare to a slower pace. All energy drained from her. They'd made it.

"Close the gate and draw the bridge." Mael jumped from his horse still holding his sword ready to defend himself. The men outside rushed toward the castle, but halted as the iron gate started its downward path followed by the creaking of the bridge hoisted up and away from the entry.

"Me laird!" came the shout from the group on the other side of the gate. "We dinna understand. 'Tis your loyal friends! Rallied to your side and this be your gratitude for our efforts?"

"Be ye loyal, then my gratitude I shall express to ye on the morrow. Be ye traitors, then robbed of your prize ye be this night," he yelled as the gate crashed to the ground and the doors boomed shut behind it. The final sound was the drawbridge hinging shut against those on the other side.

"Welcome back, me laird. We just made ready to escort ye." The men stood by their horses, some had had time to mount them.

"Stand down and guard the walls this evil night. Julian, bring two men to stand watch along my tower walls and a third to guard my entrance." The men rushed to do as ordered while he took brisk strides to her and drew his arm about her waist, lifting her from the horse. He held her close against his side as they ran up the steps into the castle.

Julian fell in behind them. With his sword still drawn, Mael seemed ready to meet an ambush inside the Great Hall. The large room was deserted. The blankets and bedding were askew as some had used the tables while others had made pallets on the floor. It was clear the men had been roused from their sleep.

"What goes here?" Julian huffed behind to them.

"Assassins roam the hills," Mael explained. "They crawled out from shadows to ambush us on our way from Fernmoora."

"Me laird!" Julian huffed behind them.

Mael led her toward the tower. Mrs. MacRay met them on the steps. She covered her cries with her hands when she recognized them.

"Me laird, such a ruckus there be outside the walls."

"Aye, Missus MacRay, assassins rule this night."

"Me laird?" The woman's wrinkled face screwed up into a confused look, with dawning understanding widening her eyes. "Me brother, Ian, me laird?" She looked anxiously past them.

"Safe," Mael answered not breaking his stride as they climbed the stairs to his chambers. "Ian guards Ishabelle this evening at Fernmoora," he threw over his shoulder.

"But how? Me laird? Ishabelle left here but shortly prior your arrival. She rallied the clan to escort ye to the castle."

Mael jerked around, nearly tripping Jeanne with the sudden movement.

"Ishabelle came here?"

"Aye, she feared assassins readied to ambush ye in the valley. She rode to Locklin's and roused his men."

"Aye, they were in wait for us outside the castle walls. Locklin never lost a breath of caring for me."

"They came to protect ye. Guarded the valley so ye have safe passage. They killed one assassin down near the river. This I know for your sister told me just before she left. But me brother, Ian, was not with her."

"Your brother rests at Fernmoora this eve, Missus MacRay. Ye have me word on this. And Locklin has never been my ally. I canna believe he would rally to my defense."

"I dinna know what governs a man's heart, especially Rory Locklin, but I know what Ishabelle said." Mrs. MacRay pursed her lips together.

"I daresay Locklin was the instigator of the assassins and as far from my ally as the devil be from the Son," Mael spat. "And as for my sister, she declared revenge upon my soul for the death of her husband. I dinna believe her heart be filled with concern for my well-being."

"Nae, me laird!" Missus MacRay's expression soured with a wrinkled frown. "The Tryon accompanied her. I saw him with me own eyes. He rode to Dewitt's and then on to Sumney's to rally their clans in your defense."

All I Want

"What?" Jeanne and Mael asked in unison.

"Aye." Her tired brown eyes deepened with understanding, and she hastily crossed herself then covered her mouth with her hand. She scurried from the foyer, crying unintelligible words.

"It's impossible." Jeanne looked up at him. "Missus MacRay is old with failing eyesight. It was probably one of Ishabelle's servants. Surely you don't believe Tryon is alive."

"As always the Tryon owns the night." Mael turned on his heel and with his arm still securely about her waist led her to his room. She glanced over her shoulder at Julian who frowned at her.

Mael paused outside the chamber door to give Julian some instructions. Jeanne hurried over to the dying fire.

"Ye be safe now, lass," he said upon entering the chamber. He barred the door and took long strides across the room to peer out the tall open window.

"'Tis a night of deceptions," he sighed heavily and closed the wood shutters, barring them against the cold. Finally, he lowered the sword and turned to her.

"Ye did just fine, lass." He pulled her to him, still holding the sword in one hand, ready to defend them at a second's notice.

"Do you think Ishabelle betrayed you?" Jeanne rested her head against his chest. His pounding heartbeat drummed in her ear.

"I dinna know what be in my sister's heart, be it a black heart now. I trust no one this night."

"Is that why you didn't yield when they said they were there to protect us?"

"I yield to no man. Come." He escorted her to the chair by the fire and knelt down to add more wood until it was blazing. He stood and placed his sword on the hearth before turning to face her.

"Ye need rest."

"But, Mael, Ishabelle was here. How is that possible? How could she have arrived before us? Traveled nearly ten miles, rallied the men, returned and then struck out for home? That's not possible. Is it?"

"Missus MacRay said she did."

"Yes."

"Then 'tis possible."

"But that's not what I meant."

"What do ye mean lass if not what ye say?"

"I mean how is it possible for Ishabelle to arrive here before us, without passing us on the way?"

"We dinna travel the entire time." He smiled slightly. Heat rushed over her. "There are other routes. Let your mind rest, lass. Fatigue clouds perceptions. Come." Before she could react, he scooped her up into his strong arms and carried her to his bed where he lowered her onto the soft warm mattress. Silently, he covered her with a heavy blanket then pivoted sharply on his heel to retrieve his sword from the mantel. He thrashed it against the foot of the bed several times.

"No assassins lurking beneath the covers." He paced over to the fireplace.

"Missus MacRay said Tryon was here. He can't be. He's dead. I don't understand." She snuggled under the covers and yawned. The tiredness in her body drained against the comfortable mattress. His bed enveloped her. With heavy eyelids, she watched him stoke the fire before sitting down in the nearby chair to unlace his boots. Deep waves of sleep washed over her. She blinked, straining to look at him, but her eyelids fluttered closed.

Mael stood from the chair and wiggled his toes against the cold stone floor before pacing in front of the roaring fire. He turned to look at her and unclasped the brooch, freeing his tartan. Such a mystery, yet so exciting. He'd never found any woman who could drive him to the edge of abandonment the way Jeanne McBen had.

Draping the long tartan over the chair, he grasped the shirttail and pulled it over his head. It tugged against his braid then released. He tossed it on top of the tartan and began unbraiding his hair, working the leather strip woven into the single braid.

Unhurried in his task, Mael pondered the day's events. He would speak with Locklin in the morning. If Locklin's clan was indeed a new ally then the man would be at Mael's castle door first light, demanding an apology. The last strand of leather fell free and he ran his hand through the matted hair until it fell in waves below his shoulders. If Locklin had in truth been Ishabelle's servant of revenge, then Mael had more than just a fanatical band of assassins to worry about.

When they attacked Tryon, Mael had hoped the assassins' vengeance had been appeased, but the superstitions and rumors surrounding Tryon would never die. They would merely fade into a distorted legend like so many others. He groaned against the exhaustion aching deep within his muscles and stood, unbuckling his belt. The plaid fell from him and he padded naked over to the bed where she slept so soundly. He'd tasted her passion, and it had only awakened a raging need for her. How easily she stoked him to frenzy. His desire for her grew when he climbed underneath the blanket. Gathering her into his arms, she nestled into the crook of his arm and moaned.

Though fatigued, he wanted her just as fiercely as he had on the knoll. The deadly interruption of the assassins was not something easily overcome. He would need to approach her in a gentle manner, until the tender emotions mended. He moved his hand over her curving form, so tempted to free her from the clothing. She had endured the night with a bravery he'd never suspected lay beneath her demeanor. Nor had he suspected the passion that bubbled below the façade of her muteness.

Just who was this Jeanne McBen and where was her village? Although he had vowed to solve her mystery, Mael now felt it had soared far beyond his grasp. He could no longer consider anything about her with objectivity. His breath touched her face, and a soft curl of her hair lifted from her cheek. His pulse sharpened at the innocent caress of her hair against the back of his hand. He'd never noticed how sensitive his hand was. Stroking the length of her hair with the backside of his hand, he marveled how silken her tresses were. She shifted under the movement then settled deeper into his embrace. He pulled the blanket around her shoulders and breathed in her sweet fragrance.

The stirring inside him was deep, unlike anything he'd ever felt. His stare wandered to the other side of the room, struggling to separate himself from the sensations she brought to him. Just beyond the tall window, reflecting in the panes, millions of twinkling pinpoints of light canopied the late night. He glanced down at her. Aye, his heart was possessed as surely as if she'd jailed it with lock and chain. He frowned. He was a mawkish mass over her. Surely, she must be a witch.

The thought took root and weaved its way through his thoughts. That was the only explanation for his obsession. He had been raised on tales of men being bewitched, and their souls damned for all eternity. Powerful men, who once struck by a witch's magic had bent to her whims. Their wills broken, they'd been left mere shells once their usefulness ended. Kingdoms had been lost. Their very souls had been stolen. He jerked from her as though she'd been ablaze with fire, relieved his sudden movement had not disturbed her rest. He retraced his steps to the fireside and sank down into the chair. The dismal mood followed him and consumed his heart.

It explained so many things about Jeanne McBen. He glanced at her. And now she held his seed. Would she spawn him a devil son? It was but one time. Yet a fertile lass required but one bedding. And everyone knew once a witch took your seed, your very soul was hers. His heart pounded heavy in his chest. His offspring would be doomed for all eternity.

Ishabelle had already seen their clan suffer that fate. Mael was the last hope for the MacRaigl name. He could not let it end with a witch's spawn. He glanced at the bed. Such passion could only come from a spell. Perhaps the lass was not a witch, but had merely purchased a spell from one.

He rubbed his beard. Only a spell could pry his focus from his clan and his destiny long enough to partake in such abandoned lovemaking whilst in the throes of intrigue and grave danger. But just how did one fight a spell? Was it too late to disentangle himself from her sorceress's web? And what was her intention?

She was such an enigma with her mannerisms and language, not understanding the simplest things like riding a horse. What manner of woman could not sit a horse? And what manner of person could believe her tribe lived across the ocean? Why, that was the edge of the world. If she lived there then surely she *was* a witch.

Shivering, he jerked the rough tartan around his naked body. Witch or not, Jeanne McBen was dangerous. He stood to pace in front of the fire. Was he man enough to deny his heart so he could fulfill his birthright?

He drew a ragged breath and closed his eyes. Was he warrior enough to do battle with his own feelings and win? Was he strong enough to resist her charms? Slowly, he wandered over to the foot of the bed and stood watching her with held breath. The firelight shadows danced an erotic rhythm across her face. How could such a bonny lass be a witch? He chided himself. Nae, his reasoning was too simple. Too easy to blame his own passion upon the spell of a witch, instead of owning the thing as having been born within himself.

His gaze traced her delicate face. She was the respite after a long, dry season. To deny her was to reject the very breath he took. Mael groaned and turned his back to her. Would one night by her side matter

All I Want

now? After all, she slept. Everyone knew witches were powerless when entrapped within slumber's web.

Settling in the bed once more, he released his breath with the flow of hers. He was connected to her as surely as if they shared the same arms and legs. How was such a uniting with another person possible unless it were a spell? Befuddled with sleepiness, he closed his eyes. Slowly, amid his musing, Mael drifted off to sleep with her riding the night nestled within his embrace.

* * * * *

Jeanne grabbed the horse's mane, struggling to catch herself as she slipped from its back.

"Yeawh!" The man's voice rang in her ears. Startled awake, she sat up. "What ye be trying to do to me arm, lass?" Mael jerked from her, rubbing his arm.

"I, ah, I thought I was on the horse," she sighed and fell back onto the mattress. "Oh, God, I'm so glad I'm in bed and not racing across the highlands with assassins on our heels."

Mael supported himself on one elbow and stared down at her. He smoothed back a strand of hair from her face. "Ye are a bonny lass, Jeanne."

She covered a yawn with the back of her hand. "I'm a grateful lass and glad what I thought was a horse was actually your arm." She smiled sheepishly up at him.

Her heart leapt to her throat at the vision he created with his hair loose about his shoulders. In the flickering firelight, his smile faded.

"I have never been compared to a horse." His chuckle was low and warm. "'Tis a compliment ye aim to bestow upon me?"

"Hmm." Jeanne took in a lazy breath through her nostrils. "I guess it would depend on which end I'm comparing you to."

Mael threw back his head to release a deep-chested laugh.

"My bonny Jeanne, so engaging. The likes of which never known."

Her own laughter broke off when a strange glint flickered across his eyes. He quickly masked it.

"Ditto," she strangled over the word, confused by that haunting look. Immediately, she realized her choice of words was wrong.

"Ditto? What kind of word be that?" The apprehension in his voice alarmed her.

"It means, I find you just as engaging, Mael MacRaigl." She lifted her hand and stroked his face, letting her finger trace the line where skin and beard met.

Her gaze continued to travel down his neck to his bare chest. Suddenly, she realized he was naked. Desire raged in her, fanning downwards. She burned for his touch. Her body responded to him as though it were separate from her.

His gaze deepened and for a moment, both lay holding their breaths as the current surged between them like a streak of lightning across a night sky. Mael broke the trance and looked away.

"The rooster shall crow sooner than we ken. G'night." He turned his back to her.

Jeanne gritted her teeth, frustrated and hurt by his unexpected rejection. She had hoped they might enjoy the same passion they'd shared on the knoll. The thought of making love to Mael in his bed, protected from assassins aroused her even more. What had doused the passion she'd seen in his eyes? Her heart pounded out her anguish. She was a fool for allowing him into her heart. Stupid to have made love to a man over seven hundred years older than she.

She snorted at the insanity of it all. Mael would never accept the truth that she was from the future. He would believe her a witch were she to voice it. She studied the way his long auburn hair fell over the pillow.

The fire's light reflected his broad shoulder, exposed above the covers. She ached for him. The memory of how it felt to be possessed so thoroughly by him burned her very blood. Her clit throbbed for his touch. The sudden deep snore assured her he was asleep. Damn him!

Chapter Eighteen

"But I tell ye, me laird, 'tis true. I seen it with me own eyes, as surely as I see ye standing before me now." The young man's voice fell to her ears before Jeanne's brisk steps brought her around the corner of the Great Hall.

"And I tell ye, lad, I saw me brother-in-law laid out in the chapel and dead he was and dead he still be."

She halted mid-stride, resting her hand against the cold stone wall, listening.

"Nae, me laird, arisen from the dead he is."

"Ye blaspheme the church, do ye?"

"Nae, 'tis not a resurrection I claim, but the unholy raising of the undead, of the *vampyre*." The other man's voice was hushed.

"I shall not have these rumors cast about. The lass and I were attacked on our way home by those who believe such nonsense."

"How can I make ye understand, Laird MacRaigl? 'Tis not rumor. I seen it with me own eyes."

"And yet ye live to tell the story?"

"I dinna know why he set me free. I canna know the workings of a devil's mind. Chance be the cross I wear about me neck?"

Mael's snort was a mixture of contempt and disgust.

"Get out of my sight, Erwin. I shall hear no more from ye. If ye continue to spread these rumors, I shall exile ye. Do ye understand?"

"I understand that ye canna color the truth as ye would a piece of cloth to suit yourself. The truth 'tis the truth."

"Get out!" The power in Mael's voice sent a shiver through her. She froze, unsure whether to retrace her steps to his room or venture into the Great Hall and pretend she'd not heard.

"Do ye plan to hide in the shadows all morning, or are ye going to join me for the meal?" Mael's voice jolted her.

With trembling knees, she stepped around the corner. Her gaze quickly found his across the roomful of silent men.

"Please come in, lass. The meal could stand a bit of change." His stare moved to his men, who mumbled a few obligatory ayes.

"I didn't mean to interrupt." She did as he instructed. It was as if the entire room gasped.

"Aye, the lass found her voice." He glared at the wave of mumblings, some crossing themselves, others just sitting with mouths agape. "She had an injury, lads. Not unlike a battle wound that heals."

She could see the men were not buying his explanation. The veins in his temple throbbed, and she knew he was dealing with more than just the threat of assassins. His men were already unnerved by the claims of Tryon traveling the countryside.

"Come, lass, tell these good men about Lord Tryon."

"He's dead." She nodded to them all. "I saw him myself." She met their challenging stares. "Dead."

"So says she. And when Ian arrives by week's end, he shall tell ye the same." Mael frowned at them and offered his hand to her. She noticed how warm his was compared to her clammy one.

"The morning 'tis filled with rumors from the night." He helped her with the heavy chair.

"I have no doubt, me laird. When men become frightened they create tales to mask their weaknesses."

The low disgruntled mumbling buzzed the hall. Her pulse drummed riotous beats as the appreciative gleam rose in his brown eyes. Reluctantly, she dropped her hand from his, instantly missing his touch. The low hum of the men mumbling beneath their breaths did little to settle her churning stomach. She looked at him, but quickly averted meeting his intense stare. He was a paradox. In private he spoke of vampires and such, but in the presence of his men, he insisted there was no such thing. Was it an effort to calm their fears? She knew he stood on shaky ground, trying to claim his birthright under the assault of assassins and now the rumor of his sister's vampire husband. She couldn't imagine what he was going through. Of course, he had to dispel the rumors to keep control. The question was, could he?

She struggled to eat the meal of bread and a thin slice of roasted pork, but it was impossible to ignore the heat of his stare. It touched her cheeks, brushing over her like a painter's strokes upon a canvas.

All I Want

Excitement twisted in her stomach and fluttered to her chest. She washed it down with a gulp of red wine.

There was no further discussion about Lord Tryon, and the men quickly dispersed to set about the morning hunt. She made to rise, but Mael's large hand covered hers, and he pulled her back into the chair.

"Please a word with ye, lass." His voice was stern and absent of warmth. "I dinna attend the morning hunts until this insanity ceases. I find myself seeking a murderer around every corner. But we must discuss a matter of great importance."

She tried to still the nervous fluttering that flip-flopped in her belly. Was he going to explain why he was so distant?

"Yes?" She tilted her head slightly, wondering what was going on behind those hypnotic brown eyes.

"A question, asked in strictest of confidences." He glanced about the empty hall.

"After yesterday I thought you knew you could trust me." Her own words embarrassed her when she didn't see the expected ardor in his gaze. Instead, she met a guarded look. How could he build walls like that so quickly? He appeared unmoved by the passion they had shared. In fact, he acted as if it had never happened. A sinking feeling quaked to her stomach.

"'Tis a matter concerning Alexander Tryon." He lowered his voice into a whisper. She moved closer. The heat of her desire tingled down her arms. She clasped her hands in her lap to keep from reaching out to stroke his face. Heat pulsed between her legs. She wanted him. Would she ever feel his arms around her again? She licked her lower lip, longing to taste his lips once more.

"Yes?" she strangled out past the thick lump in her throat.

"Ye saw my sister's husband—dead?"

"Yes." She nodded.

"I received a message at dawn." He reached inside his shirt and retrieved the folded parchment that had once been rolled and sealed. The broken brownish wax had left an oily stain on the thick paper. He handed it to her, assuming she could read. The Gaelic scrawling had been written by a shaky hand. She sighed in frustration and handed it back to him.

"I cannot read this."

His confused expression softened into a gentle smile.

"Forgive me, I assumed ye were of great learning, since ye know so much about the arts." He took the paper from her. "'Tis from Ian. He tells me that Tryon—" He lowered his face so his words fanned against her ear. Excited shivers raced down her back. "He says Tryon rode with Ishabelle to rally support last evening."

She jerked from him and hurried over to the fire, unable to bear his closeness without touching him. She could not show her desire, not after his rejection last night and again this morning.

"That's not possible. We both saw his body."

"Aye." He joined her by the fire, raising his eyebrows. "But I trust Ian. He be a brave man. And a visit from Locklin at first light assured me Tryon was here."

She considered the possibilities for a moment. Taking a deep breath, she bit her lower lip. "I don't believe in vampires."

Relief flashed across his face, but was quickly replaced with that same guarded look. What was going on? Why did Mael suddenly distrust her?

"The rumor of vampire has long followed Tryon."

"Do you believe? Is that why you and Ishabelle are no longer on good terms?" Jeanne knew she trod on thin ice, but she must know.

"What happened between my sister and me remains a private matter."

She wanted to die. His cold demeanor hurt worse than anything she'd ever experienced. How could she have been so stupid to allow herself to feel anything for him? She wanted to kiss him. She needed him to hold her and tell her how much he wanted her. She looked away from his emotionless stare.

"Forgive me," she mumbled. "I didn't mean to pry. For what it's worth, I don't think Tryon's a vampire."

"But he was dead. Ye saw him." He clasped his hands behind his back.

"I saw him," she agreed. "He was dead." The awkwardness between them seemed to expand. Why was he so distant? What had she done?

"So if not vampire, then what?" Mael challenged.

She braced herself for his reaction to what she was about to say. "I think he might suffer from a disease called catalepsy."

"A disease?"

Her stare traveled up his muscular arms to his face and locked with his pensive one. She pushed her breath through the tightening in her chest.

"Yes, an illness, a disorder actually of the nervous system," she said and wrung her hands together. "As strange as it may sound, it's an illness that makes a person appear dead, even though they're alive."

"I have never heard of this," he said while narrowing his gaze on her. Suddenly, Jeanne knew what it felt like to have a broken heart. The look in his eyes severed the last thread of hope she'd held that he cared for her. She struggled to still the shaking that gripped her and willed the emotion from her voice.

"In my ti—village, we know of this illness. Before we did, there were rumors of vampires, because the victims seemed to stop breathing. The heartbeat would slow so that there was no pulse."

"How did ye know they lived then, if ye canna hear their heart?"

"We have ways. Tools to help us. Tools I don't have here." She felt like a specimen under a microscope and nervously twisted the leather lacing of her wide belt. "The victims are able to hear and see, but cannot move. They're paralyzed. Stiff, like a corpse. The paralysis can last for minutes, hours, even days."

"How do ye know all this?" He sat down on the nearby bench across from her and folded his arms over his chest. "Have ye witnessed such a victim?"

Her gaze centered on his handsome face. Her heartbeat leapt. Swallowing back the memory of their impassioned picnic, she continued.

"I'm a trained physic— Healer. Where I come from, I'm called a doctor. I was schooled about these illnesses." She groped for an explanation. "And there are other explanations for this myth of vampire. There's another illness that makes people sensitive to the sun and unable to eat garlic." She smiled as her words struck him. Mael unfolded his arms and leaned forward.

"A sickness?" he asked, with new hope shining in his eyes.

"Yes." She took a deep breath, using the moment to organize her thoughts before continuing. "It's a blood disorder. The victim cannot produce heme, which is a vital component of red blood. The irony is garlic stimulates the production of heme, but a person suffering from porphyria cannot tolerate garlic. Consuming garlic will only make their symptoms more painful. It makes them very ill." She noticed the way his eyebrows arched higher and cleared her throat. "It's a rare disease but can sometimes be passed down from one generation to another. The victims cannot tolerate sunlight. Even their hair grows thicker and faster than most."

Mael came to his feet. Her heart ached for that tender look in his eyes lost to her forever.

"Are ye telling me the truth, lass?" he asked.

"Why would I lie to you, Mael?" She pushed back the tears. She must leave or embarrass herself.

"Have ye seen these types of illness?"

"No."

"But ye know 'tis true?" he asked with a snort.

"You have to believe me."

"I dinna have to believe ye, lass. I saw Tryon and dead he was. I know Ian. I believe him. I dinna know ye. Ye could be one of Tryon's loyals for all I know, sent to seduce me over to his world." His lips pursed together.

The anger pumped to her head. She drew back her hand and smacked him squarely in the face with a force that surprised both of them.

"How dare you say that!" She regretted her earlier mourning over his lack of affection. If he believed these accusations, then he damn well didn't deserve her love. Love? Did she truly love this man?

"Ye have a powerful sting to your slap, lass." He rubbed his jaw.

"And you are a barbarian with no manners or culture," she said with her chest heaving. "Believe in your superstitions. Chase ghosts for all I care. I'm sick of this place. Vampires and assassins. This world of yours is insane! I just want to go home." She spun on her heel and ran from him, taking the steps two at a time.

Sobs jerked from her chest as Jeanne scaled the flight of stairs leading to her bedroom. Damn him! She threw open the door and slammed it so hard the icon paintings on the wall shook. She fell onto the thick mattress and buried her face into the pillow, screaming out all the pent-up frustration and anger from the past months. Her heated cries emptied in muffled waves against the linen.

She cried for Ryan. She screamed against the betrayal of Trench and the desolation of being trapped in this ancient world. But most of all she sobbed because of Mael's rejection. It tore through her very soul. Nothing was as it should be. Her life made no sense, and worse, the world she was in made less sense. How was she going to survive Mael's rejection? How was she ever going to find Trench and return to her own time?

Her emotions spent, Jeanne lifted her head and with the back of her hand brushed the wet trails from her face. A sound came from the corner of her room. She lifted onto one elbow, and turned just as he moved toward her.

"Trench!" she called out, but he was on top of her, his hand muffling her scream.

"Did you think I'd forgotten you?" His voice droned over her. "We must leave. Something has made everything shift. I've recalculated the charts. The portal will open sooner than I thought."

She tried to talk, but her words were hot puffs against his hand.

"When I remove my hand you won't scream." he demanded.

She nodded, and he removed it slowly.

"What shifted? What does that mean?"

"Our coming back must have changed things." He released her and straightened over the bed.

"There's no telling what harm you've done. A lot of people are dead because of you." Jeanne sat up with her legs dangling from the bed.

"I don't think it will impact either of us, since we're still here to continue our argument."

"Is that what you call this? I call it a *war*."

"I guess I've started one in my attempt to place my ancestor in your beloved laird's place as Chief."

"You're responsible for the assassins. Why would you do this? Mael means nothing to you. He has nothing to do with what is between us."

"I couldn't stop it now if I wanted to. It doesn't take much in this century to get these highlanders riled. Their superstitions are easily fueled." He stood over her with his fists resting on his hips. "I think Mael MacRaigl means more than just the man who saved you from the villagers. Makes me curious. What would you give to save the men in your life?"

"Stop the vampire rumors and stop your ancestor's insane vow to assassinate Mael and his sister, or I won't go with you." She moved, but he overpowered her and something pricked her arm. He plunged the needle deeper. The injection burned and coursed up her arm as the hot fluid surged into her bloodstream.

"What did you just give me?" she demanded.

"A little something I brought along in case I had an emergency. And you have become quite an emergency." He stood from her.

Her heart pounded faster, pumping the drug pumped through her.

"Mael will kill you and your ancestor." She struggled to rise, but was too weak.

"The portal returns tomorrow night for only one hour."

"Tomorrow?"

"We go back the same way we came. According to legend."

"Legend? You don't know for certain?"

Trench shrugged. "Calculated risks. If all else fails, I will become a very rich man in this time period."

"You're a bigger gambler than you are a thief," her words slurred.

"I have enough plasma protein to produce all the antiserum I need," he said, but his words were garbled.

"Not without my formula, I'll never —"

He grabbed her by the hair and jerked her head back. Her eyes fluttered open from the pain.

"If you want Ryan to live, you'll give me exactly what I want."

The world blurred with sounds echoing in waves. Her ears rang from the sudden pounding from outside her chamber.

"Open the door, lass." Mael's voice boomed from the hall.

"Damn that Highlander, he's always in my way." Trench pulled a pistol from his cape.

"No!" she wheezed. "You can't." Even in her drugged state she knew Mael could not defeat a bullet. "Kill him and his men will kill you. You won't be able to escape. You won't get back to the cave."

"You're right." He paused. "I'm too close to risk losing it because of this barbarian."

"Lass? Open the door." Impatience echoed in his voice.

"What a waste of good drugs," Trench clipped. "But I won't be far. You *will* go back with me." He turned toward the window. "I'll be back tonight."

"Don't leave me behind," Jeanne murmured as the world blackened around her.

Chapter Nineteen

"There ye be." Mael was by her side.

"What happened?" Jeanne blinked against the bright light and rubbed her aching temple.

"For a moment, I thought ye were one of those folks with that sickness."

"What?"

"That illness. Catalepsy?"

She was impressed with his mental acuity.

"But ye were sound asleep, lass. Never seen anything like it. Slept all morning ye did. 'Tis past noon."

"It is?" She managed to sit up in the bed, pulling the covers about her.

"What happened to ye, lass? I thought I heard ye talking with someone."

"I must have stumbled and hit my head," she lied, rubbing her temple.

"Let me see." He sat down on the bed and gently shoved her hand aside. The electric fire of his nearness shocked her wide-awake. She took a long breath.

"I'm fine." She pushed from him and swung her legs over the side of the bed. Her abrupt rising nearly brought her back onto the bed. His strong arms steadied her.

"Lie back down."

"No." She shoved from him, determined to put as much distance between them as possible. She staggered over to the chair he'd vacated near the fireside and dropped into it.

"Perhaps ye need a healer?" He started for the door.

"No," her voice trembled with emotions rampaging in her.

"Then allow me to fetch ye something to eat." His tone vibrated with warm concern but edged with a guarded note.

She glanced up at him. The pained look in his eyes quickly faded, replaced by that empty stare she was growing to hate.

"I'm not hungry." Her stomach pitched at the mere thought of food. A side effect of the drug, she surmised. Where had Trench gone? He'd be hiding because no one could get past the double guard on the walls, unless there was still a traitor among them. If Trench succeeded in his plans, Mael would surely be assassinated, and she would remain trapped in the past, without Mael. The future would belong to Trench.

Tears burned her eyes, but she sniffed them back. She couldn't do anything until sunset. Darkness would be her ally. Until then she intended to resolve this matter with Mael. She would not carry this pain back to her own time. She had to know what had happened to make him distrust her.

"Then what may I do for ye, lass?"

She met his dark brooding look. Despite the turmoil raging in her, she still wanted him. She needed to feel him. She was obsessed with thoughts of him. Was it possible she was addicted to him? She almost laughed out loud.

"Just what is it you want to do for me, Mael?" she countered, daring him to reject her, again. He walked over to the window and peered out into the bright sunshine. Her heart sank.

"I can aid ye in finding what ye search." He glanced sideways at her then turned back to the window.

"Who said I searched for anything?" She wanted to touch his shoulder, force him to turn to her. She longed to press the issue until he revealed his true feelings, if he had any for her. Instead, she clasped her hands together in front of her.

"I can tell when a person hides a truth. A certain look cloaks all they say and do." His white linen shirt stretched under the movement of his muscles, defining his physique like a second skin.

She swallowed the flames fanning to her groin.

"Ye protect a secret. A mystery I felt close to solving on the knoll."

Heat rushed to her cheeks and burned her eyes. It was the first time he'd mentioned their lovemaking. She seized the opportunity.

"I thought we had something special, Mael. But ever since we returned to MacRaigl Castle, you've been distant."

He bowed his head feigning interest in his boots, and then raised his stare to hers.

"Aye."

Exasperated, she raked her hand through her hair and collapsed against the back of chair.

"Then explain it to me, please."

"Explain?" He tilted his head and gave her that infuriating blank expression.

"You know damn well what I'm talking about."

"We were nearly murdered on the knoll, Jeanne." His eyes filled with so much emotion, her breath rushed from her. "Ye understand my guard was down, otherwise I would have heard their approach. I nearly got us killed because of my passion for ye. I canna allow that to happen again."

"What?" She blinked at him. That was *not* what she'd expected to hear.

"I tried to blame ye. Tell myself ye were a witch, or Tryon's own, but I know in my heart ye cannot be either. I blame myself. 'Twas a stupid thing for me to do with assassins running about the hills." He shook his head.

"You've been avoiding me because you think it will keep me safe?"

"Aye." He jerked his head in a short nod.

Laughter bubbled to her chest. The irony of it grabbed her and wouldn't let go. He was trying to protect her by avoiding her but Trench had still managed to nearly kidnap her. If only Mael knew the truth then the confused look washing over his face would be one of anger. It was hysterical. She struggled to compose herself.

"Ye find this amusing, do ye?"

She watched the dark color rise over his face, and the light in his eyes dulled.

"No. No," she said, gasping to restrain her laughter, "just relief. I thought you hated me."

"Hate?" Mael stared at her. "Lass, 'tis not hate I harbor for ye. Nae, never hate."

She stood and stopped just inches in front of him, so close that his breath touched her skin like a caress.

"Then show me, Mael. Show me that you don't hate me." She reached out and pressed her hand against his chest. Her body welcomed the sensation of his hardness beneath her palm. It was a balm to her senses so starved for his touch.

After tonight she would be gone. He would be lost to her forever. What harm would there be in making love to him one last time? At least she could take the memory of his love back with her. That could be enough for her, Jeanne tried to tell herself, knowing it would never be enough.

His large hand covered hers and his stare searched her face. She opened her stare to allow him to see she didn't hide any emotion from him. Surely, he could see that in her look.

"I canna, lass." He pulled away and stepped around her, heading for the door.

She wanted to crumble into dust right there. It was his final rejection. There would be no other opportunity to amend the damage done by the assassins' attack. Her knees trembled under her when he opened the door. He paused briefly to glance over his shoulder.

"Forgive me," he said in a low, strained tone.

She watched with tears cascading down her cheeks as he closed the door behind him.

Mael bowed his head and paused just outside the chamber, flattening his hand against the door. He drew a ragged breath. Abandoning her with her heart shining huge in her eyes had been the hardest thing he had ever done. To make love to her was all he could think about, but he had a clan war to stop. He could not afford to be distracted. He would not place her in such jeopardy again.

"Me laird." His captain ran up the stairs.

"Julian?" He looked up in time to see the other men trailing behind the stocky Scotsman.

"We caught a stranger scaling the wall outside the lass's chamber."

"We left him in the Hall. Restrained."

"Thomas, stand guard at the lass's door. Dinna allow anyone to enter." He nodded for Julian and the other man to lead the way.

"What does he have to say for himself?" Mael asked as they descended the tower and turned onto the landing above the Great Hall.

"He claims the lass a witch," Julian frowned.

His pulse sharpened.

"He does?"

"Aye. Says the assassins belong to her legion. He claims the lass is one of Tryon's whores."

Mael glared at his clansman. It was one thing for him to accuse her of being one of Tryon's loyals, but quite another to have someone else accuse her. He tightened his hands into hard fists by his sides, restraining the urge to smash them into the man's bearded face.

"I want to hear what this black-tongued liar has to say." He shoved past Julian and bounded down the stairs.

The man sat in a straight-back chair with his ankles bound with a coarse rope. He wore the black and brown plaid of the Fareley clan. His head was bowed over his chest, and a trail of fresh blood stained his yellowish shirt.

When Mael stopped in front of him, one of the men drew the steel blade of a sword underneath the man's chin and lifted his head so his bloodied, swollen face was visible. Mael winced at the harsh beating his men had obviously given the assailant.

"Your name?" He met the swollen-eyed stare, unable to tell if the man was awake or unconscious.

"Fareley," he slurred between bloody bruised lips. "Deamond, me given name, but me clan calls me Fareley."

"Fareley?" Mael leaned against the mantel. "Ye lost? Ye appear to be a long way from your home, Fareley. Are ye the son of Donald?"

"Aye," came his response, dripping with hatred.

"A tanaiste came to run me through with his own sword, did ye?"

"I came for Tryon's property."

"What property might that be?" He braced himself for the man's response. Dreading, yet daring him to speak it.

"The witch ye protect. She's the spawn of the devil himself. As long as she lives, Tryon's power over our land shall never cease. She must die."

"The lass be neither witch nor Satan's seed."

"Ye can be so certain?" he laughed.

"Aye. Of that I can!"

"Then explain what I found along the tower wall leading to her chamber," He reached inside his shirt and retrieved an odd-looking weapon.

All I Want

Mael stepped closer and took the long tube-like thing the man handed him, careful not to prick himself with the fine, thin tip.

"'Tis her witchery, Laird MacRaigl."

"Indeed?" Mael turned the odd contraption between his fingers. It had a long stopper that he moved up and down the hollow tube.

"And what might this weapon be?"

"'Tis a witch's weapon," he hissed and moved as though to jump Mael. Several men came up behind him and pressed his shoulders into the back of the chair.

"A weapon?" he asked, unable to control his laughter. "For a fly perhaps. For a man, 'tis but a thorny prick."

His men joined in his laughter.

"Ask her what 'tis," the man challenged. "And when she tells ye 'tis a needle, ask her how she sews with it."

"A needle? 'Tis what ye think?" Mael glared at the man then laughed again.

"Ask her what she would be using such a needle for, me laird. And when she tells ye, then ye shall know I speak the truth."

"Ye are daft, Fareley, me lad. Take him away, will ye?" Mael stared down at the odd contraption and noticed the numbers and bars that ran its length. What was this object? He'd never seen anything like it. Surely Jeanne would not know what it was. Still, he watched as his men took the struggling man from the room. What if she did?

"What do ye want us to do with him?" Julian stood watching him.

"What do ye think I want done with him?" Mael frowned at his clansman.

"Would mean a clan war to kill their tanaiste," Julian warned. "Fareley Clan has long been allies with MacRaigls." Julian ran his hand through his red hair.

"Until now. Do ye believe his story, then, Julian?"

"Me laird, we all know the lass 'tis different. Something sets her apart. Why would Fareley risk so much were she not a witch?"

"Of greater importance, Julian, how did Fareley *enter* my castle? That shall be where we look. Not toward the lass, but the traitors within our own walls who gave Fareley entrance into our home. And why does a clan tanaiste undertake such a mission? They scurry about my castle abundant as rats. How can they manage to do so? I want the man responsible found and brought to me."

"Aye, me laird, me men question the guards along the west wall as we speak. But ye must not turn a deaf ear to what Fareley speaks. 'Twas not ye Fareley sought to kill, but the lass." Julian's lips pursed together.

"They wish to kill her because she be a witch? Are ye certain 'twas not me the assassin sought?"

"Aye, me laird. Dinna ye rescue her from the villagers? Were they not about to burn her as a witch? The Fareleys still believe in witch power and gaining it in a kill."

"Cullen began the rumors. Incited his own against us and formed a band of assassins. He drives a wedge of fear and suspicion between my own clansmen. The Fareleys obviously joined forces with Cullen de Mangus and sent an assassin to kill me, yea, but a few nights hence. Do ye forget so easily? They attacked my sister and her new husband. Cullen, the cunning bastard he proves himself to be, hopes to goad me into a war."

"Aye, and if ye kill Fareley, who he likely convinced to murder the girl to gain her powers, then we have the war Cullen itches to wage."

"So we lie besieged with fanatics, Julian, not rational men."

"Kill the lass and all this shall cease," Julian insisted.

"Nae!" He turned his anger on his captain. "Killing the lass shall only make them stronger. Nae! The lass shall not be harmed." He turned on his heel, but Julian was not to be put off so easily.

"Me laird!" He halted Mael at the door. "Please, me laird, at least ask the lass about the weapon before we take vengeance upon the Fareley Tanaiste, I beg thee. If what ye say 'tis true, then I shall kill Fareley meself. But what if ye be wrong? What if the lass proves to be part of the plot against ye? Ye keep her close to ye, believing ye protect her, mayhap she lulls ye into believing her loyalty lies with ye. 'Tis only a matter of time before she murders ye, perhaps in your sleep."

Mael could not restrain his outrage any longer and picked up the nearby chair. Yelling, he crashed it against the stone wall. Julian took a cautious step back. Mael glared at him.

"The lass 'tis no assassin laying in wait! Nor does she cite verse and cast spells like a witch!"

"Then no harm in the asking. Have her prove her loyalty. For all of this began the night she arrived. Think on that, me laird. If she passes the test, then I shall personally run Fareley through with me own sword."

Mael bowed his head and drew a long breath. "Await my word." He stared at the object in his hand then marched toward her chamber.

"Does she sleep?" he asked Thomas who stood in front of the door.

"I canna tell. No sound comes from her chamber." He stepped aside to let Mael enter.

She stood looking out the window and pivoted when he entered. Surprise and relief washed over her face. He marveled at how unskilled she was in masking her feelings. She had donned her bedgown and in the late afternoon light, her slender silhouette was clearly revealed through the veil of blue fabric. His heart throbbed and his body responded to her sensuality with his cock thickening hard.

"Mael?" Her eyebrows arched high above her blue eyes.

"My pardon for the intrusion, lass." He closed the door behind him.

"I wasn't expecting you to return." She lowered her gaze, trying to hide the red-rimmed telltale signs that she'd been crying.

He wanted to gather her into his arms and comfort her. He had caused those tears and hated himself all the more for what he was about to do.

"My men found someone along the outside wall, and I was hoping ye might be able to help me."

"What?" She clasped her hands together in front of her. Trench! They had captured him? He met her trusting gaze, struggling to ignore the pained look that suddenly settled there. It ran deep, but she struggled to conceal it from him.

"He was caught leaving your room from the window outside. He'd been here."

"He had? Is that what he claims?" She moved over to the fire and stood behind the heavy chair, staring into the flames.

"He claims ye witch and that with this," he said and held up the object in front of him, "he claims with it, he could take away your powers."

Her laughter rang in his ears, making his throat close. Slowly, he moved closer, and held the weapon in front of her. He studied her reaction when she glanced down at the object. Her face drained of color to a sickly pallor.

"He had that?" her voice trembled.

"Can ye tell me what this might be?" He handed her the weapon.

"Why do you think I should know what it is?" She handed it back to him without so much as a glance. "Where is this man?"

"Locked up." He cocked his head to one side, trying to gauge her concern. His heart rammed hard against his chest. The last thing he wanted to believe was Fareley's accusation. It just wasn't possible. He knew her. He had made love to her. His feelings for her were raw. He'd never known any woman like her. She was all he could ever want.

"Where'd he say he got it?"

"Outside the tower wall. Just below your window."

"I still don't know why you think I would know anything about it. I would like to face my accuser." She stiffened her spine and squared her shoulders, tilting her chin in a challenging way.

"Aye?"

"I want him to explain what he was doing outside my chambers and why he thinks *that*," she said, nodding at the object, "could harm me."

"Perhaps he hoped to prick ye with it. Like a pincushion," he laughed, trying to ease her into trusting him again. "Fareley has long been known for his wild imaginings."

"Fareley? That's the name of the man you captured?" Her expression shifted with her forehead wrinkling in a confused expression.

"Aye. Ye know him?"

"No." She shook her head.

"So why would he lie, Jeanne?"

"Why wouldn't he lie, Mael?" She stared at him without flinching. Her sudden calmness disarmed him.

"Ah, lass, 'tis so tangled a web we find ourselves ensnared within. It grows tighter each time we twist. Distrust hangs within my castle as though tapestries suspended from the very walls. I dinna want to accuse ye of anything. Do ye see the position they place me in? If I kill the traitorous bastard Fareley, then his clan shall surely seek revenge.

"If I allow him freedom then me own clansmen shall believe his story. I shall need to find ye a place of safety, for they shall surely turn on us both. I dinna wish the war I start with Fareley's death. But if a part of the assassination plot, then he shall surely die! Ye understand, lass, I canna kill a man unless I can be certain of his guilt. To kill an innocent man would be—"

"Kill?" She rushed over to him and grabbed his forearms. Her touch flashed white-hot through him. "My God, Mael. Why must you kill him?"

"He was trying to climb into your chambers, lass. He was sent here to kill ye. Dinna ye understand?"

She released her hold, turning her back to him, but not before Mael saw the tears cascading down her cheeks.

"I understand more than you could possibly believe, Mael MacRaigl."

"Do ye now?" He moved to stand behind her.

"Your men captured only one man?" Her words were so low, he had to strain to hear them.

"Aye."

"Did they mention another man? A tall, thin man with thick black hair and a pointed chin?"

"Nae, why should they?"

"Because if you question Fareley, he will tell you that he assisted this man into my chambers."

"He was here?" Mael's heartbeat pumped heavier in his chest. "Did he harm ye?"

"No," she said and shook her head, "but that object in your hand?"

"Aye?"

"He had it. He had it filled with a liquid that he injected into me."

"He *what*, lass?" Mael couldn't understand what she was talking about. Surely, she was daft. Then he remembered Fareley's words. *Ask her what she uses it for.*

"That object, it's used to inject fluids, drugs, ah…liquid herbs, into the body. It's called a syringe," she informed him.

Relief washed over him. She had not called it a needle, but she did know its purpose. She frowned at him.

"It's a hypodermic needle."

His ears rang with the word. Mael gritted his teeth together and gripped his fist into a hard knot by his side, while his fingers closed tighter around the small tube.

"Needle?" he repeated, numb by her admission. "Just how do ye sew with this?" He raised it in front of her.

"I didn't mean that kind." Her nervousness struck him full force. His worst fears were confirmed. "Damn it, Mael. Don't you see what's going on? How can I get you to understand?"

"The truth remains a simple thing, Jeanne."

"No, this truth is more complicated than any lie," she groaned and turned from him, collapsing into the chair as though she were a limp piece of material. He watched the emotions play over her face.

"What truth?" He stood over her, holding the needle in front of her.

"I'll tell you, but you aren't going to believe me."

"Why would ye think I dinna believe a truth?"

"Because this truth is too difficult to believe."

"Tell me, Jeanne lass." He kneeled in front of her and took her hands in his, so that the needle was cupped between them. "Ye must try. I canna kill an innocent man, but I canna let any harm befall ye."

"I just don't know where to begin," she said and took a jerky breath. "It's all so complicated."

He reached out to touch the softness of her cheek. She was so lovely. He wanted to protect her, but unless he knew the truth, he could not help her.

"There's a man. His name is Trench. We're colleagues, or we were."

"Colleagues?" Mael struggled to understand the word.

"Clansmen," she explained.

"Aye?"

"Only he betrayed me. I'm a doctor, as I told you before. I don't know how to say that in your language. I know I am not making any sense. Oh Mael, don't you understand? I'm not just from a different place but from a different *time*."

All I Want

"Time?"

"I can't explain how it happened, it just did. Trench stole something that belonged to me and he went through this—this cave in the hills. I can't show you where it is, because I was injured when I came through it. A woman, Verica, who lives outside the village rescued me and nursed me back to health. The villagers thought she was a witch. Trench is the one causing all this chaos. He created the rumors and stirred up your clan. He's the one organizing and sending the assassins. Please, I see it in your eyes, you don't believe me. Mael, you have to trust what I am telling you is the truth."

"Ye say ye are from—"

"The future. I come from the year two thousand and five. I was born in nineteen hundred and seventy-four."

Mael jerked from her. "Damn ye, lass, I wanted to trust ye, believe in ye, but ye canna trust me enough for the truth. Ye give me lies and silly talk of traveling through the hills in time."

"Mael!" Jeanne grabbed his arms. "I'm telling you the truth. I swear by all that is holy."

"Blasphemy!" He pulled from her. He was going to get away from her as fast as he could. This woman was indeed possessed. Only a demon's spawn could speak such things.

"Mael!" She collapsed in tears as he threw open the door.

"Stay away from me. Ye have been hexed!" He slammed the door. Julian was standing several feet from the landing and came running up to him.

"Guard this door and let no one in and no one out. She canna leave unless I am the one who comes for her."

"Aye. 'Tis something amiss?"

"Mind ye own affairs, Thomas, and ye shall live to see your bairns grow to manhood." He stomped down the stairs to his own chambers.

Slamming the door behind him, Mael quickly noticed the draperies had been drawn, a small fire set in the grate and the candelabra lit, all in expectation of his evening respite. The table beside the fireside chair supported his usual mug of mead. Groaning, he eased his weary body into the chair, and gulped down the ale.

The pounding on his door irritated him further.

"Enter," he yelled and took another swig.

"If ye drink like that all night, ye might be able to dull your pain enough to sleep." Ian peered around the door before entering.

"When did ye arrive? There are assassins about."

"Aye, they seem more plentiful than hounds chasing a boar. I met a few. We now have two less to worry over."

"Do ye try and kill yourself?"

"Nae, trying to stay alive and see that ye and the lass live through the night." Ian handed Mael the scrolled letter, sealed with the mark of Tryon.

Chapter Twenty

Jeanne tried to regain her composure. She could not let Mael kill an innocent man, yet she could not stay and allow herself to be caught up further in this tangled mess Trench had created.

She must find the cave and return to her own time. She had fallen for a man who was long dead before she was born. Hundreds of years before. God help her, she wanted him more than anything in life. But she had to return to her time. Even her feelings for Mael could not take priority.

"Damn it." She pulled the nightgown over her head to don the soft deerskin dress. She jerked the linens from the bed and tied them together. How could she expect Mael to understand things that would not exist until seven hundred or more years from now? Sometimes she had problems remembering they were real. Now he thought she was a witch. What next?

Tying her hair back with a piece of leather, she swallowed back the tears. Her old life was simple. She had an enemy — Trench. That was the only conflict and complication she'd had. In her old life there was no Mael MacRaigl. She was going home and no one was going to stop her, not Mael and certainly not a clan war.

Cinching the linens together, she tied them around the heavy poster bed, and hurried to open the window, peering down the three-story drop. The early night was brisk and dark with a faint light of the rising moon glowing just behind the tree line.

She doused the candles then leaned out the window. The dew scents of night greeted her with a cold breeze whipping her ponytail about her face. She searched the grounds for guards and found the silhouettes along the curtain walls standing with their backs to her. The guards along the courtyard were gone. Perhaps they had retired for the night. The enemy was outside the castle walls, lurking somewhere in the shadows. They didn't expect anyone to *escape* from the castle. Her heart pounded harder. What if the assassins were waiting for her? Trench had said he'd return at dark.

She tossed the linens out the window, yet could not help hesitating as she thought about Mael. He would be lost to her forever. She sucked in the cold air. He was already lost to her.

Gathering the back hem of her dress, she brought it forward and tucked it securely through her wide leather belt so her legs were free to scale the wall. Peering at the long drop to the ground, she braced herself for the enormous task.

"Oh, man." She crawled out of the window. The moon hung low in the sky just enough to bathe the countryside in a faint silvery haze.

Carefully, she stepped off the windowsill with her heart pounding like a drum in her chest. She held onto the makeshift rope with all her strength, took a deep breath and managed to release her death grip on the sill. The linen rope held her. Her mouth was an arid desert as she swung out over the courtyard, suspended from the open window. Slackening her hold, she swung against the tower wall and her shoulder slammed into the wall. She groaned under the impact, but lifted her foot, struggling to set it against the wall. The soles of her leather slippers scraped against the rough stones. She dangled there, holding onto the sheets with all her might. A gust of wind blasted through the courtyard and spun her around like a toy. Regret filled her. She refused to look down, knowing if she did, fear would paralyze her. Instead, she concentrated on the tower wall and planted her feet so she could lower herself down its length.

It was hard work and Jeanne's legs trembled under the effort. Her feet slipped out from under her, and she bit her lip to keep from crying out as she slammed against the stone wall.

Her pounding heart matched the fast, short breaths rasping from her. She lifted her legs and regained her position. When she was only a few feet from the ground, she froze, suddenly remembering there were lots of dogs roaming the castle grounds.

Suspended almost five feet above the side courtyard, her hands ached against her grip. She took a deep breath and prepared to face whatever obstacles were between her and the castle wall. She released the sheet and landed on the ground.

Her legs wobbled under her as she crouched down in the darkness and rubbed her sweaty palms against the smooth fabric of her dress. She'd done it! Looking up the long cylinder that seemed to stretch forever into the night, she was amazed at her feat. Suddenly, voices drifted down to her. She looked up and saw the two guards leaning against the tower wall overhead. She froze in her place until they finally shifted and turned to the outer wall and the glen below. She ran along the wall, careful not to make a sound and headed for the west end of the castle yard to the stables.

She would need a rope to climb over the moat wall. The thought of the task paralyzed her. She'd made it down the tower wall, but the moat wall was more complicated. She had cold water to fight and possible hyperthermia. She paused by the tack room door. How was she going to cross the moat? Swim? Her mind raced. What could she use for a float?

The water would be freezing. If the guards did not stop her and if she survived the swim, then how would she climb out of the moat onto the other side? She needed more than one rope. Jeanne reached for a second rope and slung it over her shoulder, and then headed for the south end of the castle, knowing that it was the least likely area anyone would suspect since it was the highest part of the castle. What if Trench returned for her and found her missing? He had said he would be close.

She dismissed the worry, choosing to focus on getting across the moat first. Once she'd accomplished that she would find Verica. The old woman could show her where the cave was. After all, Verica's family were the portal guardians. If she could reach the cave before Trench, she could find a way to stop him. Ryan's very life depended on her. She swallowed hard. The future of her world depended on her.

She climbed up the walkway and tied the rope to a stone column and then dropped the line over the side. She heard a faint splash below.

What manner of creatures swam in the moat? Her heart skipped a beat. Her imagination was rampant with ancient stories about castles and dragons. Of course, those were less frightening than the microorganisms that no doubt bred prolifically from the sewage runoff of the garderobes. Her stomach pitched, and she quickly rethought her plan. She stared down at the forbidding watery expanse. Her attention shot to the drawbridge. It was secured against the night. She had no choice.

"Get a grip, Jeanne," she murmured, but panic was a living, breathing thing inside her. It was as real as each ragged breath she drew. Glancing back at the castle with its golden lights flickering in the long narrow windows, deep-chested sobs threatened to betray her.

"Mael." She closed her eyes against the pain. She would forever mourn the loss of his love and forever curse fate for its cruel twist. Their life together had been doomed from the beginning.

Securing the dress hem once more beneath her belt, Jeanne grabbed the thick rope and straddled the top of the wall. She sat trying to judge the distance. The water would be cold. She had only a few short minutes to swim across to the other side before she would be overcome with hyperthermia. She tried to gauge the shoreline and the steep rocks that jutted in an erratic descent into the moat.

She shivered, realizing her dress would weigh her down, and unfastened the belt, pulling the dress over her head. Wearing only her overblouse, she tied her dress into a bundle and secured the belt around it. She tied the belt around her waist with the bundle centered her back. Her teeth clicked together.

Sitting on the cold wall, hidden among shadows, she glanced at the guards at the other end of the castle. Their voices pitched high as though arguing followed by a few shouts. She knew that someone would pay for allowing Fareley to slip past their watch. It was obvious Mael had a traitor within his own walls. Her heart tugged. After tonight Mael would be lost to her forever, left behind in the ancient past. She swallowed the bubble of grief threatening to burst to the surface. She looked down at the dark water. Her pulse pounded harder. Another bone-chilling blast of wind whirled against the walls.

"Okay, just like in therapy. I can face my fears." She grabbed the coarse rope and swung herself over the wall. "God, I'm going to fall."

* * * * *

"Do ye not understand what your sister says?"

"I understand her letter." Mael tossed it into the fire and watched with great satisfaction as it blazed and quickly burned to ashes.

"Ye could very well be the most stubborn man I know. She offers ye her protection."

"Protection extended by Ishabelle and her *dead* husband." Mael downed the last dregs of ale.

"She's your blood. Ye disregard her concern and doubt what the lass, Jeanne, told ye?"

"I know people canna come through a cave and appear on the other side in a different time."

All I Want

"Ye know this for certain?" Ian challenged. "Just as ye know Ishabelle could not arrive at the castle before ye? Or Tryon rides the winds of night?"

"Ye do me wrong, Ian. Ye challenge me to disprove myths and legends to ye, when by their very nature they were created."

Ian shook his head. "Be that as it may, the assassins be real. They roam everywhere, and ye must find a haven until we can snare them all." Ian's face wrinkled with a pained expression.

"Nae. Their numbers be too many. Within my grasp lies the power to end it all, this very eve. I shall not start a clan war over the lass. I ordered Fareley set free."

"Ye dinna." Ian leaned forward in the chair.

"Aye. I did." He noticed the worried lines creasing Ian's face.

"Then ye must take your sister's offer immediately. Ye and the lass must return to Fernmoora this very night."

"I shall stay here with my clansmen. Ride with Jeanne McBen if ye trust her. But be warned, witches can be deceptive. Prepare to do battle with a spell." He downed the mug of ale and lifted the pitcher to pour another one.

"Witch? The lass? Are ye daft?"

"Nae, bewitched," he chuckled lowly.

"Bewitched and in your cups, I say." Ian shook his head as he stood, but paused by the door to give Mael a disgusted look. He left the room not bothering to close the door behind him.

"Stand aside." Ian's voice echoed from the stairwell.

"Nae, Ian MacLaoren. I stand aside only for me laird. Stand down."

Mumbling under his breath, Mael stood unsteadily to his feet and walked to the open door. He leaned against the door jamb and squinted up the stairwell.

"Let the bastard pass, Thomas."

Thomas was quick to do his master's bidding, stepping aside so Ian could enter Jeanne's chamber. He heard Ian mutter a few choice names at the lad. Perhaps he'd best attend the matter. Mael climbed the steps to the landing above and nodded to Thomas. Ian stood outside the door and turned to cast a dark frown in his direction.

"Be off with ye, ye old goat," he scoffed and watched Ian enter the room. It was not long before he hurried back into the hall.

"'Tis empty!"

"What?" Mael suddenly felt very sober and ran past Thomas into the chamber. He quickly espied the open window and hurried over to it, noting the tied linens leading a limp trail down the side of the wall. "Be damned! The lass escaped!"

Thomas joined them and peered out the open window. "Nary a sound I heard," he assured Mael.

"Get a torch," he barked at Ian and raced down the stairs and out the tower into the courtyard.

"Halt!" The sound came from the West wall. Mael paused and turned in its direction, climbing the stairs to the allure with Ian on his heels.

"What goes?" he asked the guard and quickly surveyed the moat below.

"An object in the water from the South wall."

"'Tis the lass," Ian wheezed behind him. A cascade of arrows arched from the towers and pierced the water around the dark object floating in the water.

"Cease. Dinna attack the lass," Mael yelled, frantic that his men had harmed her.

"Hold your arrows, lads!" Julian's orders echoed across the cold waters below.

"She canna make the shore. The water's cold shall claim her." Ian shook his head.

"Jeanne!" Mael yelled and ran down the walkway on top of the wall to get closer. "Jeanne, come back! Dinna do this! 'Tis madness."

His heart pounded wildly. She was not stopping. She acted as though she'd not heard him.

"Get my horse. Open the gate!" He turned back, running toward the tower so he could descend to the courtyard. "Get my soldiers mounted."

"Look!" Ian pointed at the shore where shadows rose from the ground, and a large object was tossed into the water. Its splash crashed against the still night. Several men climbed onto the wood raft and rowed out to her.

He watched them drag her onto the log raft and was relieved she was safe.

"Jeanne!" He felt as though his heart was being ripped from his chest. "Jeanne!"

"She betrays us. She proclaims herself one of them! Just as Fareley swore!" Julian spoke from the tower stairs.

"Nae, ye fool!" Mael turned to him. "She sacrifices herself for us all." He glanced back and saw the men return to shore and hoist her from the raft. He yelled against the pain tearing through his very heart. "Jeanne!"

He was helpless to stop her. Helpless to keep them from lifting her up to the man on the horse. It had to be the one she'd spoken of, Trench.

"Your horse, me laird." the lad called up to him. Mael rushed past Julian down the tower stairs and into the courtyard. He jumped onto the horse's back and dug his heels into its sides. His war cry claimed the night as he led his men through the open gate and over the bridge. He quickly saw the movement ahead. The sound of swords scraping free of their sheathing assured him, his clansman had seen it, too.

"Julian, take your men and give chase to the band there, riding east." He pointed to the silhouettes racing across the glen.

"Aye." Julian raised his sword and the soldiers gave chase.

"Ian, ride with me." He turned to his friend, knowing the man was not fit to ride in pursuit, but all he could think about was saving Jeanne. "Close the gate," he yelled back at the castle guards, and the men who remained to defend it.

"Ye know where she travels?" Ian yelled to him.

"To a cave." Mael dug his heels into the horse's ribs and bounded out toward the village.

"What cave might that be?" Ian asked.

"The cave she used to travel from her time!" he spat.

* * * * *

Jeanne shivered as she rode behind Trench. It was dark and her overshirt was soaking wet. She'd heard Mael yelling at her, but knew she couldn't stop. If he believed she had betrayed him so be it. She had to do this. Trench coaxed the horse past the village and toward the rising hill.

She worried about Verica, hoping her friend was okay. She shivered violently and when Trench stopped midway up the hill, she slipped from the saddle and he dismounted, slapping the horse on the rump.

"We go by foot from here."

She untied her belt and hastily unrolled her wet dress. Shivering uncontrollably, her teeth clicked together as she pulled the icy garment over her head.

"Here. Put this on." Trench tossed her the fur cloak he wore. "Can't have you dying on me," he sneered and started up the hill. "That damn highlander's a stubborn son of a bitch. Looks like he's following us." He pointed to the glen below them.

Her pulse spiked. Two dark riders raced across the valley floor.

"He'll be too late." Trench grabbed her arm and jerked her behind him. "You're so damn predictable, Jeanne. I knew you'd try to stop me. All I had to do was wait and let you come to me."

The thought of going home was overwhelming. The terror she felt with Trench paled in comparison to the relief of being back where she belonged. At least in her own time, she might have the resources to stop him. In the twenty-first century she wouldn't have assassins leaping out from every shadow. There were no such things as witch-hunts or vampires. And there certainly wasn't Mael MacRaigl, just his descendant carbon copy. Her heart tugged at the thought of leaving Mael. Tears welled in her eyes. She would never see him again. When she returned to her time, he'd have been dead for over seven hundred years, a mere name in the annals of history. The pain stabbed deeper into her very soul, if there were a descendant, then Mael would find someone else to love and bear his children. The sob ripped from her chest.

"A little more of a climb, then we're there." Trench paused to shine the flashlight on his watch and cursed.

"We've less than thirty minutes. Once we get home, you're going to make me a very rich man, Jeanne."

* * * * *

"Which cave?" Ian caught up with Mael, driving his horse to match the gallop of Mael's stallion.

"One is but a short ride, the other requires more stamina," Mael threw back at him.

Ian winced and shifted in his saddle, holding his chest.

"Ye take the one closest the village." Mael turned his horse toward the hill. "Beware, Fareley's release has only taken them by surprise. Once they recover, they shall mount a more aggressive attack."

"Aye." Ian reined his horse, heading over the hills along the ridge overlooking the village. Mael drove his horse further up the steep terrain.

The moonlight was enough to guide him. The horse climbed the rocky cliffs toward the meadow that ran to the highest point along the ridge. He had spent many a youthful day exploring the crevices and caves along the highlands that overlooked the village. He knew every turn, every stone, and every shrub along these mountains. If Jeanne believed she had passed through a cave into a different time, then this would be the cave. This was where he would find her.

Perhaps she was under a witch's spell herself and a victim of Tryon's powers. Mael's chest swelled with hatred for his brother-in-law and what he had done to the MacRaigl family and now to Jeanne McBen. If she were mad, it was certainly Tryon's demonic doings.

He guided the horse through the precarious ravine and came out on the higher rise of the second ridge. Here, he carefully dismounted and led the horse through the narrow passage that opened into the hidden meadow. In the moonlight, the glen's short grass was draped in a sea of mist. A distant call of an owl echoed along the lower region. He climbed higher, pausing to lean against the mammoth boulder that marked the end of the long climb and the beginning of the mystical meadow filled with such stories that most sane men avoided the area completely.

He quickly espied the stone wall neatly tucked underneath a mossy overhang and climbed straight up the rocky hill toward it. At the end of the marked path was the mouth of the cave. The magical cave. So entranced by the potential magic, he'd explored it thoroughly on his tenth birthday, spending several nights within its belly waiting for the full moon to crest the ridge and create its magic, uncertain what to expect. And he had returned home disappointed when nothing had occurred. Disillusioned, he had focused on more tangible things like swords and riding.

"Easy now." He patted the horse's neck when it jerked alert at the sounds coming from the hill above them. He tethered the reins to the lower branch of a nearby tree and unsheathed his heavy sword. He had never contemplated the cave's legend again until Jeanne's tale of traveling from the future through a cave. Had she witnessed the cave's magic? Could she truly be from the future?

Silently, he climbed the steep path along the stone wall. Perhaps Tryon had filled her mind with the legend as a way to trick him. He ascended the rise. Muffled voices echoed from the cave. His gaze quickly found the faint golden glow flickering from the irregular jagged opening.

The cave was nearly as wide as it was high. Just as he remembered. He entered with his sword poised in front of him. His path lit by moonlight that faded within the streaming light ahead.

"Hurry up," the male voice echoed. "We've only a few minutes left."

He didn't recognize the voice, but knew the accent was similar to Jeanne's, and the words equally as strange. Was it Trench?

"How much further?"

Mael halted mid-stride at the sound of her voice.

"Two hundred feet or less. See?" Sharp laughter followed.

"My God! It's open." Her voice was a mere whisper, racing through the hollow in the mountain. It was maddening not understanding what they said. He could see their shadows against the wall.

"You thought I was lying? Couldn't get my wagon back up the steep incline, so I had my men take it apart and reconstruct it. As good as new. Proved a safer place for storage until I was ready to leave." He nodded toward the large wagon.

"I just need to push this slightly into the portal, just one small end and it'll be sucked into the vortex. Here." He shoved Jeanne against the wagon. "Push! Getting home was the uncertain part. By my calculations, it just opened. Push, damn it!"

She did as he ordered and the wagon creaked forward touching the undulating opening. It rolled from them and was jerked into the opening.

"Thank you, Doctor," he laughed and pushed her toward the opening. "That was the hard part. Now we go home at long last. I won't miss the lack of conveniences, but I admit I'll miss the drama."

Mael took a step forward as the flickering shadows danced over the cave walls.

"Untie me. I won't escape. I *want* to go home."

Anger pumped hotly through Mael. His Jeanne sounded so nervous. He envisioned her at the mercy of this vile faceless creature.

"I've no doubt, Jeanne. But you don't necessarily want *me* to go home. Why do you think I drugged you? But that damn highlander interfered. Stop fidgeting."

"What about Ryan? Is he okay? When can I see him?"

Mael's jaw clenched tighter at the name. Her frightened voice chilled him. He gripped the hilt of his sword, poised to strike at the precise moment.

Mael gritted his teeth. White-knuckled, he took a step forward, then paused when her low reply echoed to him. He was unable to make out her words.

The strange light from the depths flickered and dimmed, then flickered brighter.

"What's happening?" Her fear seized him, and he moved toward the bend in the tunnel.

"The portal's closing. We must go!" Trench's voice was shrill with panic.

Something was happening for even the man seemed alarmed. Mael rushed through the cave toward the glowing light, but froze at the sight of the watery bluish orb at the end of the cave.

It fanned out in shafts of yellow light resembling the sun. The man was dragging Jeanne toward it. The yell that parted his lips came from a place deep within. He lunged for the man. Jeanne glanced over her shoulder and cried out. Jerking free, she ran toward the light.

"Jeanne. Nae!" he yelled with his sword drawn and ran in front of her, catching her by the waist. He swung her away from the light. She was safe in his arms. He had saved his beloved.

"Let me go!" she screamed and writhed against his hold. "Please! I have to go." She tried to bolt into the light, but Mael held her firmly to him then turned on the man.

"I have all I want, Jeanne. All the blood *and* Ryan. I'll find your disc without you," Trench darted past them. He dove into the brilliance, escaping through the narrow opening as though it were a hoop.

Amazed, Mael released her and stared at the place where the man had vanished.

"No!" She raced toward the light, glancing back at Mael.

"Forgive me," she spoke in Gaelic.

"Jeanne, nae!" Mael reached for her. His hand closed over her arm, and he jerked her away from the circle just as it shrunk into a small blue dot and vanished.

"No!" she yelled and beat her fists against his chest. Jerking free of him, she ran to the darkened end of the cave. "No! No!"

He walked over to her and touched the cave wall. The hole was gone.

"Oh God! No," she wailed, offering no resistance when he gathered her into his arms and carried her from the cave. He held her as she sobbed. Taking slow steps, he carried her outside.

The early morning rays of sunlight greeted them. He brushed the tears from her face, met the look in her eyes and his heart ached for the pain in their depths.

"Now I'll never get home. I'm trapped here for the rest of my life. My brother will die. They'll all die." Her lower lip trembled. She looked away from him and squinted against the harshness of the new day.

Chapter Twenty-One

What had he done? Mael reproached himself. How could she ever forgive him?

"Why did you stop me?" she asked as he settled her into her bed.

"I wished only to save ye." He raked his hand through his hair. "He just disappeared."

"He went back to my time."

"Aye?" Mael considered her words. He listened to her weeping for some time before speaking again. "Peace, lass, I know ye hate me. But I vow to ye, I shall see ye returned to your own time since by my hand I trapped ye here. Just dinna hate me, lass. I canna live with your hatred."

She lay in the bed with her knees drawn up to her chest and stared up at him through blurry eyes.

"You think I hate you, Mael?"

"'Tis in your eyes when ye look upon me. I saw it back in the cave when I grabbed ye."

She sighed, feeling completely spent and numb.

"I don't hate you, Mael." She reached up and stroked his face. "I never could. I hate my circumstances and that Trench escaped. I hate what he'll do to my world. But I could *never* hate you." She brushed her hand along his beard.

"I hear the words, lass, but in your heart ye will forever blame me. Ye shall never be able to find peace."

She met the deep understanding mirrored in his eyes. Pain quickly filled their brown prismatic depths. Her heart tugged.

"I blame Trench," she said, "never you, Mael. I know you were only trying to protect me."

"But ye dinna believe I can get ye home, do ye?" His expression softened, and the sadness in his eyes eased for a brief moment. "I shall find a way, lass. I vow to ye, I shall." His intense stare did little to reassure her.

She didn't know whether to laugh or cry at his delusion. The legend claimed the portal only opened every seven hundred and fifty-five years. It would not open again until 2005. Her mind ached at the paradox it all created. It had arrived sooner than anticipated. Perhaps Trench's interference in history had altered the pattern or perhaps it was as Verica had said — a living thing with its own cycles.

He reached down and stroked her cheek with the backside of his hand. Tendrils of delight shivered down her. A tear slipped between her lashes and raced to his finger. He caught it and slowly lifted his finger to his lips.

"Even your tears are sweet nectar to me."

Jeanne reached for him and found his kiss. The kiss she had hungered for since that fated day on the knoll. Her sorrow faded, replaced by the joy of his touch. Gently, Mael pulled from her.

"Why, Mael? Why do you turn from me? Especially now, when I need you so much?"

"Do ye believe having ye for my own as I have and now having to eventually give ye up 'tis an easy thing? How can I send ye back if ye hold my heart in your hands?" He reached for the door. "If ye wish to return to your own time, Jeanne, then we must remain distant. If ye choose to stay with me, then I belong to ye, forever."

She sat up. Mael was hers? Forever? She could have everything she'd ever wanted in this man. Suddenly, her excitement transformed to grief. To have him would require sacrificing Ryan. To stay would mean turning her back on the entire future of the world. The choice was so unfair. Again, it was no choice.

"I have no way to return to my time. You know had I the choice, I could not stay, Mael. To stay means I sentence my brother to death. To stay means Trench will rule the future and all who live in it."

"Aye, lass and so it remains." His sigh was as heavy as her own. He retraced his steps, and sat down on the bed.

"I canna be without ye, my Jeanne." He gathered her into his arms.

She clung to him. A steady stream of tears rolled down her cheeks. She longed to hold him forever.

His hands warmed against her back as he drew her deeper into his embrace. All thoughts faded from her. His hardness pressed against her. A deep longing gripped her and radiated to her pussy. She wanted him. She needed him. This time she would lay in his arms all night, uninterrupted.

"Ye shall always belong to me." His lips found hers and she gave in to the comfort of his touch. If only she could have it all. Save her world and remain with Mael. To be his was more than worth any of the conveniences she'd known in her modern world. With Mael she had found life and a vibrant beautiful world.

Her fingers worked his braid. Each twist she loosened sent a new shiver of excitement coursing through her. His kiss was strong and eager. She abandoned the braid and ran her hands down his powerful back to his waist, digging among the tartan wool, until her fingertips touched his leg.

Her flesh to his was magic. Instant relief and comfort. She let her tongue twist around his, enjoying his passionate play. She moved her hand around his leg, and found his hardened cock, erect, hot and throbbing.

She broke from his kiss and shifted onto her knees, pushing her hands against his chest, until he finally relented and lay down against the pillows. She shoved the kilt aside, revealing his strong powerful legs and his erection.

Lowering herself to his cock, she took it between her hands and opened her mouth, letting it slip past her lips, twisting her tongue around its stiffness. His deep groan assured her all thoughts of the portal and assassins were gone. Power rose in her. The power to tame and bring a man of his strength to erotic ecstasy. She moved her tongue over his cock and sucked against its tip. He growled and before she knew what had happened, found herself on her back with his lips tracing small kisses over her abdomen to her pussy.

His tongue found her clit and danced erratic flicks, bringing her arousal to rapid heat with need and hunger. She moaned and writhed under his artful lovemaking until she couldn't stand it any longer.

"Fuck me, Mael," she groaned. "Now!"

He lifted his head, gave her a lopsided grin, and mounted her, slipping between her spread legs. He grabbed her by the thigh and hoisted her leg to his shoulder and slipped his swollen cock into her. It filled her with raging heat. He pumped in and out of her, and she rolled her hips to receive each thrust.

"I want you!" she whispered and lifted her hips to receive him. Her words seemed to excite him. He drove his cock deeper into her pussy and turned his face so his lips sucked against her leg. He lifted her from the bed, bringing her toward him and shifted so he now lay beneath her. He groaned when she straddled him and lifted from his cock slightly then lowered herself onto his throbbing shaft.

She flattened her hands against his chest and lifted forward, allowing herself to move up the length of his cock, and teased him, threatening to pull from him all together. He grabbed her buttocks and eased her back down his cock.

Giggling, she lifted from him again, but this time, he was not so gentle and seized a cheek in each hand and jerked her back onto his lap, holding her at the waist. He thrust into her.

"Did you think I was going to dismount?" she asked, unable to stop the giggling tease.

"Nae, lass, I dinna realize ye knew how to ride since ye do such a poor job with a horse," he laughed and slapped her ass. It startled her, but also sent pulses of pleasure throbbing to her clit.

"Oh, I shall ride you better than any horse, me laird."

"Aye, lass, ye seem more adept with this kind of riding," he chuckled.

It was such a warm, deep satisfied sound that sent her pulse pounding harder. If ever bliss had a moment of bursting to life, this was it. She ground against him, rolling her hips and stroking his steely cock. She teased him, moving slow, then quickly, then setting the pace to a slower grind.

"Teasing wench," he groaned and Jeanne found herself on her back again while he plunged his cock harder into her. The slapping sound vibrated in the chamber and she wrapped her legs about his waist, longing to hold him inside her forever.

His hard muscles flexed beneath her hands. She wanted to feel every inch of him, taste every part of him and possess fully. Her mind was liquid warmth. All thoughts of what had happened fled. There was only Mael. He was all she wanted and for now, being with him was all she needed.

All I Want

Streaks of hot pleasure shot up her spine. Firm lips captured hers as he plunged in and out, driving his frenzied passion through her. Her clit throbbed against each thrust, her own need driving her to grind against him, longing for more.

Her desire twisted from deep inside and spiraled up, bursting bright against her eyelids, throbbing in spasms, coiling and releasing, clamping against his hardness inside.

"Mael!" Her release captured her voice and roared to her head, bursting in wave after wave of intensity.

"My Jeanne. Never leave me. Promise me."

Reality shattered the enchantment. Jeanne pressed her lips into his neck and longed to forget everything but him.

* * * * *

"'Tis three days now, lass, open the door," Mael called from the other side of the door.

"Go away. I want to be alone," Jeanne sobbed, unable to control the emotions still seizing her since the morning after Trench had escaped. The same morning after Mael's ardent lovemaking. It had been a sweet release from so many things, but the light of day had revealed harsh truths. She could never go back to her time. Trench would rule her world. Mael was a constant painful reminder of her failure to stop Trench.

Over the course of the following days, she had sunk deeper into depression. At one point she feared she'd never be able to claw her way out. The weather turned colder and the first snow fell over the highlands. She stood with the fur wrapped about her, peering out at the bleak scene then padded from the window to stand in front of the roaring fire.

She avoided Mael. His absence only darkened her mood. She had failed to rescue Ryan and mourned her brother. He was now at the cruel mercy of Trench as was the entire world.

There were dark moments within the timelessness of night when she feared she'd go insane. She climbed back into the bed, pulled the covers underneath her chin, and slept once more.

When she awoke the next day, she lay peering between the curtains hung around the bed. She stared at the long tall windows where brilliant sunlight struggled to enter through the draperies. The winter storm was over. She sighed heavily. She had no purpose to rise, no reason to prepare for the new day. The same desolate truths she'd contemplated the day before would fill the day.

Each day the servants moved in and out of her room, bringing food, emptying her chamber pot, and occasionally one of the maids would attempt to help her groom by offering her a boar's bristle brush, or a basin of hot water. Jeanne would turn over in the bed, shutting her eyes to the world. She lay contemplating the fine stitching along the hem of the bed curtains, noting her mind was cloudy with the dull repetition of despair when the door jarred open.

"I came to get ye up and readied for the day." Missus MacRay barged into the chamber, jerking the bed curtain open.

"Dare you be so bold?" Jeanne sat up, glaring at the intruder.

"Aye, that I am. As the housekeeper for me laird, I decided to set ye from this bed." She jerked the covers off Jeanne and flung them to the two younger women who stood just inside the doorway.

"Get out!" She tugged against the remaining covers the old woman tried to pull from her.

"I dare not leave ye here to wallow in your grief. Whatever the cause, I care not. I know that ye blame me laird for your sorrows, but know that he is but half a man since ye took to your bed three days hence."

"No!" she screamed. "Get out! All of you!" She jumped from her bed, but cringed when her bare feet touched the harsh cold floor. She rushed over to the dying fireside and picked up the empty washbasin. "Leave!" She flung it at the two chambermaids. The wooden bowl slammed against the wall and splintered into pieces. The maids screamed and ran from the room. Their footfalls resounded from the stairwell as they fled her attack.

"Now, see what ye did?" Mrs. MacRay stood with her arms akimbo. She scrunched up her round face into a disapproving frown.

"Leave!" Jeanne held the pitcher above her head.

"And if I dinna? Will ye break open me head with that?" Mrs. MacRay's expression softened, and the look in her eyes shaded from anger to pity.

Suddenly the pitcher was heavy, and Jeanne lowered it to the table. Her knees weakened with the deep sobs rising into oceans of tears that spilled down her cheeks.

All I Want

Mrs. MacRay's big arms came around her. It was maternal comfort the other woman offered, and she seized it, letting the pain rush from her. She gasped with sobs as the housekeeper stroked her hair and murmured comforting words.

"There now, lass. 'Tis time to call an end to this suffering. Ye do no one good and only yourself harm. 'Tis time," she soothed.

Her emotions fully spent, she brushed back her tears and turned to the fire, embarrassed by her breakdown. She hugged herself against the chill of the room.

"Ye be just as stubborn as he." Mrs. MacRay set about pulling the heavy draperies open. The morning sunlight blasted into the room. Its warming rays moved over her back. Through blurred vision she turned to watch the housekeeper move about the chamber, picking up discarded clothing and the half-eaten soup from her evening meal.

"Ye are a fine match for me laird. As I said, I dinna know the reason for the rift between ye, but he lives all alone, having disowned his only living kin." She stopped her work and turned her full attention to Jeanne. "If ye have a warmth within your heart for him, lass, then turn to him with it, I beg ye."

The dam she'd set against her earlier breakdown trembled with pent-up emotions for Mael. She bit her lip and turned from the housekeeper's knowing look.

"Me brother, Ian, and meself helped the old laird raise those twins. Me husband died the year before and a comfort the bairns gave me." She didn't move, but continued her story, even though Jeanne had her back to her.

"No wee ones of me own, ye see, and with Mael and Ishabelle, in many ways they filled the place me own bairns would have held.

"And me brother, Ian, his wife died but a few weeks after me lady. Gave birth to a stillborn son, she did. I thought Ian would lose his mind and so the duties bestowed upon him to see to the twins' raising was a blessing for his heart's sorrow as well. Two blessings to two people. 'Twas a mystical omen.

"So ye understand, we may be the laird's servants, but in his heart and ours 'tis more. 'Tis a family, not of blood, but just as binding. The MacRaigl clan has always been different, lass. Stronger, closer, 'tis until…Ishabelle married the Tryon and cursed us all."

Jeanne spun around.

"You can't blame Ishabelle for this war. It was a man from *my* ti— clan who set Cullen de Mangus against Mael. He started the rumors and incited the assassins."

"Your loyalty shows and 'tis good, lass." Mrs. MacRay ignored her defense. "I shall send one of me lasses up to help ye with ye hair, if ye promise not to throw anything at her." She winked. "Hot water and soap will see ye feeling better." She didn't wait for Jeanne to respond and left the chamber.

Jeanne stared after her. The woman had not heard a word of Jeanne's confession. Exasperated, she fell into the chair. What was she to do now? If she were, in truth, trapped for the rest of her life somewhere in Medieval Scotland then Mael was no longer off-limits.

She contemplated her choices. Returning to her own time was impossible, regardless of Mael's new quest to find a way. The maid returned and brought a fresh bar of soap and another basin. She left as silently as she'd entered. Slowly, Jeanne bathed in front of the fireside.

An hour later, the two chambermaids returned and assisted her in washing her hair. It was a luxurious process and over an hour and several braids later, they left. She felt renewed and determined to rise from her feelings of helplessness.

The rap on the door startled her and before she could call out, it was shoved open.

"No longer trapped within the covers of your bed?" Mael stood in the opening with his hands clasped behind his back.

Her stomach lurched and seemed to turn upside down.

"Come in, Mael." She noted the dark circles underneath his eyes and the tired, drawn lines creasing his forehead.

"I feared ye still pined." He closed the door behind him, but did not venture further into the room.

"My brother was all the family I had, Mael, and he's lost to me forever." She wiped the tears from her eyes. "So you can understand my grief."

"Aye, ye do your brother no good by taking to your bed."

"True." She turned her back to him and stared blindly out the window.

"What do ye intend to do now?"

"I don't know."

All I Want

"As I told ye before, Jeanne lass, I shall see ye returned to your home."

She couldn't prevent the laughter bubbling from her chest. He suffered ridiculous delusions if he truly believed he could return her to her own time.

"The portal *closed*, Mael. It's gone—for another seven hundred and fifty-five years. At least the portal to my world. My time. It's over." She stood in front of the window and stared down at the snow covered landscape and courtyard below. There was no hope of ever going back. "This is my home now." The thought burst into bloom.

"It *can* be your home, Jeanne. But can ye be happy here?" Hope resonated in his voice, but when she lifted her gaze to his, there was only lackluster emptiness in his brown depths.

"I can be very happy with *you*." She took a deep breath and waited for his response.

"Ye fulfill my fondest dream, lass, yet there shall be a way for ye to return home."

"So you say." She shook her head and turned her back to him. "But you've yet to tell me what it is."

"Not yet."

"Whatever," she shrugged. What was the point of this? For the first time, she contemplated life in 1250 A.D. Scotland not as an intruder, but as a participant.

If this were to be her home for the remainder of her life, then she needed to join the rest of the world. She turned the thought over and paced the length of the chamber, pausing to stare out the window once more at the courtyard below.

"I shall see ye returned. I pledge my vow to this," Mael insisted and moved toward her.

"Let's just say you can't, okay? It isn't possible, and I must live here in MacRaigl Castle for the remainder of my life. What then, Mael? What will I do?"

"Ye are free to do what ye please, lass. What prevents ye from a life? What keeps ye confined to this room?"

"You do, Mael, with this insanity about returning me to my home." She unfolded her arms and took a deep breath, filling her lungs.

He seemed to contemplate her for a while then finally spoke.

"Would it make life easier for ye, if I dinna mention the plan until I have it worked out and ready to implement?"

"Yes." She let the long breath flow from her. She must deal with the facts. That's all there was. She was a scientist, and the facts told her there was no way home.

"Then it shall be so, Jeanne. My castle, 'tis your home."

Her cheeks rushed warm with the feel of his stare.

"Rumors have it that ye now become like Ishabelle and soon shall lurk about as a creature of the night. Should ye join me in the break-the-fast everyone shall witness this lie canna stand the light of day."

Jeanne heard the nervous catch in his voice, which he quickly cleared with a gruff cough. Her heartbeat pounded in her chest.

"I shall, Mael." She wondered why he had not moved to hold her. It was one thing to say the words of finality about her returning home, but another for him to accept.

"All ye need do, Jeanne, is ask, and I shall see that ye have it."

* * * * *

Several days passed and she busied herself tending to the servants' minor complaints. Her thoughts turned to her friend and teacher, Verica. Was the old woman well? She longed to go to the village but memories of the angry mob that nearly hanged her prevented her from striking out across the snow-covered hills. Perhaps come spring she would.

Mael kept his distance. Every day she wanted him more. She missed his attentiveness, his touch. She reassured herself that in time they could find a life together. Time might heal the hurts. She stopped him on his way out of the Great Hall early one morning.

"A word with you, Mael?"

"Aye, lass."

"You said I could ask for anything?"

"Aye."

"I would like a bathtub made." She glanced from him to the door.

"A bathtub? I have one in my chamber, lass."

"Yes, but I wish to have my own. I wish to bathe regularly in a tub. I am quite tired of bathing from a basin of water."

"What? But ye are not bloody from battle. Too much bathing shall make ye sick. A weekly bath suffices enough."

"Where I come from, Mael, we bathe daily."

"Daily?" He laughed out loud. "No mystery why your world 'tis dying."

"Will you do my bidding? I will also need hot water brought to me every night. Can you do that for me?"

"Aye. If it shall serve to make ye happy." His brown eyes reflected shards of passion.

Jeanne swallowed the rising fire and managed a short nod.

* * * * *

The chambermaids entered carrying a stack of folded linens, followed by the young man who had been her guard. He carried a wide wooden barrel that he set down in front of the fire.

The maids began to line the barrel with the sheets, draping them over the rough sides. It was great to be rid of the sponge baths. When she'd lived with Verica she'd taken frequent baths in the cold river. Suddenly, she was filled with delightful anticipation over having a tub bath. One maid handed her a bar of soap scented with sweet herbs.

"A razor?" Jeanne asked.

The women frowned at her.

"A knife?"

Warily, the three women left, mumbling among themselves. She frowned and decided she was pushing her luck asking for the knife. A knock sounded on her door and the older maid entered, holding up a small knife.

Jeanne smiled and thanked the girl. She barred the door then nearly skipped to the tub. She shifted the two bathing screens so the fire's warmth was trapped then eased into the luxurious bath. She could not remember when she'd enjoyed a bath so much. She took her time and worked the soap's lather into her hair then rinsed the soap from her hair with the extra buckets of water.

Afterwards, she dried her hair in front of the fire, feeling renewed. It had been several years since she'd created a French braid in her hair and without a good mirror she had to start over several times. She donned a smock, selecting a beige pair of hose and gartered them at the knees.

She went over to the wardrobe and ran her hand over the five kirtles. She appreciated her wealth in gowns. Few women owned more than a couple. She chose the purple gown embroidered with gold and green floral swirls. Next, she selected a tapestry-style shoe, silently thanking Ishabelle for her good taste in clothing.

Pausing in front of the small wall mirror, she turned sideways, patting her braided hair then reached for the door. She emerged from the chamber as a new woman—a medieval woman. Would Mael be pleased with her transformation? She swallowed the rising knot.

Thoughts of Trench threatened to send her back into the depression. Jeanne bowed her head, trying to separate her current life from her past.

"I cannot prevent that future." She took a cleansing breath of air. She was here for the duration and did not intend to spend it grieving. She deserved happiness.

Trembling, she started down the spiral staircase that led to the Great Hall. She wondered about Mael and if they might have a future together. Was that feasible? Her pulse spiked, and her breath quickened. Dare she even think of such possibilities?

His rich baritone laughter echoed from the Great Hall. Her pulse pounded harder, and her knees weakened when she stepped off the last riser. The heat rose from the room along with tempting aromas. Her stomach rumbled in response.

Immediately, her stare found his, and heated yearnings to feel his touch rushed over her. She licked the dryness from her lips and took a deep breath. Amid the din, several diners looked up from their conversations and meals but quickly averted their surprised glances as she made her way across the crowded expanse. Low murmurs followed in her wake.

Mael stood from his conversation and started toward her. A new wave of whispering washed over the room. She noticed the way his kilt swung with his determined gait, venting above his knees. Her pulse slipped a beat then raced frantically in her chest when his lips spread into a welcoming smile.

Everything in her seemed to melt into a hot pulsing mass as he drew closer. She halted in the aisle between the long, crude tables. The aroma of cooked pork and strong ale mingled with the hint of yeast bread and that ever-present scent of the Highlands. Her stomach did flip-flops as he extended his hand. She saw the appreciation in his eyes and was rewarded for her lengthy toilette.

"Welcome, fair Jeanne."

She grasped his hand, hoping he didn't notice how her palms were sweating. His brown eyes glinted with an unspoken question as he guided her toward his table, with one hand on her waist.

Jeanne managed a faint smile at the greetings the men and some of the women gave her as they passed.

"Sit here." Ian was quick to his feet, vacating the chair beside Mael's place and forcing everyone to change seats to make room.

"Good evening, Ian," Jeanne smiled warmly at his friendly face. She sat down beside Mael, and someone placed a bowl of hotchpotch in front of her. One thing she had noticed about this century was the heavy use of spices not so much for enriching flavor but for masking spoiled meat. She was appalled how little was known about common sense food preparation. She marveled that the human race had survived such primitive conditions and thought of the plagues of the food industry from her own times and shuddered.

A mug of mead was placed in front of her. Self-conscious, she ate slowly and glanced about the Hall, surprised that the meat was fresh and delicious. Several men stared at her, and a few nodded. She immediately recognized the guarded looks, followed by low comments. Mael downed the ale, staring at her. She met his twinkling gaze and smiled slightly, bowing her head.

"Did you trim your beard?" She leaned over to him, trying to gauge the shorter length of his beard.

"Aye," he chuckled.

"Why? It's winter. I'm sure it protects you from the cold."

"Barbarians ignore social morés. I am not a barbarian."

"What?" Jeanne blinked at him.

"We have our ways, but dinna mean we live ignorant of the world. I know that most no longer sport the hair beyond their shoulders, and the face made clean-shaven."

"What are you talking about, Mael? Fashion?" Perplexed, Jeanne stared at him. She tried to keep the laughter from bubbling to her lips.

"I suppose I am. Would not harm us to modernize our ways a bit."

"Modernize?" She could not stop the giggle. She reached to touch his arm and the feel of his muscled arm beneath her fingertips excited her. "I don't mean to sound unkind. I just don't understand what's going on. I mean what is this about?"

"I just wanted to give ye something more refined to look upon." He reached up and covered her hand with his. His eyes shone huge with tenderness.

"You did it for me?" Her eyes stung with hot tears.

"I certainly dinna do so for them." He nodded at his men.

Her smile rushed from inside her and spread over her lips.

"Careful, lass." Ian leaned over. The ale coated his breath. "'Tis a heart he seeks. Yours," he whispered in her ear.

"What ye saying there, Ian?" Mael leaned over her and glared at the older man. The heat from Mael's body radiated over her.

"I say, when shall we call out Cullen?"

Jeanne sensed Mael's muscles tense.

"We shall discuss another time, Ian," he nearly growled at the other man.

"Ye have neglected the problem too long as 'tis."

"'Tis my problem to do just that."

"'Tis a problem for our clan and if ye want to be made Chief, ye shall take care of Cullen without further delay." Ian leaned closer, trapping her between their conversation.

"Must ye spoil the night?" Mael leaned in to whisper to her, "My apologies. Ian is *less* civilized than the rest of us." His face was inches from her and his hot breath fell over her lips. Her arousal was instant. She couldn't move.

"Another man was killed today," Ian announced.

Chapter Twenty-Two

Mael straightened in his chair and glared over her head to Ian.

"Why do ye wait until now to inform me? Why do ye wait to spoil the lass's night?"

"I dinna plan the timing, me laird." Ian spoke louder, and the hall stirred with hushed voices. "Just the way it unfolds this very eve. Emmett was murdered just after sunset."

Mael's breath left him in a huff as he stared out over the crowded room. Wood scraped against wood, and the room appeared to stand en masse and face their long table.

"We canna stand by and let the Mangus join with the Fareley clan. Others shall follow," one of the men spoke.

"Aye, now 'tis the time to put the murderers down."

"'Tis time to seize your birthright, MacRaigl! MacRaigl!" the chant rose louder. Sword hilts banged on the tables and fists slashed the air.

"Ye old manipulator," Mael cursed Ian, who slumped back in his chair with a satisfied smirk.

What had she just witnessed? Had Ian been waiting for her recovery so he could push Mael into claiming the Chief role of the clan? Why had Mael delayed confronting the rebels? What war tactics was he playing?

"Enough!" Mael banged his cup onto the table. The silence was a wave that started along the front row of men and rolled all the way to the back of the hall. "I shall meet with the Lairds on the morrow and settle this once and for all."

A boisterous cheer went up and soon the room filled with shouts. A bagpipe wheezed into a tune and a reel broke out among the diners. He fell back into his chair with a thunderous sigh, glaring behind her to Ian.

"There now, Ian, are ye pleased with yourself? Now we have a war on our hands."

"Nae, now we shall have a Chief." Ian raised his cup in a toast.

Jeanne sat watching the frenzy of the Hall grow and swell as though it would burst from the very walls. The bagpipes ground out the lively music. Her stomach tied in knots, and she sat back from the table unable to eat.

"Come, lass." Mael offered his hand and stood from the table.

She placed her hand in his. Excited pulses moved up her arm as she let her fingers lace through his. How she loved the way his hand felt. He escorted her from the hall amidst the cheers and wishes for a lovely evening, leading her to the shortest route from the room, which was the side courtyard.

Once outside, the blustery fall wind tore through their clothes, as though the mischievousness of the hall had been unleashed onto the world. She shivered and his arm came around her, with the folds of his tartan warming her. They walked in silence toward the tower and he handed her up into the doorway, then moved around her, leading the way up the winding stairs. Her heart slammed against her chest when he stopped outside his chamber door and turned to her.

"A word with ye is what I ask," he spoke before she could voice her objection and swung the door open. The gentle plea in his eyes melted her prepared refusal. She stepped past him into the room.

A fire crackled from the fireplace giving the room a seductive gold light that washed over his face. He secured the door behind them and motioned her to warm herself near the fire while he poured them a silver chalice of wine.

"To your recovery." He pushed the goblet into her trembling hand and touched his to hers. The metal clink broke the silence accompanied by the popping and spewing of the fire.

"Mael," her voice quivered.

"Shhh." He lifted the goblet to his lips and sipped the wine.

She clutched hers between icy fingers, staring up into his fiery eyes. Her mouth dried and suddenly the room was scorching. She tilted the cup to her mouth and downed the wine as though it were water. The alcohol rushed through her and buzzed warmly to her head. His fingers closed over hers, trapping them against the cold, smooth goblet.

"I wanted this night to be a pleasant one, but Ian had his own plans."

She trembled. His closeness filled her senses and when he took the goblet from her, she had to clasp her hands together to keep from throwing her arms around his neck.

"Do ye know what kind of evening I planned for ye?" He took her hands in between his. They were large hands that completely consumed hers. All she could do in response to his question was swallow the knot tightening in her throat.

"I planned for ye to enjoy an evening of fun in the Hall with special dishes prepared just for ye and this fine wine. I wanted to dance with ye and watch ye laugh. Then once I'd charmed ye silly," he said, spreading his lips into a disarming smile, "I would bring ye here, to my bed." Mael leaned over her and let his lips brush her cheek. "And here I would undress ye, shower your silky body with kisses then take ye as I have never taken any woman."

The light touch of his kiss sent wave after wave of delight down to her feet.

"Mael." His name tugged from her. His kiss slipped up her neck to her ear.

"Then I was going to hold ye in my arms all night, my Jeanne." His hot breath scorched into her ear with his words lingering in her mind. His arms formed a loop about her, and he pulled her to him. He was intoxicating. She slipped her arms around his neck. Her passion cascaded over the walls she'd erected. Her need throbbed between her legs.

His lips poised on the arch of her neck while his tongue darted its own teasing path. He smelled so wonderful of soap and some other scent she couldn't place, but it was enchanting. He had even trimmed his beard for her.

"It has been so long since our time together on the hill and then that night when Trench—"

"Hmm." She nuzzled her face in his hair, cradling his head and allowing her fingers to explore his thick braid. She needed to see him without the braid, with his hair as wild as his passion.

"A man in great agony has been my lot." His hands moved over her and pressed her harder into him. His hard cock brushed against the folds of her clothing.

Nimbly, she unbraided his hair, letting the thin slips of plaid and leather fall forgotten to the floor. His breath released hot against her flesh as she combed her fingers through the wavy lengths. His hair fell below his shoulders midway to his back.

She luxuriated in him. He was powerful, and though a savage by modern definition, he was everything she wanted. And she wanted him, now. Turning her head, she reached for his kiss.

Her lips melted into his. Their groans entwined and lashed together. His back was rigid and his brawny muscles flinched under her touch. She kneaded his back, arching herself so her hips ground into his hard shaft.

This proved more than he could endure for he quickly grasped her buttocks and pulled her against him, lifting her from the floor. He carried her with him to the massive hand-carved bed and gently lowered her to it.

"My Jeanne," he moaned against their kiss. She tore at her clothing, trying to free herself so she could feel his hardness against her. He lifted from her and stood over the bed with the golden glow of the fire silhouetting him. He jerked the brooch free of his tartan, and it fell from his shoulder. He was so unaware of the effect his pose had on her. His long wavy hair fell about him and the ties of his linen shirt lay partially unlaced, revealing his chest.

The tease was more than she could bear. A deep-throated moan ground from her. His attention shot to her like a flash of lightning, and in one swift movement, he freed himself of the plaid. It fell to his feet.

"Mael," Jeanne gasped, letting her stare travel his physique. He was a mass of muscles. He had muscles she never knew a man could have. His six-pack would make a modern man look puny. He took long strides to her. His cock was erect and bigger than she recalled. She tugged against the confines of her own clothing, but her fingers merely fumbled in the effort because she was so mesmerized by him. She worked the laces of her bodice and finally slipped from the bed, so she could step out of the gown.

She turned just as he closed the distance between them. Eagerly, she stepped into his embrace and entwined his neck within the loop of her arms. His powerful muscles flinched under her touch. His kiss was hungry and demanding. Once more, his passion overwhelmed her, becoming hers with a need of its own. She lifted her leg around his hip and his hand slipped to her thigh, pulling her into him. His hot cock throbbed against her heat now molten between her legs in her need to feel him inside her.

All I Want

He broke from her kiss, tearing a groan from her and nibbled down her neck to the base of her throat. She reared back and displayed the length of her neck for him to explore, while his hands kneaded her back, slipping to her hips. He lifted her and set her onto his cock, slipping between the moist lips of her pussy, and pulled her down onto his length. She writhed under the sensations, gasping with the sheer pleasure each thrust gave to her as he fucked her standing up. His hand slipped around her other thigh, and he brought her legs around him so that she rode his waist while he supported both of them with his strong legs. He drove his cock into her, thrusting in and out. His other hand bore down on her shoulder. Jeanne met his thrusts with her own, riding him in a wave of delightful sensations. He was as solid and hard as any boulder erupting from a hillside.

He shifted and slid her onto the edge of the bed, gripping the poster with one hand while he continued to pump himself into her. He planted one hand by her head and grasped her buttock with his other, pulling his cock in and out in a tease with a breath of hesitation before driving it deeper into her. The fire crackled and roared brighter behind him, and Jeanne clung to his corded arms, longing to taste his lips against hers.

As though truly of one mind, he lowered his head and locked his lips with hers. The sound vibrated in her throat, and a hot tear slipped from the corner of her eye, rolling from her face into her braided hair. Her very soul seemed to break from her body and rush to meet his.

She moved her hips so he slipped in and out of her pussy with hard thrusts. His heat increased, driven by her own passion. He slammed his cock into her with his balls slapping against her. She ground her hips in a circular motion, longing for him to come, and knowing she could not restrain her own climax any longer, she released under the passion and heat. Her body jerked in wave after wave of ecstasy as she came hard. She grasped his buttocks and pulled him into her, longing to be lost forever in the moment. The second current pumped up her spine like a rolling wave. The heat pulsated from her clit until unleashed, the sensation roared all the way up her back and out through the top of her head in one shuddering, powerful burst of orgasm.

She cried out, feeling herself close around his hard cock, longing to feel it all over again, basking in the delightful sensations he'd brought her. He thrust his cock harder, with a quickened rhythm. He ground himself deeper into her, groaning out his pleasure until his passion burst and exploded deep inside her. Shuddering, he reared back and released a deep satisfied groan. His breath tunneled a heated path over her.

She trailed the backs of her hands up and down his back through the heated rivers of sweat, cooling his body with her movements. He jerked in a continuous rocking as his orgasm ebbed and receded. He leaned over her, panting, bowing his head between his wide shoulders.

His cock still throbbed inside her. She lowered her legs to the mattress with a satisfied sigh warming her entire body. Neither of them spoke. It required too much energy. They lingered in that space of extreme satisfaction and stared at each other in the dimness of firelight.

Mael supported his weight on his elbows. The undulating surges gripped him and carried him through the pulses of such pleasure he knew he'd die of sheer joy. He hung his head and watched her round breasts rise and fall. His tongue longed to taste their rosy nipples, but he was frozen in place, unable to muster the strength to unlock his arms and collapse onto the mattress beside her.

His gaze melded with hers, and he wanted her more than the previous moment when he'd spilled himself into her. Lazily, her lips parted into a contented grin. She raised her hand and trailed an index finger along his flexed arm.

Taunting goose bumps chased after her fingertips. Mael lifted his head slightly when her hand moved up his arm again. He brushed his lips against her finger then sucked it into his mouth. His tongue made love to her finger. He sucked harder. His stare found her blazing one, and the heat in his body surged once more to his groin. He smiled at her startled expression as his hardness grew inside her. His desire raged anew.

She tugged her finger from his mouth, but he nipped it between his teeth and tenderly pressed his bite into her skin. The reaction was greater than he'd anticipated for she flattened her hands on the mattress and lifted herself to him. Mael released her finger and caught her eager kiss. He shifted and gently pushed her back onto the mattress. Supporting himself on his hands, her fingers played the line where his beard and smooth skin met. He smiled against her kiss.

"What is it?" She pulled from him.

"Happiness." He covered her next words with his kiss and gathered her to him, rolling her on top of him. He lay on his back, marveling at her beauty as she settled on his cock. Seductive strokes up her arms rewarded him with her soft wanton moan.

"I want to see ye with your hair unbound." He began working the massive plait and soon freed her hair, working his fingers through its thickness.

A groan rode his breath as she lifted from him then lowered herself down his steely shaft, moving it in and out of her pussy. She was moist and hot and ready for him. She rode him harder, lifting her hips from him, pulling from his cock and lingering long enough to drive him to the edge of control, only to lower herself onto him once more, driving his cock deeper inside her. She threaded her hands through his, and lifted his arms above his head.

"Ye torture me, lass," he groaned.

"I'll shackle you, Mael of the MacRaigls, and show you just what torture is."

The thought sent excited shudders through him.

"Ye torture me as 'tis, my love."

Her full breasts brushed against his chest then lifted from him again. Her hips undulated as she ground against him. Mael cupped her breasts in his hands and closed his eyes with the sudden surges coursing through him. He released her soft mounds and relaxed against the mattress. His hand scraped the dirk's sheath entangled in the bed linens with his tunic.

"Will ye be mine, Jeanne?" he murmured up to her.

Perspiration glistened on her satiny skin. Her eyes reflected the fire of her love.

"I *am* yours, Mael."

"Then will ye join me in a handfast?" he whispered, struggling to stave off the insistent excitement demanding fulfillment. It took all his willpower to rein his desire.

"Handfast?" she slurred and rolled her head to one side, her hair cascading wildly over her face, falling against her shoulder.

Mael sat up and held her to him, grasping her hips between his hands.

"My God, ye are so comely, my Jeanne." He buried his head between her breasts, letting his tongue flicker over one nipple.

Her throaty moan greeted his tender nibble. His other hand closed over the hilt of his dirk as he pulled it from his sheath, dragging the corner of his tartan with it. He straightened from her, and she broke her rhythm momentarily to glance down at his hand.

"Dinna fear," he said to quickly reassure her, "ye know I would never ye harm." He lifted the short knife and slipped the blade into the tartan and sliced the material into a narrow strip.

"What are you doing?" The concern in her voice was absent of fear. Mael was relieved by her trust.

"A handfast, my Jeanne. See?" He held up the strip of plaid and gave it to her.

Poised with him still erect inside her, Jeanne sat on him with a curious expression replacing the heated one of desire.

"Mael?" She seemed exasperated with his interruption.

"An act of my passion, my Jeanne. Do ye ken?"

"Is this a custom?"

Mael could not resist the laughter that rumbled from his chest.

"Aye, can be consummated, but generally the ceremony comes first with many in attendance." He moved under her and was rewarded by her quick response of rolling hips. "But I want to do this now. At this very moment. Do ye object?"

"Oh Mael, you truly possess a romantic soul." She planted a kiss on his forehead.

"Aye," he shrugged, feeling self-conscious. Gently, he lifted her from him and rose onto his knees beside her. "But I wish to seal my love for ye. This is the way. A handfast. What better time to partake than during the moment of consummation?"

She kneeled in front of him, and Mael followed her wide-eyed gaze at his glistening erection.

"I promise I shall not keep it from ye for very long." He adored the way she blushed in front of him. The rosy color washed all over her beautiful body. His heart pounded harder, and the pulsing in his groin demanded release.

"Come," he said and rose from the bed. "We shall do this in front of the fire." He met her gaze and was lost in her blue eyes. Beads of sweat formed along his spine. He reined in the excruciating need for her as though it would erupt any moment. He wanted her more than anything he'd ever wanted and tonight he was going to make her his. He lifted the knife.

"What's with the knife?" Her attention centered on the threatening blade.

"An instrument of ceremony. Do ye have yours?"

"Ceremony?" she gulped and held up the plaid.

His gaze fell to her full breasts. He ached to taste her, suckle her and lay her back onto his bed and fuck her. He reached for the goblet and dipped the blade into the wine.

"The blade is man and the wine is woman." He lifted his left palm to hers.

"I thought it was the wrists." Her eyes widened on the knife. "Don't you cut the wrists to bind?"

"For my clan 'tis the palms we bleed, instead of the wrists, for they symbolize the love we each hold within the palms of our hands. Ye hold my love, my heart, within your hand, my Jeanne." He drew the blade across his palm and winced under the slight cut. His blood rushed in response. And he cupped his hand to pool the blood.

"I pledge my heart to ye, Jeanne McBen. To thee I belong and no other. In the presence of all my ancestors, by the name MacRaigl, I give ye myself, mind, body and soul. Forever and always."

"Mael?" she cried out, when he seized her hand.

"Do ye take me, Jeanne McBen?" He held her palm in front of the knife. Her hand trembled against the blade as he poised to finish the ceremony. It seemed an eternity. His breath caught in his chest as he waited for her reply. What if she said no? He could not hold the thought in his mind. There was only one answer. She had to love him.

"Oh Mael!" she gasped between sobs. "Of course I take you. You are all I want." She bit her lower lip and squinted her eyes shut in anticipation of the knife's cut.

He did the deed quickly but she still pulled from the sudden pain. His hold tightened around her wrist. He pressed her cut into his and clasped their palms together.

At first, Jeanne tried to jerk from the contact of his blood then reminded herself it was safe. She released a ragged breath and watched as he slipped the plaid from her other hand and wrapped it about their hands. He then tied their left hands together.

"The binding is not tight, so either can be free whenever so desired," he smiled down at her and gathered a loose curl between his fingers, and tucked it over her shoulder. Their breaths filled the room, and the heat from the fire radiated around their naked bodies.

He bent over her and claimed her lips, nearly bruising them in his fierce passion. Tears burned trails of joy down her throat. Their bound hands were crushed between their bodies. She broke from his kiss and raised her hand along with his above her head, so she could feel his hard body pressed against hers.

He guided her back to bed, taking care their hands were still bound together. She sat down on the mattress beside him and his other arm came around her while the hand he'd bound to hers brushed against her cheek.

"Now we are tied by our blood. No man can claim ye his. My wife ye are, Jeanne. I vow this night that we are one for as long as there be love."

"Is that what we just did, Mael? Married?" Realization seeped in through the fog clouding her thoughts. Hot tears rushed to fill her eyes. She could not marry Mael. If she did, how could she ever leave him were she to find a way back to her own time?

"Aye, ye are my wife." He lowered her to the bed and gently separated her legs so he could ease between them. "For a year and a day." He planted tiny kisses over her face.

"A year and a day?" she repeated.

"If ye dinna wish me husband at the end of that time, we simply shall no longer remain married. But," he said and drew their hands still tied to each other over her head onto the coolness of the pillow, "if ye claim me husband at the end of that time, then so I shall be as long as there be love betwixt us."

"You married me?" She still couldn't believe what had just happened.

"Me seed ye already had in ye, Jeanne, now I give ye me married one." His lips covered hers. The wanting returned stronger than before, and all worries fled. All she could concentrate on was her husband.

He slipped between her legs and plunged his swollen cock into her pussy. She lifted her legs and wrapped them around his waist, moving with each thrust, rolling her hips with delightful sensations rushing up her spine.

Chapter Twenty-Three

Jeanne rode the night in wave after wave of ecstasy held in the sensual arms of Mael MacRaigl. Her husband. She considered herself a modern woman and fairly sophisticated, but she quickly learned she knew very little about the art of making love. She'd never known there were so many ways for a man to please a woman. Mael was a master and some of his techniques Jeanne had never heard of, much less contemplated. Had her world lost more than she realized? How could a whole way of human sensual love have been lost in the years between his and hers?

She wondered about these things as she lay in the early morning hours, with his arms and legs entwined with hers. His chest rose slowly beneath her head with his strong heartbeat pounding against her ear. Raising her hand, she examined the fresh cut and slowly wound the discarded fasting plaid around it, securing it into itself.

"What do ye ponder so?" his voice startled her.

"I thought you were asleep." She nuzzled into the warm curve of his neck, reveling in how it felt to press her body against his. Her lips found his, and she was lost again in his passion.

He spread her legs and traced his tongue from her belly button over her stomach to her pussy. He flickered the tip of his tongue against her clit, while thrusting two fingers into her, just enough to make her writhe and undulate under his rhythm. He sucked against her clit, nibbling ever so gently, sending streaks of pleasure up her body. He fucked her with his fingers drawing rasps of pleasure from her until she burned too hot, then he stopped, sending her into an agonized wail.

He flipped her onto her stomach and she rose on her knees. Lifting her hips so she could receive him, cool air brushed against the damp lips of her pussy but was quickly replaced by the heat of his cock. He grasped her hips and drove himself inside her, plunging his cock deeper.

"Take me, Mael," she said, moving against his thrusts, longing for that pinnacle of pleasure he'd spoiled her to expect each time. He rubbed his fingers against her clit and rammed his cock into her pussy, pounding her harder. Her heat rose and fanned through her body. She cried out as it exploded, ringing in her ears as waves of release climaxed in her. He came with her and huffed against her ear, groaning. He ground into her and pressed harder with a final thrust, then collapsed with her onto the mattress, panting. Sweat bonded them as they lay with his cock still throbbing inside her. He slipped from her, not moving, with his head buried in the pillow beside her. He released a deep-throated groan of pure satisfaction.

"That's what my world calls a quickie." She glided her hand over his muscular shoulder, tracing the sinewy outline down his strong back where his torso narrowed to his waist. Her heart skipped a beat when she let her touch move over his buttocks, admiring their indented sides and firmness. She flicked the dark spot on the side of his buttock, but it didn't move.

His laughter fanned hot from the pillow.

"'Tis not a fleck but a part of me."

"What is it? A birthmark?" She rose up to examine it and quickly realized it was a tattoo.

"The mark of my *máthair's* family. Her *máthair* was French, but her *máthair's* family lived here on this land before the MacRaigls and were renowned for their gift of the second sight. They were known as Picts," he said with his voice lowered an octave. "Not many in my clan know of my heritage. 'Tis best they dinna know." He folded his arms underneath the pillow and glanced over his shoulder at her, clearly enjoying her examination.

"Why would you need to keep your heritage a secret?" She traced the tattoo that wound into a Celtic knot of great detail and intricate lines with her fingertip, then bent lower to kiss it. He chuckled.

"The Picts were fierce warriors, but they were conquered by their enemy. Most were killed but some of the conquerors took the women for wives. The Picts were feared for the powers they held. And ye know how my clansmen believe in superstitions."

Jeanne had to laugh. She bent over to nibble at his buttock. He flinched under her small bite.

"Ishabelle has the sight. Like myself, she, too, bears the mark of our ancestry. Only two living people know about the mark."

"Ian and Missus MacRay?" she asked.

"Aye." His voice bore out his appreciation for her astuteness. "'Tis the legacy of the mark that it remain secret and be received soon after birth."

Jeanne lowered her lips to the tattoo and kissed it, again feeling such a part of him that her heart filled to bursting. When she released her kiss, he moved, pulling her into his arms and back onto the mattress with him. He was so much larger than she, but she felt safe within his embrace.

"I love ye, my Jeanne." His words drifted over her like a lullaby.

* * * * *

The sound awoke her like the blast of a trumpet. What was it? She squinted against the harsh sunlight streaming through the window.

"Mael?" she called out and looked about the deserted room. He was gone! She lifted her hand and stretched her palm wide. The cut stung in response. She must put a salve on it before it became infected. She made a mental note that she must tend to Mael's cut, too.

The fire in the grate still burned bright. She smiled. He must have added more wood before he'd left. Only where had he gone? Dragging the bedding with her, she tripped over to the long window and opened the shutter.

The courtyard was crowded, and the sound that had awakened her sounded again. Dogs. Her heart pounded harder. The pack of hounds reared their heads back and howled in unison.

"The assassin's scent lingers!"

Her pulse quickened as she recognized his voice and scanned the courtyard for him. She pressed her face against the window and looked down the side of the building where he apparently stood on the steps.

"We shall find him," Ian's voice drifted from below.

The groom led Mael's horse across the courtyard. He stepped from the castle. The morning mist seemed to roll from the moat to greet him. Patches of snow still clung to the mountainside. Her heart pounded a frantic beat in her throat. He wore a dark brown tunic with his plaid pinned and belted. He slung a dark fur wrap over his shoulders, his hair hung in one thin braid on either side of his face. Jeanne squinted and pressed her forehead against the cold glass pane. He had some kind of markings on his face.

"Set the hounds loose," his voice boomed, and the ropes around the hounds were removed.

She struggled to unlatch the window so she could call out to him. He swung into his saddle, took the sword from the servant and then reined the stallion from the courtyard toward the bridge.

She pivoted and was out the door, descending the stairs as fast as she could with the cumbersome bedding. When she reached the bottom landing, she threw open the courtyard door but she was too late. It was deserted. The thundering sound of the horses crashed against the high-pitched wailing of the dogs as they bounded over the drawbridge.

She slammed the door and retraced her steps to Mael's chamber. Tossing the covers aside, she jerked her clothes from the floor where she'd so hastily discarded them. Every detail of their night as husband and wife sent waves of need throbbing between her legs. He'd taken off to God knows where. She would ride after him. The thought of staying in the castle awaiting his return was maddening. Hurrying from the chamber, she descended the steps and entered the Great Hall. Only a few servants remained, cleaning up after the morning meal. She quickened her stride, noting the confused looks of the women sweeping the floor and spreading new rushes and herbs.

"Where is Ma—the Laird?" she demanded, surprised at the possessive tone in her voice.

"The men pursue the one who murdered Emmett." The woman glanced up from her work.

"What are ye about this morning, lass? Me laird said ye were not to be disturbed and ordered a plate be sent up to ye." Mrs. MacRay stood in the doorway leading to the pentice, the covered walkway between the Great Hall and the kitchen. Her sleeves were rolled to her elbows and her hair, dripping from the heat in the kitchen, was caught in an elongated cap.

"How was Emmett murdered?" she asked, frowning at the way the woman looked at her as though she knew Jeanne had spent the night in Mael's arms. She raised her chin slightly.

"The same as all the others. Puncture marks and all the blood drained."

The room spun around her. Jeanne felt as though she were hyperventilating. Trench had gone through the portal. She reached for the chair, but missed. Mrs. MacRay was quick to steady her.

"There, lass. Sit down a bit." She helped Jeanne into the chair. Her mind raced with the possibilities. The old woman pulled a small pouch from her pocket and shoved the foul leather purse underneath Jeanne's nose. Holding her hand up in front of her, she fought to push it from her.

The older woman halted in her attempt, grabbing Jeanne's hand in hers.

"What have ye done?" She held Jeanne's palm up to her. The woman mumbled something then bowed to Jeanne. "Please forgive me, me lady. Me laird said nothing to me. I knew not a handfast had been made."

Jeanne stared from her palm to the housekeeper, uncertain what to say.

"I understand your consternation to find your bridegroom missing from your bed this morn." Mrs. MacRay regained her composure. "I shall prepare a celebration for this evening." She started to turn, when Jeanne reached out and grabbed her by the arm.

"A word, Missus MacRay."

"Aye?" The woman paused, her expression fell when she met Jeanne's look.

"A secret you have fallen upon. One your laird obviously wishes to keep since he failed to share it with you this morning."

"Aye?" Her large face scrunched up into a perplexed scowl.

"Until he decrees our union in public I beg you keep our secret."

The woman's confusion waned in her eyes then she patted Jeanne's hand.

"I understand. The timing would not be right until he secured his place as Chief," she said. "I understand why he chose ye for his wife. Ye think like a MacRaigl already, lass. I shall prepare a plate for ye and have it brought to *your* chamber?" Her heavy eyebrows arched high as she waited for Jeanne's response.

"Yes, my chamber, for now," she said and sighed with relief. Perhaps it would be best to retreat to her chamber until Mael returned. Besides, she needed to tend to her cut. She could not risk anyone else noticing it.

Once inside her room, Jeanne set about dressing the cut. Jolting currents streaked in her stomach. Nervousness coiled in the pit of her belly. How could there still be one of Trench's victims when she had witnessed his return to their own time? It wasn't possible. She couldn't eat the bread and venison Mrs. MacRay sent to her. At length, she spent the day pacing her chamber as though she were a prisoner. The only conclusion was Trench had shared his secret with his clansmen and left his tools behind so they could continue terrorizing the world. The last reddish rays of day slipped behind the mountains, and the coldness of night settled over the village and behind the castle walls. The men had not returned. Her fear became reality.

The rap on her door startled her.

"Your meal, lass." Mrs. MacRay's muffled voice followed. Without waiting for a response the servant entered carrying a tray and set down on the table. "Haggis, barley bannocks, crowdie, a bit of cheese, and a nice pitcher of heather ale to wash it all down. Perhaps your appetite returns with the setting sun?"

"Perhaps."

"The men shall not return this night," Mrs. MacRay announced as she stopped by the door. Jeanne sat down at the small table by the fireplace.

"You received word from them?" She could not mask the hope in her voice. She felt Mrs. MacRay had become her ally since they now shared a secret.

"Nae. I see the hope shining in your eyes. They shall not journey at night. Had they found the raiders, they would have returned by now. 'Tis worrisome being separated so soon after your marriage." Mrs. MacRay closed the door behind her.

Jeanne didn't dare speak her deepest fear that the assassins had perhaps found Mael and his men, first. She had not developed a taste for haggis, but managed to eat the Scottish dish as long as she didn't think about it being made from a sheep's stomach, ignoring the ingredients used to stuff it. If she concentrated on the liver and heart of sheep or beef combined with oatmeal and onions, she'd never be able to swallow it. She ate but had to rush to the garderobe soon after. She suspected some of the meat was spoiled and was grateful Mael's castle had a private toilet for his chambers. She must train the cooks on proper curing of meat and other basic hygiene. She spent the remainder of the night making several quick trips to the garderobe and paced her chamber worrying about him.

The next morning, feeling better, but tired, she awoke to the vacant place beside her. She stretched out her hand, letting it glide over the cool linens.

"Mael. I want you," she whispered, with an edgy rawness tingling between her legs.

She dressed quickly and ventured to his private solar, hoping to find some comfort in being surrounded by his books and other possessions. The stone floor was identical to hers, but unlike her chamber this one held rows of bookshelves along the circular walls. She felt as though she were on a treasure hunt, knowing that her brother would have been envious of her finds. She closed her eyes and said a prayer for Ryan and another one for Mael.

Her pulse sharpened when she realized an illuminated manuscript lay open on the narrow tall table. Was it possible? She marveled at its antiquity. The thought of its value in her own time made her mind whirl. She wondered if it had survived to 2005.

Her fingers caressed the left-hand page. It was completely covered with hand-drawn Celtic patterns. How had Mael come to possess this book? She knew about St. Columba and the monastery he'd established in Iona during the late 500s. She'd even visited the abbey on her last trip to Scotland. Could this be one of the Saint's books or was it a more recent work? She would ask Mael when he returned.

She reasoned boundaries might not have been as defined in the past and since Irish monks had been known to travel all over the European continent, it was possible such a monk had stayed with Mael's ancestors. She regretted her own limited knowledge of Scottish history and wished she could translate the text. If she only had a computer. She snorted. In her own time, she would have done a search and found all the historical data she needed. She soon became frustrated and left the haven, hurrying across the courtyard past the kitchen.

Her mind wondered about her place within the clan. The last few months' events had cemented the suspicions surrounding her. If she were going to remain in this time with Mael, then she must first focus on damage control.

Once he announced their marriage she would undertake educating Mrs. MacRay and the kitchen staff about boiling water and handwashing with boiled water and soap. From there, she would eliminate spoiled meat from their diets and teach them how to cure it or even smoke it. Granted she had never participated in such chores, but she'd read enough over the course of her life to make a reasonable stab at it.

With the waning of day, her concern for Mael grew even more. Walking toward the East tower, she hoped to find some comfort in the small chapel and climbed the steps to the second floor. Standing outside the door, she was overwhelmed with an intense feeling of…familiarity. She reached for the latch but hesitated. She had never ventured into the chapel, feeling out of place with the morning prayers some of the castle residents tried to maintain until the replacement priest arrived.

According to Mrs. MacRay, the last priest had fallen victim to a fever. Spoiled meat, no doubt, Jeanne winced. She had never known Mael to attend the informal prayers and wondered if he had when the priest had officiated.

She leaned forward so her ear flattened against the door and strained to hear if anyone was inside. Slowly, she pushed to heavy door open and blinked against the darkened room. Immediately, her attention was drawn to the series of stained glass windows offset behind an archway. In front of them was an altar covered in white linen. A large gold cross and tall tapers lay in wait of the new priest.

She swallowed the thickness in her throat and took a hesitant step into the private chapel. The walls appeared to be stucco and painted in a brilliant gold. As she moved closer to the altar, her breathing quickened. The windows had been scaled to the size of the room with two small scenes in each one. All five of them were capped with an arched panel of glass that reflected a gold Celtic knot. The windows were rich in colors and intricate designs depicting scenes from the bible.

She stood in the center of the room with the silence ringing in her ears. The chapel was bathed in soft afternoon light that faintly touched the stained glass. She could imagine how brilliant it must be with morning sunlight blasting through them.

The silence seeped into her loneliness. If she lost Mael, then what would she have to sustain her in this world? How would she make a place for herself? She'd have to leave this area and go where no one knew her. It would not be easy. It would be a harsh life.

The chapel darkened. Panic moved over her and wouldn't let go. She'd been cast in a role she'd not chosen. It was uncomfortable being suspected and feared in the eyes of the world. She would not become a martyr to the legacy Trench had left in his wake. She would show the villagers and those within the castle walls that she was no one to fear, if it was the last thing she did. She would make a home here for herself and Mael.

Her pulse quickened. God, where was he? Was he safe? Was he hurt?

"Come home to me, Mael," she whispered.

* * * * *

They had tracked the rebels for two days. Mael was ready to return home. He'd gone to the Great Hall for the morning meal when they'd been interrupted with the news. The traitor had been identified. When confronted, Angus Hamilton had bolted for the gate only to be slain by the guards.

There were those who knew of his blood tie to Cullen de Mangus, and the plot began to unfold. Hamilton had been responsible for letting the assassins into MacRaigl Castle. He had guided Fareley and Trench inside using the west wall entrance.

Fareley, upon hearing the news of Hamilton's death, had rallied a band of raiders and rode hard to the North to carry the news to Mangus and escape the MacRaigl clan. Mael knew this was the moment Cullen de Mangus had awaited. It was the spark that would ignite an all-out clan war. It must be stopped.

There had been no time to bid Jeanne farewell. His wife. The thought warmed him yet made him impatient to have this business finished. They tethered the horses in the forest at the base of the mountain. From here, they would travel by foot.

The Highlanders scaled the rocky terrain running along the vast ridges and jagged cliffs. Guided by the fading afternoon light, Mael was desperate to catch Fareley and his men before they reached Mangus. By sunset, his men were exhausted and he ordered a rest by a tumbling stream. Tearing off pieces of bread from the packed loaves, the men sliced chunks of cheese before passing the food about. It was all followed by skin flasks of mead.

"We must take advantage of the night," Mael told Ian as they sat a short distance from the others.

"Your men be spent, Mael. Give them rest."

"The clouds are rolling in. It shall be a dark night. 'Tis our best weapon. We can reach Fareley while he rests."

"Nae, ye push the men beyond what's human."

"What we fight 'tis not human."

The air stirred colder, and Ian mumbled an aye under his breath.

"We rest a while, then we move up the mountain." He pointed at the distant ridge. "The fires of their camp will guide us. They go no further this evening."

Ian looked where Mael pointed.

Under the cover of night, Mael led his men toward the enemy's camp. They scaled the top of the steep mountain in silence, moving with the agility of those born in the Highlands. With swords drawn, the band crested the mountain on the other side of the encampment.

It was darker than any night Mael could recall. He studied the small fires scattered throughout the clearing. Like ghosts, Mael and his men encircled the sleeping men. They stood poised over the raiders awaiting his signal.

Mael squatted down beside a sleeping man, careful not to make a sound and poised the tip of his sword inches from Fareley's neck. He glanced about to make sure everyone was in place.

"Fareley." His voice boomed into the night. Fareley bolted awake, as did the rest of the camp. The men scrambled for their swords, only to find the point of their enemies' blades at their throats.

Fareley's eyes widened with terror. Mael pressed the blade closer to his neck.

"Were I the devil ye claim me, Fareley, then dead ye and all your men would be." Mael sat back on his heels and stabbed his sword into the ground inches from Fareley's head.

The man jumped from the blanket and rolled to his feet, wielding his sword. Mael stood with his arms extended from his sides. "Yet ye and your men live. Twice I spare your life. And twice ye brandish your sword. Yet, I dinna fight. Why would your enemy spare your life twice?"

"What is your ruse, MacRaigl?" came Fareley's challenge. His square face contorted with angry lines.

"None. I come with a treaty in my other hand. This night we stop the madness that was created in our land by an outsider. We unite our clans against Cullen de Mangus. Together we fight the true enemy of our clans. What say ye? Do ye take my treaty to your chief?"

All I Want

Fareley stumbled in his place and looked about the camp. He gulped then turned back to Mael.

* * * * *

Jeanne had heard the horses galloping over the drawbridge and rushed for the door, but stopped before lifting the latch. She wanted to run down the steps and into the courtyard, but she could not trust herself to remain composed when she saw him. He had to be alive. He had to come back to her. The last thing she wanted to do was put Mael in an awkward position with his clan. If he intended to keep their handfast a secret, then she would not betray him. Instead, she hurried back to the window and watched as the men dragged in through the castle gate. The courtyard swelled as their families ran out to greet them.

Immediately, she saw him swing down from his horse and receive several slaps on the back. Her stare burned against his face, dropping to his torso. How she'd missed him. She longed to feel his body against her. She wanted to feel him inside her. She was already spoiled to his amorous care. He'd washed the war paint from his face. His hair fell in several long braids about his shoulders.

He moved through the crowd. She admired the way he carried himself with his broad shoulders squared. Her body tensed in response to the image he cut in his kilt. God, he was sexy! The moistness rushed from her, wetting her thighs. She thought of her own time, and how a man with Mael's magnetism would have quickly captured the public's adoration. A woman fell into Mael's arms. Searing rage burst in Jeanne.

She pressed her face against the cold green-tinted glass and gritted her teeth against the newfound jealousy when the woman locked her lips against Mael's for a long passionate kiss. Jeanne clenched her hands into hard fists by her sides. She reasoned the woman was just caught up in the moment, but when another woman encircled her arms around Mael's neck and bestowed an equally passionate kiss upon his lips, she nearly broke her own resolve to stay in her chamber.

"What's going on?" she fumed, and stared down at the women as one after another greeted the laird. Was it a tradition? The bristling along her spine eased somewhat. Okay, so it was a tradition, still, he was *her* husband. Her breath latched in her throat. She *was* married. She longed to be the woman in Mael's arms, receiving his hungry kiss she knew so well. The memories of the night they'd shared before he'd left had sustained her over the last two days. She'd never missed anyone so much.

Had they found the assassins? Was the threat over? Had Mael succeeded in uniting the clan? If he had been successful, then he would be Chief.

"Victory!" The chant started as the crowd undulated toward the castle.

Her joy crashed around her. Now Mael was the most eligible man of the clan. The women would be standing in line for a chance to be the new chief's mate. The pain started near her heart and drove to her stomach. A sickening pain, it left her empty and frightened. Another cheer went up from the crowd below, and the mass of people climbed the steps and poured into the Great Hall.

She must rush downstairs and join her *husband* in his victory. Now they would be free of Trench's rumors and superstitions. They could be together.

"What are you doing, Jeanne?" she asked out loud and bumped her head against the thick glass pane. "You don't belong here." She stared down at the vacated courtyard, so symbolic that she be closeted in her chambers watching. She would always be an outsider. Not even Mael's love could change that. She did not belong in this time. She could not belong to him. History must have held another woman by his side. How could Jeanne step into her place and take all this from her? Searing pain stabbed her very soul.

Tears poured from her eyes. She was here by accident. This had not happened before. Trench and she had interfered with what had been. But how could she not love Mael? How could she refuse her own heart? Her other life felt so distant, like a dream. She had been a research scientist. She had a brother. Ryan! Yet it all felt so remote as though it had been another lifetime. She flattened her hand against the cold window, allowing its smooth icy surface to siphon the heat from her fingers.

Her heart pounded harder. How could she embrace a life with Mael? She brushed the tears from her cheeks. It could work! She ran out of the room toward the Great Hall and the loud sounds of celebration.

"To the new Chief, Mael! Long live the Clan MacRaigl."

The boisterous cheers echoed and were followed by clashing mugs of grog.

All I Want

"MacRaigl!" The crowd cheered. Jeanne paused, leaning against the wall of the stairwell. Mael had won. He was the new Chief. The knot in her throat burned against pent-up tears. He had managed to defeat his enemy. How many men had died, though? All because of Trench. Yet Mael had won! He deserved to be the leader of his people. The cheering from the Hall filled her with pride. For the moment, her love for him was all that mattered. She could not resist the wide smile that parted her lips when she heard his deep infectious laughter.

"To the Clan MacRaigl!" he cheered.

"Aye, now ye need a wife, Mael," came a shout from the men.

"Wife. Wife. Wife." The din was deafening even where Jeanne stood as the men pounded fists, sword hilts and mugs on the tables in accompaniment to their chant. Soon, it grew into a frenzy. Several drums pounded out the chant, followed by the sudden wheeze of a bagpipe. A song took up the passionate chant. Several cheers went up.

Jeanne took a deep breath. It was such a moment of pride that she could not contain the rampaging emotions. She could not descend the steps fast enough to join him.

The scene burst in front of her like an epic movie. She had to remind herself it was real. The Great Hall was filled beyond its large capacity. Not only had the castle residents joined them, but it appeared the opposing clan was in full attendance. She noted the black and brown tartan plaids of the Fareleys as the highlanders danced to the song.

He spotted her and quickly disentangled himself, taking long strides in her direction. She pushed her way through the celebration toward him.

"My Jeanne!" Mael wrapped his arm around her waist and swung her from the floor. Twirling her about the Great Hall, he held a mug of grog in his other hand.

"Oh, Mael." Her breath jerked from her as his arm tightened. "I'm so glad you're back." She glanced over him doing a quick inventory to make sure he'd not been injured. "Congratulations." She tilted her head so she could see into his brown eyes and met his love shining in their golden depths.

Mael relaxed his strong hold and let her slip down the full length of his body to the floor. The Hall was wild with revelry. Music, food, drink, and dancing whirled around them as the Highlanders celebrated their victory and their new Chief.

"So what do ye think, my Jeanne?" he yelled above the din.

"It's wonderful, Mael. You deserve to be Chief. You're a man of great honor and wisdom."

"Aye?" He paused with a perplexed frown deepening his forehead. "So say ye, lass?"

"Aye, me laird," Jeanne said and grinned up at him, "so say I." The frenzied heat pumped to her chest. The need to press her lips against his and explore his mouth was more than she could stand.

"The ceremony shall be later, but tonight we celebrate." Mael's smile disappeared replaced with an intense expression that shuddered through her. He drew her into his arms. His hard chest pressed against her breasts, as he crushed her to him. His face was inches from hers. She could easily slip up on her tiptoes and taste his lips. Who would notice?

"What do ye say to my next act as Chief?"

"What would that be, me laird?" She trembled with the excitement of his closeness.

"A few wee MacRaigls to fill our chambers, my Jeanne."

Chapter Twenty-Four

Jeanne's mouth fell open. Thunder roared in her ears. The room spun around.

Mael reared back to release deep rumbling laughter.

"'Tis how ye react whenever a man asks ye to bear his children?"

"Children?" Her pulse pounded riotously, and the pain returned, this time piercing straight through her heart.

"Of course, my Jeanne. Dinna ye want to have my sons?"

"I cannot think of anything more wonderful," she choked with hot tears searing her throat. Her voice masked the sadness. So truly a wonderful thing it would be, too. Mael's children! Her mind whirled. It was the one thing she could *never* give him. And the only thing she could do to help solidify his success as new Chief. The bitterness of life's cruelty was too much. She swallowed back the tears and looked away.

The celebration pitched higher. Mael tossed his mug to the floor. It spilled and clattered underneath their feet as he grabbed her hand and pulled her toward the door leading to the garden.

Several shouts and cheers went up as the couple left the Hall.

"Aye, Mael, me lad, get started on those bairns right away with ye," a man called after them, followed by a loud roaring cheer. The reel pitched louder and shouts gave way to laughter and dance.

For the moment, she felt accepted and free of the stigma surrounding her. She realized it was spawned by the revelry, and Mael's new position as Chief. The cold air blasted her hot cheeks. He pivoted and gathered her into his embrace, letting his hand trail down her cheek.

"Mael," she breathed. "You're intoxicated with the moment. Do they know of our handfast?"

"Nae, lass. All in good time."

"Mael." She gasped for air but he tugged her closer to him. His lips sought hers, and his tongue slipped between her half-spoken protests. Jeanne knew it was impossible to reason with him. It was better to join in the gaiety of the moment and discuss it when life grew somber once more.

His passion flamed, consuming her with hot strokes of desire. He tightened his embrace, and she drew hers around his neck. His long braids brushed her cheeks. Slowly, he lifted his head, reluctant to release her lips, stealing several smaller kisses in the wake of his retreat.

"I love ye, my Jeanne. I love ye as a man loves a woman. As a soul loves its other half. Dinna ye understand? Fate decreed ye mine. Destiny brought ye home to where ye rightfully belonged. It dinna matter how or why or even when. All that matters 'tis we were meant to be together. Canna ye see? So clear a thing 'tis."

She pulled slightly from him and bowed her head. Tears slipped between her shuttered eyes. She couldn't look at him. If she saw that look in his eyes once more, it would surely break her heart. "I missed you so. I was so worried."

He gripped her arms and jerked her into his kiss, covering her chilled lips with his warm hungry ones.

"Ye are mine forever, Jeanne McBen," he breathed against their kiss. "Be with me, forever."

She couldn't say the words that would erase the apprehensive look she'd seen in his eyes. Her heart pounded harder under the pain of her denial. She moved her lips but the words would not come. She must tell him the truth. She must tell him there would be no children. Not with her.

"Keep the other words silent, Jeanne. At least for this night, say naught of what I see in your eyes." He placed his forefinger over her lips as though he could seal the words within her. "I dinna want to know. Not this eve."

"Mael—"

"Shhh." He leaned over and reclaimed her lips. The revelry from the Hall intruded on them. "This night shall be ours." He scooped her up into his arms and turned for the tower's side entrance. She buried her head in the curve of his neck, luxuriating in his warmth as the wind whipped through them. He took the steps effortlessly and kicked open the door to his chambers.

"Mael. You have guests. You can't leave them like this," she protested as he kicked the door closed.

All I Want

"Lass, this be the one night I can do as I wish. I am the new Chief." His deep laughter filled the room with a warmth all its own. The fire in the grate crackled louder, and he released her gently so her legs slid down the length of his hard body. The touch of her legs against his aroused her.

"Jeanne, my love." He drew her to him.

"I can't do this, Mael."

"Ye can't love me, Jeanne?"

"I can't pretend that we're going to be together forever."

"I dinna ask ye to pretend, Jeanne."

"Then what are you asking of me, Mael?"

"To love me, Jeanne," he said and released the brooch on his tartan, "and to allow me to love ye. As our vows said, as long as there be love we shall be together." The plaid fell full-length to the floor. With a quick jerk against his waistline, the rest of the nine yards of material fell from him. Her gaze riveted to his torso, where his shirt fell midway to his knees. His erection pressed against the material, tenting it in front of him.

Her pulse quickened.

"No man has ever loved a woman as much as I love ye, Jeanne."

"All men in love say that, Mael." She tried to keep her own emotions in check by not allowing herself to believe his words.

"Aye? But do they mean it? I mean it, Jeanne MacRaigl."

Her senses prickled at the sound of her new name. She warmed with his possessive tone. Yes, that was the word. Mael completely possessed her. Everything about him consumed her. His hands trailed over her. His kisses touched her body everywhere. How could she deny him?

She opened her eyes and stared up at him.

"Ye are as much a part of me as my arms or my eyes."

"Mael." Her mouth dried, and her gaze widened when he crossed his arms over his chest and grasped the hem of his shirt. She took a few steps back.

"I shall show ye just how deep my love for ye is, Jeanne."

She stopped when she came up against the bedpost. He took long strides toward her while pulling the shirt over his head. Her heart pounded so loudly in her ears, Jeanne couldn't hear what he said. It didn't matter. She stared at his lips as they formed the words. She knew what he said, but she knew what their futures would become. He would resent her. She could not give him the dynasty he was expected to create with his new wife.

"Ye are me *wife*, Jeanne. Love me as your husband. Don't be afraid of our passion."

He walked naked across the room to her. The fire's golden light danced over him, revealing muscled arms and the thick hair that matted over his chest then raced in a tapered line to his cock. It was engorged and erect. Her pulse quickened. She tried to raise her stare but it was riveted to his cock. How well she knew it could please her, fill her and fuck her until she felt she would disintegrate from wanting him.

Her breath escaped her, and her knees trembled weaker. Mael swooped her into his arms and laid her on his bed. His fingers worked the laces on her leggings and then moved to untie the lacings of her dress.

"Ye are my one true love, Jeanne, forever stirring in my blood and stealing the very breath from my soul."

Their shadows merged and danced a rhythm all their own across the stucco walls. Her breath rushed from her. It was just as she had seen that night so long ago on the hillside with the other MacRaigl. It was this moment she had remembered. How could that be? Had she been remembering this moment or had she seen into the future? Panic surged through her but quickly fled in the comfort of his love.

He ran his thumb over her nipple until it hardened then closed his lips over it. He stroked her hip, moving his hand to cup her pussy, while he sucked and tugged against her nipple. Her mind reeled under the onslaught of tingling sensations pulsing to her clit.

"Ye are my wife, Jeanne, and that shall not ever change," he whispered in her ear and covered her lips with his once more. His fingers teased against her clit. She lifted her hips, writhing under the friction of his fingers. She whimpered when he slid his fingers and entered her, moving in and out, fucking her with their long thickness. She was wet and ready for him. He slid between her legs, guiding his hardened cock inside her tight pussy and groaned.

"I missed ye. How I longed to feel ye, to slide inside ye last night, instead of lying beneath the stars, shivering beneath my skins."

All I Want

"I was lonely for you too," she said, and wrapped her legs around his waist. His heart slammed against his chest. He wanted to hear the words she had yet to say to him since his return. What had happened during his absence? Why was she distant?

"Ye take me fully, my love. I want ye to ride me all night. I shall bring ye great pleasure." He thrust his hot cock into her, groaning as he slid in and out of her moist tightness. She moved under him, inciting him beyond control. She moved her hips and tightened her pussy against his cock just at the right moment, pulling him deeper into her. He fucked her harder, longing to bring her to climax with him and was rewarded when she tightened against him, throbbing, jerking against the orgasm. He came immediately, incited by her orgasm, ramming himself as deeply as he could inside her, never wanting to leave her.

* * * * *

"Nae, we had an agreement." Fareley's face reddened as he turned to face Mael and Ian.

"And our agreement I honor."

"Nae, we destroy the Mangus. All of them. 'Tis the only way to end the uprising."

Mael pivoted on his heel and paced the length of the fireplace, pausing to warm his hands in front of it.

"I shall not annihilate an entire family," he yelled.

"Me clan agreed. As chief of your clan, ye must hear me out. I carry my chief's wishes. If a war ye wish to abate, then your clan must agree upon this action. The Mangus shall stir the pot again and next time, I canna assure me people shall resist joining him. His branch has strength in their beliefs. Their magic—'tis powerful."

"Superstitions," Mael ground out the word.

"Be they such or naught, dinna matter when the tally be taken, me laird, shall be the same—war. We must strike while both our people still ride the dregs of celebration in honor of the MacRaigl clan's new chief. Striking a common enemy will solidify the pact between our clans, and the new loyalty shall remain intact."

Mael bowed his head.

"Laird MacRaigl shall take your council and send for ye when he reaches a decision." Ian moved to usher Fareley from the private chamber, but Fareley sidestepped him and closed the space to Mael.

"Indecision will bode ill for your dream of a peace betwixt our two clans. A vision canna be realized without action to preserve it. Ye hold it in the palm of your hand. Dinna let it slip between your fingers because ye grow a conscience. Mangus' seed must be stopped. *All* of his seed. Not just the old man. All of them. Ye canna have the bairns age and seek revenge upon your lands."

"Leave!" Mael yelled. His stomach churned with what the other man was demanding he sanction.

Fareley mumbled under his breath and stomped from the room. Mael heard the door close behind him. Ian returned to the fire and stood beside him.

"Ye know he speaks the truth. Settle it now in one swift blow or settle it again and again with each generation."

"I shall not be known as the chief who slaughtered innocents. I shall not have that resting upon my soul for all eternal damnation. 'Tis not the legacy I envisioned I would create." Mael glared at his friend.

"Then how shall ye resolve the threat?"

"I dinna know. But I shall think of a solution that dinna sanction the murder of women and children. Never did I slay a woman or child *before* I was Chief, and I shall not do so now that I am. Mark my words."

"Whilst I must agree with ye, me laird, 'tis talk of a secret deed." Ian cleared his throat. "This deed could very well end the luxury of choice should it became known."

Mael turned to face him, noting the wary look reflecting in his mentor's eyes.

"What secret deed?" He studied the way Ian seemed to weigh his words before he spoke.

"'Tis about ye and the lass."

"And who spreads this?"

"Only one and she does so to me in private, 'tis me sister."

Mael frowned and raked his hand through his lengthy hair.

"Then bid your sister to spread naught rumors, but confront me with her concerns."

"Ye did handfast with the lass?" Ian stiffened his stance as though physically bracing for Mael's anger.

"Aye." Mael nodded, unable to stop the smile that spread over his face. "And I long to shine it from beneath the cloak of secrecy." He

All I Want

rubbed his gloved hands together. The leather moaned under the friction. "But for now, I deem it remain private. Until 'tis peace within the clan. 'Twas an act of the heart and not of the mind."

"So I guessed," Ian said with a nod, "for she be a comely lass and could make ye a good wife."

"Aye. At long last I found the woman I sought all these years." Mael released his breath, glad to have someone he could discuss it with. It was the most joyous thing in his life, and yet he dared not own it in public.

"Ye be wise in keeping it from the people. They yet to trust her fully and still there be whispers behind her back."

"What do they say?" His muscles tensed with his need to protect Jeanne flaring.

"The same," Ian swallowed. "Beneath her appearance lies a witch in league with Tryon. Ishabelle's betrayal when she married Tryon was yet part of a plan. It all makes for a foul kettle of rumors and ye now have another pot of unrest stewing."

Mael closed his eyes. How was he going to resolve all that faced him? Everything hung in a fine balance. A misguided decision and he could doom himself and all who followed him. A careless word and all he had worked for could be destroyed. The wrong approach and his people would never accept Jeanne as his chosen wife.

"Ye know what ye must do, Mael," Ian's voice cracked. "The ceremony looms before ye and as new Chief, ye now must rule your people with a tempered heart. One tempered by your *mind*, with reason." He stepped toward Mael, his blue eyes widening in a pained look. "'Tis reasonable to expect your people to accept the lass?"

"Nae." Mael hung his head and released the burden of his choice with a ragged sigh. "Nae! I canna do what ye ask!" Mael balled his fists by his sides, struggling to control the rage. It rumbled from his very core to his chest.

"Ye must!" Ian insisted. "The lass shall be your death! The death of our clan! 'Tis fair to forfeit all of us for your own desires?"

"Nae!" Mael yelled and shoved Ian against the wall, pinning his arm underneath his friend's throat. "Ye ask *too* much of me," he growled between his teeth. "Dinna ask me to do this! I canna do it. I canna."

Ian clawed at Mael's arm pressed against his throat.

"Ye have no choice, man. Ye sit as Chief. Ye must put your clan before her or any other lass! Before your own wants," Ian strangled out.

Mael pushed against him, and then relaxed his hold. Ian slumped forward, coughing and rubbing his throat. Mael fell into the nearby chair.

"For the sake of the clan, ye must break your vows with the lass." Ian straightened.

Chapter Twenty-Five

Jeanne nestled under the covers and molded her body to his back. She glanced through the small gap in the curtains surrounding his bed. Faint light fell across the stone floor leaving fairy dust in its trail. How she'd loved to run though such streams of light when she'd been a child. She nuzzled her face in his long brown hair. Since their handfast, he'd shared her bed every night, and she had never known such happiness.

Mael had explained that the handfast meant they would live as a married couple for a year and one day. At the end of that time, if they felt it was a mistake, the marriage would be annulled. It seemed a fair system, especially to the woman. She had observed the women seemed open about their sexuality — at least among the MacRaigl clan, oftentimes as aggressive as the men in making their intentions known. She released a lazy sigh, delighting in the warmth they shared beneath the covers.

"Good morning, my love." Mael squeezed her hand, and turned over to face her.

Eagerly, she settled in the warmth of his arms, resting her head on his chest.

"What is all the commotion outside?"

"They prepare for Martinmas in a few days."

"What?" she blinked.

"We call it Samhain."

"Sav-en?" she repeated.

"Aye. The church claimed it and now 'tis known as Old Hallowmas. Dinna ye hear the talk about the bonfires?" he asked and lifted her hand to his lips, pressing a kiss into her flesh. She tingled with delightful shivers.

"I didn't really understand it."

"'Tis a quarter day to mark the waning of the sun. We light the fires to aid the sun in its power."

"You believe in all this?"

Mael stroked her hair.

"My ancestors did for hundreds of years. 'Tis the feast of the dead. When we honor those who have gone before us and those passed since the last Samhain."

"How do you honor them?" She traced a circle with her finger through the hair on his wide chest.

"We leave a plate of food for the souls of the dead just outside the door and light a candle in the window to guide them to the land of eternal summer. We shall bury fruits and food from the harvest so they have food for their journey."

She lay with her head on his chest, listening and realizing what she had considered history and superstitions were for Mael and all those in this world, a way of life. Even though he may condemn things as superstitions and feel himself to be a man of sophistication, he was still a man of his times.

Again, she was keenly aware how wrong it was for her to be here. She came from a world of technology and fast food where tradition was something mostly forgotten. She sighed and clung to her husband, lest she be swept away in a whirlpool of insanity so deep she'd never resurface.

"What?" he asked, lifting from his rest to look into her eyes.

"Nothing." She tried to hide the pain she knew was in her eyes.

"Nae, sadness shines in your eyes. Did my words upset ye?"

"I just realized how little I know about your world. It's so different from where I come from."

"Tell me then." He settled into a sitting position while she rested her head on his chest. "Tell me about your world, Jeanne." He stroked her hair.

"You would surely think me daft, or worse, a liar."

"'Tis so different from my world?"

"In every way. We have machines that fly at great speeds over metal cities, carrying people all around the earth. We've sent men in these machines to the moon and beyond."

Mael threw back his head and laughed deeply.

"See? I told you it was impossible to believe."

"Ye truly want me to believe these tales?"

All I Want

"They are the truth." She pursed her lips together and decided such things were too fantastic for him to comprehend, and it might be safer to tell him about her work and her family. "My father was a great man in his time."

"Tell me about him."

"He was a man of great vision and science. He knew the healing arts and was considered a man ahead of his time." She tried to choose words she felt Mael could relate to and continued her story. "He prophesied the coming of the disease that now plagues my world. But no one listened. And I inherited his work after he and my mother—" her voice cracked. She could not force the words past her sorrow.

"The pain remains too strong for ye, Jeanne. Dinna speak it." He bent over her and planted a tender kiss on her forehead.

"But I need you to know about my family. My mother and my father were scientists. I don't know how to say that in your language. They were leaders in their professions."

"And ye followed their passion?"

"Yes, that's a good way of describing it. I like that." She stroked his abdomen with her hand, marveling at how strong he was.

"What happened to your *máthair* and da?"

"They were killed." Jeanne swallowed, trying to keep the emotion from her voice, but it cracked with tears. "My father was a colleague, a clansman, of Trench's. My parents stopped by his home the day after New Year's." She didn't ask if Mael celebrated a New Year, obviously they acknowledged the change of seasons.

"Why did they make this journey to his home?"

"Trench had some papers concerning my father's research so they went to pick up the research notes. It was very classified information, not the kind of thing you'd send over the internet." She paused, what was she doing? Mael wouldn't know what the internet was.

"Internet?"

"It's a form of communication like a great hall of information. Like your solar only everyone in the entire world can use it. I mean, they don't actually travel to it because it's not really there. Well, it's…ah, never mind. It doesn't matter. They went to his home to retrieve these documents. Trench was out of town, on a journey, and he left the package at the gate of his home. These papers supposedly held the key that would unlock my father's research." Tears spilled down her cheeks.

"Trench had vicious guard dogs." She shuddered, and he tightened his arms around her. "But he always kept them locked up whenever expecting guests." Her voice broke off. Tears cascaded down her face. "I tried to help them. Tried to climb over the fence. I flagged down a cop, a peace officer, and he killed the dogs, but it was too late. I know now, Trench murdered my parents."

Mael held her closer to him.

"Why would he do such a thing?"

"Because my father was going to stop him. Trench's science didn't care about risks. He only wanted results. It didn't matter who suffered years later. Trench put what he wanted before the needs of his people."

Mael's entire body stiffened.

"What is it?" she asked.

"Nothing." He squeezed her tighter and planted a kiss on her head. "Tell me more."

"He didn't care the world would suffer. He lived for the research. He was possessed by his own desires. So he ignored the warnings. He completely dismissed those who tried to reason with him. One of them being my father. Trench and those following him created this tragic disease that became known as 'Next Gen'. He saw a way to have everything he wanted and he took it. And once he had created the disease, thought he could find a cure then sell it to the sick for an outrageous price. But there was just one drawback—he couldn't find the cure."

"So ye continued your father's work in hopes ye might solve the puzzle? Was that when Trench befriended ye?"

"More than that, he was my benefactor. He—" Her voice trembled over the words. "He saw that I was accepted into the finest medical school and sponsored me in a research fellowship after my parents' deaths. But now I know he'd planned it all. I believe he murdered my parents to get a formula that didn't exist, and when I followed their research, he entrapped me, stole my work and would have killed me, too." Jeanne shuddered with the familiar wave of terror. Mael held her tighter and whispered in her ear.

"I understand." He kissed her again. "I understand now why ye have such a fear of dogs."

"All dogs. Not just the kind that attacked my parents." Jeanne fought the waves of trauma. Slowly, it eased and averted the usual path. She relaxed, grateful Mael's presence somehow intervened.

"Ye lie safe from that world, my Jeanne. Safe with me. I shall not allow any harm to befall ye." His lips slid over hers. She marveled at the tenderness in their possession. Their kiss bloomed into a heated urgency.

She moved her hand over his matted chest and down to the hardness of his cock. Her fingers closed around his thickness, and he groaned against their kiss.

"Mael," she moaned.

"I love ye, my Jeanne."

She slid her lips from his kiss and traced small trails down his massive chest to his cock. She held him between her hands, allowing her strokes to press just hard enough to elicit a groan from him.

Tenderly, she lowered her mouth to his hard shaft and sucked his cock, moving him in and out of her mouth.

"I canna wait," he groaned. "I believe 'tis a time which demands a 'quickie'."

Her laughter was muffled against the pillow as he turned her on her stomach and lifted her to her knees.

"And do ye have a term for this?" he asked, entering her with his thickness filling her. She gasped at the intense pleasure the position afforded her.

"Yes, we call it the doggie position."

"Doggie? Does that mean the men of your time must bark and fetch?" he asked but didn't wait for her response. Instead, he grasped her by the hips and jerked her into his thrust.

"You really are a rutting stag," she giggled and moaned when his fingertips found her clit and massaged her aching heat.

"More than ye can ken, my love." He ground himself into her. His fingers rubbed against her nub providing just the right friction she needed while his other hand cupped her breast, teasing her hardened nipples with gentle, firm pinches.

He was right, their passion demanded a "quickie". The urgency roared and peaked when they came together. The walls of her pussy clamped around him and he rested his head against hers, stroking her breasts, letting his fingers trail down her abdomen.

"I so love quickies," he groaned.

Laughter filled his chambers as she collapsed on the bed with him rolling from her.

* * * * *

"I don't understand, why did you marry me if it's to always be a secret?" Jeanne planted her hands on her hips. The tender remnants of their lovemaking evaporated in her anger.

"My patience is worn thin, Mael. The servants all know I spend every night in your chamber. We can't keep the marriage secret much longer. The rumors are growing by the day. And I'm tired of wearing these gloves hiding the most joyous thing to ever happen to me." She threw the black leather gloves at him, missing his head and landing on the bed behind him.

"'Twas not how I planned it, lass. The truth be known I dinna plan it at all. 'Twas an act of the heart."

"Or maybe an act of the anatomy?" She turned from him. Fire roared through her, lodging in her chest.

"I understand your anger, but ye dinna need to wound me more than I am."

"Are you saying you want out of our handfast pact, or whatever you call it?" She pivoted to direct her anger in the fiercest glare she'd ever bestowed on anyone.

"Nae, nae!" He moved to embrace her, but Jeanne stiffened against his hold.

"Then what are you saying?" She tried to calm the fury roiling in her.

"I need to remain in my chambers and ye in yours until—"

Jeanne jerked from him, but he quickly pulled her back to him.

"Until I can finish this business with Cullen de Mangus."

"Mangus?" Jeanne screamed. "Trench's ancestor? Oh, God, Trench continues to destroy my life even from the future."

"Jeanne." He engulfed her with his arms. "My Jeanne. I love ye, more than life itself. I would do anything for ye. Do ye believe me?"

She couldn't respond. Anger silenced her attempt.

"Do ye believe me, Jeanne?" He pressed for a reply.

Reluctantly, she nodded. The tightness in her chest eased. Her love for Mael melted through the sting of their enforced separation.

"I canna quell the rumors within my own walls. Trench's threat lives beyond his time spent here."

"But you're the Chief, Mael. You can do whatever you want. If you decree we're married, then the clan will have to accept that."

"Under normal circumstances." Mael bowed his head.

"Normal?"

"Jeanne, the rumors seep into my castle as though water seeping through the walls. Ishabelle has not escaped the stories surrounding her. New gossip is added each day. And ye, Jeanne, the rumors followed ye from the village. They never died. With Hallowmass on the morrow, I take my oath. It fuels the rumors. This shall be for just a short while, my Jeanne."

"This is such a mess." She wrapped her arms around him.

"I shall bring it to an end, soon, I promise." His voice was deeper than usual and held a sadness in its depths.

"How will you stop Cullen?" she asked and pulled slightly from him.

"Ye need not worry, Jeanne." A strange glint pierced his brown eyes.

"I'm not a simpleton, Mael. What are your plans?"

"I shall negotiate. If that fails, then I must convince him we harbor no witches or demons."

"But as long as I'm here, Mael, you shall have rumors and gossip."

"Nae, lass. As long as Ishabelle and Tryon roam the highlands, I shall have this shadow. Yours shall pass, but would not aid my mission to announce our handfast in an untimely fashion. Can ye understand?"

"I'm so sorry, Mael. I've added to your burden." She raised her hand to stroke his bearded face. His hand covered hers.

"Nae, my sweet wife. Ye be the one joy shining in my life. To push ye to the side and not claim ye as my bride 'tis my greatest sorrow. My uncle once told me the true mark of a chief should be to lead his clan through troubled times in spite of personal sacrifice and sorrow it may bring."

Jeanne felt guilty for adding to his burdens. She was a liability. She shivered. He would be better off without her. She should leave. She should go somewhere else, perhaps England or France. Her thoughts tumbled over themselves. Mael tilted her head back and bestowed a fierce kiss to her lips.

His touch sent her into a mindless whirlwind. All she could concentrate on was him. To wake and not find him lying beside her was going to be impossible. She tightened her arms around his neck.

"I shall miss you in my bed," she sobbed and buried her face in his shoulder.

"And I ye. But for this moment, I want to take ye, Jeanne, one last time before we separate."

She lifted on tiptoes and seized his lips with hers. Her aggression excited him. His cock hardened and rose between their bellies.

"Come," she whispered and led him toward the bed where only moments earlier she'd made love to him upon waking.

"This shall last us for some time. I dinna think I can breathe without ye near, my Jeanne."

* * * * *

The last rays of day were mere slivers of light cascading through the tall windows of the Great Hall when Jeanne entered. She had taken great care in her dressing, choosing the deep purple gown with gold braid. Opting for a pale lavender fillet of silk and a matching barbette, she disliked the wide strap that came underneath her chin. She wore the small hat with purple brocade and material that matched her gown. Her hair was caught in a bold mesh crispinette, and she felt she looked the part of lady of the castle.

Even if Mael would not claim her publicly, she had heard the rumors. The chambermaids had snickered and giggled all evening while they helped her bathe and dress. Finally, she had forced confessions from them. Their secret handfast was no longer a secret. There was nothing left to do. Mael would now be forced to claim their marriage this very evening, and she intended to dazzle the entire clan with her presence. She would end all rumors once and for all and prove she was worthy of their Chief. She would redeem herself and win their loyalty.

She stood on the landing and surveyed the Great Hall. Hallowmas had begun. Candles had been placed in the windowsills and several women moved about the enormous hall lighting them. She sought her

All I Want

husband in the crowd. Her heart skipped a beat when she saw him. He looked as though he had stepped from the portrait she had seen hanging above the mantel in the twenty-first-century castle. He sat at the large table and paused briefly in his conversation, just long enough to glance at her as she stepped from the landing. Her smile was involuntary, but his frown wasn't. He turned back to his conversation.

The blood rushed to her face from the sting of his rejection. Was that his response to the rumors? Ian hurried over and quickly placed her hand in the crook of his arm.

"Good evening, lass. Ye look most fetching." He escorted her to the seat across from Mael instead of her usual place beside him.

She struggled to maintain her composure, but the angry trembling shook deep in her and threatened to crumble her nonplussed exterior. This was not at all the reception she had anticipated. She stared at the bench with humiliation stinging her cheeks.

"I thought ye might enjoy the company of a different dinner companion. After all, I have been accused of selfishness where your attentions are concerned," Mael offered without so much as a glance.

There was a low, halfhearted chorus of ayes from the roomful of Scotsmen. He scowled at them before turning his attention to her once more. "So, to remedy this, I placed ye at a more convenient table where all can enjoy the delight of your company, lass."

"I am flattered, me laird," she choked and averted his stare, not wanting him to see what she knew was reflecting in her eyes. It was not possible to mask the hurt of his public insult. He could have warned her about what he had planned to do. Damn him.

She had spent her first night alone and was miserable. It was true he had spoiled her over the last month as her attentive husband. Now this! She fought the bitter tears and vowed not to let anyone in the Great Hall see just how devastated she was by his public rejection. Somehow, she managed to engage in pleasant conversation with the men at her table. The celebration grew, and the children played about the hall in some kind of Hallowmas game.

There were empty places set as according to tradition for those who had died the previous year with the hope their departed loved ones might join their celebration. It all intrigued Jeanne and she tried to focus on the traditions of the night—anything that would help her get through the evening in her seat of shame.

She saw the woman enter the hall. She had never noticed the blonde at any of the meals and wondered who she was. Her long, curly hair was gathered in a single strand tied into sections with colorful strips of cloth. Immediately, she recognized the tartan as belonging to the Fareley clan. Rage replaced shame. She glared at the way the woman's hair cascaded all the way to her waist. Strings of what appeared to be pearls were laced through the weave of her hair. Her beauty was striking, and all of the men in the Hall seemed mesmerized.

The woman walked confidently toward Mael's table as though she had done so many times before. She paused and said something in a low murmur to him, then sat down in the empty chair beside him. Her place! Oh, he did not have to go that far.

She swallowed the burning tears and stared at the plate of pork. She refused to lift her gaze when the young woman's giggles shrilled up an annoying scale. Mael responded in deep laughter and Jeanne cleared her throat. Grabbing up her goblet, she washed the bitterness of her humiliation with a mouthful of wine. After what seemed an eternity, the laughter became intolerable.

The message was louder than any public proclamation he could have issued. She had been replaced, by the token of the clan's newest ally. She could never compete for the clan's affections now. She was fair game, as it were, to any man. Their handfast had been broken.

How could Mael have done this to her and in public? Not claiming her wife in public had been humiliating enough, but to disclaim her in public left no doubt in anyone's mind that talk of a handfast had only been a rumor. If any chose to continue to believe it true, then certainly, all who witnessed this evening knew it was over. In modern terms, he had just divorced her.

Jeanne wanted to scream at him, even though she knew why he had chosen to publicly supplant her. She looked about the Great Hall. His tactic had worked. The atmosphere had shifted. The dark cloud hanging over them had been replaced with a spirit of festivity and fun.

She forced herself to look at him and regretted it the moment her gaze settled on the scene. The woman sat nuzzling Mael, her arms locked behind his neck while she whispered in his ear. Rage pumped through her like a jet engine.

Was this part of his grand scheme too? Was it necessary to carry the farce this far? Did he think this would stop Cullen de Mangus? Was this the old feudal form of preventing war? A marriage between the enemies? And she no doubt could give him a whole brood of little MacRaigls. Her stomach pitched. She felt so betrayed! She sat staring at her plate, desperately clinging to what little control she could maintain over her raging emotions.

"Are ye going to just sit there and not touch your meal?" Mael frowned from across the table. Everyone stopped eating and turned their stares on her.

Oh, she was quickly learning to hate him!

"The excitement of the evening, me laird." She glanced into the gaze of the other woman whose lips curled up into the most vicious female smile of triumph Jeanne had ever seen. She dug her fingernails into her other hand lest she lunge for the woman's face. Primal emotions rocked her. Fire raced from her feet to her head as though she would explode.

"Please excuse me, me laird, I heard rumor there was dancing this eve." Jeanne looked around the silent room. She prayed he cared enough about her to allow her a gracious exit. She met his stare. Pain pierced his eyes, but he quickly masked it.

"Aye?" His voice boomed louder than necessary. "Musicians! Let the dancing begin."

"Then ye must favor me with the first dance, me laird," the Fareley woman cooed. Jeanne gritted her teeth refusing to watch what she knew would be yet another possessive touch from the bitch. Feeling self-conscious, she dared not glance up when she heard the chairs grate against the floor. He was going to dance with her, too! She would not allow herself to be humiliated further.

The court musicians began the strumming reel, with the bagpipes whining into the melody. Jeanne stood from the table and on wobbly legs made her way toward the closest exit, which led to the small private bailey along the South wall, not one she normally took, but she had to escape. She rarely visited the farthest courtyard since it led to the upper catwalk and was the long way back to her tower chambers, but tonight she would have crossed through the fiery rivers of hell to escape the room. She pushed the door open and closed it solidly behind her.

Leaning against it, her composure crumbled. The noise inside rose and the driving beat of music and stomping feet matched that of her breaking heart. The bitter wind whipped about her as she climbed the exterior steps to the crosswalk. She would enter the chamber towers from the top. She knew she'd have to face the night guard, but she didn't care, she could not have made the great length of the Hall without breaking down. She'd had to escape his cruel exhibition. Damn him, he could have at least warned her. Love! He didn't know the meaning of the word, or he would have prepared her. Yet, hadn't she seen sorrow in his eyes, however brief?

The night was freezing with a howling wind tearing over the castle walls whipping about the deserted courtyard with a fierceness to match her inner storm. She struggled to hold the pain of the evening but it bubbled past her lips. The cold embraced her like an unwanted lover. Sobbing, she hurried from the steps and along the allure. Perhaps that was the very scene Mael had wanted to create. The anguish rushed over her from its dark recesses and encased her, dragging her into its lonely depths. She was trapped. Mael was a jerk to do this to her in public, even if she understood his reasons! If only she had the comfort of his love in private, but even that had been taken from her.

So absorbed in her sorrow, Jeanne did not hear the movement in front of her, or see the shadows move from the arched walkway until it was too late. She was quickly overpowered as the hooded creatures seized her upper arms and held her struggling between them.

"My apologies." The female voice spoke from the darkness, and a figure cloaked in scarlet velvet stepped into the faint light.

"Ishabelle?" Jeanne blinked at the woman.

"I truly dinna wish it come to this, Jeanne," she said with a deep sigh, "but my brother will not answer my letters. He refused the protection I offered. He places himself and *ye* in great danger and could end in both your murders before this crisis of a clan war passes."

"What clan war?" Jeanne jerked against the men. Her arms ached under their hold. "What are you talking about? Mael just ended that threat."

Ishabelle took a step forward and raised her hands to the outer edges of her hood. It fell to her shoulders. Her long reddish hair flowed in vibrant masses and spilled over the folds of material down her back.

"Ye are naïve, my dear," she smiled as though sympathetic. "Cullen shall not stop until he has his war. He stepped onto this path and is the kind of man who shall follow it to the very end."

"But Mael reached a truce with the Fareley's clan. They eat at his table." Jeanne shook her head. "Mael just made a very bold public demonstration of that bond," her voice trembled.

All I Want

"They declared a truce and sent that whore to my brother." She paused. "Aye, I know about the woman. But they still plot against my brother. And *ye*. The assassins still roam the hills. I have my own spies who keep me informed." She motioned to the men holding Jeanne. They released her, and she stumbled forward, quickly drawing up all her height so she stood toe to toe with Mael's sister.

"So what is it you want?" She met Ishabelle's hard look.

"My brother safe. For him to live. I shall not have his life destroyed because he fell in love with the wrong woman." Her voice was calm and absent of emotion.

"Like you did with the wrong man?" She regretted her words immediately when she saw the anger rise in those brown eyes, so similar to Mael's. Ishabelle raised her hand. She braced herself for the sting of the slap, but it never came. Opening her eyes, she met Ishabelle's icy smile.

"Ye speak of things ye dinna understand. My brother's passion has him besotted. And in an act of impulse he performed a handfast with ye."

Jeanne glared at her.

"Your secret was no secret. Even if I dinna possess the second sight, the rumors reached Fernmoora. Everyone knows. And though he tries this very eve to break the agreement with ye through his little demonstration just now, the damage has been done. He canna stop it any more than he can stop the return of the sun come morning."

"What do you want, Ishabelle?" she asked, letting the contempt she felt for the woman drip from her words.

"I want my brother to regain control over the clan. With ye here, he never shall. Do ye understand that much, Jeanne?"

"So what are you going to do? Kill me?" Panic replaced anger. She wouldn't put murder past Ishabelle. She would not go without a fight.

"I dinna want my brother's hatred. Nor do I wish ye dead, Jeanne. Just out of the way."

"I would have been out of the way had your brother not interfered." Her resentment rose to her chest and pumped through her anew.

"What do ye mean?"

"You wouldn't understand." Her voice was caustic and resounded with the anger seething in her. "I tried to leave, but Mael interfered."

"Then ye have no objection. It shall be easier. Ye come with me, and my brother can return to his life."

"You're going to kidnap me?" she laughed but when she met Ishabelle's determined glare, her laughter caught in her throat.

"I let it rest with ye, Jeanne McBen. Do ye have feelings for my brother?"

She looked away from her probing stare. Her skin became clammy under the other woman's regard.

"Good. Ye dinna wish to see my brother murdered because of ye."

"Murdered?"

"The assassins plot to capture ye, to lure Mael into defending ye. And I know my brother. He shall defend with no regard for his own life. He is but one man and soon even his own clansmen shall turn against him. All because of ye.

"So ye see, Jeanne, no matter what motions he goes through this evening. It dinna matter. Cullen de Mangus cares not for the public displays he postures. Everyone knows his heart belongs to ye. Can ye live with my brother's—your husband's—death upon your soul?"

"Why do you think I hold so much power over what happens to your brother?" She centered her glare on the other woman, hoping Ishabelle could sense her outrage. "What have I to do with the Mangus family and their plotting?"

"Dinna the assassins first appear shortly after Mael saved ye from the villagers who wanted to hang ye as a witch? Ye appeared out of nowhere and soon after that all the killings began."

"The ones you and your husband have been blamed for committing?"

Ishabelle took a menacing step forward. "Be *very* careful. I dinna have the forgiving heart of my brother."

Jeanne swallowed hard, "Okay, Ishabelle, try this on for size."

"Your language is so strange, Jeanne." Ishabelle's forehead furrowed.

"Yeah, that's true enough. I find it humorous that you think I'm the reason for the assassins when your brother believes it's *you* who turned the clan against him."

Ishabelle's demeanor darkened. She could hear the low drawn breath that exhaled without vapor into the cold night.

All I Want

"Were it not for me, my brother would never have been able to claim his heritage."

"I don't understand."

"Our time draws nigh. Ye are marked for death. 'Tis but a matter of time."

"How do you know this?"

"One thing that canna be controlled when rumors are unleashed, 'tis how they grow and become something other than what they were intended. These rumors have manifested into vengeance against *ye*, Jeanne, and Mael because of his insistence to be with ye."

Time seemed to stand still. Ishabelle's words echoed in her mind. The assassins were after *her*? Had Trench poisoned them so much that they actually believed she was responsible for the deaths? She shook herself from the haze clouding her mind. Trench had been thorough. How could she ever exonerate herself and Mael?

"Jeanne, the time draws near. Ye must decide. Stay and die. And my brother dies with ye. Is that what ye want?"

"Of course not." She stiffened her spine and glared at Ishabelle. "But like I said earlier, after tonight's demonstration I don't think it's a problem. He just publicly dissolved our handfast. So no one believes he loves me. His attentions are now with that *woman*." She managed to still the trembling in her voice. The welling tears were pushed from her eyes by a gust of wind.

"Ye truly believe he no longer loves ye?"

"I believe he is trying to save his people."

"Then ye must see that he succeeds. Ye must come with me."

Jeanne looked toward the Great Hall where the golden flames danced in the tall windows. The music and laughter echoed from inside. The pang of desperation drew her breath. She turned back to Ishabelle.

"I'll go with you," she finally consented. "But I must tell him in private." She turned to leave, but the two goons were quick to restrain her again.

"Nae. Stand down." Ishabelle moved closer and drew her arm around Jeanne's shoulders. She shuddered from the instant chill of the contact.

"Jeanne." Ishabelle guided her over to the ledge overlooking the garden below. "Mael shall not let ye go. Dinna ye know? Never has he been so bewitched with a lass as he is with ye."

"Right. I saw how bewitched he was this evening, and it wasn't with me."

"As I said before, I dinna care what he does tonight. Ye know as well as I, 'tis ye who holds his heart in your hands. The question is will ye protect it?"

She bowed her head, struggling against the emotions. She knew in her heart Mael loved her, but it didn't stop the pain she felt.

"I can't just disappear. He'll search for me."

"Aye. And when he finds no trace, he shall give up, believing ye found a way to return to your own time."

Jeanne gasped and pulled from her.

"Ye thought I dinna know? I know more than ye ken." Her smile was pure amusement. "We can each have what we desire the most. I gain my brother's life and he regains control over his people and his lands. And ye, Jeanne, can return to where ye belong. Makes a tidy resolution for us all."

Her pulse spiked.

"You know how I can get back?"

Ishabelle's confident smile burst a spark of hope in her. Another breeze gusted between them, lifting a wisp of Jeanne's dark hair over her eyes.

"Can you help me return to my home, Ishabelle? To my own time?"

Ishabelle raised her hand and brushed back the lock of hair from Jeanne's face.

"Aye. But the question is, Jeanne, how much are ye willing to sacrifice to make it possible?"

Chapter Twenty-Six

"What did you give me?" Jeanne held her hand to her head. Her words slurred as she tried to lift her head. The world reeled in front of her, and she was reminded of another time when the twenty-first-century Mael had taken her to Scotland.

"It shall pass," came Ishabelle's response.

"Where are we?" She focused on the flames in the grate. Tapers flickered in the drafty room and she realized they were in a solar. "Are we at Fernmoora?"

"Aye. We haven't much time. The night still lives and we must perform the rite quickly so ye can return to your time."

"Rite?"

"Ye come from such a modern time yet ye dinna know the ways, Jeanne. How is that? Are the ways lost in your world?"

"A lot is lost in my world."

"The feast of divination is a night when we can peer into the future."

"I don't understand."

"'Tis the first of the new year, Jeanne, when time cycles back into itself. The natural order of the cosmos dissolves this night, returning to its primordial chaos, preparing itself to reestablish a new order for the next year. Dinna ye know this in your world?"

"In mine, it's just Halloween, not New Year's Eve and time is linear."

Ishabelle burst into a chesty laugh.

"How do ye think ye could travel in time if it dinna bend back into itself? Even the novice of seers knows this."

"I've read concepts and theories."

"This eve, Samhain, 'tis a night of magic. It exists outside the realm of all time. On this eve, a seer can view any other point in time."

Jeanne listened intently. The concept was often discussed in her time period. It certainly was not a new theory and obviously Ishabelle believed in it.

"If a seer is *very* good, she can sometimes alter the pattern of time and thereby place certain elements within the new order, but it must be done before the sun rises on the New Year just as the order is reset."

"What certain elements?" She leaned forward in the chair.

"Ye, my sister-in-law," Ishabelle acknowledged her relationship for the first time, and her heart tugged as she realized she'd never have a normal relationship with Ishabelle. They were literally from different worlds.

"Are you saying you can put me back into the stream of time?" Jeanne snorted.

"In a manner of speaking, yes. But I canna do it on my own. I require ye assist me in the incantation and ye hold the key to its success."

"I do? How?" She was fascinated how matter-of-factly Ishabelle talked about time. She actually believed what she just said.

"Ye must possess the desire to return, Jeanne. 'Tis not something I can give ye. It must come from deep inside by your own free will. And I can only return ye to your starting point. It is a matter of resetting patterns on their proper course. I canna take ye to any other time."

"I have no choice. I must return."

"But do ye want it more than ye want to be my brother's wife?"

"That's not fair, Ishabelle. You cannot force me to choose anything over Mael."

"Life is filled with such choosings, sister-in-law."

Jeanne bowed her head to hide the tears. She startled when Ishabelle came over and put her hand on her shoulder. She looked up into brown eyes that reminded her so much of Mael that she sobbed.

"Your heart is a wee thing to break in order to save my brother's life."

* * * * *

"I was wrong to embarrass the lass." Mael shifted his weight in the saddle. He glanced at Ian who had dismounted. He reined his steed and signaled for the men to halt.

All I Want

"Ye did what ye thought best. Ye had no way of knowing the lass would be so hurt that she would run away." Ian groaned, flexing his legs from the saddle.

"'Tis old ye be," Mael jeered and guided his horse over to Ian. He bent over and slapped him hard on the back.

The yelp from the other man made Mael pause.

"My pardon, Ian, I dinna know how severe your pain was."

"Aye." Ian straightened his spine with slow puffs of air as he struggled against the pain. "The lass gave me herbs for the pain. I wish I could recall the name. She made a special tincture for me."

"Aye, 'tis bright, the lass, full of knowledge of the arts."

The village lay below them with early morning sounds echoing from the glen.

"Ye grow old, Ian," Mael teased.

"Old be it?" Ian reined his horse. "I recall not too long hence I was wounded in my fight with your would-be executioners."

"Aye. Ye ole goat."

"Where do ye think the lass went?" Ian squinted through his bushy browed eyes at the village.

Mael sought the answer to that question, wondering if Jeanne had somehow returned to her own time. He knew if such a thing were possible, it would have been during the wee hours of Samhain. The thought of never seeing her again ripped through him like the piercing of a sword in battle. Pain radiated through his chest and wrung him out with its fleeing.

"She knows no one, save ye, where could she possibly go?" Ian spoke again.

Mael thought back to the night he had first seen her. The villagers had been outraged. Surely she would not go back there or would she?

"The lass had a friend in the village, an old woman named Verica, but she's dead."

"Are ye certain?"

"I have nae word of the woman since the lass came to MacRaigl Castle. The old woman disappeared." He kicked his heels into the horse's ribs and led the small band of men down the mountain into the village. "I desired to find the old witch and bring her to the castle for a surprise visit. A nice gift for my bride." Mael led the way through the village recalling the night he had first seen Jeanne.

His lifelong search for his soul mate had ended the moment his gaze had locked with hers. He had known she was the woman he had waited for all his life. Now, he squinted his eyes against his agony. She was gone.

* * * * *

"Nothing," Ian muttered and turned from the doorway of the cottage.

Mael slammed the door. The cottage appeared to have been abandoned some time ago. Verica must have died.

"Where else would Jeanne go?"

"Ishabelle!" He met Ian's stare.

"Ishabelle would not be giving the lass haven. She always believed the lass was danger. Besides, the lass ran away from ye. If she has sought refuge with Ishabelle then she be serious about not wanting ye."

"Nae, once I explain my plan, she shall be more than eager to return to MacRaigl Castle."

"And what plan might that be?"

"The plan of returning her to her own ti—land."

* * * * *

Jeanne woke with a start and blinked against the glorious morning. She gazed about the unfamiliar room then collapsed back into the soft mattress with a sigh of realization. The incantation and spell had failed.

Ishabelle had been furious and blamed her for not being of pure enough heart to empower her travel back within the circle of time. She could not argue with that truth. To leave Mael with a willing heart was impossible, even if she believed Ishabelle was capable of transporting her into the future. She only had Ishabelle's belief that such a thing was possible.

So now she was a guest at Fernmoora. This was to be her new home, Ishabelle had informed her, at least until the next Samhain when they would try again. In the meantime, Jeanne had an entire year to cleanse her heart of all resistance.

She rolled over on her side. All she could see were endless years of cleansing and failing to journey into the future with Ishabelle always blaming her and not the fallacy of her own art. Her stomach knotted.

Flattening her back onto the mattress, Jeanne straightened her arms to her sides, gliding her flattened palm along the mattress in the vacant place beside her. The coldness assaulted her fingertips. She ached for Mael's warmth beside her. What had he done when he'd discovered she'd left? Did he feel the same pain she had felt seeing him with another woman?

Tears stung her eyes, blurring her vision. She turned over on her stomach to bury her sobs in the pillow. How could she live without him? Even if it were possible to return to the future, how could she leave him?

Sudden thoughts of Ryan pierced the pain of losing Mael, but quickly circled back to her problem with Ishabelle. Her sister-in-law could not be trusted, and neither could anything she said. Ishabelle was obviously insane to believe she could place Jeanne inside a time stream, or whatever she had called it. Yet, had anyone ever told Jeanne she would travel through a portal in a cave, she'd have thought them crazy.

She heaved a sigh and flipped over once more, resting the back of her arm over aching eyes. She groaned, recalling how distraught Ishabelle had been only a few weeks earlier, and talked about her husband coming back to her. Jeanne lay in the bed for what seemed like forever, before mustering the courage to face her new home. Dressed in her only clothes from the night before, she ventured downstairs.

The castle was quiet, not at all like Mael's. There were no aromas of freshly baked bread wafting in from the kitchen across the courtyard to tempt her rumbling stomach.

"Hello?" she called out into the eerie silence. There was no response. Timidly, she descended the curving stone staircase. A chill rushed over her. Where was everyone? She paused on the landing before daring to travel down the interior corridor to the Great Hall. Certainly, she'd find someone there.

She quickly surveyed the room. The long tables were bare. She ran her hand along the rough table and marveled at the lack of even a single crumb. The air stirred cooler and she hugged herself, quickening her stride, resisting the deep longing to rush back to her chamber for the fur wrap Ishabelle had loaned her. Instead, she pushed the door open and stepped into the bright light. Cheerful birds greeted her from the courtyard.

Cold wind pushed against her, and she immediately regretted not donning the heavy cloak. Surveying the valley beyond the great towers, she was amazed at the stillness within the castle walls. Where was everyone? She shivered and quickened her stride.

Her previous visit to Fernmoora was still fresh in her mind and she was able to find her way about the massive estate. It was a similar layout to MacRaigl Castle, however, no guards perched in the towers or along the castle walls. It was clear that Tryon Castle no longer had any fear of attack. She marveled at the power of superstition, then sharply reminded herself of her own fallacy in going along with the beliefs of a self-proclaimed seer.

A sudden movement along the main tower wall drew her attention, and she was startled to see several guards. Looking about the courtyard, she realized what she had earlier believed to be shadows were in fact guards perched along the allure. She hurried toward what she hoped was the kitchen. Upon entering, she halted inside the doorway. An elderly man raised his head from a bowl of porridge.

"Aye, lass?" He blinked his red-rimmed eyes. "Where did ye come from?"

"Where is everyone?"

"Asleep." He spooned the thick mixture into his mouth.

"Where are the servants?"

"Asleep. Some are about tending the animals."

"I don't understand." She stared at the deserted kitchen, noting the dying fire in the grate.

"What's to understand? My master and my mistress sleep during the day and live during the night."

"Your master?" Her limbs weakened.

"Aye." The old man spoke between mouthfuls.

"What of the servants?"

"The cook is about. She tends our meals along with a few maids who tend the vegetable garden in the side courtyard during the season."

"And you?" she questioned.

All I Want

"I oversee the grounds during the day, but I shall not stay beyond sunset."

"And why is that?"

"Grandfather?" the child's voice echoed from outside. "Grandfather?" The second call held a tremor of fear in its pitch.

"Me granddaughter, Lillie." The bench scraped against the stone floor when he stood. "In here, lassie." His voice did not ring with the feeble tone she'd anticipated.

"Grandfather! Ye dinna wake me so I can help ye." The blonde-haired girl rushed inside but froze in the doorway when she saw Jeanne.

"I started earlier this morn, lassie. Laird Tryon set extra tasks for me."

"But I *always* help ye, Grandfather." She was near tears, and the old man opened his arms wide. The child rushed into his embrace.

Jeanne placed the girl's age to be around seven or eight years old. She stole a sideways glance at Jeanne.

"Who is she?" Her long hair cascaded in ringlets over her shoulders down to her waist.

"A new one. Have ye had your meal this morning?"

"Nae." The child shook her head. A tiny gold earring in her left ear jangled with the motion, but her wide-eyed gaze never left Jeanne.

"I suppose you're hungry as well?" he asked Jeanne then shuffled over to the fire. "Fetch a bowl." He nodded to the cupboard in the corner.

She reached for a wooden bowl and handed it to the little girl.

"Lillie's a pretty name," she spoke in the child's native tongue.

The girl jerked the bowl from Jeanne and rushed over to her grandfather.

"Is she like *them*, Grandfather?" she whispered.

"Not yet." He spoke so softly, Jeanne had to strain to hear him. He swung the pot on its hinged arm away from the fire and slopped the porridge into the girl's bowl. The guarded look never left her blue eyes as she watched Jeanne retrieve another bowl and take the ladle the old man offered.

"No cream this morning, Lillie, love. The milkmaids have yet to return. Eat your meal, now, and ye can help me collect the eggs."

"Wonderful! I love to collect the eggs."

Lillie looked up at him with open adoration shining in her cherubic face.

Jeanne spooned the thick porridge into the bowl then sat down on the bench across from Lillie. Still eyeing her suspiciously, Lillie spooned the porridge into her mouth and ate hurriedly. All the while, the child glanced toward her grandfather as he moved about the kitchen adding wood to the fire as though she feared he would leave her alone with Jeanne.

"My name is Jeanne. I arrived last night. Would you care to show me about the grounds when you finish your chores with your grandfather?"

Lillie glanced over at her grandfather, who tossed his bowl into the large barrel filled with water. He looked up.

"If ye like, Lillie. Would be a safe thing for ye to do."

Lillie contemplated Jeanne as though deciding whether she could trust her. At length the child turned back to her breakfast without a comment.

"I must be about," her grandfather announced. "Stay and finish your meal with the lady, Lillie."

"Nae, wait for me, Grandfather." Lillie jumped from the table and rushed to scrape the remains of her half-eaten meal into a nearby barrel. She dropped the empty bowl into the water where her grandfather had deposited his. Shoving her hand into his, she skipped alongside him.

Jeanne took an uneasy breath when the door slammed behind them. Tryon was alive? Her pulse quickened. Apparently, her diagnosis had been correct. It was an eerie feeling knowing that only a skeleton staff ran the castle by day. It was clear Tryon had used the people's superstitions to gain his power. Sleeping during the day would be a logical choice for one sensitive to the sun. It would also be reasonable for his wife to adopt the same schedule as well as the general household.

So he had transformed the limitations of his disease from something his enemies could perceive as a weakness and had masterfully made it a strength. Combined with the backdrop of superstitions and mystical practitioners such as Ishabelle, it had the perfect makings of a reign of fear. It was rare to come across a person with catalepsy. She wanted to talk with him, that is, if she could really talk with the man and not the myth.

All I Want

Her stomach rumbled. Reluctantly, she finished the bland mush then put the bowl in the same water barrel the old man and little girl had used. She stood staring about the kitchen, noting the large fireplace with its pots and kettles waiting to be used. Suddenly, she felt as though she were the only person in the world. Life had slowed to a crawl now that she no longer dodged the next assassin lurking in the shadows. Absently, she wondered what it had been like to microwave a bagel. She had learned to live without so many modern conveniences. Until now, she'd had little time to miss their absence. How she missed her morning stop by the coffee shop. It seemed like another lifetime, almost as though she had awakened from a dream she'd had about a future world.

Her sudden nostalgia tugged deeper into longings which circled back to the new constant in her life—Mael. If only she could talk with him. She needed to feel his all-engulfing embrace and hungry kisses. Hugging herself against a shiver, she left the kitchen. It was the first time she had actually been alone since coming through the portal. Verica had been the first to befriend her, then there had been Mael. Her pulse quickened as she recalled his fierceness the night he had rescued her from the villagers. Never had any man looked so sexy. She sighed.

The pain of his loss bore down on her. Even the brilliant sunlight that greeted her as she emerged from the cold kitchen could not raise her spirits. Squinting, she marveled at the warmth covering her cheeks, which was quickly chilled by the lashing wind. The sound of chickens clucking angrily brushed past her in a gust of wind.

Curious, and not wanting to reenter the lifeless castle, she turned toward the farmyard and quickly found the young girl assisting her grandfather in the chicken coop. Her delighted squeals each time she retrieved an egg from underneath a hen made Jeanne smile with memories of her own childhood and Easter egg hunts.

Lillie turned to show her grandfather her latest find when she glimpsed Jeanne standing there. She waved, hoping to calm the child's earlier fears. The smile was faint as Lillie raised her hand in a slight wave. Taking a deep breath, Jeanne continued to watch until the last egg had been gathered.

"Look at all the eggs I found." Lillie ran over to her and pointed to the basket her grandfather carried.

"You're the best egg gatherer I've ever seen, Lillie," she nodded.

"Aye," the old man huffed with pride then headed for the kitchen.

"I'll help, Grandfather."

"Nae, Lillie, go play."

Lillie's face scrunched up and then she looked at Jeanne.

"I can show ye about the castle now if ye like," she offered and dug her hands into her fur cape as it flapped about.

Jeanne nodded, grateful to retreat from the wind into the Grand Hall. Lifting her skirts, she climbed the steps and entered behind her young tour guide. Unexpected emotions flooded her with the memory of the last time she'd been in MacRaigl Castle's Great Hall. She took a deep breath and struggled to suppress her sorrow.

MacRaigl Hall would be empty this time of day with servants adding new rushes and spices to the floor in preparation for the new week. The men would be off on their hunt, and Mael—her heart pounded harder. He would be about daily duties among his clansmen. He would listen to their problems, help those who needed assistance and resolve disputes.

Had the woman stayed the night? Would he have taken her into his bed so soon? Jeanne shook her head and closed her eyes against the thought. She hated herself for allowing such torturous images to invade her thoughts.

"Are ye ill?" The child touched her hand.

She looked down at the girl and shook her head.

"Ye look sad."

"I am." She squeezed the girl's hand.

"When I feel sad, I go to the top of me mistress's tower, to the secret room."

"Secret room?"

"Want to see?"

"Yes."

Lillie's smile widened, revealing a missing tooth. Holding Jeanne's hand, she led the way to the tower stairwell. A cold current whirled past them as they climbed the winding steps.

"They won't hear us. They're asleep," Lillie whispered.

"They?"

"Me master and mistress." She pointed to the second-floor chamber door.

Jeanne looked down at her, longing to explain away the superstitious aura that cocooned Tryon and Ishabelle.

"Ye dinna believe me?" Her lower lip jutted out. Without warning, Lillie released her hand and rushed over to the door, pushing her slight frame against it.

Jeanne scaled the steps to stop her from interrupting the couple.

"You can't just barge in there and wake them up," she reprimanded the child.

"They shall not hear. I visit them often when the guard is not about."

"Guard?" Jeanne swallowed hard.

"Aye. He usually stands there." She pointed to a nook along the long window shuttered against the light.

"Where is he?"

"Eating?" She shrugged her tiny shoulders. "The garderobe? He dinna guard all the time. Not like he should," she whispered.

"What would Laird Tryon do if he knew?"

The child's eyes widened. "Nae, dinna tell me master. Jeremy be me brother. I would not want him harmed. Please." The child gripped her hand, chubby fingers digging into her flesh.

"Shhh. I won't say anything, Lillie. I promise." She took a ragged breath, feeling the child's anxiety as her own. She recognized the fear in Lillian's eyes, just as she'd felt for Ryan. She bowed her head.

"Going inside their chamber will alert them that Jeremy's not at his post," she warned, thinking it would prevent future intrusions.

"They dinna hear when they sleep. 'Tis the reason Jeremy guards them. He must be their eyes and ears during the day."

Before Jeanne could react, the child shoved against the door and it creaked open.

"Lillie!" She reached for the girl, but the child was too fast and slipped into the darkened room away from her grasp. She hurried after her.

The heavy draperies were drawn against the morning light. Immediately, she spotted Lillie standing at one of the bedposts peering between the brocade panels.

Tiptoeing across the room, her fingers itched to seize the child and usher her from the room before the Tryons awoke. Lillie glanced back at her and bobbed her head with long curls bouncing about tiny shoulders.

"See?" she whispered and pointed, only she didn't point at the mattress. Her short finger stiffened upwards inside of the canopy. Jeanne mused how similar children were—even centuries apart they still enjoyed teasing adults. She closed her fingers around Lillie's arm and dragged her toward the door.

"Dinna ye see—"

She clamped her hand over the girl's mouth and rushed her outside, closing the door solidly behind them.

"Why did ye do that? Ye dinna even see. Ye spoiled it." Lillie stamped her foot and walked away, heading for the stairs. She ran down them and out the door into the courtyard.

Catching up with her outside, Jeanne called to her.

"Lillie, you can't do that ever again. It's not right to spy on people while they sleep."

"Ye spoiled the fun. Now ye shall not see them, and I shall not show ye the secret room." She stomped off, leaving Jeanne in the courtyard staring after her.

* * * * *

Jeanne spent the remainder of the morning in her chamber, sitting in front of the fire while the scene of Lillie in the Tryon's bedchamber replayed over and over in her mind. Children had very active imaginations she reminded herself, yet the picture of Lillie pointing up at the canopy piqued her curiosity. Just what would she have seen?

Eventually, the silence of the castle grew loud and she couldn't recall ever feeling so alone. She missed Mael and couldn't bear the thought of another woman in his life, however superficial it might be. Sorrow welled in her and spilled down her cheeks. Then the most painful thoughts penetrated her grief. If she had in fact met his descendant in her time, then— She wailed and covered her cries with her hands, pacing across the room, longing to run from the realization. Mael surely would wed another and sire children. She felt as though her very heart ripped through her flesh, leaving her an empty hollow shadow.

Throwing herself onto the bed, Jeanne wept for the life and children she would never have with him, until spent, she drifted off to sleep. It was a fitful rest, with an occasional noise jerking her awake. Sometimes she rushed to the window and peered down into the bailey only to see one of the servants skirt across the yard toward the kitchen. By early afternoon she had counted five servants, noting two more guards had taken posts. Every now and then she would see Lillie skipping alongside her grandfather.

The sun moved past the west wall and with it distant aromas wafted from the kitchen stirring her stomach into a rumble. Steeling herself for the cold welcome she knew awaited, she donned the fur and hurried to the kitchen. The people inside halted their conversations. A middle-aged woman sat at the end of the rough table. To her right sat Lillie and her grandfather. Jeanne noticed the young man sitting beside Lillie had red hair, and the same look in his eyes as the others—fear.

"'Tis the lady, I told ye about, Missus McLarty," the old man spoke to the woman who was obviously in charge of the kitchen, for she stood and set about preparing Jeanne a plate of venison stew.

She plopped it down on the far end of the table.

"Thank you. I am Jeanne McBen."

All eyes stared up at her as though she had spoken a foreign language.

"Ye arrived with me mistress?" the young man beside Lillie finally spoke.

Taking up the bread, she sopped the stew. She had learned that most people carried their own eating utensil with them—a dirk. She didn't have one so she picked up the meat with her fingers and ate.

"I arrived late last night," she nodded.

"Ye best keep the hours of your hosts, me lady." Mrs. McLarty wiped her hands on a stained apron and sat back down to finish her meal.

"I don't know that I can do that." She sipped from the wooden mug.

"Not right for a lady such as ye to be dining with such as we. Me mistress would not be pleased," the cook insisted.

"I'll talk with your mistress when she awakes."

There were some muffled comments from the far end of the table, and she sneaked a glance at Lillie, who quickly hid behind her grandfather.

"How long will your visit be, Lady McBen?" the old man braved. They all awaited her reply.

"I don't know," she sighed, feeling the desperateness of her new life.

"Best ye leave whilst ye can," the old man mumbled with a low chorus of ayes and nods from the cook and young man.

Chapter Twenty-Seven

Dusk settled over the valley with the red sun hanging just above the mountain ranges. Jeanne drew a long breath of crisp air before closing the tall balcony door and turning into the room. She paced in front of the crackling fireplace. The lack of sleep the previous night weighted her eyelids. She longed to stretch out on the bed, but had waited all day for Ishabelle to make an appearance. She couldn't risk missing her.

Maybe just a quick nap. She lay down on the thick quilted cover and stared at the fading sun beyond the window. Just a short nap then she would go downstairs and find Ishabelle.

She startled awake. A movement came from outside the door. Her breath caught in her throat when the knock resounded. Gathering her wits, Jeanne set about lighting a taper from the low-burning fire.

The knocking grew louder.

"Just a moment," she called and nearly tripped in her haste to answer, sliding the bolt from the door. It swung open with the harsh torch light from the stairwell piercing her eyes.

Ishabelle's eyes gleamed with bold amusement. She wore a dark purple dress, cinched at the waist, revealing how slender she was.

"I dinna mean to startle ye, Jeanne." She stood holding a tray covered with a white linen cloth.

"Ishabelle," she said and swallowed the nervous quivering the woman's mere presence caused. "I was just enjoying the sunset and fell asleep."

"Sunset? My dear, Jeanne, 'tis much later. The sun shall rise soon." Ishabelle drifted around her and lowered the tray to the table then moved to stand in front of the fireplace. Jeanne marveled at the way she moved as though a part of the very air.

"I brought ye something to eat. Some mutton stew and a nice heather ale to wash it down. Eat." She gestured to the covered tray.

"I slept all night?" She rubbed her neck and strained to clear the sleep from her mind. The fire leapt higher creating a wall of light and shadows behind Ishabelle.

"What did ye do all day?" Her voice was veiled and belied her pretense of concern.

"I find it strange that you operate your household like this, Ishabelle. What is the reasoning?" She yawned.

"I dinna understand."

"Is this a game?" Her stomach rumbled as the faint aroma of roasted lamb drifted over to her. "I mean, is that what you're doing? Playing games with me?" She met Ishabelle's wide-eyed glare. Its force hit her with a jolt of pressure. She took a step backwards feeling as though she had been knocked off balance. How was that possible? She was still asleep, she reasoned.

"I have not brought ye here for game-playing. Now eat your stew like a good lass." She moved her hand so fast, Jeanne could have sworn the linen drifted from the tray on its own.

She relented and sat down to the meal, still in a mental fog. Her stomach rumbled louder as the smell of the stew entered her nostrils and her mouth literally watered and filled with the taste of mutton stew. Such an odd sensation as though she had actually eaten the stew. Shaking, she picked up the spoon and retrieved a small piece of lamb with broth.

"Eat, Jeanne." Ishabelle's voice vibrated through the haze. "I prepared the stew myself, just for ye. Do ye like it?" Her smile was stiff and cold.

Jeanne's stare locked with her hostess's icy one. Goose bumps traveled up her arms. She strained to break free of Ishabelle's stare and was reminded of the feeling she'd had so long ago in a diner parking lot with another MacRaigl.

"It has a different flavor to it," she swallowed. The stew raced down her throat to her stomach. A sudden heat coursed through her. It was as though her senses heightened followed by a surge of energy that literally bolted through her. She gasped and clutched at her rumbling stomach.

"Secret ingredients," Ishabelle's smile broadened. "Makes the stew have a bit of a kick to it."

"Um." She took another bite. Each bite exploded with layers of unique flavors. What were they? It wasn't a delicious stew, yet she craved another bite of lamb, another sip of the broth. With each spoonful she was left wanting more until to her dismay, it was gone.

Ishabelle beamed down at the empty bowl, obviously pleased with her culinary skill.

"There now. Do drink your ale, my dear. The stew needs a bit of ale to complement the spices."

Jeanne obeyed, taking a small sip of the light ale. It filled her senses with the smell of yeast and she suddenly felt dizzy. Absently, she wondered about the alcohol content. The thought slipped from her. The buzz was stronger than any she'd ever felt. She forced her attention on Ishabelle.

"I've had to wait all day for you to make an appearance, Ishabelle. After your little experiment failed last night, you just disappeared. So what do we do now since your magic didn't work?"

"I offered ye a way home, Jeanne McBen. Do ye now insult my generosity?"

"Oh please." She stood but the room titled sideways, settled quickly. "You offered to use your magic to send me back to my time because you want me out of the way. Out of Mael's life. Only your magic failed. And now you feel you were being generous to me?" The anger pumped through her, but she felt as though she were moving in slow motion. "Is it generosity to keep me prisoner while you fulfill your own agenda? I hardly think so. I would call it deception because you deceived me in order to get me out of your brother's life."

"Ye deceive yourself, Jeanne McBen. 'Twas your own heart that kept ye here in my time. Nothing more. As for my brother, I make it my concern to know everything that affects him and the future of the MacRaigl clan. 'Tis my duty as *seer* to protect my clan, any way I can.

"I know about the man who incited Cullen. He poisoned Cullen de Mangus' mind. And now he has returned to your time from whence he came, only he left Cullen burning with a passion to destroy my family. Cullen shall not rest until all of us lie dead." Her brown eyes glistened with determination. "I shall not allow that to happen to my family."

"Yes, you've made that quite clear." She clasped her hands together in front of her, attempting to still their trembling. How could Ishabelle know all this? Perhaps a part of her was truly a seer. She shook her head against the odd sensations trying to engulf her. The ale was more potent than she had realized. Jeanne made a mental note not to drink ale upon awaking ever again. Regardless if it was customary to have ale with morning meals, her system was too modern for such robust living.

"Ye merely became an obstacle to my brother's destiny."

"What destiny is that?"

"Ruler of this land, of course. He was marked at birth as the rightful heir. He was destined to be Chief. I shall do whatever I must to assure he fulfills that birthright. And that requires him to marry and bear children, for only they remain the true legacy once our time is finished."

Jeanne's pulse quickened. Mael would fulfill that legacy without her. She had met his descendant.

"Had ye remained with him, there could be no legacy."

Her stare hardened on Ishabelle.

"I know of the disease that plagues your time. It makes the women sterile. And the men are dead within months after succumbing to *Next Gen*. I also know about your antiserum." She moved over to the window where the moon hung just above the dark mountain range. "Your serum can save your world. Ye have a destiny as well, Jeanne McBen, but it dinna lie here, in my time. Your destiny resides with your own people. Ye must save them, just as I must save mine."

"How...how do you know this?"

"I *am* a seer. Ye discredit me with something ye were unable to accomplish last evening."

She was amazed at the woman's refusal to accept she had failed to do what she'd claimed she could.

"I saw ye before ye ever came through the portal. Unbidden, I watched, helpless to stop your arrival. I dreaded the day ye would come. I knew what your arrival would bring. And I knew what I had to do. So I positioned myself to counter the destruction ye would bring."

"If you knew all that," Jeanne said, pausing to still the tremor in her voice, "then you know how I tried to return to my own time when Trench did."

"Aye. Ye were earnest in your quest to fulfill your destiny. 'Tis why I offered the sacred gift to ye. But ye were unwilling to give up my brother, so it bound ye to my time. 'Twas not my magic that failed last evening, but *your* lack of conviction. And now Trench shall discover the missing equation he so desperately needs. Perhaps not in time to save your world, but to save those who have money enough to pay whatever sum he commands for your cure. But in the end, your kind shall limp along through time until it has recovered from this plague and once more rebuild its numbers."

"My kind?" she asked. "What do you mean by that?"

"I realized last evening ye shall never be able to transcend time through your heart. 'Tis your heart that keeps ye anchored to my brother." She leveled her gaze on Jeanne.

Uncomfortable under her regard, Jeanne tried to avert Ishabelle's stare.

"However, I can offer ye another way." The woman released her gaze. "Are ye willing?"

"Oh, great." Weak-limbed, she plopped down in the chair with a sigh. "What is it this time? Do I have to drink some putrid witch's brew? Perhaps you want me to dance naked around a standing stone during a full moon. And when this fails, too, are you going to blame my unwilling heart?" Her stomach churned noisily.

"Be careful with your sarcasm." The tone of Ishabelle's voice snapped her to attention. "Making jest of those things ye canna understand means ye risk losing all hope."

"I have a newsflash for you, Ishabelle, I've already lost all hope." She vented her anger, longing to rile Ishabelle into some kind of demonstration of all this magic and seer power she boasted. Frustrated over her failed attempt to save Mael and return to her time, Jeanne realized being at Fernmoora was futile.

"Ye may still be able to save your world." Ishabelle acted as though she'd not heard a word she'd said.

"What?"

"But there's always a price for what we want and 'tis no different with this. Are ye prepared to pay the price for *this* kind of hope, Jeanne?"

"You just don't give up. You should be a used car salesman. Again, it lies at my doorstep that I must be the one to sacrifice for something you want to give to me."

"I offer ye the greatest gift of all the world, but to accept it, ye shall no longer be like others."

"Then who would I be like? You? And what is that? A sleep-deprived former widow with delusions of being a grand sorceress?"

"Your humor fails ye for ye know the truth within your soul. I offer ye the gift to never die, to live forever. As a scientist ye must surely be curious." One of her eyebrows arched high above her unnerving stare.

"You're insane." Her bravado wavered. "I tried your way. It failed. There's no way back. So, I've reached a decision. If I must be stuck in your time, I'll at least have a life with my husband. Your approval is not needed. I'll find a way to make this right with him." She pivoted and started for the door, but halted with a start when a shadow emerged from the hallway. The man stopped just inside the opening. She staggered backwards with her breath rushing between parted lips.

He wore a red and black tartan with full regalia and a linen shirt. She trembled under his intense regard.

"It's not possible!" she gasped.

Alexander Tryon's lips slid into a cold, satisfied smile. He was a tall man, with broad shoulders and stark black hair plaited into one thick braid that ran down the center of his back. His features were sharp and refined. His pallor reminded her of chalk, but it was his eyes that captivated, yet shocked her. They were solid dark with no white showing.

"I dinna believe ye met my husband. Alexander, welcome our guest, Jeanne, the one I told ye about."

"And did ye have a nice, long rest, Jeanne?" He nodded slightly to her, but his dark gaze swiftly found his wife. "Did ye give our guest your special stew, my dear? She must learn to keep the schedule of our household."

"Aye. The first step toward transformation has begun." Ishabelle's smile was one of triumph.

Her pulse pounded harder. What had they given her? Fear pierced her heart, ripping it with cold, sharp talons.

"My dear, we have a slight problem." He moved past Jeanne, stretching out his open hand to his wife. "It appears Jeremy has been neglectful of his duties. As I prepared to retire, I discovered *this* on our chamber floor."

Jeanne's breath tightened in the center of her chest. She swore her heart stopped beating for the briefest second as she strained to see past

All I Want

the man's shoulder to his outstretched hand. She leaned forward trying to see what the object was. He pivoted in one fluid movement, and she found herself staring up into his depthless eyes. The trembling chill started in her chest and fanned out to her fingertips. The air stirred colder. She shivered against the bitter freeze.

"'Tis a child's." His wife held the tiny loop to the light, drawing Jeanne's attention to the world outside. The moon had disappeared behind the mountain range. Her gaze fell over the couple and the loop Ishabelle held higher to examine.

Her breath rushed from her as she recognized Lillie's earring.

"I daresay 'twas that brat, Lillie," Ishabelle continued. "If she has been spying on us again—"

"I shall have a word with Jeremy." His voice chiseled into the air.

"A word, my love? Do ye believe that strong enough a reprimand?"

"Ye may be correct, my sweet. A first-time offense warrants a verbal reprimand. A second time requires sterner measures." He stared down at Jeanne. "Did ye see the old man's granddaughter about?"

She nodded, unable to push a sound past the tightening in her throat.

"Tell me where ye saw her," he demanded as one accustomed to giving commands and having them followed without question.

"During the morning." The words pushed past her attempt to hold them in her mouth. "She was helping her grandfather gather eggs, then again at the afternoon meal."

"Ye ate with the servants?" His fine-lipped mouth slit into a severe disapproving frown.

"I told ye, Alex. Her cooperation is nonexistent." Ishabelle handed her husband the gold earring. "I daresay she was with the little orphan when she spied on us."

Locking her arm through her husband's muscular one, Ishabelle leaned against him. Her breast brushed his arm, and his attention swiftly deserted Jeanne. She watched him smile down at his wife.

"My beautiful wife. Of course Lillie is enamored of ye." He bent down to kiss her. "I most certainly am."

Their passion stirred and Jeanne looked away when Ishabelle pressed her lithe form against him. He released her lips to trace the length of her neck.

She could have sworn she heard a hissing sound as he nuzzled his wife's neck. She glanced at the fire and realized it must have been damp wood sizzling from the flames.

"The night fades, my love," Ishabelle purred while caressing his cheek with the back of her hand.

"Aye, 'tis a shame." His lips covered hers, and Ishabelle drew her arms around his neck.

Jeanne recognized her opportunity and turned for the door.

"Dinna leave so soon, Jeanne," he commanded without breaking from his embrace with his wife. "An answer I await. Did the child come to our chamber whilst we slept?"

"Let your guard answer," her voice cracked, betraying her attempt to sound unmoved by his powerful presence.

"No, I require an answer from ye." He turned to her, his arm still tight about Ishabelle's waist.

Jeanne met his gaze again and was slightly relieved to see a faint glint of white in his eyes, however abnormal. She swallowed and longed for a glass of cold water to ease the dryness strangling her.

"Do I frighten ye, Jeanne?" His eyebrows arched higher.

She took a deep breath, willing her hammering pulse to calm.

"Is that what you want? I admit, I find your lifestyle a bit unusual and unnerving, Laird Tryon."

"Lifestyle?" The cold hollowness of his laughter vibrated in the room. She froze in its unearthly peal. "She truly *is* from the future, my dear. Her language bears it out, 'tis just as ye saw, my gifted love. She shall bring us much amusement." He planted a tender kiss on Ishabelle's forehead.

"We have nothing to hide from ye, Jeanne," Ishabelle spoke.

"No? You may think you have me fooled, but I know your magic is just an illusion built upon fears and superstitions." Crossing her arms over her chest, Jeanne felt very helpless against the two of them. Ishabelle's look swept across the room leaving an icy trail in its wake. Jeanne shivered.

"Ye are young and very naïve, Jeanne, if ye think ye can hedge my questions." Alexander frowned. "I ask ye once more. Dinna try my patience further. Was the child in our private chamber?"

All I Want

The need to tell him the truth choked in her throat as she willed it back. She sensed that somehow he was responsible for the compulsion to confess. She would die before she betrayed the child.

"Ask your guard," she breathed, rushing to speak before he regained control over her. "I don't work for you." Her voice sounded braver than she felt. She dropped his stare and focused on the floor. The sound was like a growl and grew into a snarl and she knew if she were to look up, she'd see him standing there with his teeth clenched and lip curled back. She didn't dare look. A shiver snaked down her spine.

"Nae, Alex," Ishabelle cooed. "She dinna understand just yet. Once she has acclimated to our way, she shall become more cooperative and understand the severity of this matter. She needs time for it to grow inside her. But we dinna have the time to question her any further. Look. We have a more pressing matter to attend." Her voice pitched higher with obvious concern. "The night, 'tis spent."

Jeanne glanced up. The couple stood in front of her, facing the window. She quickly saw the brilliant pink sky and said a silent prayer of thanks.

Alexander turned to Jeanne and moved to stand in front of her. "Ye shall answer my question the next time we meet, Jeanne McBen. Upon your very life ye shall answer." He brushed past her and out the door with Ishabelle following close behind. She stopped in the doorway and pivoted to face Jeanne.

"'Tis a very unwise thing to go against my husband, a man accustomed to the respect he deserves. He dinna tolerate insult any more than he tolerates negligent guards and their mischievous sisters." Her stare punctuated the warning. "Ye would be wise to remember that when next he questions ye. Until then, sleep, Jeanne, we shall return for ye. Sleep…" her voice echoed in a whisper that spiraled into the chamber. She then turned, closing the door behind her.

Jeanne rushed to slide the bolt snuggly in place. She staggered, barely able to stand. Gasping for breath, she fell against the heavy door.

What had she been thinking? If the rumors *were* true, then she had tempted fate with her refusal to confirm their suspicions. What had she been thinking when she'd agreed to come here?

Alexander Tryon was not a man to let such defiance go unpunished. Her heartbeat leapt to her throat. Hurriedly, she glanced about the chamber. Alexander Tryon's presence still hung heavily in the air. What if there truly was a secret room or passage as Lillie had claimed? She could use it to leave Fernmoora, but she must first warn Lillie and her brother.

She stumbled toward the chair. Why was she having such a difficult time walking? She faced the window as the sun rose brilliantly over the mountains. She would pull the chair over to the window and watch for Lillie. There was plenty of time to escape before Ishabelle and Alexander awoke. Her ears rang and a rush of heat leapt from her stomach as though she were on fire. What had Ishabelle put in that stew? Or had it been the ale? She staggered to the table and picked up the bowl, holding it to the firelight and rubbed her finger against the inside curve of the bowl. The dark stain streaked down her finger. Shaking, she held it to the light.

"Blood?" she rasped. Realization drummed hard beats in her chest. The room spun, and her knees weakened. "No."

Chapter Twenty-Eight

Jeanne jerked awake, struggling to get her bearings. She was lying on the floor in front of the cold fireplace. She pushed into a sitting position. What time was it?

The sun hung low in the sky. She cursed under her breath. In spite of her good intentions, she had missed the entire day. Why had she trusted Ishabelle? Suddenly, she recalled the blood in the stew and convulsed at the thought. Disgusted, she hurried across the room and out the door, determined to find Lillie. Once outside, she ran across the courtyard toward the kitchen and threw open the door. The old man smiled with relief flashing in his tired eyes. Lillie gave her a guarded glance, telling her the child had yet to forgive her for spoiling yesterday's game.

"I thought ye had fallen into the schedule of me master and mistress," he said.

Jeanne shook her head.

"Can we finish our look about the castle, Lillie?" she invited. The little girl looked up at her grandfather who nodded.

"Aye." Lillie's smile widened. Jeanne smiled back with relief.

"Always shy in the beginning, but once she finds her tongue, she'll talk your ears off," he laughed.

Her tiny hand was cold as she slipped it into Jeanne's on their way to the Great Hall.

"Do ye wish to see them now?" She released Jeanne's hand and ran in front of her toward the main tower.

"No, Lillie!" Jeanne ran after her. "You can't."

Ignoring her, Lillie ran up the stairs.

"Jeremy!" The child's voice rang up the turret as she rushed over to the young man standing on the landing. He stooped to receive her hug.

"I wanted to show her. She dinna believe."

He settled Lillie on his knee.

"There now, what did I tell ye? I canna let ye inside. 'Tis not safe. Should Laird Tryon discover—"

"They know about yesterday," Jeanne said, interrupting them.

Both Jeremy and Lillie turned to her with terrified expressions.

"They found your earring, Lillie."

The child groped at her ear where the ring used to dangle. "I thought I lost it in the chicken pen."

"Laird Tryon will not let this go unpunished." Jeremy's face was nearly as white as Tryon's had been.

"I daresay you're right." Jeanne looked at Lillie, more concerned for the child's welfare. "You should leave. Get far away from here."

"Dinna leave!" Lillie's arms tightened around his neck.

"I shall not leave, Lillie," he consoled with his arm about her then looked up at Jeanne. His round, freckled face scrunched up in a worried frown. "The Tryon would surely find me." The lanky youth released Lillie and stood to his full height. He scratched his head, absently running his hand down the long braid that traced one side of his face.

"You could hide in the mountains," Jeanne suggested.

"Ye dinna understand the power of me master. 'Tis nae place I could hide. Were I a bird, he would find me still."

"Jeremy." Lillie's eyes were wide with fear.

"Hush, little dove." He scooped her into his arms. She hugged his neck. "The Tryon shall not harm me. I am his favorite since I was but your size." He jostled her and managed a nervous laugh.

"The room. Ye could hide in the secret room." Lillie's face brightened.

"Nae, little one. 'Tis nae secret to them." He set her down.

"What *is* this room?" Jeanne asked, chewing on her lower lip. There should be some way to save the young man.

"It leads to a passage that runs underneath the castle all the way to the river. Lillie discovered it. If Laird Tryon knew we had knowledge of it—" His voice broke off and his blue eyes clouded with the obvious direness of his situation.

"Then you must use it to leave. You should leave now, while you can. Where is it?"

All I Want

"Nae, dinna tell her," Lillie pouted.

"Running would be foolish." He shook his head and smiled down at Lillie. "The Tryon shall not harm me, little one. But ye must be off. Dinna worry about me." He winked at Lillie. "'Tis almost sunset, and ye must return to Grandfather."

"Come, Lillie, we shall find your grandfather," Jeanne offered, anxious to see her off so she could talk some sense into Jeremy.

"Nae!" Lillie jerked from Jeanne's attempt to take her hand. "Had ye not startled me and dragged me from their chamber, I would not lost me earring. 'Tis your fault. I hate ye!" She burst into tears and sprinted down the stairs and out the tower.

Jeanne stood on the staircase helpless to console her. She couldn't save either of them from Alexander Tryon's wrath.

"She is but a child. 'Tis me fault for allowing her to wrap me about her finger." Jeremy shook his head. Her own helplessness was mirrored in his blue eyes.

"You must leave, Jeremy, while they still sleep. I'm afraid what he will do to you. He was enraged."

"A worse fate would await me once Laird Tryon caught up with me. Until that time, he would take his anger out on me family. On Lillie."

"There has to be some way." Jeanne raked her hand through her hair.

"Fear not for me," he insisted and took a deep breath. "Me lady understands the ways of a child. Lillie shall be reprimanded but she shall not be harmed."

"I saw the look in Laird Tryon's eyes and Ishabelle was not very understanding."

"What would ye have me do? Flee and abandon me sister? Would ye have her face the Tryon in me place?"

Jeanne gasped with realization, but before she could reply, a shout from outside interrupted them.

"Grandfather." Jeremy rushed past her, taking the steps two at a time and bounded out the door.

Jeanne was hard on his heels.

"She just jumped on the horse and rode off. Where does she go? Why would she do such a thing?" The old man pointed toward the gates.

Jeremy rushed past him with Jeanne running as fast as she could. She caught up with him in the stable.

"Saddle a horse for me," she ordered the groomsman.

"Nae. I shall fetch her. Someone must guard me laird and lady." He grasped her hands in his. "Someone I can trust. Who can explain with her *heart* when they awaken why I abandoned me post."

Jeanne looked up at him as he swung onto the horse.

"My husband, your mistress's brother, Mael of the clan MacRaigl. He is the new Chief. He will grant you sanctuary. Do you know him?"

"Aye. I accompanied me master there weeks hence to warn of assassins."

"Travel there as fast as you can and tell him I sent you and Lillie to him." Jeanne reached up and touched his hand.

"I shall not forget ye, dear lady." He dug his heels into the horse's sides and yelled. She stood watching him as he raced from the castle after the child.

As she turned for the tower, Jeanne's heart pounded harder at the sight of the sinking sun. She scaled the steps, panting. She must stall Ishabelle and Tryon in their room. Somehow, she must gain more time for Jeremy and Lillie. Her legs carried her toward the room and with each step, the air grew heavier.

Catching her breath, she stood in front of the heavily carved door and listened. Had they awakened during the ruckus? Alexander Tryon would waste no time sending for Jeremy. He did not strike her as the kind of man to let unfinished business linger. She smoothed her clammy hands over her cloak and leaned against the door. No sounds came from the room. She pushed against the massive door and it creaked open just enough for her to slip into the darkened room. The air was cold and dense within the shrouded room.

She stood just inside the room and allowed her eyes to adjust to the dimness before venturing further. She looked beyond the bed to the windows where the draperies didn't close completely against the fading day, leaving enough of a gap for her to see the brilliant shards of piercing rays along the mountaintop. Sunset had begun. Her pulse throbbed to her throat. Soon, shades of pink and purple would streak the sky, and darkness would fall. She trembled as she took a step forward.

Her legs wobbled beneath her. Pausing at the foot of the canopied bed, her breathing quickened. She tried to still the quaking in her body by clutching her trembling hands together. The sound of her panting breath filled the room.

Her gaze slipped over the curtains encasing the massive bed. She raised her hand. Her fingertips brushed the heavy gold and red brocade. The material's coldness seemed to suck the very warmth from her. She jerked her hand away. Gathering her wits, Jeanne stared through the two panels. Her breath hung in her throat.

She leaned forward and peeked through the narrow slit. There was only darkness. Tilting her head, she held her breath and strained to hear their slumbering breaths, but there was only unnatural silence. She let her hand slip along the side hem of the panel and gently tugged it from itself. Her eyes ached as she widened her gaze, intent upon seeing the couple vulnerable in their sleep, but she only found a neatly made bed. Her mind rejected what she saw. It wasn't possible. Where were they?

Recalling Lillie's outstretched gesture the day before, and how the child had pointed up into the canopy, Jeanne's pulse jabbed a gasp from her. Licking her lips, she moved her gaze up the solid silk lining of the interior panel. It slipped over the deep gold tint shimmering from the last rays of day.

Her heart slammed against her frantic thoughts. Her breath pumped in short rapid jerks. She pushed her stare over the elaborate post and gold tasseled cord suspended down its length to race beyond, forcing it up. She had to know. But she didn't want to see. She wanted to run. Her scalp tingled, and shivers crawled down her back.

She leaned back, lifting her head, allowing her gaze ascent up the tall bed. Her breath tunneled down her throat. Her mouth fell open for there at the very top of the elaborate canopy, just above her, were Ishabelle and Alexander. She covered her mouth, trapping the scream. Disbelief rampaged through her. It was not possible! They appeared to be suspended, lying facing down toward the mattress. They were still as though dead. How could they be some ten feet above the mattress? Her mind reeled with what her eyes commanded was there. The room spun around her.

She stumbled backwards. Numb in disbelief. The room darkened, and her stare flashed to the window. The sun had slipped behind the trees. It was night. Dread replaced her questions and hammered terror through her.

The current of air swept from the bed toward her. She spun on her heel toward the door, but the sound behind her made her turn. She glanced over her shoulder just as the dark shadows floated from the ceiling and swept in a rush toward her like falcons descending upon its prey. Her scream ripped through the deserted castle.

* * * * *

"Here," Mael called out to Ian, "I found it. 'Tis through here. Just as I remembered."

Crouched over, carrying a wooden box, Ian hurried along the slope of the riverbank.

"Aye, dinna appear to have been used for some time." His voice rose and fell with the roar of the rushing river below. "I thought it only legend. How did ye know?"

"When I was a lad and roaming the hills, I decided to see for myself if the legend of Tryon and his secret passage were true."

"Did ye now?"

"Aye. And what a surprise. It took me nearly all day to find it and I climbed the stairs, but just as I was about to enter, the light from the bottom stairs disappeared behind the mountains."

"And ye escaped unscathed?" Ian huffed behind him.

"Curious I was, a fool I wasn't. I dinna explore further, but lit across the hills back home and never ventured back. Yet here we be about to enter the devil's liar at sunset. And to think the fool in me waited 'til I be older to finally emerge." Mael scoffed but his attention snapped to the sound a few yards from where they stood hidden from the guards. A horse darted from the castle and bounded over the bridge.

"Who goes?" Ian asked.

"Appears to be a child. We must hurry." Mael wasted no time slashing the bramble from the opening with his sword. A second rider came bounding over the bridge, and they flattened their backs against the moss-covered embankment.

All I Want

"A runaway," Mael clipped then shoved from the hill, sheathing his sword to his back. He entered the black tunnel. "Careful, Ian, 'tis blinding dark."

It was slow going as Mael groped his way through the winding tunnel, often times missing the crude steps that climbed the hillside leading to Tryon's castle. His eyes ached for light as he continued to lead the way toward the top of the hill.

His thoughts raced ahead of him. What if he were too late? What if his sister had— He could not allow the thought into his mind. He quickened his stride and his foot slipped against the damp stairway.

"Easy now." Ian's voice echoed from below. "Would be a long tumble down for us both."

With his hand in front of him, Mael followed the curve of the narrow passage walls. Suddenly, their path was blocked by a barricade.

Ian's labored breath sounded behind him.

"The door?"

"Aye." Mael ran his flattened palms along the wooden door. When he touched the cold metal, he sighed in relief. He closed his hand around the curved handle and jerked it up. The door groaned upon its hinges. He wasted no time and pushed it open.

"Where are we?" Ian asked.

"An inner room," he whispered and felt his way along the stone wall.

"How will we find the passage?"

"Along the wall, 'tis a lever to release the door. Help me find it." Mael ran his hands over the wall, desperate for light. His senses played tricks on him and at times he wasn't sure of his direction.

"I've found it," Ian whispered from behind him. Mael turned at the sound of scraping as the hinged stone door released. He shoved his way through the narrow opening and stepped outside. The torchlight blinded him and he shielded his eyes from its piercing rays. Ian followed him from the secret room onto the round landing that led up the tower.

"Now where do we go?" Ian rubbed his eyes.

"Down," Mael smiled, pleased they had managed to enter Tryon's haven without detection. If he could locate Jeanne, he could get her from the castle before the devils discovered them.

The terrified scream sliced the air. The hairs along his neck bristled.

"'Tis Jeanne!" Mael drew his sword and ran down the steps, taking them two at a time. Ian drew his sword too, and still clutching the box, followed Mael.

As they neared the landing, the air grew heavy. It was as though a blanket had been drawn down over them. The force bore into every stride they took. Mael glanced over his shoulder and saw Ian collapse on the winding stairs behind him.

"I canna move. Me legs grow weak. 'Tis a spell," Ian heaved and struggled to rise, but fell back. Mael strained against the force and with labored steps retraced his steps to where Ian had collapsed. Ian handed him the sacred box.

"Ye must go without me. I dinna the strength to resist," he groaned. "The holy water rests inside the box."

Mael pushed his way down the steps to the lower landing.

Suddenly, the pressure released, and he fell to the floor. He grasped the wall for balance, tightening his grip on the box.

"The devil's lair grows cold," he tossed over his shoulder to his defeated companion above. He braced himself against the icy blast of air whipping along the stone stairwell and rushed past him.

"The bastard attempts to hold me with his witchery."

"Nae," came the female voice from the landing below him. The wall torch sputtered with the cold wave of air that surrounded him.

Mael looked down at her.

"'Tis I who holds ye prisoner," Ishabelle said with a triumphant smile. "Why are ye here, my brother?"

"I came for my wife. Release her."

"She came of her own free will."

"Nae." Mael opened the box and removed the ornate silver cross. The torch on the wall sputtered and reflected against the metal. The reflection came to rest in a harsh glint on Ishabelle's face. She cried out and shielded her eyes from it.

He seized the opportunity and darted past her and down the stairs to the main floor, knowing she must have come from where she held Jeanne prisoner.

"Nae!" Ishabelle's screech filled the tower.

When he rushed toward the chamber door, Ishabelle flew past him and blocked it.

"She dinna wish to be with ye."

"Stand down, ye bride of the devil. Ye once were my beloved sister. I dinna wish to kill my own blood, but keep me from Jeanne, and I shall."

"Jeanne!" His voice boomed down the dim corridor. "Are ye in there, lass?"

"Leave her, Mael. She canna make ye the father of a great country. Let her go. She has made her choice."

"What choice does the lass have?"

"A choice of life eternal. She can join me and—"

"Never!" Mael held up the cross again, but this time he retrieved the small vial of holy water and uncorked it. Ishabelle's gaze sharpened on the two sacred instruments and she shielded her face with her hands.

"Ye are my *brother*."

"Stand aside. Dinna force me, Ishabelle."

"Nae. I canna let ye throw away the future I worked so hard to prepare for ye." Her words halted him.

"*Ye*? Prepared for me?"

"Do ye think the branches reunited by themselves? Did ye truly believe 'twas their own initiative?" Her laughter was low. "My brother, ye know not the power of superstition, yet ye would douse me with this holy water and attempt to redeem my soul with a cross held to my flesh?"

"What do ye claim, Ishabelle?"

"My alliance and marriage to Alex was what sealed the unification of the clan, dear brother. Least ye think the Fareley rushed to give his clan's allegiance out of a higher calling of his soul? 'Twas the threat of Alexander Tryon and myself who blackmailed him into the peace.

"And when I presented the mighty chieftains of our clan with the choice of peace, or the wrath of the House of Tryon, they were most eager to unite and exalt ye to your rightful birthright."

"'Tis a lie! Your *marriage* created the rumors and incited the assassins," Mael yelled. He didn't want to hear her words.

"I foresaw all that has transpired. I saw your Jeanne before she emerged from the cave and I knew the turmoil she brought to our world. I saw Trench and how he would manipulate Cullen. So I knew I had but one choice. My marriage ultimately kept the clan from complete rebellion, dear brother. 'Twas Alexander and I who rallied Fareley to your side when Cullen began his plot to overthrow ye."

"Ishabelle." His breath knifed through his chest. He felt the truth in her words. "Ye gave yourself up to save the clan? By becoming the hunted? Why?"

"I saw it long before it began, my beloved brother." She stared at him with tears pooling in her eyes. "I saw your Jeanne and the evil creature who came through the portal before her. I saw the malice he spread across our land. I had to stop him. I had to assure ye fulfilled your destiny. But he escaped before Alexander and I could capture him. After all I have sacrificed, do ye think I would let a mere lass undo all I accomplished for our blood?"

The cross slipped from his grip and clamored against the floor followed by the vial of holy water. The glass shattered against the stones, pooling at his feet. Mael sank to his knees. The sacred box tumbled from his grasp, joining the other weapons of his final battle.

"Shhh, my brother. I shall never let ye be sacrificed for their greed." Ishabelle knelt beside him. He clutched the velvet sleeves of her gown. His anguished cry tore from him and he slammed himself against the stone walls.

"Nae!" he yelled. "Tell me ye dinna do this all for me!"

"We united the clan, all save the Mangus, and Alexander travels this very night to stop that seed which spawned it all. My husband shall see our enemy's seed never takes root. This night he shall set things back on their proper course and restore the natural order of life."

"Ishabelle," he choked. "Ye sacrificed your life."

"Shhh," she stroked his head, "'twas my choice, my beloved brother, and do it all again I would. And soon, it shall all be restored."

The tidal wave of emotions drowned him. Grief ebbed and receded only to ebb again with each piercing thought of what Ishabelle had sacrificed for the common good of the MacRaigl clan and for him. She had orchestrated it all so he could be laird.

He longed to turn back the pages of their history together, back to their time of innocence. If only he had realized what she was about. He should have known. Her motives were always noble. Her single-most

All I Want

thought had always been to preserve their land and assure their legacy survived.

"Mael!" Jeanne's voice called to him in the darkness. "Mael." She stroked his forehead, planting tender kisses along his face. When he opened his eyes it was Jeanne's face that greeted him. Her gentle spirit dried the tides that seized him. Dazed, he looked around for Ishabelle.

"She's gone." Her mouth covered his. He drank her kiss, clinging to her as his touchstone. She pulled from him and held his face between her hands.

"Mael! I've missed you." She sandwiched her shoulder underneath his arm and helped him to his feet. Weak-kneed, he stumbled with her into the chamber where she deposited him into a nearby chair.

"You're so cold. You're in shock." She jerked the quilt from the bed and wrapped it about him, then knelt at his feet. "What happened, Mael?" She held his hand between hers.

"I came to take ye home, Jeanne." His words were a low rasp.

A shadow darkened the doorway, and Jeanne jumped to her feet, with her fists balled to her sides ready to fight Ishabelle. When she saw Ian leaning against the doorframe, she relaxed.

"Ye heard?" Mael glanced up at his friend.

"Aye. I heard it all."

"Here." She shoved a mug into Mael's hand and rushed to hand the skin flask to Ian. "Heard what? My scream?"

He stared at her delicate oval face, her luminous blue eyes filled with such concern. His heartbeat pounded louder in his ears. Mael raised his hand and let his fingers stroke her silky skin. She grabbed his hand between hers and kissed his fingers.

"My Jeanne. Ye have captured my very soul. To let ye go is my curse in life."

"Let me go? Now that we're together again, we shall never be apart." She bent over to kiss him. "I promise."

"Ye canna make such promises," he choked against the powerful wave of emotions and pulled her into his lap. Her lips tasted sweeter than he remembered. He dropped the mug, and the ale spilled over the floor. He drew her against him, inhaling her essence until every pore in him breathed her. His beloved.

Ian cleared his throat and turned from the chamber, closing the door behind him.

Mael broke from her and held her from him. "We have so little time, Jeanne." His breath caught in his chest when he met the loving look in her blue eyes. He lifted his hand to stroke her hair from her face.

"What do you mean?" Confusion creased her forehead.

"Our time has come to an end, my Jeanne. I canna prevent it. 'Tis too late."

"What are you talking about?" Her body trembled in his arms.

He pulled her to her feet with him and held her tight. His embrace stole the breath from her. She pushed from him, gasping for air.

"I wish to I hold ye and somehow keep ye with me," he said, his voice a deep bubble of anguish. He gathered her into the folds of his arms once more.

"Mael, what has happened?" she asked, tugging from him, searching his darkened eyes.

"Ishabelle has discovered a way to return ye to your own time." He cradled her face between his hands.

"Oh, that? She tried during Samhain to place me into a time stream or some such nonsense, but she failed. I realize how futile it was for me to come with her. There's no way back to my time." She smiled up at him.

"But there is." His eyes watered with bitterness. He recalled all the times he'd looked into those beautiful eyes. This would be the last time he'd ever gaze into their warmth. His entire body quaked. Dread seeped through him.

"Tryon rides the wind to see that ye are returned to your time."

"What?" Her forehead creased.

"He goes to stop the seed."

"I don't understand." Her stare darted as she searched his face, struggling to comprehend what he was talking about.

"Tryon seeks out Cullen. He shall kill Cullen de Mangus this very night."

Her face paled.

"Dinna ye understand?" His hand bit into her tender flesh. "Tryon goes to stop the seed! He stops it—before it can ever be sown."

Her expression shifted as realization sunk in.

"No!" She tightened her grip on him. "That means I would never come back in time. And I would never know you, Mael. That none of this would happen!" Her breath came in hot puffs.

"I dinna know, lass. I only know Trench would never breathe a moment's harm to ye. A true paradox of events we shall face," he tried to laugh, but the sorrow pierced his efforts, and the sound was more of a groan. He tightened his arms around her as though he could prevent her from leaving him.

"Mael." She buried her face into his broad chest, longing to stay in his arms forever. The thing she had sought since first journeying through the portal had arrived, and all she wanted to do was escape it.

"I don't want to leave you, Mael. I want to be with you." Sobs racked her as she clung to him. She wanted to run. It was as though she faced death and knew there was no escape. Her future would be a world without Mael. Tears streaked down her cheeks.

"I dinna want to lose ye, my Jeanne, my beloved wife." He clutched her closer.

She startled at the sudden popping sound.

"What's that?" she cried out and looked about the room.

"It has begun." Ishabelle appeared the doorway. "My husband has set the world back upon its natural course. Soon, our world shall return to how it was meant to be. Goodbye, Jeanne McBen." Her lifeless gaze centered on Jeanne.

"Mael!" Jeanne rose onto her tiptoes and locked her arms around his neck. "I love you too much to leave."

The world elongated then contracted around her. Her own movements were jerky and stretched as though moving through a force so great that it sapped all of her strength.

"Jeanne." His words ground out in slow motion.

She lifted her head and stared into his eyes. The world melted into layers where movement was like taffy being stretched in front of her.

"No!" She tightened her arms around him.

"Remember me." His hand warmed against her cheek. His lips covered hers. She pressed herself against him, hoping she could hang on to him. Suddenly, he was jerked from her. Jeanne reached for his outstretched hand. "We are one for all eternity. Remember me," he repeated. His strength shone in his eyes. "Remember me."

"Mael!" Jeanne screamed between sobs, but he faded from her as the brilliant blue light that had delivered her to that time engulfed her. "Mael!"

Chapter Twenty-Nine

"Cullen's death has brought peace to the highlands," Ian commented and glanced over at Mael.

"Aye, the glen has returned to its normal rhythm of life." He sat staring into the fire, reliving every moment he had shared with her. His heart felt as though it would surely burst from his loss.

Over the past months, the rumors had transformed into legends and were told and retold around firesides on cold nights. They were the story of his love for Jeanne, the witch who had vanished into thin air, the story of a man and woman who were split apart by an evil man who roamed the nights and fed upon the innocent. Their tragic love story began to inspire songs and fill maidens with bittersweet dreams of true love.

Mael spent his time solidifying the bond between the chieftains in the valley. He threw himself into his role as Chief, serving his people with all his energy, until exhausted, he'd collapse into his cold bed. But his sleep was plagued with memories of her.

His dreams were filled with Jeanne, his beloved. He would wake himself up calling out her name and reaching for her in their bed. Every morning was the same. He would climb from the lonely bed and set about his daily tasks, but memories of their time together haunted his every waking moment. Soon, the grief bore him down.

His longing grew more intense with each passing day until the burden of his loss was intolerable. Unless he could find some hope of being reunited with her, Mael knew he could not continue to draw breath. At length, he sought the only person who could give him that hope.

"What ye want at my door?" Ishabelle glared up at him.

"Ye know why I find myself here, Ishabelle. Will ye make me beg?"

"Just to have the satisfaction of knowing that which ye condemned ye now seek? Aye."

"'Tis only because of my love for my wife that I come to be at your door."

"And 'twas only because of my love for my husband that I am here as well. Do ye see how much alike we are, my brother?" Her smile was sad. "We both loved people neither of us could have as we were, but because of what we felt for them, we can sacrifice all that we are. But ye have a destiny to fulfill, Mael. Ye have no heirs for what ye have created. How do ye plan to accomplish your destiny without heirs?"

"I dinna know. I can keep the land safe and fight the battles I must fight. I am married to my Jeanne as long as there is love between us."

"And she now lives some seven hundred or more years from this world. In her time, ye are long dead and turned to dust."

"Nae!" Mael shook his head refusing to believe what she said. "'Tis one year and one day this very day. The love remains."

"And why ye find yourself at my door?"

"I canna break the vows. I'm bound by heart, forever, and yet I canna ever leave our people to seek the gift of Samhain for the future."

"The Samhain gift would not work to place ye in the future, only return ye to your own time. And so remains the final choice which would satisfy both of your commitments."

"I beg ye. Help me, Ishabelle." Mael extended his hand to her.

She stared at his outstretched hand.

"Then, we shall do just that, brother," Ishabelle said and stepped into his embrace. Mael held his twin and knew the kinship they had once shared. "Ye shall serve our people and keep the lands safe. And then one day ye shall find your Jeanne again." Ishabelle whispered in his ear, "Ye shall have your wife once more. I promise."

* * * * *

Penington, North Carolina
May 12, 2005

"Congratulations, Sis." Ryan leaned over and kissed Jeanne on the cheek.

"I couldn't have done it without you." She linked her arm with his, noting the older her brother got the more he looked like their father.

All I Want

With a pang of sorrow, she turned to face the crowd gathered in front of the University steps.

"Doctor McBen? How did you conclude it was blood type that decided the carrier? Who was the first donor for the AB negative blood?" the reporter asked as she descended the podium.

"A family member was the blood donor." She winked at Ryan.

"Your brother?" The reporter shoved the microphone in front of Ryan.

"An ancient family member provided the necessary DNA sample that started me thinking about possible blood types and proteins." The happiness of the moment faded into inexplicable sadness.

"What is it?" He drew his arm around her shoulders. A stray strand of blond hair fell over his forehead.

"I don't know." She shook her head.

He guided her toward the awaiting limousine. Concern reflected in his blue eyes, but was quickly masked when she looked up at him.

"I'm okay," she said.

"How does it feel to have saved an entire world, Doctor McBen?" The Scottish accent jarred her. Jeanne halted mid-stride. When she turned, she locked stares with the man standing in the shadows beneath a large oak tree. Her breath latched in the base of her throat. His auburn hair was pulled behind his head in what appeared to be a braid.

"Have I done that?" Her pulse sharpened when his lips spread into a teasing smile. Ripples of delight tingled down her back. Every nerve ending in her body came alive with a twinge of fire when she glimpsed the naked desire burning in his eyes.

"Ye have done just that, Jeanne McBen." He winked then turned back into the shadowy grove of trees. She looked about the throng of people, desperate to find him, but it was as though he had vanished. Had he been an illusion? He seemed so familiar that she nearly called out his name. What had that name been?

"Who was that?" her brother asked.

"I'm not sure." She continued to search the engulfing crowd.

"Doctor McBen, please." The police officer stood impatiently by the open car door. "The crowd's getting aggressive." Just then he was knocked backwards, but was quick to shove the assailant back behind the line. Without ceremony, the policeman pushed Jeanne and Ryan into the limo, slammed the door, and then pounded on the roof. The limo sped from the curb and out of the University parking lot.

She looked back at the crowd just as the limousine moved through the gate. He emerged from the wall, beneath the thick row of crepe myrtles. He was dressed in a pair of black slacks and a crisp white shirt. A memory sparked. She knew him. But from where?

"Who *is* that man, Jeanne?" Ryan followed her stare. "He sounded Scottish. Did you meet him in Scotland during your research trip?"

"I'm not sure," she murmured and bit her lower lip, straining to see him as they rounded the curve.

"You really need to rest before the banquet tonight. You know, this week's going to be busy with all the parties and interviews. I think you're booked on every talk show."

"I know," she mumbled, but her mind had been captured by that smile and pair of brown eyes that seemed to hold all the answers she'd ever sought. Who *was* he? Something stirred, like a memory, only she could not hold on it and it retreated.

They returned to their parents' home, a large antebellum house restored to the last detail. Once inside, Ryan paused in the foyer to look through the day's mail while she climbed the winding staircase to her room.

Suddenly, the scene of a tower staircase flashed in front of her. She froze on the steps. The stone wall was cold and smooth against her hand as she balanced her climb up the tower. Voices echoed up the massive stone structure. She turned to look over her shoulder. Ryan raced up the wide staircase past her, but stopped on the landing.

"What's wrong?"

"I thought I—" she gulped.

"You okay?"

"Yeah," she nodded. "I'm fine. Really." She resumed her climb.

"I'm meeting the gang at the lake for a few hours. I'll be back in plenty of time. You mind?" He flashed a bright smile but didn't wait for her response and ran to his room, slamming the door behind him.

"Have fun." She mentally shook the feeling of déjà vu from her mind and continued down the hall toward her bedroom. Her footsteps were muted by the Aubusson runner that graced the length of the hallway.

All I Want

She entered the bedroom and closed the tall double doors behind her. Her breath escaped her in a long uneasy rush. What had just happened? Her heartbeat pounded louder in her ears.

A slamming door sounded from Ryan's part of the house followed by running footfalls down the stairs.

"I'm gone!" he shouted and slammed another door.

She sat down on the crocheted-canopy bed and took a long breath. She could not shake the feeling. Ryan's singing came from the garage below followed by the door sliding open. Soon the revving of his motorcycle filled the side yard as he sped out of the driveway and down the street. She listened for the sound until she could no longer hear it.

Images flashed in front of her, mental pictures that seemed to transform into actual visions. In the past, whenever she had such images, she chalked them off to fatigue from crazy work hours and lack of sleep during the long months of research. This past month, however, the frequency and intensity of the visions had grown, penetrating not just her dreams, but her waking hours, like on the staircase. How could her imagination be so powerful as to create the sense of touch? She could have sworn her hand had been against a stone wall and not the wood banister.

She lay down on the bed and closed her eyes, willing the tumbling thoughts to stop. She just wanted to rest, escape all thoughts and go into a deep, mindless sleep. The banquet that evening was too important to arrive frazzled. She needed sleep. Ryan would accompany her. Her dress hung in the closet, her accessories were selected.

She took a deep breath. Her younger brother was all the family she had left. She knew their parents would have been proud of this day. She rolled over on her side, facing the window. How she wished they were alive to share her success. She blinked as she watched the rays of sunlight send shafts of gold into the room, stirring dust particles in their heated trail. She let her mind unwind and soon fell into a deep sleep.

"Remember me. Remember me. My Jeanne." His voice echoed in her mind. She moaned. "Remember me." Jeanne tightened her arms around his strong neck. She wanted to stay with him. "We are one for all eternity. Remember me."

"Don't let me go! Please, don't let me go!" she gasped between sobs, waking herself up. She sat up in bed, panting. Sadness gripped her and would not let go, even when she swung her legs over the side of the bed and pushed herself away from the dream.

"God, what's wrong with me?" She willed her breath to slow. She glanced at the clock and was relieved it was only four in the afternoon. She had plenty of time to get ready. As guest of honor, she'd been given strict instructions to arrive exactly thirty minutes after the gala had begun.

She sat on the edge of the bed with her hands resting in her lap, unable to release the desperation she'd felt in the dream. How could an emotion from a dream linger with such intensity? A tear slipped over her eyelid and fell onto her hand. She reached to brush it off, turning her palm up, but her attention froze on the scar. She traced the pattern with her index finger. The scar ran from beneath her forefinger in a diagonal line to the heel of her hand. Yet another mystery for her. How could she have so serious a cut and not recall it?

She pushed back the rising fear. As a scientist, she was intrigued. But it was only a momentary intrigue. Whatever it was, she didn't want to remember. Somewhere in the far recesses of her mind, she knew the sorrow she felt in her dreams would become greater than she could bear if she remembered how she'd cut her hand. She sensed the two were linked.

"Remember me." The words resonated around her. She knew that voice with its melodic Scottish brogue. Instantly, she thought of the man that afternoon.

"Well, that's insane." She stood from the bed. "I don't know any Scotsmen." She ran her hand through her hair and examined herself in the cheval mirror. Her dark hair fell below her shoulders. When had it grown so long? She frowned at her reflection and picked up a strand of hair along the side of her face and twisted it between her fingers. Unconsciously, she began to braid it.

She watched her reflection as though she were separate from the person in the mirror. She stood staring at the braid as it slipped from her hand and cascaded the length of her jaw to her chest. The feeling of déjà vu brought with it the same deep sadness of her dreams. Dark pain engulfed her and bore down on her. Tears spilled from her eyes.

Why was this happening to her? This should be the happiest day of her life and all she could do was mourn the death of some unknown emotion. Was this the onset of clinical depression?

All I Want

"Mael." The name tumbled from her lips. Jeanne snapped alert. Who was Mael? How could she call out for someone she didn't even know?

"Get a grip, Jeanne, before you lose it," she reprimanded herself and pushed from the dresser. Squaring her shoulders, she brushed the tears from her face with the backs of her hands and made a firm resolve not to indulge in the melodrama any further. It was over. Whatever her dreams, no matter how sad she felt afterwards, they were only dreams.

Over the following days, her resolve was quickly destroyed as her dreams became more frequent with amazing minute details.

Passion spent in the man's arms set against an ancient time filled her dreams so much all she wanted to do was sleep. She eagerly escaped into her dream world, where her dream lover waited night after night. Other vignettes of people and scenes, of riding horseback over a wild countryside filtered through the dreams, interrupting her ecstasy in her lover's arms.

She heard an ancient dialect and in her dreams spoke it. The ending of each dream had one constant thought that always left her anxious and angry. She had to stop a man determined to destroy everything she loved. Was it the Scotsman from the press conference? Was he more than just a curious onlooker? She had not seen him since and with her last public obligation over in two weeks, she looked forward to getting back to work. She would lose herself in her research and crowd out all other thoughts, especially her dream lover.

* * * * *

"It's good to be back in my lab," she told Ryan and collapsed in her chair, powering up her computer. She was not scheduled to open her lab until next week, but she couldn't resist taking a detour during their midnight run for donuts and coffee.

"Do you think you can settle back into a normal life? I mean, Jeanne, you're the twenty-first-century Jonas Salk. You've been on the cover of every magazine, tabloid and every talk show. Every news net site has you plastered on it. This past month has been so—"

"Enough." She scrunched up her face. "It's been tedious. But we have all the funding we could ever want for any kind of research, Ryan. It's something every researcher dreams about."

"We? You want me to help you?" he asked with his smile widening.

"You have to finish high school, and then on to college, but I need my favorite brother helping me out." She winked at him and propped her feet on the desk, crossing her legs at the ankles.

"Yeah, slave labor. That's what you really want."

"You have to be good for something. Who else would go out and get me coffee and donuts in the middle of the night?"

"I'm on my way." He reminded her so much of their father.

"No, I just wanted to stop in. I'm not going to work." She raised her hand in a gesture to stop him.

"Sure you are. I know—" he halted mid-sentence. She followed his stare to her hand. "What's that?" He grabbed her hand and turned her palm up. His blue eyes narrowed. "When did you cut yourself?" His forehead furrowed deeply as his forefinger traced the long red slash. "That's a recent cut only a few months old."

"It's nothing," she shrugged and pulled from his grasp. She still had not been able to recall how she'd hurt herself, but she couldn't let Ryan or anyone know what was going on. She couldn't afford to have them suspect what she already did, that she was having some kind of breakdown. It wouldn't be unusual after witnessing so tragic a thing as their parents' deaths. She squinted against the painful memory.

"That's a serious cut. I don't remember you having a bandage or doing anything to your hand."

"I had a few wounds from the attack." She averted his stare so he would not see the pain she knew still lived in her eyes. She didn't blame her brother for their parents' death anymore than she blamed him for her own injuries. They had been his dogs, but no one could have known the animals would turn on them the way they had. Such things were inexplicable.

"I'm going for coffee." He lifted his gaze to hers. "What kind of donuts?" he asked lightening his tone, attempting to change the mood.

"Lemon-filled? And some plain? I might as well stay and do some work," she shrugged at his smug look of *I told you so*. "There's some cash in the armrest in the car."

"Got it covered. If they don't have any fresh ones out of the oven, I'll wait. So don't get worried if it takes a while," he called as he left the lab.

She shirked off her lightweight jacket and settled behind the desk while the computer loaded her latest program. She set up the protocol for her current experiment that she'd started just before all the press frenzy. Now she wanted to get back to the work.

Invariably, her thoughts turned back to the man in her dreams. He seemed so real. Whenever she awoke she could still feel his kiss fresh on her lips. She touched her tongue to her lower lip. How could a dream be so real? In her dreams, her passion was taken to the edge of her senses. She had powerful orgasms even in her sleep, always awaking with a feeling of sadness. To use an old Southern phrase, she could easily describe it as a pining.

Her computer made a series of beeps, and she nearly jumped from her seat. Taking a deep breath, she reined in her nervousness and responded to the prompt by entering her password. She sat back as the file loaded. Again, her mind wandered. She could see him so clearly in her dreams, but his image escaped her when she awoke. Perhaps she should go back to the counselor. This could be part of the trauma she had suffered when her parents had died, although she couldn't see the connection. So engrossed in her musings, she didn't hear him come down the hall and had it not been for the squeaky door hinges, he would have entered without her realizing it.

"They must have had some hot ones all ready for you," she said.

"At least one."

She jumped from her desk. The man from the press conference stood in the doorway of her lab. Adrenaline pumped wildly through her.

"How did *you* get in here? This is a secure building. No one is able to get in without an ID."

"I believe this is all the ID I require, Jeanne lass." He held up his left hand, mirroring the mysterious scar on her own hand.

Her breath rushed from her. She felt she was going to faint and gripped the edge of her desk. She fell back down into the chair. Slowly, she turned her palm up and looked from hers back to his.

"I wasn't sure if ye would keep the mark, but since I did, I knew ye had to have it, too." He closed the distance between them in long, fluid strides.

"Who are you?" She reached for the alarm button underneath her desk.

"Dinna send for them, Jeanne. I'll not harm ye. Ye should know I could never harm ye," he soothed. She stared up at him. The scene of a parking lot flashed in front of her. He stood dressed in the same white dress shirt and dark trousers. No, it was a meadow. She shook her head.

"I'm tired. Yes, that's it. I'm having a *complete* breakdown. I knew it was just a matter of time. I've had all the warning signs." She clasped her cold hands together and continued to talk to herself, desperately trying to ignore him. "I just didn't want to admit it. I have so much work to do. I can't afford to be ill." She rubbed her eyes and tried to clear the vision in front of her from her mind. "Now my hallucinations are talking to me."

"We think our dreams are just dreams, but oftentimes, they are memories of a past life spent in another time. Another place." His voice was seductive. God, how could anyone have a voice like that? Well, they couldn't. It was proof she was delusional. She ignored him, closed her eyes. When she opened them, he'd be gone. She peeped through her eyelashes.

"Oh, man, you're still here." She jumped to her feet.

"I'm always here, Jeanne."

"How do you know about my dreams?" She struggled to contain the rising panic.

"Dinna ye remember me? *One for all eternity.*" His face stretched into a wide warm smile.

"But, I thought… I mean—" Tears sprung to her eyes. She stared at him, unable to pull her gaze from his.

"I'm not a hallucination, Jeanne. Do ye remember Fernmoora? And Ian? And how he was wounded in the attack? How ye sewed up his wound and how he stayed behind with Ishabelle? And on the ride back to my castle we made love for the first time, after our picnic on the knoll?"

The blood rushed from her head all the way to her feet. Her mouth dried, and the room threatened to fade with the intense ringing in her ears.

"Remember how I teased ye about the way ye could not ride a horse? And of course, there was Trench, back then, only now, he never existed in this future because Alexander killed Cullen de Mangus so Trench could never be born. Never harm ye."

"This can't be happening." Tears stung her eyes.

"I'm real, Jeanne love." He moved closer. She stared, blurry-eyed at him.

All I Want

"You're a vision, a creation of my own thoughts, as such you're not solid mass." She continued to argue with herself, but when he touched her hand she screamed.

"Shhh. Dinna ye remember me? Look at your left hand. The palm. Ye canna deny it. The night we married. The handfast." He moved closer and once more touched her hand, only this time, he picked it up between his, pressing her scar into the matching one on his hand. Jeanne trembled as memories flooded back to her.

They cascaded like water over a damn. Scotland, a massive room with aromas filling her nostrils and bagpipes playing. It was like watching a movie in fast forward. She trembled as another lifetime played in front of her, but it was her lifetime. It belonged to her. How?

"Mael?" She covered her mouth with her other hand. Slowly, she reached up to touch his face, tracing an imaginary line along his jaw.

"Aye love, 'tis me," he said, turning her palm upside down, planting a tender kiss along the line of her scar.

"I don't understand," she said, still trying to piece the fragmented scenes together, accepting they were memories of when she had shared that lifetime with him.

"I've waited seven hundred and fifty-five years, five months, three days, six hours, thirty-eight minutes and," he said, pausing to glance at the wall clock behind him, "five seconds for this moment. The moment I would reclaim ye as my wife, Jeanne McBen MacRaigl."

He flattened his palm against hers once more. A current shot through her, jolting her as though struck by an electrical impulse. Her heartbeat was a riotous pounding. She met his deep stare and felt as though she was being drawn inside him. His presence filled her. Her senses responded to him, and her deep longing burst to heat.

"Let down your defenses and allow me to show ye."

"I'm afraid."

"Ye have nothing to fear, my Jeanne."

She let her fingers thread through his and stepped into his open embrace.

"Ye see? That first step always was your hardest." His handsome face brightened with a smile, and her heart flip-flopped. Could it all be true? Was he her husband as he claimed? From another time?

"Try not to analyze it, lass, just close your eyes, and ye shall remember it all."

He touched his lips to hers. His lips were chilled, though it was warm outside. The touch of his flesh against hers sent Jeanne into a higher awareness.

She drew her arms around his neck and returned his kiss. Suddenly, her mind was filled with scenes once more. The diner downtown and a man who had stolen something from her. They argued, and she fled the diner. Mael had been there.

His kiss deepened, his tongue parted her lips, and she welcomed him. Her defenses dissolved under his passion. Scene after scene flashed before her as a lifetime expanded and inflated with colorful, powerful memories within her mind.

His arms tightened around her, and his tongue teased hers then claimed her mouth for his own. She broke from his kiss and stumbled backwards, gasping for breath.

"It's true," she sobbed and stood staring at him. "How can it be? Oh, Mael." She covered her mouth with her hand. "You found a way." She rushed back into his arms, scattering kisses over his face. "But how? Did you find another portal?" She kissed him between sobs and laughter. She touched his clean-shaven face, remembering his beard, remembering it all.

"There was always a way, Jeanne," he said with a shrug, "all things have a price. But never too great for the chance to be with ye again."

"Mael," she said with sudden realization. "Please tell me you didn't. Not for me." A sinking feeling fluttered in her stomach.

"Would ye happen to know where I might find a good hematologist?"

"Oh Mael," she said and fell into his arms, "what have you done? Tell me you didn't give up your soul."

"Whatever the price, my love, 'twas worth it to be with ye again. I have lived long enough to find ye again." His kiss consumed her. Her arousal was immediate. Electric twinges pulsed to her clit. She needed to feel him inside her. His hand cupped her breast and his fingertip smoothed over it, rubbing her nipple until it hardened. She pressed her body against his, feeling his rigid cock against her leg. Her hands glided up his back. His muscles flinched under her touch, and she felt the excitement course through him.

He grabbed her by the waist and effortlessly lifted her onto the desk, shoving the papers aside. They fell in flutters to the floor. He leaned over her and lowered his head to her neck, pausing slightly at the pulse in her throat, and then sought her rising breast. She groaned when his hand freed one of her breasts and his lips covered her nipple, sucking and tugging.

Her senses pounded through her. Heated desire stoked with his suckling of her breast.

His hand traveled over her stomach. Her pussy rushed moist as the raw aching traveled to her clit in anticipation of his touch. It was just like her dreams. His touch was the same and made her wet and needy. She longed to feel him inside her.

"'Tis good ye remember, Jeanne. I was so afraid ye had forgotten me," he said and glided his hand over her stomach and rubbed his hand against her jeans, massaging her pussy with the palm of his hand. She reached for the zipper, but he found it and the zip sound broke between their heated breaths. Her pulse raced as her pants opened and he slipped his hand beneath her panties. Her clit throbbed harder when his hand brushed against her stomach and traveled to her pussy.

The heat roared with a raw aching where she longed his fingers to touch. She held her breath in anticipation of the pressure of his fingers. He found her nub and stroked his fingertips against its swollen hood. She bit her lip as the waves of pleasure pulsed against his fingertips. She undulated under his stimulation and groaned when his fingers slid down and plunged deep inside her.

Her response seemed to incite him for he jerked her pants away so her ass smacked against the coolness of her desk. He freed her legs from the pants. She wrapped them around his waist, welcoming him home.

"My Jeanne." He kissed her hard, drawing her into his embrace while she fumbled to unzip his pants. He pushed her hands aside and released his hard cock from the confines of his slacks. Her fingers closed around his heated hardness and guided him to her moist pussy. He pushed his cock past the wet lips of her pussy and plunged deep, groaning low as he moved in and out, slowly at first. His passion exploded, and he fucked her harder, pulling his cock out so its tip teased the inside of her opening then rammed deeper. He filled the ache her dreams had started. She was back with her husband! Tears of joy slipped from her eyes. He whispered Gaelic phrases in her ear. His heated breath carried the poetic words proclaiming his undying love.

She moved with him, their heat rising in urgent need. He nibbled against her breasts, and then raised his head to stare down at their bodies joined together once more. Fire leapt in her and he crushed her to him holding her as though he feared she'd disappear from him. He pumped his cock into her and she writhed under his lovemaking, luxuriating in the extreme sensations pulsating through her. The fluttering rose up her spine. He groaned and reared back, pressing his hands against the desk as he ground himself deeper into her.

She twisted under the uncurling fire that etched waves of delight, until her urgency grew, and pressed her clit against him. She pushed and strained against the rawness pulsing in her pussy. The fire exploded from her clit, traveling up her spine, with her spasms gripping his cock. They rocked against the climax. She gasped for air and pulled him to her, panting, stroking his face, murmuring her love in his ear.

His lips found hers. His tongue twisted around hers and recoiled, then captured hers once more. He moaned and broke from her kiss to flick his tongue inside her ear, sending a cascade of warm shivers over her.

"Mael!" she cried, her voice bubbling over in a mixture of laughter and sobs. "My magnificent husband," she said and held his face between her hands. "You *are* still my husband, aren't you?" She searched his eyes, his molten passion still glowed in their depths. "It's been so long. But we're still married, aren't we? Our handfast was to bind us for that one year and one day, and then we were to claim it a marriage if there was still love."

"Aye, my beautiful *wife*. There is still love, is there not?"

"Oh yes, yes! There is." She showered his face with kisses.

"Ye are all I ever wanted, my Jeanne."

The End

Enjoy this excerpt from
All I Need
© Copyright Sally Painter, 2005

All Rights Reserved, Ellora's Cave Publishing, Inc.

Frankie's dark stare shifted over her when he leaned forward and closed the gate behind them. The heavy metal slammed shut. She jerked around, trying to shake the foreboding sense she'd just entered a prison. Of course, that was ridiculous.

"Oh man! What an incredible night this is going to be." Amy squeezed her arm.

"What do you think, Dani?" Lillian turned to grin at her.

Her stare widened on the three-storied high ceiling, the ornately carved statues and the gilded furniture. Even the tables were massive wood with marble tops. But most alarming were the suspended cages where men and women held in bondage struggled against their chains and leather collars. Dark booths were more like beds with red velvet draperies fringed in gold— some open, but most closed, revealing teasing glimpses of couples. Women with leather thongs twisted and moved over men dressed in leather chaps, while others wore Speedos. Danielle tried to swallow past the dryness in her throat.

"I bet you've never been to a place like this," Minnie leaned in to whisper.

"You bet right." Rising heat fluttered over her. A part of her was shocked, even horrified by what she saw, while another part of her found it just so...very exciting.

"What do you think, Dani?" Minnie used her nickname and gestured to the room.

"I think I've been out of circulation way too long, if this is what the single scene is all about nowadays."

This seemed to amuse Minnie for a moment then she simply nodded and moved away from them, disappearing into the surging crowd.

"Well, I guess most of the people at work would be shocked by this place," Amy spoke above the pounding music.

"I daresay any normal person would be shocked." Lillian gestured to the corner of the room where Minnie now stood waving at them.

"We have a booth?" Amy asked. "Wow, this woman knows how to make people snap to attention."

"Yes, she does," Danielle murmured to herself, staring at a man across the room. He stood out from the crowd, mostly because of his handsome looks, but also because, unlike everyone else in this club, he wasn't wearing black. She followed her friends to the procured booth, casting a wistful look in his direction. His dark gray suit highlighted his broad shoulders and attempted to disguise his muscular arms. He wore a red and gray brocade vest with gold, embossed buttons. The final touch was a black tie with a gold tie chain.

His unrelenting gaze smoldered over her face, searing down the length of her neck to the low neckline of her birthday dress. Danielle tried to look away, but she was captive to his presence. She willed her legs to take her in the opposite direction of the booth, where he now appeared to be waiting for them. Waiting for her. Quickening heat pumped through her.

He tilted his head slightly and her pulse jumped. He was staring right at her with a slow grin parting his lips. Excited shivers raced down her spine tingling her nipples hard.

"That's Armondés!" Lillian grabbed her arm and squeezed. Amy pivoted to look at them with her eyes wide in an exaggerated expression of surprise.

"Oh my God! Do you see him?" Amy gasped. "Why is he watching *us*?"

Lillian looked past Amy then back to Danielle.

"He seems to be watching our birthday girl here."

Danielle recognized the name, *Armondés*. The owner of the club. Her knees weakened but she continued to walk toward him.

"Watching her? I'd say more like devouring her." Amy mouthed the words, *lucky you*.

"Come on," Lillian locked her arm through Danielle's.

"Please! Can we have a little bit of control, ladies?" She jerked free of her friends' arm locks. "You act as though I'm some kind of sacrifice to the guy."

"Sacrifice?" Lillian released her hold and flashed Amy a warning glare.

"Sorry, Dani," Amy relaxed the deathlike grip. "He's just the most eligible and desirable man ever. Other than that, he's nothing."

"You just don't understand, Dani. Amy has this big crush on him." Lillian sneered at the other woman.

"Oh, like you don't? Thing is, Dani, to have Armondés looking at you like that, I mean he's really interested in you. That's what all the women here are panting hot to have happen to them. You're just so lucky!" Amy literally trembled beside her.

"Amy, you have no shame. I swear, Dani, she's like some high school kid. Gets all hot around Armondés. She's impossible to work with. If she keeps it up, I'm going to ask for a transfer across the street to your building. I'm serious, all she talks about is Armondés this and Armondés that. I have to listen to her all day long. You're lucky you don't work in our building!"

"Oh, like you don't talk about him?" Amy pouted. "I saw the way you went after him last Saturday night, but he took that blonde up to his suite, didn't he? Not you, babe."

"My turn will come, Miss Amy. You're just jealous that he bought me a drink and hasn't once noticed you."

"Am not! And so what if he bought you a little piddling drink. He still left you down here staring into your vodka."

"Look, Amy, do you want to make this about last Saturday or are you going to let it be about Dani?" Lillian challenged with restrained anger edging her words.

"You're the one who started it by saying I had the hots for him," Amy defended.

"Well, honey, you do," Lillian jeered.

Danielle stared at them unable to believe what she was hearing.

"Whoa!" She finally interrupted them. "Just what's wrong with y'all? You've never talked to each other like this. Ever since you first came to this place, you both act...well, different. Is there something I should know before we go any further?"

* * * * *

"That's her," Minnie slipped her hand around the column of the booth and leaned toward him.

"I know," Armondés spoke, not daring to break his stare. He gauged Danielle Rivers to be about five-eight, and lithe, but very voluptuous with well-rounded hips, a small waist and larger than average breasts.

"They're real," Minnie spoke and shifted to stand beside him. "I can tell."

He ignored her, keeping Danielle's gaze locked to his. He watched the way her hips swung ever so slightly, teasing him with their unconscious rhythm. Something he'd not felt for several months stoked to life — desire.

"Do you feel resurrected?" she asked and once more he ignored her.

Danielle Rivers was irresistible. From her dark brown, long, silky hair and deep chocolate eyes to her full lips, currently pursed in a tense, uncertain expression, she was the woman he sought. If he must marry to save himself from the curse, then this woman would do nicely.

"She's lovely." He watched her move closer.

Enjoy these excerpts from
Fated Mates
© Copyright Delilah Devlins, Sally Painter,

Charlotte Boyette-Compo 2005

All Rights Reserved, Ellora's Cave Publishing, Inc.

Warlord's Destiny
By Delilah Devlin

Mora felt a tremor rumble beneath the polished, marble floor of the great hall, so explosive was the swell of conversation that arose at the warriors' arrival.

They were seven, dressed in furs and leather, armed with bows slung across their shoulders and scabbards at their sides.

She couldn't drag her gaze from the man at the head of their formation, striding toward her—her husband in name, if not yet by deed. Although she had never seen him before this day, she knew it must be him, for he looked the fiercest, the strongest—only one such as he would be chosen to rule from amongst their ranks.

He was from a race of barbarians, seemingly as proud of their reputation for brutal warfare as their orgiastic sexuality. The latter, Mora could well believe for the man stalking her now looked every inch a sensual marauder.

A shiver of awe bit the base of her spine and trembled upward until the fine hairs on the back of her neck stood erect.

Taller by a head than any Mellusian, his broad shoulders nearly blocked out the sight of the two heralds dogging his steps as they attempted to halt him. He seemed not the slightest bit interested in following protocol by waiting for his name to be addressed to the assemblage. As if anyone attending the ceremony hadn't already guessed who he was!

He'd also eschewed the fine wedding tunic Mora's mother had personally designed—an embroidered silk affair that would have stretched absurdly across his bulging chest and arms.

No, he wore a vest of gray animal pelts that parted at the front, no doubt to tempt a woman's gaze to ogle his obscenely muscled chest and follow the dark arrow of hair down his hewn abdomen. The black sueded leather that encased his legs, strained over thickly corded thighs and the alarming swell of his manhood.

Mora's heart tripped, and then fluttered like the wings of an *aradil*.

Her mouth dry, she forced her gaze upward to look at his face, but found no comfort there.

Lord Tetrik of Kronak—his name was as harsh as the angles of his square jaw and the sharp blade of his nose. His hair was dark like a moonless sky and worn like the old warriors in the paintings in History Hall—hanging past his shoulders with small braids on either side of his inflexible face. But his eyes frightened her most of all—chips of blue ice froze her in place as his gaze found hers across the noisy hall.

He would have to know she was his bride. She wore her wealth and importance in the weighty jewels studding her hair and gown and encircling her neck. She saw fury in that first glance. Had he already guessed he'd been cheated of the true prize? That her rich adornment was a ruse?

Love Me Tomorrow
By Sally Painter

He slipped past her hatred and found recognition. The same recognition now reflecting in her liquid chocolate eyes. His heart was a staccato beat. She knew they were kindred spirits, too. What would she do now that she, too, knew? In spite of his attempt to control his thoughts, Mecah couldn't help wondering about her. How could it be that he had to travel millions of light years from his home to find his kismet mate? The irony was too much and he released the welling emotions in a laugh.

"You find this humorous?" she asked, reinforcing her persona, bolstering her energy against his probing. At that very moment she knew, just as he did—they were made for each other. Designed by a greater purpose to come together at this fated moment.

His thoughts unleashed to explore deeper, needing to know everything about her. Intuitive females who evolved to her level not only knew the secrets of the universe, but had a greater appreciation of the art of lovemaking. Orgasms were achieved using their minds as well as their bodies. He'd heard all the legends of such highly evolved women and their abilities to reduce a man to little more than a sex slave. He watched the emotions struggling to escape her rigid control. Oh yeah, he'd gladly be her sex slave. The response to his musings tightened in his crotch.

"Get up," she barked.

Embarrassed by the telltale sign of his arousal, he stood from the blanket. Immediately, her attention was drawn to his erection bulging beneath his tan pants. A slight smile lifted one corner of her mouth.

"You have a strange reaction to being captured, ah…"

"Name's Mecah, Captain Mecah. And what can I say? I appreciate a beautiful woman," he grinned.

Secrets of the Wind
By Charlotte Boyett-Compo

"Do you not want a man who will make your blood boil one moment, and then make it flow like hot molasses in the next as his fingers ply your flesh? Do you not desire a man who will take you soaring to the highest mountains then cradle you gently in his arms as he settles you back to earth?"

"Your Majesty," Chas protested, her voice a whine of complaint.

"I am told that when he laid hands to you in the marketplace, you were seen to shudder as though a lightning bolt had traveled the length of you. Is that correct?"

"While it is true I felt a charge from his touch, I…"

"Did you not call him Enlil?"

"Aye, but I don't have any idea…"

"Enlil," the queen said, "was the Lord High God of the Winds in ancient *an Iaráin*. His wife was Ninlil. That phantom woman you were in the distant past called out to her lover."

"That is only speculation," Chas denied.

"Had you heard the name before? Is it one you commonly use?"

Chas groaned with frustration. "No, Your Majesty. The name was new to me."

"No, it was love calling to love, Chastain. Ruan Cosaint is the reincarnation of an old, old love and he is the man for you, lass," the queen said, her statement brooking no argument. "And you are the woman for him! You were meant to be together! The mystic says so!"

"But when he finds out you hired me to…"

"Don't let him!" the queen snapped and rose from the bed. She smoothed the skirt of her gown. "Men don't need to know everything a woman does, lass. The sooner you learn *that* lesson, the better off you'll be!"

When Queen Annalyn left her, Chas went over the information regarding her heritage and realized she was crying. She had been trying for so long to find out whom she had been, who her parents were, the reason Charlton Neff and his wife, Catherine, had adopted her, it was a relief to finally have answers. To learn she had been of noble blood? Unexpected and totally surprising. No wonder the Tribunal did not want her to know of her heritage.

As to the Gaelachuan queen's assertion that Chas and Ruan were fated to be mates? Well, she thought as she swiped at her tears that remained to be seen.

Why an electronic book?

We live in the Information Age—an exciting time in the history of human civilization, in which technology rules supreme and continues to progress in leaps and bounds every minute of every day. For a multitude of reasons, more and more avid literary fans are opting to purchase e-books instead of paper books. The question from those not yet initiated into the world of electronic reading is simply: *Why?*

1. ***Price.*** An electronic title at Ellora's Cave Publishing and Cerridwen Press runs anywhere from 40% to 75% less than the cover price of the exact same title in paperback format. Why? Basic mathematics and cost. It is less expensive to publish an e-book (no paper and printing, no warehousing and shipping) than it is to publish a paperback, so the savings are passed along to the consumer.

2. ***Space.*** Running out of room in your house for your books? That is one worry you will never have with electronic books. For a low one-time cost, you can purchase a handheld device specifically designed for e-reading. Many e-readers have large, convenient screens for viewing. Better yet, hundreds of titles can be stored within your new library—on a single microchip. There are a variety of e-readers from different manufacturers. You can also read e-books on your PC or laptop computer. (Please note that Ellora's

Cave does not endorse any specific brands. You can check our websites at www.ellorascave.com or www.cerridwenpress.com for information we make available to new consumers.)

3. *Mobility.* Because your new e-library consists of only a microchip within a small, easily transportable e-reader, your entire cache of books can be taken with you wherever you go.

4. *Personal Viewing Preferences.* Are the words you are currently reading too small? Too large? Too… ANNOYING? Paperback books cannot be modified according to personal preferences, but e-books can.

5. *Instant Gratification.* Is it the middle of the night and all the bookstores near you are closed? Are you tired of waiting days, sometimes weeks, for bookstores to ship the novels you bought? Ellora's Cave Publishing sells instantaneous downloads twenty-four hours a day, seven days a week, every day of the year. Our webstore is never closed. Our e-book delivery system is 100% automated, meaning your order is filled as soon as you pay for it.

Those are a few of the top reasons why electronic books are replacing paperbacks for many avid readers.

As always, Ellora's Cave and Cerridwen Press welcome your questions and comments. We invite you to email us at Comments@ellorascave.com or write to us directly at Ellora's Cave Publishing Inc., 1056 Home Avenue, Akron, OH 44310-3502.

The Ellora's Cave Library

Stay up to date with Ellora's Cave Titles in Print with our Quarterly Catalog.

To recieve a catalog,
send an email with your name
and mailing address to:

catalog@ellorascave.com

or send a letter or postcard
with your mailing address to:

Catalog Request
c/o Ellora's Cave Publishing, Inc.
1056 Home Avenue
Akron, Ohio 44310-3502

Cerridwen, the Celtic Goddess of wisdom, was the muse who brought inspiration to storytellers and those in the creative arts. Cerridwen Press encompasses the best and most innovative stories in all genres of today's fiction. Visit our site and discover the newest titles by talented authors who still get inspired - much like the ancient storytellers did, once upon a time.

Cerridwen Press
www.cerridwenpress.com

Discover for yourself why readers can't get enough of the multiple award-winning publisher Ellora's Cave. Whether you prefer e-books or paperbacks, be sure to visit EC on the web at www.ellorascave.com for an erotic reading experience that will leave you breathless.

www.ellorascave.com